P

THE CAPTAIN'S BRIDE

"American Joshua Fairbourne is in London on business and to find a wife. He has his sights set on a docile woman he thinks will be his ideal, when a whirlwind named Anabelle Crosbie spins into his life and turns it topsy-turvy.... As always, Ms. Jarrett takes the high seas by storm, creating one of her liveliest heroines and a hero to be her match. Readers are sure to delight in Anabelle's sometimes outrageous schemes and fall in love with Joshua, hoping to see them return in another book in the Fairbourne chronicles. Hurrah for a new series!"

—Kathe Robin, *Romantic Times*

"The queen of colonial romances has another winner.... Miranda Jarrett is the admiral of the historical sailing romance and *The Captain's Bride* is at her usual level of excellence. The story line is superb and filled with nonstop action, and the lead protagonists are a delightful, intrepid couple. The surprise ending is simply a pleasure to read. Another great tale that is on an even keel with the top of the Sparhawk series."

—Harriet Klausner, Amazon Books

"*The Captain's Bride* is a fabulous colonial sailing romance that is loaded with action and high-seas adventure. The lead characters make a classy couple as they passionately duel with each other and fight to survive their ruthless enemies. Miranda Jarrett continues to be top sea dog of the historical romance."

—*Affaire de Coeur*

And cheers for Miranda Jarrett

"Miranda Jarrett knows how to put life and love into her pages and make you believe every word."

—Rendezvous

"Miranda Jarrett is a hit with seekers of powerful, moving love stories. . . . She researches her time period meticulously to breathe life into her characters, and it pays off in stories women adore."

—Meg Grant, WCAU-TV/CBS News

"There is no doubt that Miranda Jarrett knows how to bring the sting of sea spray, the bite of the cutlass, and her passion for colonial adventure to readers like few others. A sparkling talent!"

—Kathe Robin, Romantic Times

"A marvelous author . . . one of romantic fiction's finest gems. . . . Each word from Miranda Jarrett is a treasure, each page an adventure, each book a lasting memory."

—The Literary Times

"A spectacular author. . . . Miranda Jarrett is the queen of eighteenth-century American historical romance. . . . If you haven't read her, then it's strongly recommended that you do, because [her books] are some of the best fiction of the nineties."

—Harriet Klausner, Affaire de Coeur

"When Miranda Jarrett writes of love and romance, her fans eat it up. . . . She maintains a personal tradition of romances that are action-packed, thought-provoking, and emotionally riveting. . . . Richly deserves her title as one of the greatest writers of colonial romance of our times."

—The Suburban & Wayne Times (PA)

Books by Miranda Jarrett

Captain's Bride
Cranberry Point

Published by POCKET BOOKS

For orders other than by individual consumers, Pocket Books grants a discount on the purchase of **10 or more** copies of single titles for special markets or premium use. For further details, please write to the Vice-President of Special Markets, Pocket Books, 1633 Broadway, New York, NY 10019-6785, 8th Floor.

For information on how individual consumers can place orders, please write to Mail Order Department, Simon & Schuster Inc., 200 Old Tappan Road, Old Tappan, NJ 07675.

MIRANDA JARRETT

CRANBERRY POINT

POCKET BOOKS

New York   London   Toronto   Sydney   Tokyo   Singapore

This book is a work of fiction. Names, characters, places and
incidents are products of the author's imagination or are used
fictitiously. Any resemblance to actual events or locales or persons,
living or dead, is entirely coincidental.

An *Original* Publication of POCKET BOOKS

POCKET BOOKS, a division of Simon & Schuster Inc.
1230 Avenue of the Americas, New York, NY 10020

Copyright © 1998 by Miranda Jarrett

ISBN: 0-671-00340-2

First Pocket Books printing June 1998

10 9 8 7 6 5 4 3 2 1

POCKET and colophon are registered trademarks of
Simon & Schuster Inc.

Cover art by Ben Perini

Printed in the U.S.A.

For Jake,
mirabile dictu:

Because all the best lines
were yours

CRANBERRY POINT

One

Off Cape Cod
1720

*E*verything had vanished.

The pale strip of beach, and the rocks above it, the ragged wind-bent pines on the far side of the dunes, even the wheeling, diving gulls that had followed her this morning: all of it was gone, swallowed up in the wet, gray nothingness. Who would have dreamed a winter fog would come in this fast?

Serena Fairbourne held the tiller of the little single-masted sailboat as steady as she could, her fingers numb with the cold despite her heavy mittens. She knew she shouldn't have waited so long to leave Denniman's Cove for home, no matter how good her reasons had been for lingering, just as she knew she was something dreadfully close to a fool to be out here now, alone on the bay. At least she hoped the dark green water that lapped at the boat's sides belonged to the bay, and not to the ocean that lay beyond. Please God she hadn't strayed that far with the ebbing tide, or she'd never find home again.

She shoved the hood of her cloak back from her face, straining to hear any sounds that might guide her toward the shore: the bell from the meetinghouse on the hill, a fisherman's call, even a dog barking for his supper.

But there was nothing.

Nothing.

She swiped a mitten across her forehead to brush her damp hair back from her forehead, the fog wet and chill on her skin. The worst thing she could do in a boat was to panic. That was what her oldest brother, Joshua, always said, anyway, and he'd been sailing since before she'd been born. She took a deep breath to calm herself, determined not to be afraid. Fairbournes weren't afraid of anything. Her brother said that, too.

But still her breath hung in nervous little puffs before her face and her heart thumped painfully within her breast, and now all she could remember were Joshua's horrifying tales of those lost at sea, swept overboard into the icy waters, struggling vainly in the waves until—

"Ahoy there, y'infernal bastard!" roared a man's furious voice from the fog. "Shove off now, less'n you mean to haul us all down to the devil wit' you!"

Instantly the steep side of a deep-water sloop loomed out of the fog before her, the black-painted planks rising high as a wall as the sloop's path angled across hers. With a gasp Serena threw all her weight against her boat's tiller, desperately trying to sheer from the path of the much larger boat.

"Shove off yourself!" she shouted back, her fear swallowed up by anger as her boat bobbed clumsily in the other's wash. "And may the devil take you as one of his own!"

"By all the saints, it's a woman!" A second man appeared behind the first at the rail, a tall man, all in black, his face hidden by the wisping fog and the shadow of his hat's brim. "Haul aback, I say! Haul aback directly!"

"Haul aback yourself!" retorted Serena. She'd barely managed to turn in time, and now the two boats were sailing side by side on the same course, the space between them not more than a dozen paces. "Where are your lights, sir, your bell? What kind of foolish ninnies go about silent as the grave in a fog such as this?"

The first man, the bearded one, swore impatiently. "And what manner o' sorry female would go out in a boat on her lonesome in such a fog? Answer me that, y'yowling, dim-witted strump—"

"Enough, Davis," said the tall man, his voice deep and easy with the certainty of being obeyed. "The lady needs our assistance, not our insults."

"Thank you," said Serena stiffly. Too late she realized that the captain's order—for surely the tall man must be the master—to haul aback had been directed at his own crew and not at her, for the sloop had slowed to keep pace with her little boat, the distance between them narrowing further. Why, why had she let her temper get the better of her again? Shrieking insults across the water like a fishwife was not something to be proud of, and the tall man in black was being generous—*very* generous— to refer to her as a lady. And the dear Lord help her if Joshua ever learned of this!

Self-consciously she tried to smooth her hair, aware of how bedraggled she must look in her salt-stained cloak and muddy petticoats and hairpins sticking out every which way, and in a boat so small as to be called a peapod. She wished she could see the man's face as clearly as he must see hers, and the unevenness of her situation made her feel doubly vulnerable, bobbing alongside in the water a good ten feet below him.

"I have rather lost my bearings in this fog, sir," she began again, this time with a certain belated primness, "and if you would be so good as to advise me as to the proper direction to the harbor at Appledore, then I shall be on my way myself."

"Appledore," repeated the man, rolling the name off his tongue with a booming flourish. "Come aboard, sweetheart, and I shall carry you there directly as my guest."

"Oh, but I mustn't!" said Serena hastily. After spending all her life in a seaport town, she knew too well the

3

perils to women who trusted strange sailors. While this captain seemed gentlemanly enough, his accent marked him as an outsider, a foreigner, not from their county, and as for that cavalier "sweetheart"—ah, she must be wary, wary indeed. "That is, your offer is most kind, sir, but not necessary at all."

"Not necessary, you say." He shook his head, perplexed. "Yet I cannot in easy conscience let you simply vanish away into the fog."

Serena nodded eagerly. Clearly the man didn't like being refused, but then, what man did? "Of course you can. Your pilot can tell me the way to Appledore, and that will be more than sufficient. You needn't worry over me. I am quite skillful in a boat."

That was not the truth, neither the *quite* nor the *skillful* nor any combination of the two, and Serena's conscience twitched uneasily. Like most Appledore women, she could handle a boat well enough in fair weather, but she did know when she'd crossed her own limitations as a sailor. Yet a dubious truth did seem preferable to being kidnapped and ruined and sold to some Martinique brothel, or whatever other untoward fate this man might wish for her.

"Doubtless Appledore lies just through that fog," she continued, nervousness rushing her words. "Likely no more than a stone's skip away."

But the tall stranger had no interest in skipping stones. He motioned to the sailors behind him, and instantly two long boat-hooks appeared over the side of the sloop, catching Serena's little boat and pulling it snug against the sloop's dark planks.

"No, no, you cannot do this to me!" cried Serena with growing panic, swinging her mittened fist at the nearer boat-hook. "I told you I didn't wish to come aboard, and I still don't! I *don't!*"

Swiftly she bent to grab her only weapon, the long-handled rake she'd used for scalloping. If she could knock away the boat-hooks, then perhaps she could push herself clear enough to escape. That was her best chance, her only hope.

But now even the rake seemed to be against her. The wooden teeth snarled in the single sail's lines, forcing Serena to struggle to work it free as her heart pounded with frustration and fear. Abruptly the line gave way, and with a startled gasp she tumbled backward into the puddle in the bottom of the boat, nearly losing the rake over the side in the process.

"Let me help," said the man as he dropped into the boat with alarming agility. "Here, take my hand."

"I'll take nothing from you!" cried Serena, settling awkwardly onto her knees as she tried to untwist her tangled cloak. Her hood had flopped over her eyes, and all she could see of the man now were his buckled shoes. "And who gave you leave to be in my boat, anyway?"

"You refused my hospitality, so I took that as an invitation to try yours instead. Now come, give me your hand and we'll set you upright. There's a good lass."

She swatted away his hand so hard that the boat rocked back and forth in clumsy sympathy.

"The devil take you," she declared, trying to sound braver than she felt as she struggled to find her footing, hampered by the rocking of the boat and her twisted petticoats and the way her hood had once again fallen forward over her eyes. Blindly she groped for the rake, her fingers finding and tightening around the oak handle. "And I am *not* your good lass!"

But before she could lift the rake, the man put his foot squarely over the handle, trapping both the rake and her hand with it.

"Your goodness, or lack of it, is of no concern to me," he said. "Which is fortunate for you, seeing as you seem to have precious little of that admirable quality, particularly for a woman. *Especially* for a woman. Now come, up you go."

Before Serena realized what was happening the man took her by the wrist and swung her up onto the bench to sit beside him, with only the tiller between them. His fingers on her cold skin were warm and strong, his touch disturbingly proprietary. With a frightened gasp she finally managed to shove the hood back from her eyes, then nearly gasped again as, at last, she saw the man's face.

"There now," he murmured, his voice low, as if sharing a special confidence with her alone. "That's far better, isn't it?"

"Better?" repeated Serena foolishly, unable to bring more than that single word squeaking to her lips. *"Better?"*

She was twenty-two years old, old enough, she'd believed, to have seen something of the world and the men that ruled it. But she'd never seen a man such as this one, not even in Boston, a man so supremely, outrageously sure of himself: a strong mouth and a stronger jaw, an arrogant hawk's beak of a nose, black hair and black brows and black lashes and eyes that were bluer than a summer-bright sea. And oh, the size of him beside her, so much larger, so much more grandly *male* that he seemed to fill the little boat entirely.

"Yes, better," he said with a mild patience that proved he was completely aware of his debilitating effect on womenfolk as a rule. "Or would you have preferred to continue drifting out to sea?"

Her first inclination was to strike him silly, to smack her open palm across his smug, handsome face. Having three older brothers had given her precious little patience with male condescension. But she'd lost her temper once already, squalling and squawking when she'd feared their boats would collide, and she wouldn't give the man the satisfaction of doing it again, any more than she wished him to know of the strange puddle of warm confusion he'd momentarily reduced her to.

No, reason and a calm, measured demeanor would be her best weapons now. Her only weapons, really, since he'd kept his shoe firmly across the rake.

She dared to meet his eyes again, dared herself to remain unaffected. "I wasn't drifting out to sea. I was perfectly in control, excepting for the fog."

"Oh, yes, the fog." He nodded agreeably, but the glint in his eyes showed he no more believed her claim than she did herself. "So you said earlier."

She pulled one mitten off to tuck a wayward lock of her hair back behind her ear, wishing her fingers and nose weren't so red with the cold and her clothes so bedraggled. Not that she cared what the man thought of her, of course—she reminded herself sternly that she didn't care in the least—but in comparison he looked as if he'd just stepped from a carriage in London instead of dropping into her boat from a sloop in the fog on Massachusetts Bay.

His greatcoat and breeches were beautifully tailored, the superfine wool a deep, midnight blue, nothing homespun, and not the black she'd first thought. The buttons on his waistcoat and at the side of his knees—very large, masculine knees, leading to equally masculine, muscular thighs and other masculine things she shouldn't consider—were polished brass, stamped with tiny flowers, and his linen was the best holland, better than most men she knew could boast for Sabbath wear, and finished with a neat pleated frill at the cuffs. To dress like this he must be a prosperous captain indeed, especially considering he could not be much older than herself, and self-consciously she once again smoothed her rumpled skirts over her knees.

"It is very bad today, most dreadfully bad. The fog, I mean," she continued, hoping she wasn't really babbling as much as she feared. "Far worse than I can ever remember at this time of year. Nigh as thick as clabbered milk."

"Indeed." The corners of his mouth twitched upward, something that Serena suspected happened often. "'Thank you' would be sufficient, you know. Or is the custom different here in your colony?"

"Of course we thank others in Massachusetts," she said defensively. "But only when they deserve it, and I do not believe that you do."

"Even when I've done exactly as you wished?"

"If you'd done as I wished, you'd have stayed aboard your own vessel!"

He sighed deeply, too deeply for any man not suffering from blackest melancholia, and far, far too deeply for Serena to regard him with anything other than outright suspicion.

"And here I'd thought I'd come to your rescue," he said mournfully. "Playing the gallant hero and rescuing the fair maid from her distress."

"I am not in distress," she said sternly, "nor am I this wretched fair maid you fancy awaiting your rescue."

"No?" He raised one brow with feigned surprise. "Ah, sweet, how sadly then you've misled me!"

Serena's cheeks grew hot. *He* was not the one who'd been misled. She should have known better than to refer to herself as a maid, or rather to deny that she was one, which was not what she'd intended at all. Blast him for twisting her words about so! No man in Appledore would ever presume to speak to her like this. But then, this particular man wasn't from Appledore, and he'd clearly no notion of how one addressed Miss Serena Fairbourne, unless one wished to be addressing her brothers next.

And in an oddly perverse and confusing way, Serena was almost glad he didn't.

"I have not misled you, and I wish you would stop pretending that I have," she said with as much dignity as she could muster. "Now please go back aboard your sloop and leave me in peace."

"Not possible, I fear." He sighed again, and settled his arm comfortably on the tiller between them so that his sleeve brushed against hers. "I'm not enough of a sailor to go dancing across the waves, even at your bidding. Can't you see how we're already well on our way? But

8

once we reach your Appledore, I'll be happy enough to oblige."

Belatedly Serena realized that the boat was moving through the water, drawn by a towline that bound it to the larger sloop. With a little cry of dismay she twisted around on the narrow bench, her face to the wind as she stared back out over the stern at the white-flecked wake they'd churned through the waves. How could she possibly have let herself become so distracted by the man beside her that she hadn't noticed?

From the wind she guessed they were in fact heading toward Appledore, as he said, but in Appledore her problems would only grow worse with him beside her. After what she'd done earlier this day and where she'd been, she needed to slip back into the harbor unnoticed, to return this boat she'd borrowed and run back to her house along the back paths through the marsh to Cranberry Point so she wouldn't be seen or questioned. But to be towed in instead like a prize for everyone in town to remark would bring questions she didn't wish to—no, *couldn't*—answer, and it would all be this man's fault.

"There now, didn't I tell you I'd rescued you?" he said, his smile widening to a wickedly satisfied grin.

"But you cannot do this!" she cried indignantly. "Hauling me off against my will as if I were no more than an old piece of lumber! It's kidnapping, you know, pure and simple! *Kidnapping!*"

"Oh, aye, and I'm the wickedest old Turk in creation for trying to help you. Now come, lass, sit neat beside me and tell me of this Appledore."

She glared at him, wishing he were not as big, not as charming, not as strong, not as comfortably settled in her boat as if he owned it, so that she could shove him over the side as he deserved. "What I'll tell you of, sir, is the stout new gaol where you'll be spending the night. Double walls and iron bars, and a brick floor, too, to keep you from burrowing out."

"What a disheartening beginning." He swept off his cocked hat with a flourish, holding it with both hands in his lap, and frowned a bit as if to concentrate. "Let me offer this instead:

> *The nymphs of Appledore are most wondrously
> fair,*
> *With Neptune's own gold in their gossamer, ah,
> hair,*
> *Mermaid-daughters of the mariner's keep,*
> *Where salty zephyrs bring fresh rose to their
> damask cheek.*

At least that fits *you*, sweetheart."

"What it's fit for is the rubbish heap," declared Serena promptly, but not before her own damask cheeks flushed hot to betray her. She'd never heard such nonsense before, not from a man's lips, anyway, and she wasn't prepared for the effect. Yes, that must be it: unfamiliarity. That must be *all*. Empty compliments were empty compliments, no matter how prettily they were phrased nor how handsome the messenger.

So why, then, could she not bring herself to break her gaze from his?

"Rubbish?" he asked with a showy, heartfelt sigh of disappointment that still couldn't undermine the merriment in his eyes. "Considering I'd no time to beckon a muse properly, I judged it rather fine."

"Then you misjudged. 'Mermaid-daughters of the mariners' keep,' indeed! Whatever does that *mean?*"

"But you remembered the lines, didn't you? My humble effort cannot be so appallingly bad then, can it?"

Lord help her, he had dimples, too, charming little brackets to a smile that held altogether too much charm already. And she wished he'd return his hat to his head, so she wouldn't be distracted by the way his thick, dark hair streamed back from his forehead, the black silk ribbon on his queue fluttering in the wind.

"Oh, yes, it can." She narrowed her eyes, striving not to be distracted. "I still say you misjudged, and badly at that."

"I don't in matters of literature," he said, tapping his forefinger on the crown of his hat, "nor among ladies, either. I'm considered a deuced fine judge of both."

"Then you should know better than to go about calling decent women 'nymphs,'" she declared, but somehow her words seemed unable to convey any of the primness she'd mustered earlier. It had been much easier to do when she'd been frightened of him, and now, somehow, she wasn't. "I am not quite sure what a nymph may be, but I'm certain it's wicked. It sounds that way. *Very* wicked. And we are respectable women in Appledore. Excepting perhaps some of the sluttish ones that serve at the taverns."

"I shall remember that," he said without the least contrition. "Every word. Especially that part about the sluttish ones."

"Rubbish," she said again, slipping back onto her seat on the bench beside him. "Everything you say is. Honey-sweet words with nothing behind them. 'Tis all naught but rubbish."

"Then we must agree to differ, lass," he said. He brushed her cheek with his thumb, sweeping away a stray bit of her hair with a touch that was perilously close to a caress. The merriment faded from his eyes as his fingers spread to cradle her cheek against his palm. "For you *are* a most agreeable mermaid-daughter."

The last thing Serena expected him to do then was to kiss her. Or maybe it wasn't the last, but the first. Maybe she'd expected it from the beginning, deep down behind her conscience, for otherwise she would have slapped him outright, the way he deserved, or at least shoved him away. She wouldn't have let her eyes flutter shut as his face neared hers, or tipped her head to one side for her mouth to meet his, or parted her lips for the last, helpless sigh of protest to escape and vanish over the waves.

To let a stranger kiss her like this was undeniably wrong. Yet the longer his mouth moved against hers, the more right it felt, making her heart race and her blood run faster in her veins, and her head turn as dizzyingly light as the wisps of fog surrounding them. He might think of a dozen elegant ways to describe this kiss, but she knew only one: *magic*.

Yet when at last they broke apart, he had no elegant, teasing words to offer. He wasn't laughing now. Instead his expression seemed curiously confused, almost bewildered, as he searched her face, his fingers still lingering across her cheek.

Serena's heart fluttered oddly in her breast, a strange mixture of hope and joy. For all his teasing airs, perhaps he was no more in the habit of kissing strangers than she was herself. Could he perhaps have felt the special magic between them, too?

But if he had, he didn't admit it, instead only shaking his head. "I should not have done that, sweet," he said softly. "If you but knew the promises I've made, and now have broken. . . ."

Swiftly she drew back from his hand, her cheeks stained bright with shame. She had been too occupied with her own position to think of his. He could be betrothed or even married, someone else's sweetheart or husband or father.

"What you must think of me," she said, her words stumbling over themselves. "Lord help me, I've never been so bold, and I must beg your forgiveness, surely I must, and—"

"Hush." He placed his forefinger across her lips to silence her. "No begging, no apologies. A practice of mine, born of much experience, you see. I should not have kissed you, no, but I cannot in truth say that I regret it. Nor, I pray, should you."

"Nay, you do not understand—"

"But I do, lass," he said gently. "I understand everything."

He smiled then, a smile that turned his charm bitter-sweet with the regret he swore he did not feel. "Now come, speak to me of other things instead. That fine bucket of cockles, shall we say?"

"Cockles?" she repeated, as much confused by his abrupt transition as by the unfamiliar word. She followed his gaze to the water-filled oak bucket of fresh shellfish that sat wedged in the boat's bow before them. "Ah, you mean the scallops."

"If that is what they're called here," he said, leaning away from her to look into the bucket.

"Scallops," she said again. No regrets, he'd said, no apologies: if he could do that, then so could she. She'd intended the scallops to be her alibi when she returned to Appledore, and they could just as easily serve the same purpose now. "I raked them myself this morning. 'Tis the season for them to be sweetest, you know."

"I didn't." Heedless of his fine linen cuffs, he plunged his hand into the bucket, running his fingers through the water and across the heaps of fluted shells—rose, lavender, pale lemon, deep blue—with undisguised fascination. "All the ones I've seen at home were only white, but these, these are much more handsome. Almost like wildflowers. But what's this?"

He held his dripping hand outstretched to her. In his palm lay a pair of shells of striated pink, shading like a sunset from deepest plum to pale rose. Though the two shells were still joined together at the hinge like wings, the animal within was gone, the concave interior empty and clean.

"A sorry catch this makes for fisherfolk," he said, tossing the twin shells lightly in his palm. "No prize for the market here."

"Oh, don't throw them away, please!" she cried, lunging for the empty shells before they vanished over the side of the boat. "I know they're worthless, but I kept them because—because they were beautiful."

"Then so shall I," he said, his fingers closing over the shells. "To remind me of you, for the same reason."

Over his hand their eyes met again, the power of his gaze alone enough to make Serena's breath tighten in her chest. He was welcome to the shells. She'd need nothing extra to remind her of him.

But no apologies, no regrets . . .

"Appledore, sir, a point to th' starboard," called the sloop's pilot from over their heads.

"Ah, sweet, so your home beckons at last," said the stranger, breaking the spell between them. Carefully he tucked the scallop shells into the pocket of his coat as he rose to stare across the water. "And a fair place Appledore looks to be. No marvel that you are so fond of it, and so eager to return. What better time for us to make our adieus?"

"But wait, captain, please," said Serena quickly as the men in the sloop pulled her boat closer. "Please, I—"

"Not 'captain,' lass," he said as he prepared to untie the line that held the two boats together and climb back aboard the sloop. "I've no right to that title or any other, by birth or by merit. Except, of course, as a rogue. That's the one title I've earned."

"But you never told me your name!"

"And neither, sweet, did you." With the rope in his hands as a guideline, he swung himself away from her boat and climbed up the shallow footholds carved into the sloop's sides. Over his shoulder he smiled at her one last time, a smile that failed to reach his eyes. "In my heart you will always be my misplaced mermaid, beckoning from the fog, and you can think of me as your gallant savior, rescuing you against your will."

Already the two boats were separating, carried apart by the wind and currents, and belatedly Serena hurried to set her own course for the shore. By the time she could look back, the sloop was slipping away into the fog, and she could just make out the stranger's face and the hat waving in his hand.

"Farewell, Mistress Mermaid," he called, "and may Neptune always watch over you in my place."

She waved her hand in return, staring after the sloop long after it had disappeared. At last she lowered her hand, carefully touching her fingers to her lips where he'd kissed her. Then with her head bowed, she steered her course for home.

. . . and no regrets.

Two

Responsibility, as a rule, did not sit well with Fitzgerald Crosbie.

To avoid it he'd seen a good deal of the world and its amusements in his twenty-five years, perhaps more than was his fair share. But as the youngest son of an Irish baronet and the grandson of an English peer, he'd been born to certain expectations, and so far he hadn't been disappointed, at least not in any way that had left lasting damage. His gifts included his mother's charm and his father's temper, and enough of a fortune in his own right to grant him all of the comforts of the heir, but none of the inconvenient obligations. He didn't like obligations any more than he liked responsibilities, yet now, standing here in the middle of this rutted lane while the snow seeped into his boots, he was very soon going to be confronted with both.

His *favorite* boots, too, the ones with the yellow tops, the devil rot this infernal ice and snow and the scapegrace sister who'd led him here to this godforsaken town in the first place.

He sighed, his breath coming out in a little puff of impatience in the icy evening air. Why hadn't Anabelle run off with a Neapolitan *Conte* instead so he might have followed her to some place more agreeable? Even a heathen corsair from Barbary would have been an improvement, for at least the desert would be warm. But Anabelle, being Anabelle, would lose her heart to an overgrown sailor from the colonies, some great orangutan of a sea-captain who'd practically carried her away over his shoulder, or so the tale had gone around London. Not that Gerald doubted the gossip. Where his sister was concerned, anything was possible.

He blew on his frozen fingers to warm them, and critically studied the house before him, the one that had been pointed out to him as belonging to Captain Fairbourne. Here in the colonies he supposed it would be considered fine enough, but compared to the grand house at Kilmarsh where he and Anabelle had been born, it seemed a humble, old-fashioned effort at best: square and solid with the snow piled about it, plain painted clapboards without any elegance or grace, the shutters closed against the cold and a cluster of bare trees shivering before the front door.

So this, then, was what Anabelle called home with her seafaring cicisbeo; clearly his sister had lost her wits along with her heart. No wonder Grandmother believed Anabelle could be persuaded to return with him to London. Why the devil would she choose to *stay?*

Yet still Gerald hung back. As soon as he walked up that path and knocked on the door, he'd be tossed, head first and irrevocably, into the middle of a family disaster, and Crosbie disasters were never small. The only reason he'd come here at all was that his own life was in temporary disarray.

Another minute of his own, that was all. Hadn't he already squandered ten weeks of his life at sea for Anabelle's sake? He tugged the collar of his coat higher over the back of his neck. Well, perhaps not the last day of the ten weeks: that had belonged squarely to him, and all because of the fisherman's daughter.

He smiled wryly at his own foolishness, even as the girl's face filled his memory once again. He could not name a single reason for her to be there. She was a pretty young creature, true, but he'd known far more beautiful women. Considering her humble station, she'd had some grace and wit, though nothing compared to what he was accustomed to in the ladies in London. Her hair had been a disheveled tangle, her dress coarse and bedraggled, and she'd carried the distinct scents of saltwater and fish about her person.

Yet he could not forget her. He couldn't explain why, any more than he could understand how a single, stolen, indulgent kiss had turned him as stupefied and befuddled as a green schoolboy. Leaving her alone in the fog in her little boat had been one of the hardest things he'd ever done, and he couldn't explain that, either. He'd ordered the captain of the hired sloop to go back out to sea until nightfall, giving her the chance to return to whatever wretched little house she'd call home, and him the opportunity to put her out of his mind.

Not that it had worked for him, not in the least. He'd been waiting at the rail as soon as they'd returned to the harbor, scanning the moonlit water for an unlikely glimpse of the girl in her little boat. The sloop's crew had called Gerald daft not only behind his back but in his hearing, and no wonder. He couldn't think of any better word himself.

He slipped his hand inside his pocket and once again touched the twin scallop shells. If he'd any sense he'd toss the shells in the bushes now and be done with it, and with her. But he didn't, instead shaking his head at his own foolishness. He was fond of beautiful things, too. Odds were he'd never see the girl again, and even if—

The front door to the house before him swung open, a wedge of candlelight slicing out in the dark across the muddled snow. A women stood silhouetted in the doorway, a small, round woman, bending to push a reluctant cat outside.

"There now, Tomkins, you wicked little beast," she said as she gently prodded at the cat. "You cry and cry to be let out of doors, and then the moment I leave the fire, you change your mind. A vastly wicked little beast!"

"Anabelle?" Gerald frowned as he stepped forward. He couldn't believe she'd answer her own door like this, especially to put out some lowly feline. "Anabelle, goose-girl, is that you?"

"Gerald?" Her voice squeaked upward with surprise as she peered into the dark. "Here? Faith, it cannot truly be you, can it?"

"Ah, Anabelle," he said with a mournful sigh, "who the devil else would come traipsing clear across the sea to find you?"

"Gerald!" She bunched up her skirts in her hands and ran, hopping and skidding across the snow to fling her arms around his waist. "Oh, I should have known you'd be the only one who'd understand!"

He barely caught himself from falling backward as she hurled against him. "What I understand, Nan, is that you've nearly toppled me into the mud."

"It's snow, not mud, or ice at the very least," she said with her cheek pressed fondly to his chest, "and anyway, it would take far more than little me to topple you into anything."

She pushed herself backward, holding fast to Gerald's arms as she grinned up at him.

"When did you become such a beauty, Nan?" he asked as he studied her face. "No wonder you left so many broken hearts behind in London!"

"Ha, I'll wager you can't find a one," she scoffed cheerfully. "'Tis only more of your pretty, empty words, Gerald, puffed up with charm to make me sigh."

He frowned, startled by this odd little trick of fate. The girl in the boat had told him nearly the same thing. He could hear her again in his thoughts, her teasing, throaty voice echoing in his memory. Strange that Anabelle should say it, too.

Stranger still that he'd remembered, and that he cared.

"Faith, I did not mean to make you sad, Duckie," said Anabelle contritely. "'Twas my usual empty prating, that was all."

"Was there ever any other kind from you, my own sister?" He kissed her loudly on the cheek and she squealed with indignant delight. Better to think of Anabelle, how he'd missed *her,* than some nameless girl he'd lost in the fog. When he'd last seen Anabelle at Kilmarsh, three summers ago, she'd still been running wild over the meadows and through the stables, a small, plump, merry girl with a knotted handkerchief full of sweets in her pocket and the latest litter of puppies at her heels. No matter how properly she'd been dressed at the breakfast table, by supper her cap would be lost and her silk skirts covered with blotches of mud, a constant trial to governesses and laundresses alike.

But though she'd grown no taller nor any less merry, his little goose-girl sister had vanished, replaced by this new, elegant lady who bore only the slightest resemblance to the Anabelle he remembered. She must be seventeen—or was it eighteen?—by now, and clearly her days of running through the stables with the hunting spaniels were long done. Even here in this determinedly unfashionable colony she was wearing some sort of slippery, rustling silk gown with hoops and a French back that trailed out behind her. On her feet were open-backed, high-heeled mules never meant for the Massachusetts snow, and a little feather of diamonds winked in her pinned and scented hair.

But the clothes weren't what he noticed first. No, her clothes, however elegant, were a distinctly and uncomfortably remote second.

She reached up to pat his shoulders with her hands. "You've grown even more handsome, Duckie, if such a marvel were possible," she said with approval, using her old nursery name for him. "Whatever wickedness you've found in Rome and Paris must be most agreeable. La, look at how grand a gentleman you've become!"

"Look at yourself, Nan," he said, pointedly staring

down at the rounded swell of her belly beneath the patterned silk, "and don't go lecturing *me* on wickedness."

Perplexed, she looked down, too, following his gaze, before she tipped her chin back to let the merry laughter ripple from her lips. "But I'm not wicked, Duckie," she said, laying a protective hand across her unborn child. "I'm married."

"Married?" he repeated, aghast. He'd never considered such a humiliating possibility for his sister. Of course he'd seen the note she'd left when she'd run off, but no one in the family had seriously believed her plan to *marry* her sailor. "Why the devil would you—"

"Anabelle?" The man's voice, deep and commanding, rumbled out across the snow, and his tall, black shadow filled the open doorway. "Anabelle, where in blazes are you?"

At once Anabelle turned swiftly back toward the house, her face alight with such obvious love that Gerald couldn't help but see it. Nan's husband, he thought with a shock. Of course it must be her husband. *His* brother-in-law.

God help him, it made no sense. If she'd only had an intrigue with the rascal, why, that he could understand. That was what he'd expected, the kind of thing neatly settled with pistols or swords for the sake of family honor, and the kind of thing, too, that Gerald did rather well. But Nan with a husband—a large and unpleasant-sounding husband—and a babe of their making on the way was altogether different.

"Oh, Joshua, I have the most wonderful surprise for you!" Anabelle called happily. "You cannot begin to guess who I've found out here in the snow!"

"I'll return in the morning, Nan," said Gerald quickly. There'd been surprises enough already, and he wasn't ready for more. He needed time and brandy to settle his thoughts and stop his head from spinning. "I left my things at a tavern near the water, and I'll spend the night there."

"You'll do nothing of the sort." Eagerly she seized Gerald's arm, tugging him toward the house. "You shall dine with us at the very least. Come, I cannot wait to see the look on Joshua's face when he meets you!"

Perhaps she couldn't wait, but Gerald certainly could. "Then better you should see it by daylight, Nan. Tomorrow's soon enough."

"Anabelle?" The husband's voice rumbled more ominously now. "Is there something amiss, lass?"

"Not in the least! I—that is, we—shall be there directly," she called back, then lowered her voice for Gerald alone. "Now you *will* come with me, Fitzgerald James Rockingham Crosbie. You are likely the only member of our family who shall ever deign even to meet Joshua, and it won't hurt you to do it now."

"That's all well enough, Nan, but—"

"Please, Duckie," she said softly, beseeching in exactly the same way she had years ago when coaxing him into some shared mischief. "Please. For me."

Gerald sighed heavily, patting her chilled little fingers as they dug into his sleeve. And, just as he had then, he did as she wished, walking at her side to the house like a man to the gallows.

The gallows, ha, he thought grimly as they reached the step. At least Jack Ketch smiled at his victims. Captain Fairbourne was not nearly so welcoming.

"Who in blazes is this, Anabelle?" he demanded. "You go to open the door for the cat and come back with some blessed pretty-boy!"

Gerald bristled, but Anabelle hurried between them before he could speak. "Hush, Joshua, you hush this moment!" she said, obviously with fond and considerable practice. "This is not some mere pretty boy, though I'll grant you he is remarkably comely. Nor do pretty boys grow in our orchard for me to gather up like windfalls. Not that I've noticed, anyway. No, this is my brother, come clear from London to wish us well."

She looked expectantly at Gerald. For her sake, he swallowed his irritation, and his pride with it, and swept his hat from his head to bow. "Fitzgerald Crosbie, sir," he said curtly. "Your servant."

The other man eyed him warily. "Joshua Fairbourne," he said, yielding nothing, "but I expect you know that already to come here after my wife."

"My *sister,* sir," said Gerald sharply. Anabelle's husband or not, he still would call the man out if he continued like this. "And I'll thank you, sir, not—"

"Now you hush, too, Gerald!" interrupted Anabelle, waving her hands impatiently before her. "Faith, you're no better than a pair of squabbling mongrel curs, both of you! If it weren't so cold tonight, I'd go fetch a bucket of water to toss on you, too, just as I would the dogs. Now come inside, to the parlor, and let us close this door before we all turn to ice where we stand."

There was precious little risk of that, decided Gerald grimly, not with tempers as fired as this. But he dutifully followed Anabelle and her husband inside as she'd bidden, pausing in the hall with her to unbutton his greatcoat while Joshua went ahead to the parlor.

"Joshua is not so very fierce, Duckie," she whispered as she helped him shrug free of the coat. "And neither, for that matter, are you."

"Then tell that to him, Nan, not me." He handed his hat to the shy-faced serving maid who'd also taken his greatcoat from his sister. He smiled his thanks to the girl, who flushed to the ruffles of her linen cap, bobbed an unsteady curtsey, and fled. The world might have turned upside down where his sister was concerned, but at least other things seemed to be mercifully unchanged.

Anabelle swatted his arm. "And I wish you to behave that way, too. It was one thing for you to go poaching among the kitchen and scullery maids at Kilmarsh, but it is very different here. You dawdle and toy with a girl here, and you'll have all her outraged family after you."

"So why the devil can't I be outraged on your behalf?" he demanded. "Don't you remember who you *are?* Finding you actually wed to this low-bred scoundrel and swelling up with his child in the bargain—that's a great deal for me to swallow, Nan, a great deal indeed."

"Then I shall give you one more bit to choke upon, Gerald," she said, her fierce whisper a determined match for any persuasion he might muster. "I love Joshua. I love him more than anything or anyone else in all creation, and I would do anything or go anywhere to be with him. Forever and ever, Gerald. That is what I vowed when I married him before everyone in the meetinghouse, and that is what I believe, with all my heart."

"You wed him before witnesses?" Gerald sighed. This was considerably worse than Grandmother had led him to believe, a disaster of the first order even among Crosbie disasters. "Though a meetinghouse wouldn't seem to be quite a proper church, especially here in the colonies, and the minister wouldn't be quite a proper minister. If we slipped a bit of gold into the right pockets, then perhaps—"

"Oh, Duckie," she murmured, almost mournfully, as she rested her hand on his arm. "I *love* him. Can't you understand what that means?"

And as he looked down into his sister's face, he realized he didn't. He liked women, liked them very much, in fact, from those distant, giggling kitchen maids at Kilmarsh to the grand, languishing ladies that graced the king's court; and women in return liked him with equal ardency. He'd been merely amused and entertained by some, and more attached to others, with whichever was the most recent one generally holding the firmest grasp on his interests, as was the case with the fisherman's daughter. But in perfect honesty Gerald could not say he'd loved any of them. Not the way his sister meant the word, anyway. Not to the point that he'd abandon his family and his honor and his fortune and his place in the world for the sake of another. No woman had ever dared ask that of him, nor had he offered such a sacrifice. It was, quite simply, beyond all reason.

Beyond reason for him, and for Anabelle, too. The challenge for him would lie in convincing *her*.

Gently he patted her hand. She really hadn't changed that much after all. Beneath the brocaded silk she was still his foolish, merry, little sister, and she still needed him to help her out of scrapes.

"Oh, aye, Nan, I understand," he said lightly, and when she rewarded him with a glowing smile, his conscience troubled him in only the slightest way. He was, after all, acting for her own benefit. "We'll talk later, you and I, when we won't have to worry about vexing your husband with the tedium of old family tales."

She tucked her hand into the crook of his arm. "I should like that, Gerald, above all things," she said happily. "Now come, and make yourself agreeable."

For her sake, and her sake alone, he would. But to ignore the black look that Joshua Fairbourne launched his way when he entered the room was not easy. The man stood before the fireplace with his legs spread and his hands clasped behind his back as if mastering his ship's quarterdeck and crew rather than his front parlor, and his thick black brows were drawn together into a glower fearsome enough to squelch any mutiny.

If he'd deigned to smile, thought Gerald grudgingly, he might be called handsome, in a dark and grim-faced way, and his coat, though plain, was cut well enough to display his height and the breadth of his shoulders. Though there was nothing genteel about him, Gerald couldn't really fault Anabelle for falling under the man's spell. That much he could understand. Women admired a well-made man. For sheer robust size, she would have been at a loss to find his match among their peers in England or Ireland, either. Outside of her brothers, that is, and unconsciously Gerald shifted his own shoulders as he thought of how dearly he'd like ten minutes in the yard with Captain Joshua Fairbourne to prove it.

"You must sit here, Gerald, here by me until supper is served," said Anabelle as she sank down onto a green harrateen settee and patted the cushion beside her. "Is not this green quite the most delicious color you have ever surveyed?"

"Oh, delicious, indeed," murmured Gerald, not missing his host's disdainful *harumph*.

"It should be the most blessed bloody green in New England, for what it cost," declared Joshua. "Must have gold thread woven in it, too."

Gerald's eyes narrowed at the other man. Right now he didn't give a tinker's dam for one green over another, not with this bully of a sea-captain goading him, but nothing, not even Joshua Fairbourne, was going to make him hurt Anabelle's feelings. She did in fact have much to be proud of, for from the mahogany tea table to the gold chinoiserie mirror to the French porcelain in the corner cupboard, the parlor was the most elegantly appointed room he'd yet seen in the colonies. However her husband had made his fortune, clearly Anabelle was doing her best to spend it, and at a good pace, too. Gerald hoped she'd drain his coffers down to the last shilling.

"Anabelle is a lady of the most exquisite taste," he said evenly, though the challenge behind his words was clear enough. "No *gentleman* would doubt it."

"It is a most genteel green, yes," said Anabelle nervously, looking from one man to another as she tried to steer the conversation back to safer waters. "Though in Boston the shopkeepers do not yet have an eye for such things and believe that a drab stone blue is still the fashion. Blue, la!"

"That is because in this distant place they've never had a well-born lady like you to inform them," said Gerald with a slight bow in Anabelle's direction that pointedly excluded Joshua as much as it honored her. "Isn't that so, Nan?"

But to Gerald's surprise Anabelle didn't rush to agree, the way he had expected. Instead she looked away from him and across the room to her husband, and though her cheeks were flushed—with shame? embarrassment? uneasiness?—her lingering smile was without question entirely for Joshua.

Damnation, was she lost to him already?

"Pray bring Gerald a glass of whatever you are drinking, love," she said with a cheerfulness that sounded forced to Gerald's ears. "I would not have him questioning our hospitality."

Silently Joshua poured from the heavy bottle on the marble-topped sideboard and handed the tumbler to Gerald.

"Rum," he said curtly. "New England rum, and the best such in the world."

Slowly Gerald took the tumbler, his fingers curling around the heavy glass. He did not care for rum and never had. It was too sticky-sweet to his taste, too coarse in its flavor. But if he'd leveled one challenge toward Joshua, then Joshua in turn was handing him another of a different kind in this glass.

With a long, deliberate swallow he emptied the tumbler and returned it to Joshua. " 'Tis well enough," he said carelessly, ignoring the fiery path the rum was burning down his throat. "But there is a plantation on Jamaica that brews better. Lord Tockhamton's holding, on the north side of the island. His rum makes this taste like—"

"We'll be dining *en famille* this night," interrupted Anabelle hastily. "Mr. Foster was to join us, but he sent word earlier that he was indisposed. We're to have a splendid turkey-meat pie, Gerald, and leeks dressed in butter, and a winter cheese that—"

"She's not going back, mind?" thundered Joshua. "Damnation, she's mine now, Crosbie, and I'm not giving her up."

"La, what foolishness!" said Anabelle with a nervous trill of a laugh as she stepped between them. "As if I could belong to either one of you, as if I were no more than another bit of livestock!"

"Then why the devil is he here?" demanded Joshua, thumping his fist against the mantelpiece.

Gerald took a single step closer. "Because, sir, I care for her welfare. I care for my *sister.*"

"Oh, yes, and what better reason, Joshua?" said Anabelle quickly, resting a restraining hand on the broad front of her husband's waistcoat. "Gerald is my brother, my favorite brother in all the world, or at least of the three from which I must choose, and it is right for him to be here to wish me—to wish *us,* Joshua—happiness. Isn't that so, Gerald? Gerald?"

Gerald didn't answer. He couldn't. His outraged temper was choking him too much to let him. To see his sister standing there before him, her sweet, besotted face turned upward to appeal to the man who'd seduced her, who'd ruined her, even sliding her hand wantonly across the bastard's chest without a morsel of decency or shame—it was very nearly more than he could bear.

But he *would* bear it. For Anabelle's sake, though the little ninny didn't know it, and for the sake of their family's name, he would do it. In a land of savages and rogues, he would remain a gentleman. He would not lower himself to become one of them, however great—and this was great indeed—the provocation.

Instead of hurling his empty tumbler the way his frustration demanded, he set it down on a table with infinite, excruciating care. He would make his excuses and leave now, and return in the morning when he could speak to Anabelle alone. Perhaps then she'd listen to him, perhaps then she'd see the sense . . .

"Faith, that must be our other guest now," said Anabelle breathlessly, cocking her head at the sound of the front door opening. She pushed herself away from Joshua and smoothed the front of her petticoats. "How agreeable it was of you, Gerald, to produce yourself on a night when I was short a gentleman, and to help me to balance out my table places properly."

Before Gerald answered the parlor door opened, and he turned on his heel to greet the newcomer. She swept into the room with a sudden rush of cold air from outside to carry her forward in a rustle of heavy silk and didn't bother to wait for the maidservant to announce her. Not that Gerald would have remembered her name even if he'd heard it called; her appearance alone was enough to strike him both speechless and unhearing.

She would, he knew, have that effect on most men, at least those who weren't already laid out on their biers. Her face was rosy from the chilly night, her full lips reddened, her honey-colored hair loosely knotted and pinned with the exact degree of artlessness to enchant. Her eyes glowed bright with anticipation and pleasure, and Gerald would have given an unspeakably large sum to keep the happiness in her smile, at least as long as he could see it. Her plum-colored gown displayed the pleasing roundness of her figure, proving that she was tall enough to move with the grace of a goddess, but not so large as to overwhelm.

Aphrodite, then, decided Gerald, not Juno: an exceptionally perfect Aphrodite, stepping from her open shell and into his life. Lord, what was it about her that turned him into a poetical dunderheaded halfwit?

Anabelle hurried forward, her mules slapping gently against her stockinged heels and her arms outstretched in welcome.

"Oh, how pleased I am to see you, dear!" she cried happily as she brushed her lips across the taller woman's cheeks. "I have such a surprise for you, such a wonderfully fine surprise! Come here now, and meet my favorite brother."

With their hands firmly clasped, Anabelle triumphantly led her toward Gerald, unaware of how all the happiness had drained from the other woman's face while her eyes had rounded with startled surprise.

"Miss Serena Fairbourne," began Anabelle, "might I present to you my brother Mr. Fitzgerald Crosbie, new arrived this very night from England. I promise he'll cause you no harm. He's sworn to me to behave."

She laughed merrily. "Now, Gerald, your turn. I should like to present you to Miss Fairbourne. There, sweetly done, wasn't it? I shall expect you two shall have the world in common, for Miss Fairbourne is Joshua's only sister."

No, she wasn't, thought Gerald as he automatically took Miss Fairbourne's fingers in his own and bowed over them.

She wasn't Miss Serena Fairbourne, the only sister to Captain Joshua Fairbourne. She couldn't be.

She was his misplaced mermaid-lass, God help him, and tonight there wasn't a wisp of fog within sight for him to blame.

Three

Serena stared down at the top of the man's head as he bowed gracefully over her hand. No, he wasn't just a man, any more than he was her nameless gentleman in the fog. Now he had a name and a family to go with it, and to her hideous dismay, that family was her own.

"Your servant, Miss Fairbourne," he murmured. He raised his gaze to meet hers, his eyes even more intensely blue than she remembered. "I am honored."

"Honored? Ah, yes, Mr. Crosbie," she stammered, belatedly remembering to drop a curtsey the way her brother expected her to. Because she hadn't been born a lady like Anabelle, she'd been late learning about curtseys and tea pouring and other genteel niceties, and she didn't always remember to do what she was supposed to or when. And as for now—now she'd consider herself fortunate if she didn't topple over onto the floorboards from absolute and complete mortification. "That is to say, ah, I am the one honored, Mr. Crosbie, or rather the, um, the honor belongs to, ah, to me."

Oh, dear God in heaven, she didn't dare look in

Joshua's direction, not after such a stumbling, stammering disgrace to the Fairbourne name!

She spread her skirts the way Anabelle had showed her, lowered her eyes, and tried again. "The honor is mine, sir."

Was she imagining it or was he holding her fingers in his own longer than was proper? Was the warmth in his eyes the spark of amused, shared confidence, or only a reflection of the fire in the hearth?

And worst of all, how dreadfully much had he told the others before she'd arrived?

"Oh, la, Serena, you needn't be so formal, not among family," said Anabelle, giving Serena's arm a fond little pat. "And he is family, or rather my family, which considering how I am your family now, too, having married your brother, makes my brother your family as well."

Serena nodded mutely, unable to add anything of her own to her sister-in-law's explanation. Anabelle often spoke in such roundabout confusion. When Joshua had first married her, there'd been times that Serena hadn't the slightest idea what she'd said, but tonight Serena's own head was spinning so that Anabelle almost made sense.

"Set the man free, Serena," rumbled Joshua with benign exasperation. "He doesn't need your help to stand upright."

Serena jerked her hand away, her face growing hotter than she'd dreamed possible. Gerald Crosbie must have said nothing of meeting her earlier for her brother to still be so agreeable. There was some small grace to be found in that. If Joshua had heard she'd been out alone in the fog in a boat, let alone that she'd let a stranger kiss her, he'd have had her head the moment she'd entered the room.

"Forgive me, Mr. Crosbie," she began yet again. "I did not mean—"

"No more titles, Serena, I beg you no more!" scolded Anabelle cheerfully. "Now come, you must give my brother your hand one last little time so he can lead you into supper. 'Tis not so very difficult, is it?"

" 'Tis not difficult at all," agreed Gerald before Serena could, his voice as deep and full of charm as she remembered. Gently he reclaimed her hand and placed it in the crook of his arm. His coat was made of the most beautiful shade of silk velvet, somewhere between deep blue and green, and the plush beneath Serena's fingers was made softer still by the golden brown squirrel that lined it. She'd never seen any man wear silk velvet—for that matter, she'd never seen a woman wear it in Appledore before Anabelle—let alone a silk velvet coat lined with fur and edged with silver braid, but instead of seeming womanish, the soft luxury of the fabrics by contrast only made the sharp edge of his masculinity more unsettlingly apparent.

He smiled down at her, giving her hand a possessive squeeze. "Step lively now, Miss Serena, else we won't reach the table before Anabelle perishes."

Anabelle sighed, one hand resting upon her belly as she turned her face winningly up toward her husband. "That *is* the honest truth, nothing less or more. Faith, I believe I could eat the entire roasted bird myself!"

Joshua's face relaxed as he gazed down at her, his adoration for her so clear in his expression that self-consciously Serena looked away. It was often that way with her brother and his new wife, she thought wistfully, as if they'd forgotten she were in the same chamber. But the obvious love between them made Joshua's angry hostility toward Gerald even more inexplicable and disturbing as well.

She hung back in the doorway, watching Joshua settle his wife in her cushioned armchair at the head of the dining table and nearest the fire. Anabelle's ever-present appetite might well be the only "honest truth" to be found among them. Lord knew Serena was hardly free of secrets herself. Her visit that morning to the sad little house on Denniman's Cove, becoming lost in the fog, meeting—and kissing—Gerald Crosbie long before he'd come here, all of these were things she'd wish in turn to keep from her brother. But how long, she thought uneasily, could she trust Gerald Crosbie to do the same?

"I pray you're not harboring a stray doubt or two about me yourself, Miss Serena," said Gerald, his voice now low and suggestively confidential, for her ears alone, the same voice she remembered from the boat. "Or perhaps there is a secret of your own that you wish to share?"

She glanced at him sharply, wondering how he'd come so near to echoing her misgivings. "A secret shared ceases to be a secret."

"Not if it's shared in confidence," said Gerald lightly. He had a way of watching her with his eyes lazily half-closed that reminded her of a sleek, sleepy cat, ready to pounce on a careless mouse. "And I can assure you, sweet, that I was every bit as surprised as yourself to learn of our, ah, our connection."

"It was no surprise to me, not in the least," said Serena swiftly, determined not to be that careless mouse. "Anabelle has spoken of you many times."

Gerald smiled, his sleepy eyes suddenly alight with fresh appreciation. "Well played, Miss Serena. We shall, I think, get on quite well as kin."

Anabelle rapped her hand impatiently on the arm of her chair. "No more whispers in the hall, Gerald. From the way you're loitering and lingering you'd think I charged a tariff for my hospitality."

"Not at all, Nan," said Gerald easily as he guided Serena to her chair. "And what a charming table you do manage here in the wilderness. You could set a fashion for rustic airs. *En famille sur la glace,* eh?"

Serena sat, her back very straight against the carved mahogany, and tried to ignore how Gerald's fingertips had brushed across the bare skin along the nape of her neck as he pushed in her chair. There was much here she didn't understand, and it wasn't just the French words that had made Anabelle laugh so merrily. Carefully she spread the linen napkin across her skirts, trying to decipher Gerald's meaning while she avoided his gaze from the opposite side of the table.

Appledore wasn't wilderness and hadn't been for years and years, not since before her grandparents' time. It might not be as grand a place as Boston, to be sure, but it wasn't some tiny backwater trading post, either. There was a meetinghouse with a tall white spire and a bell, a wind-driven gristmill and a market, a dockyard and a chandlery, a ropewalk and a blacksmith, shops and taverns, houses and farms. Gerald Crosbie had only to use his eyes to see what a fine, prosperous town Appledore was.

But maybe that was the problem, not with Appledore, but with his eyes. Maybe he was so accustomed to London and Dublin and all the other great cities of Europe that he couldn't see the appeal of her own hometown, at least not at once.

Yet for him to tease Anabelle about the table she set made no sense at all. The serving girls, the pressed linens, the tall polished candlesticks, the French porcelain so fine that the light shone through it, even the dainty little forks at every place: all of this struck Serena—and the rest of Appledore, too—as the height of well-bred gentility. Certainly she and Joshua had never dined in such style before he'd married Anabelle. Then, before they'd learned better, they'd eaten the meals she'd cooked herself from pewter plates on a bare table before the kitchen hearth. Those had been happy times, too, for all they'd been so drab and unfashionable.

Lightly Serena's fingers stroked the plum-colored satin of her skirts. When Joshua had brought the silk to her from Martinique last year, she'd thought nothing could be more elegant, so much so that she'd been half-terrified to cut into it. But to Gerald Crosbie and his sleepy blue London eyes, she likely looked as foolishly provincial in her best silk as she had on the water this morning in her most practical linsey-woolsey homespun.

"*Sur la glace,*" repeated Joshua, his large hands resting

on the table on either side of his untouched plate. Unlike Serena, he'd sailed to enough foreign ports to learn bits of a dozen different tongues. "Means 'on the ice.' We're eating dinner on the ice? What the devil is that supposed to mean?"

Anabelle grinned, another forkful of turkey pie poised on her fork. "'Tis only a jest, Joshua. Compared to Ireland, Massachusetts is a veritable haven of ice and snow. Even you can't deny that, love. Duckie intended no slander, so don't you seek it."

Joshua's freshly shaven chin dropped lower toward his chest as he gazed down the table to Anabelle. "*Duckie?*"

"'Tis not his real name, of course," admitted Anabelle wryly, her eyes dancing as she glanced at her brother. "But Duckie suits him, too, you see, not because of any true likeness to a duck—though I'll grant he can quack most creditably if he's had enough claret—but because he was so very good at playing Ducks and Drakes on the lower pond at Kilmarsh. I vow sometimes he could skip a stone a dozen times across the water, while I could never progress beyond three. Isn't that so, Duckie?"

Gerald sighed with bemused resignation and shook his head. "A nursery name that Nan, alas, insists on remembering," he said as he sipped the wine from his goblet. "But then, Captain, even you must know how it is between you and Serena, between any brother with a vexing imp of a younger sister? Childhood is filled with countless quarrels and reconciliations, insults balanced with secret names kept from all adults."

In wordless sympathy Serena looked toward her brother, his face impassive as stone as he hid behind his pride. As children they'd shared none of these things because, quite simply, they'd had no childhood together. Joshua had become the head of their orphaned family when Serena had been a baby and he'd been only nine and already gone away to sea for months at a time. He'd done well for them, moving swiftly from cabin boy to seaman on a privateer, then to shipmaster, and, finally, to captain of his own vessels, finding success and rewards far, far beyond what anyone in Appledore had expected of him. But the price her brother had paid as a boy in return would always exceed whatever gold he'd earned as a man, and Serena was one of the very few who knew it.

And for all he'd done for her sake then, she would not abandon him now.

"Oh, aye, Joshua knows exactly what you mean," she said, striving to emulate Anabelle's teasing banter, "but he's far too gentlemanly to tell tales on me."

She didn't dare look at her brother, but she still could hear him, clearing his throat uneasily before he spoke.

"No, Josh, don't deny it," she said quickly, and flashed a nervous smile at both Gerald and Anabelle. "I won't have him defend me when I don't deserve it. We both know perfectly well what a trial I was to him when we were children."

The younger of the two maids hurried to Anabelle's side, dipped a hasty curtsey, and bent to whisper a message before scurrying back toward the kitchen.

Anabelle's face had grown suddenly serious as she squashed her napkin in a soft heap upon the table. "Like it or not, there's an end to my party," she said with a sigh. "Jacob Hallet's youngest son has fallen from the ladder to their loft whilst playing cat-and-mouse with the twins, and poor Jacob can't decide whether to be cross with the boy or to be worried sick to death himself. A broken leg, from the sound of it. I must go, of course."

Gerald leaned forward with obvious concern. "But surely you don't mean to go yourself, Nan."

"Damnation, she won't be alone," said Joshua as he came to stand beside Anabelle, making it abundantly clear what he thought of Gerald for even asking such a ludicrous question.

But this time Gerald shook off the insult. "Be reasonable, Nan, and consider yourself as well. Wouldn't a surgeon or physician serve the boy better?"

"Not with the nearest surgeon somewhere in Boston

and the Hallets here," she said, pushing her chair back from the table with Joshua's help. "And I do indeed mean to go. Jacob Hallet is one of Joshua's men, one of his crew. He wouldn't have come to me unless he believed I could help."

"But you are a lady, Nan," protested Gerald, clearly appalled that she'd even consider going. "You shouldn't be out wandering about in the cold and darkness because of some clumsy brat!"

"He's not some 'clumsy brat,' Gerald," chided Anabelle gently as she took Joshua's arm. "He's Jacob Hallet's son, and that is sufficient for me."

Serena saw the fresh displeasure clouding her brother's face. Jacob Hallet had sailed with Joshua as long as she could remember, as much a trusted friend as a crewman, and Joshua's loyalties ran deep.

"Anabelle has a rare gift for healing," she ventured swiftly, hoping to forestall her brother yet again. The waters she'd navigated this morning were nothing compared to the currents eddying through this room now. "Though she's only been in Appledore since the summer, the people here have learned to come to her with their troubles."

But Anabelle didn't seem to have heard her. Instead a bittersweet smile played about the younger woman's lips as she paused to smooth her brother's hair.

"Oh, Duckie," she said sadly. "Can't you recall how Mama tended to everyone at Kilmarsh? She didn't care who they were or what they did or whether they worked in the fields or the house, as long as she could ease their sorrows and tend to their illnesses when they needed her. Can't you remember that much of her?"

Gerald didn't answer. Of course he remembered their mother, and likely a good deal better than Anabelle did herself. She'd been only six when Mama died, too young to have any but the simplest memories.

Too young to understand the grim, unhappy farce that their parents' marriage had been, or that the reason their mother had taken such pleasure in easing the pain of others was that she'd been so unable to ease her own. Mama had been tall and willowy, with clouds of spun-gold hair and a flawless pallor that had made her a famous belle throughout Britain. None of that same beauty had come to small, plump, dark-haired Anabelle, or so Gerald had always believed.

Until now. Now, when his sister spoke of helping this sailor's child, all he could see was their mother reflected in his sister's face, Mama's infinite kindness and the gentle way she could soothe any hurt, any pain, any—

"We'll talk tomorrow, Duckie, as you promised," said Anabelle softly, the disappointment clear in her voice as she misinterpreted his silence.

He hated that disappointment, nearly as much as he hated the sharp sensation of loss as she rose to go, away from the table, away from *him*. Not that it was Anabelle's fault. Somehow he'd managed to tangle her together with Kilmarsh and his mother and skipping stones across the still, dark water of a pond, all things he'd thought he'd never forget and now wished fervently that he had.

God help him, could he do nothing right? "Tomorrow, then, Nan," he murmured. "Tomorrow."

"Are you really Anabelle's brother?"

Serena Fairbourne stood waiting for her answer on the other side of the table, her napkin clutched before her like a white flag of surrender. The image was so ludicrous Gerald would have laughed if his head hadn't been throbbing so much from that foul-tasting rum. Surrender, ha! As if any Fairbourne would offer him decent terms for a truce, especially not with that determinedly murderous expression in her eyes.

Lovely eyes, really, dark green and flecked with gold, nearly the same gold that rippled through her hair, green and gold and fit for a mermaid, skimming through the waves to tempt—

"Are you truly Anabelle's brother?" she asked again. "There is precious little resemblance between the two of you that I can see."

"Is that so," he said evenly. No surrender, then, no truce. Well enough. He'd no intention of abandoning the field on the first day of the battle, anyway. "You know I could level the same charge at you, too."

She blushed, the warm pink washing over the roundest part of her cheeks, one of the things he'd noticed first about her this afternoon and one he'd liked at once. "Whatever can you mean?"

"I mean that you, Serena, in turn demonstrate precious little resemblance to your great black bear of a brother, either in appearance or humor, and a good thing, too, for your sake."

"If you do not see a resemblance, it is because I favor my mother," she said, defensiveness creeping into her voice. "And Joshua is not a bear."

"I'm told I favor my mother's family as well. It's Anabelle who's the black sheep in our fold. Or rather the little black bear, to carry the simile to its inevitably proper conclusion."

She frowned, as close as she'd come to admitting she'd no conception of similes, proper or otherwise. "Anabelle would be furious if you called her that to her face."

"She would laugh until she wept, as you know perfectly well. Nan's faults may be beyond counting, but a priggish sense of her own exalted place in the world is not one of them." He swept his arm grandly through the air, the soft linen ruffles on his cuff fluttering back from his wrist. "Pray sit, please, I beg of you, and continue your supper, the way my sister would wish."

She refolded the napkin with tidy precision before setting it beside her plate. "Thank you, sir, no. I find I'm no longer hungry."

"Ah." He let his gaze wander pointedly from her barely touched supper to his own. "Strange how I discover my own appetite has quite vanished, too."

She dipped her chin, her lashes sweeping over cheeks

as she looked down. She might have smiled, but with the flickering light of the candles he wasn't certain. He also wasn't certain what should happen next. A lady and a gentleman in a house empty save for the servants offered interesting possibilities, or at least it would have anywhere other than Massachusetts.

What he didn't expect was for her to take a tray from the sideboard and begin to clear away the dishes from the table.

"The servants will see to that," he said impatiently. "This isn't what Nan meant by playing hostess in her place."

"I did not intend—but no, you are right." The flush returned to her cheeks as she stepped back from the table, her head bowed, clasping her hands tightly together almost as if to punish them for erring. "It is from habit, you see. I forget myself. 'Tis best I leave for home now, before I shame this house again."

He hadn't expected that from her, either. "You do not live here, under your brother's protection?"

She raised her chin, her eyes suddenly defiant. "Do you believe I need protecting?"

The obvious answer was yes. Even if he hadn't found her lost on the water this afternoon—was it really only this afternoon?—he'd have had to say so from the way she looked now, her eyes bright, her lips parted, her breasts rising and falling just enough to make them impossible to ignore over the tight lacing of her gown. God, yes, she needed protecting.

Protecting from *him*.

"Will you permit me to walk you to wherever you're going?" he asked, deftly avoiding her question with another. "Not for protection, but companionship."

"Companionship?" She tipped her head to one side, skeptical. "From you, Mr. Crosbie?"

"If you don't find the prospect too disturbingly odious, yes, from me," he said mildly. "And you must call me by my given name."

Her eyes narrowed, the skepticism deepening.

"You must do it for my sister's sake," he explained. "We must all make certain adjustments to please Anabelle."

"Anabelle *would* have a brother like you." She sighed with impatient resignation, but still didn't use his name. "I'll fetch my cloak."

She left him only long enough for him to consider whether being Anabelle's brother was an insult or a compliment. She returned wearing a red wool cardinal, its simplicity undermined by thick, shaggy mittens, and she carried Gerald's coat and hat.

"Turn about," Serena ordered brusquely, holding his coat up for him. "Come along, before morning."

Dutifully he turned, and she slid the sleeves over his arms and slipped the coat over his shoulders. The coat's fit was snug, the tailoring exact, and she barely stopped herself from smoothing the soft wool over those same broad shoulders. What was it about the man, she thought with dismay, that tempted her to such boldness? She was no better than Bett and Sukey in the kitchen, giggling and twittering over Mistress Fairbourne's comely marvel of a brother.

"Done as neatly as Rourke," he said as he turned, buttoning his coat. "Perhaps you've missed your calling."

"Who is Rourke?" she asked suspiciously.

"My servant, and the one person in creation who keeps me both honest and presentable." He grinned as he took his hat from her and settled it on his head. "I left him at the inn near the waterfront, guarding my possessions and wooing the barmaids."

Much like his master, thought Serena as she turned the key in the box lock on the front door. She used both hands, the wool of the mittens slipping on the polished brass. "You won't be staying here? Anabelle didn't insist?"

"She tried. I declined." He reached around her to turn the key for her, his hand fitting easily over hers. "You see, I don't need protection, either."

Flustered, she pulled her hand away from his and back beneath the shelter of her cloak as she stepped out into the cold. She was already regretting allowing him to come with her. To her gate only, she resolved, and not a single step beyond it.

"No lantern?" he asked with surprise as he latched the door shut behind them.

She shook her head, shuffling her feet both from nervousness and to keep warm. "The moon is nearly full, and besides, I've walked this path so many times I vow I could do it blindfolded."

"In a seaport town?" He frowned. "You walk alone, a lady without even a light to guard you? You should show more concern for your own welfare, lass."

She smiled, as much from the surprise of hearing that "lass" as from how he had turned nearly as grim and serious as Joshua. It was wrong, she knew, to take such pleasure when so much else was at stake, but she couldn't help it.

"Ah, but I'm not alone," she said. "I have Abel."

He shook his head, not understanding, and she whistled low. Instantly a large black shadow came racing around the house, a large, black, and furry shadow that came to a skittering stop before Serena, panting and gazing up at her with undisguised adoration while his entire back quarters lurched back and forth with the force of his wagging tail.

With a little chuckle she crouched down to ruffle the fur around the dog's neck. Joshua had brought Abel to her from Barbados as a birthday surprise three years before, when all he'd been was long silky ears and enormous paws, all of him small enough to fit beneath her arm in a little basket. He had grown considerably since then, and while he'd proven to be no discernable breed, he had become her indefatigable companion and the most loyal of friends.

"You're my good pup, aren't you?" she crooned softly. "Even if you have let Sukey stuff you silly full of scraps in the kitchen, you're still my favorite lad. But here now,

there's someone new you must meet. This is Gerald, and
he is Anabelle's brother, so you must be nice to him
whether you wish to or not."

"What a delightful introduction, Miss Fairbourne,"
said Gerald wryly as he pulled off his glove and patiently
held the back of his hand out for the dog to sniff. He'd
grown up around dogs at Kilmarsh—he'd always suspected his father preferred them to children anyway—
and he knew not to rush canine acquaintance. "As long
as Master Abel won't serve me the same as he does the
kitchen scraps, then I suppose we shall get on famously.
Isn't that so, Abel?"

To Serena's surprise, the dog licked Gerald's hand and
moved closer to his legs to be petted. "Famously, ha,"
she said. "I shall be jealous if he gets on with you any
better. I cannot think of another man besides Joshua that
he even lets touch him."

"We black dogs recognize one another."

"No, Gerald, I am serious," she said, rising. "Abel is a
most suspicious dog with strangers, which makes him
good, constant company for me."

Gerald rubbed the dog's ears between his hands. "He
wasn't with you in the boat."

Serena felt her face grow warm at the mention of the
boat, and the memory it carried with it. "That is because
poor Abel is an abysmal sailor. He cannot abide boats or
ships, and begins to tremble if I so much as lead him
onto a dock. I don't believe he ever recovered from that
first voyage here with Joshua."

"I cannot say I fault Abel for that," murmured Gerald
wryly. "But I do not know as I'd trust such a friendly
pup with guarding you."

"This is Appledore, not Portsmouth or Liverpool,"
she explained. They began to walk together, their shoes
crunching on the brittle mixture of ice and crushed clam
shells that made up the path while Abel trotted alongside. "I keep from the taverns and docks themselves, of
course. That is only prudent. But I know every person

who lives in this town by name and by family, and there is not a soul who would wish me harm."

"What of the ones who come by water?"

She glanced at him shrewdly. "Are you referring to yourself?"

"No, foolish woman, for I am entirely trustworthy. Even your dog recognizes that. I meant all the pirates and smugglers and other rascals that must hug this coast."

She decided for now to let the question of his eminent trustworthiness go unremarked, along with her purported foolishness. Both statements were patently false, of course. He would know it as well as she did herself. But to deny them would lead her back into the same sort of foolish, flirtatious conversation that had ended in a kiss, and she was determined not to let that happen again.

Instead she merely shrugged. "The colony, and this coast, still make for a small world. Few would know the way past the rocks to Cranberry Point, where my house lies. Those who do know my brother as well."

"Quite a Cerebus, your brother," said Gerald drily.

She looked at him quizzically. "Is that something like the nymphs?"

"Not precisely. It means your brother makes a most excellent watchdog for you. Perhaps even better than Abel himself."

"Joshua is like that, and always has been." She sighed, a sigh that bore all the weight of a lifetime of that overbearing brother's careful watching. "Here now, mind yourself on the ice. It's especially thick through here from lying in the shadow of that wall."

But Gerald was more interested in that mournful sigh than in any snow or ice. What must it be like for Serena to always live in the shadow of such a brother? She hadn't mentioned any parents—he supposed they must be dead by now—or a sister to lighten the oppressive burden. No wonder she felt so fiercely proud of living by herself. She'd probably had to fight him tooth and claw for that much independence.

And now, of course, he had Anabelle to smother with his jealousy and rules, and he shook his head at the unfairness of it. How long would his sister's merry little self survive beneath such a husband?

His heart heavy at the prospect, he gazed out across a stone wall and snow-covered meadow toward the sea. They'd long ago left the little town behind, and now walked a narrow, rutted lane, the few bare trees gnarled and bent. It *was* a beautiful night, the blue-black sky dappled with stars and crowned by the silver circle of the full moon, the fields and marshes covered with snow as pale as the moon itself.

But all Gerald could see was the chilly bleakness of it. How narrow and empty life here must be! Anabelle could have been a duchess if she'd played her hand right. She could have had ermine on her gowns and jewels beyond counting, grand houses and hundreds of servants and a place at court among the wittiest people on earth. All the amusements and entertainments of London, Paris, and Rome could have been hers.

And yet in the hot, heady fever of desire Anabelle had traded it away for these empty, snow-covered fields and a town with fewer people than they'd had servants at Kilmarsh. What would become of her when her infatuation with Joshua Fairbourne faded, and she saw him for the overbearing bully he was? Where would she turn when she'd realized how impetuous she'd been, how fleeting passion could be?

To him, he thought grimly. To *him*. He had come this far to save Anabelle, and save her he would.

"Is that why you didn't admit to knowing me?" he asked Serena finally. "You feared your brother's bite?"

Startled from her own thoughts, she didn't answer at first, but he could see how her face closed against him in defense. He wished she weren't so much on her guard, and though he couldn't really blame her, he wished she'd smile instead. She didn't smile as often as Anabelle did, or as quickly, either, but when she did it was something a man wouldn't soon forget.

She fiddled with the front of her cloak, worrying the fabric with the thumb of her mitten. "I had—that is, I *have*—my reasons."

"Ah, reasons," he said with a sage nod. "There are so many. Indignant virtue, outraged propriety, second, third, fourth thoughts, the renewed conviction that you'd never, ever let yourself be kissed by a gentleman you hadn't met through a genteel introduction."

To his surprise, she didn't laugh. She didn't even smile. "It's all those things, yes," she admitted seriously, "but you must understand that this is not entirely my own secret to keep. There is, you see, another involved as well."

"Your brother again," he said, though with an oddly sickening certainty he knew what would follow. Watchdog or not, she was far too pretty, far too delectable, to live her life alone.

She shook her head. "Oh, no, not Joshua. No."

"A sweetheart, then?" he persisted, determined to hear from her own lips what he'd already guessed. "A lover? You'd gone to meet a man that does not have your brother's approval?"

She stared at him, her eyes round with amazement that he'd jumped to such an unlikely conclusion. Unlikely, and untrue, but still useful.

"Yes!" she blurted out in a breathless rush. "Yes, that is where I'd been, and now that I've told you, you must give me your word you'll never tell Joshua!"

He slipped his hand into the pocket of his coat, seeking and finding the shells he'd tucked inside. He could toss them away now. He'd amazed himself, really, by keeping them as long as he had. He could drop them right here on the path.

But he didn't.

"Your secret's safe, lass," he said softly. "Your brother-bear won't hear it from me."

But instead of thanking him, she shook her head.

"Please don't call Joshua a bear, or a watchdog, or anything else. He's not like that, not at all."

Gerald's brows rose with scornful disbelief. "He's all that and nothing else from what I've seen."

"But what you've seen is scarcely all." She stopped to rest her mittened hand on his arm, pleading. "My brother is about the bravest man I've ever known. He's fought in wars and against every sort of enemies, and he's never yet lost a ship to a storm or to rocks. But tonight—tonight he was scared. Scared of you, and the trouble and sorrow you could bring to him and to Anabelle."

"'Tis not so grievous as all that, Serena," he said gently, placing his hand over her mitten. Surely there'd be no harm in that. "Men will always shake their swords and stamp their feet, but it does not necessarily signal the end of the world."

She drew away, shaking her head. "For Joshua, it could," she said sadly, "and there's precious little he can do to fight back."

"I cannot believe—"

"Nay, do not lie to me, I beg you," she said, drawing her hood more closely around her face. "I understand too much for that as it is. No wonder Joshua is so frightened of you. For I am, too."

"Don't say that, sweetheart." How could she believe his quarrel was with her? He held his hand out to her, not daring to touch her yet still offering his touch, his assurances, offering himself. "I would never want you frightened of me."

He wanted to take her in his arms and tell her anything she wished to hear that would make her not be afraid, anything that would take the sadness from her lovely eyes and make her laugh and smile again. He wanted to hold her close, to slip his hands inside her scarlet cloak and find her warmth inside. He wanted to forget there was another man with a claim to her, and he wanted to kiss her again, to taste her sweetness and see if she could turn his senses upside down a second time.

"I must go," she said as she stepped backward, away from him. "I'm home, you see."

He hadn't noticed they'd come so far, near enough to the sea again that he could hear the endless *shush* of the waves. She stood before a low white fence, banked with snow, and behind her was a small clapboarded house with a single chimney that must be hers.

"Stay another minute," he said, not wanting to lose her yet. "Please."

She shook her head, taking one step back through the open gate and latching it shut between them. Abel had already bounded ahead, waiting expectantly on the stone doorstep.

"Good night, Gerald, and thank you for—for your companionship. That was it, wasn't it? If you keep to the same road, you shall be back in Appledore in no time."

He wanted to keep the image of her like this forever, her red cloak against the white snow and the dark shadow of her house, her upturned face as luminous as the moonlight itself.

"What a rare lady you are, Serena Fairbourne," he said softly. "Do you know that when I first saw you, I thought you were no more than a common fisherman's daughter?"

"You did?" she asked, her face alight with shy surprise at his compliment. "A rare lady who was also a fisherman's daughter?"

He nodded, wishing he knew what to say to make her linger. "A fisherman's daughter, there with your buckets of scallops at your feet."

"Ah. The scallops." She nodded as if there could be no other explanation. "And here I thought you were no more than a dream."

And at last she smiled, the warmth of it hanging in the cold night air as she gently closed her door and left him alone.

Four

"Mistress Fairbourne's still abed, sir," said the maid named Sukey, lavishing her announcement with a winning smile. "She won't be seeing anyone, sir, leastways 'til noon."

"Indeed," said Gerald, his own smile doubling hers. "And is Captain Fairbourne abed with her?"

Sukey gasped with scandalized delight. "Ooh, no, sir, 'course he don't be *there,* not at this time o' day! He's a proper Christian gentleman, the captain is!"

Gerald heard the muted patter of bare feet overhead and raised his gaze to find Anabelle grinning over the stair rail at him. The morning sun streamed in through a handsome arched window on the landing, and he had to admit that by daylight the staircase had better proportions and more elegant carving and turnings then he'd judged last night. He prided himself on having a fine eye for architecture; Italy did that for a gentleman. This stair was quite imposing, really, even with Anabelle's face hanging upside down above him, her hair in mussed braids flopping from beneath her cap.

"Well, good morning to you, too, Duckie," she said cheerfully. "Come up directly, won't you? And Sukey, next time all you need say is that I'm not at home. No protestations of Captain Fairbourne's spiritual accomplishments, mind? Now back to the kitchen with you and help with supper."

Sukey nodded, dipped a curtsey, and fled, but not without tossing one last smile, beyond Anabelle's sight, over her shoulder to Gerald.

Anabelle sighed with dramatic resignation. "She thinks I don't know how wickedly she behaves," she said as Gerald climbed the stairs to join her. "Mooning on as if she's no other tasks before her than to make calf's eyes at you. Though *you* didn't exactly help matters, either, asking after Joshua that way. You know that particular bit of raillery will be all over Appledore by nightfall."

"Oh, come now, Nan, don't be so hard on the girl," said Gerald, "or on yourself, either. Neither of you deserves it."

Anabelle tipped her cheek up for him to kiss and sighed again. She was still in her nightrail, a French nightrail thick with lace, the silk drawstring at the neckline loose enough for the fine linen to slip down to bare one round, rosy shoulder. Doubtless that, too, was spoken of all over Appledore, and Gerald wondered what else the townspeople had possibly had to discuss around their hearths before the Crosbies had swept up on their shore.

"I rather believe I do," she said dolefully as he followed her to her bedchamber. "Deserve it, that is. Have you breakfasted? The kettle's hanging by the fire if you wish tea, and there's still half a plate of raisin buns and honey-butter. I can call for coffee, too, if you'd prefer. That's what Joshua drinks, but these days even the scent of it makes me vilely ill first thing in the morning, and so I've banished his coffee pot to the kitchen."

The bedchamber was a large corner room paneled in jade green, a warm, welcoming room full of the bright

51

morning sun. As with the parlor below, Gerald could see his sister's hand throughout the room: the gilt-framed mirror over the fireplace, the rose-pink hangings on the bedstead, the colored prints of frolicking monkeys on the walls, and, most tellingly, the rumpled stockings and garter-ribands strewn carelessly over the back of a chair.

"You will excuse me if I return to bed," said Anabelle as she used the little mahogany step to climb into the tall bedstead. There was no mistaking her pregnancy this morning, for the nightrail did little to hide her body's plump curves. Nor did Gerald need to count the months to guess that she and Fairbourne had made ample use of that long ocean voyage from England.

Oblivious to his thoughts, Anabelle nestled down against the bolsters with a happy sigh and drew the coverlet high over her knees, tossing aside the pink-covered novel she'd been reading. "This is, you know, the one truly warm place in the house."

Gerald warmed the tea in the pot with hot water from the kettle, and settled himself in one of the armchairs, considering what argument might have a breath of a chance with her. How the devil was he supposed to convince her to return to England while she was finding so much to content her here?

"How fares that boy you went to tend last night?" he asked, searching for a way to begin their conversation. "Did he survive your ministrations?"

"He most certainly will survive, thank you," said Anabelle, "and he will flourish, not so much from my tending as from his concentrated desire to be able to thrash the brother that pushed him from the ladder in the first place. I suppose I should be grateful you bothered to ask, even if your solicitude was not well-meant."

"It's not his welfare that concerns me, Nan. It's yours. I still cannot fathom why you would go."

"Because I should," she said promptly. "Because it's good to do good for others, though I doubt *you'd* ever understand that. It's also one of the few things I can do well."

"Oh, I doubt that." Instantly Gerald thought of a number of other occupations—raising scandals, squandering doweries, leaving perfectly good husbands at the altar—that she apparently did rather well, too. "I told you before. You are entirely too hard upon yourself."

She threw her arms back against the pillows and let free a dramatic, disconsolate sigh.

"This whole wretched mare's nest is my fault," she declared, abruptly enough for Gerald to look up from his tea with surprise. "Entirely mine, Duckie. Entirely! You can't know how glad I am that you've come clear across the ocean to see it all for yourself, and I vow I shall listen to any suggestions you might have for putting things back to rights."

He stared at her with open, speechless disbelief. He never dreamed she'd see her own error, that she'd make his whole outlandish mission so easy to fulfill!

"Oh, stop gaping like a carp," she scoffed, twisting one of her braids around her fingers. "You must have seen the sorry mess I'm in from the moment you crossed that doorstep. The only thing that can save me now is a fresh beginning, except that I can't contrive how to do it for myself."

"You know," he said quickly, plunging ahead, "if you came back to London, Grandmother could set everything to rights for you."

Anabelle stopped her twisting, now the one staring at *him*. "Grandmother? However how?"

"The usual way she fixes anything," said Gerald as his confidence grew. "Being a dowager duchess does have certain prerogatives. Why, she'll simply begin calling on her old coven of friends, spinning some tale or another about where you've been hiding, and then when she's ready to launch you anew—"

"*'Launch* me?' Like one of Joshua's ships?" Her voice squeaked upward with amazed amusement. "Gerald, dearest, you are not thinking I'd actually wish to return to London, do you?"

He set the tea dish and spoon down with a clatter. "What the devil else could you mean, Nan? Mare's nests and fresh beginnings: if there's another way to read that sort of confession, then I'd like to hear it."

"Oh, poor, poor Duckie!" she said, trying hard not to laugh. "What a dreadful slattern you must think me, that I'd wish to be rid of my husband as easy as that! To go traipsing back to London, as huge as a horse, and expect Grandmother to try to find me another gentleman—oh, Gerald, it would be too, too vastly wicked, even for me!"

She laughed then, unable to help herself, and fluttered her plump little hands before her as if her merriment needed even further amplification.

And for the second time that morning Gerald could think of nothing to say. As his family's ambassador, as his sister's savior, he was an absolute failure. Yet as Anabelle's laughter bubbled around him, he also felt like a stiff-backed prig and a hopeless fool, each of which was considerably worse than being a mere failure.

"Hellfire, Nan, you needn't laugh," he said crossly. "It's not all that bloody amusing."

"It is rather, Gerald," she said, dabbing at the teary corner of her eye with the edge of the sheet. "I meant those ninnies in the kitchen, my sorrowful excuses for servants. I spoil them abominably, and I never will be able to run a decent house the way Joshua deserves. And can you imagine what sort of pitiful mother I shall be?"

He frowned, wishing she wouldn't keep reminding him in so many ways of this infernal baby of hers. Besides not wishing to envision any more precisely how she'd come to this sorry state, the whole notion of confinement and childbirth and all their unpleasant, queasy details disturbed his bachelor sensibilities.

"You will be exactly the same kind of mother as you are a silly young chit," he said, his crossness not abating a fraction. "Irresponsible and self-indulgent and a trial to all who must care for you."

"Most likely you are right," she said with infinitesimal remorse. "The greatest punishment I can foresee is that this child shall be as handsome as Joshua and as willful and wild as I, a dreadful combination, and that as its mother I shall have no end of trouble and sorrow for the rest of my days."

Gerald considered all the trouble and sorrow he'd expended on her behalf already, and she was only his sister.

"You deserve that, Nan," he said darkly. "That, and a great deal more."

"Yes." She smiled warmly. "Perhaps he—or she— shall take after his—or her—Uncle Gerald instead."

"Then may merciful God preserve the poor wee creature," declared Gerald, "because its sweet-tempered father surely won't."

"Of course he will. And to prove it, Joshua has agreed that you shall be godfather."

With a sigh Gerald leaned back in his chair. "Nan, pray do not believe that such an action will influence me one way or another. Recall that I am already godfather to several other squalling sprats within our family alone."

"You shall have to stay here in Appledore until after the baby is born, of course," she continued, ignoring him as completely as if he hadn't spoken. "But that will only be another four months or so. That is what the midwife says. Four very short, very tiny months. You will stay, Duckie? For me?"

He hadn't expected that sudden wistfulness from Anabelle, or the edge of fear in her voice, either. She was watching him closely, the sheet bunched in her fists as she silently willed him to agree. Odd how now she actually looked her age in that great rumpled bed, her eyes huge in her round little face.

Unwillingly he recalled disjointed memories of the night when Anabelle herself had been born, Mama screaming and Father drunk and midwives running every which way with blood-covered linen while no one had paid the slightest attention to him or his brothers, cowering fearfully on the stairs. No wonder Anabelle looked frightened, with that sort of woman's ordeal before her. How could he blame her? And how, really, could he leave?

"Four more months, you say?" he asked slowly. Four months was an eternity; he wouldn't be back in England before summer at the earliest, a saddening, sobering thought. "April?"

"Or May," said Anabelle eagerly. "There is no sure way to tell for certain with babies. You wouldn't wish to sail for England before then anyway, not with the great sea-storms in the Atlantic in February. Not even Joshua would venture a voyage then. But 'tis only four months, Duckie. Not so very long at all."

Four months. Four months to battle Joshua Fairbourne, four months to convince Anabelle to return to London with him, four months to overcome the cold and bleakness and boredom of this grim little excuse for a town.

Four months, maybe five. *Months*. Gerald wasn't entirely convinced he would survive.

"It's not such a fearsome responsibility, Duckie," she said forlornly, reading his reluctance. "You said that yourself. It would not take such a great effort to say yes. And you would be sharing your godfatherly duties with Serena."

"Serena?" he repeated blankly, thinking only of how Serena related to him, thinking of how she'd appeared so suddenly in the fog, of how she'd tasted when he'd kissed her. Coming to the image of Serena as another dutiful relation coerced into sanctioning Anabelle's mischief took a bit more time. *"Serena?"*

"Yes, Serena." Anabelle sighed. "I know she wasn't to your liking, Duckie. I saw it in your eyes at once. You dismissed her as plain and, well, odd, the kind of holy-hallowed spinster you've always detested, but she really is very nice."

Serena Fairbourne wasn't plain, far from it, and she

certainly wasn't detestable. His situation would be much easier if she were. "That's not the point, Anabelle."

"Oh, bah, Gerald," she scoffed. "Where women are concerned, there *is* no other point with you. Your mistresses have always been the gayest sort of *jollie femmes,* strumpety French dancers and Italian singers and goodness knows what else. You can have as many mistresses as you please since you're a younger son, and no one worries whether you'll marry well, or even at all."

"How the devil—"

"Grandmother told me all about them," she said promptly. "As a cautionary tale, I suppose. She wished me to know what sorts of wickedness I should expect, and accept, from perfectly respectable gentlemen. Can you fancy what she told me about—"

"No more, Nan, if you please. No more." He exhaled slowly, wondering how the balance of his world had spun so far from what it should be. To hear his sweet-faced little sister catalogue his past inamoratas in such detail was beyond bearing. "You'd begun to speak of Serena Fairbourne."

"Serena. Very well." Reluctantly Anabelle shifted back to the less titillating topic. "I've grown very fond of Serena, you know. Perhaps because we've both only known brothers, we can pretend we truly are sisters. And she is so very agreeable that I don't know why she hasn't married. I don't suppose she will now, though to hear Joshua it hasn't been from lack of suitors. He says there have been gentlemen who have been most attentive, too."

"But none good enough for her brother?" asked Gerald lightly, remembering Serena's breathless admission and how she'd sworn him to secrecy regarding her lover.

" 'Tis not Joshua's doing that she's a spinster," said Anabelle defensively. "I do believe he'd like little better than to see her settled and happy. The problem lies with Serena. She simply seems to have no interest in marriage, or in men, either, for that sorry matter. I cannot fathom it myself."

"No, goose-girl," he murmured dryly. "I'll wager you cannot."

He thought of Serena clutching the long red cloak around her with the shaggy homespun mittens, standing in the snow before the prim little house where she chose to live alone, still troubled by the memory of a single stolen kiss. He knew for a fact that Serena had a most admirable interest in men. He'd tasted the proof firsthand. Anabelle was wrong there. But as for the rest, his sister was right as rain.

He could not imagine two more different women, different in every conceivable way, and the first small germ of an idea began to quiver and root in his thoughts. It was, he sensed uneasily, going to blossom into a misbegotten weed of a plan, an unruly and unlovely plan that should be yanked from the garden now before its roots took too firm a grasp into his consciousness. But he left it alone, and let it grow, and God help him, grow it did.

"It's Joshua's wish that she become more genteel," Anabelle was saying, "to learn to be more of a lady. She's not had much opportunity here in Appledore. Not that I am worth a farthing as a teacher, of course, but I have tried to make her aware of, well, the *niceties* of life, to help her learn a bit about pretty things."

He thought of the twin scallop shells, transferred with foolish care and behind Rourke's back from one coat pocket to the next so he'd have them with him. No, Anabelle was wrong about Serena there, too; she didn't need any lessons at all in seeing beauty. His gaze hovered briefly upon a print of two monkeys in Chinese costumes, posed before some ruined garden folly as they danced a minuet, and he wondered idly if perhaps Serena would be willing to tutor Anabelle instead.

He tapped his fingers on the damask-covered arm of his chair, his weed of a plan sending out all manner of curling tendrils.

"It's been my experience," he said with a careless

shrug, "albeit limited, that one lady doesn't generally much care for being advised by another."

Anabelle's eyes widened with interest. "Do you mean among your mistresses? You would ask one to teach another what you preferred?"

"Wherever do you come by such notions, Nan?" he asked with more dismay than displeasure. "And the answer is no, as it would be from any gentleman with a fraction of his wits about him. Nor have I ever, ah, addressed more than one fair creature at a time. I am not some many-houri'd pasha and never have been, and I'll thank you to recall it."

"I rather wish you were," she said with undisguised disappointment. "It would be vastly more interesting."

"No," he said. "It would not. And what I meant by women was, for example, you and your various nursemaids. You and whichever of your governesses stayed at Kilmarsh for more than a week. You and Grandmother. You and any other female in God's creation."

"But it is not that way with Serena," protested Anabelle. "We are like sisters. Truly, Duckie. I have done my absolute best to behave since I've come to Appledore, and Serena has made it easy."

He lifted one brow in disbelief, unable to comprehend what Anabelle's absolute best might in fact be.

"I swear to it, Gerald, you horrid toad," she said indignantly, and hurled a small pillow toward his head. "You might ask Joshua, if you can promise not to try to take one another's heads off again. Or better yet, you should ask Serena directly. She will tell you how well-mannered I've been, and you would have to believe *her*."

He caught the pillow, and began to toss it gently from one hand to another as he rose to his feet. In a curious way, it all made a great deal of sense. He loved his sister, and Serena loved her brother. Fate could never make them in turn lovers, but perhaps they could settle for allies instead. "Then I shall call on Miss Fairbourne."

"Serena," said Anabelle, warily eying the pillow in his hands. "No matter how hard it is for you to do so, you truly must call her by her given name. For my sake, Duckie, do please try to be agreeable to her."

"For your sake, Nan, and yours alone," he said, tossing the pillow harmlessly back beside her as he made a neat bow of farewell, "I resolve to be as agreeable as a summer's day."

And with that resolution, he felt his obstreperous weed of a plan burst into full and lurid flower.

Serena crumpled a handful of curled hickory bark and tossed it into the fire, pausing as its rich, pungent scent rose up from the flames to fill the parlor. At least she hoped it would. She'd spent much of the morning pickling the scallops she'd raked yesterday and the whole house still smelled of them. Fish of any sort was well and good in a kettle or on a plate, but to her mind it had no business lingering in her house like an unwelcome guest.

Or on her hands, either, she thought ruefully as she looked down at the innumerable nicks and scratches she'd earned by opening all those scallops herself. Even Gerald Crosbie would not be so ridiculous as to mistake her for a lady now, not with hands like these, and she smiled to herself again at the memory of his idle words, and at her own foolishness for remembering them.

As if lily-white hands were all she needed to turn *her* into a lady—the sort of fine, gracious lady that Gerald Crosbie would favor and Joshua so much wanted her to become. She had tried, and she would keep on trying for her brother's sake, but the honest truth was that she would have been happier as that fisherman's daughter or wife, the way she'd been taught as a girl.

Yet she was content enough with her life as it was. Aye, content, that was it. She'd be greedy and ungrateful to feel otherwise.

"Whatever shall you do with me, Abel?" she asked the dog, who lay near the fire with his head on his paws. "Have you ever seen a more forlorn creature?"

In sympathy Abel thumped his tail against the floor. Serena smiled sadly and, with a sigh that should have been more satisfied, she swept the cornbread crumbs from the tabletop and into her gathered apron. She drew the latchstring on the door and slipped outside, standing on the worn stone step to snap the crumbs free from her apron and onto the snow for the birds.

The day was cloudless and bright, the sky an enameled blue and the sun nearly blinding as it glanced off the snow, and Serena's unwilling spirits began to rise as high as the gulls near the end of the point. She shaded her eyes to gaze out across the bay, heedless of the cold. How could anyone feel baleful or somber on a day such as this?

"Have you any crumbs to spare, sweetheart?" asked Gerald. "Any crusts to scatter before me?"

She turned swiftly to find him standing beside the fence, one gloved hand resting on the gate. "How long have you been standing there?"

"A fine greeting, that," he said with a sorrowful shake of his head as Abel squeezed past her to race happily to Gerald's side. "Perhaps we should begin again. Good day to you, Miss Serena. Have you any crumbs to spare for this weary English sparrow?"

"A sparrow, ha," she said defensively. "More like some dimwitted cockerel without the sense to keep to his roost in the snow."

Too late she wished she'd kept the way to her house secret from him. He didn't belong here, yet somehow by her gate he was managing to look both completely at home—faith, even her own dog thought so—and ludicrously misplaced, the perpetual elegance of his clothing at odds with the rough-hewn little fence that came barely to his waist.

"But I have no roost," he said cheerfully, his words coming with fleeting white clouds in the cold air. "None to claim as my special place in this land, anyway. I've flown so far from my own, you see, that I'm thoroughly lost and confused and in need of your assistance. Hence I beg for crumbs. *Your* crumbs, dear lady."

"You're perfectly free to scrabble and peck about in

the snow. Leastways I shall not stop you." She wished he wouldn't talk like this, either, bantering and saying nonsensical things calculated to make her laugh, and reminding her all too much of the boat and the fog and the kiss.

"Ah, then I *am* welcome to enter," he said with satisfaction as he unlatched the gate and stepped inside, the skirts of his coat swinging behind him as he played with Abel. "I was not certain, even without your Brother-Cerebus in residence."

"I didn't mean that," she said with swift dismay as he began walking up the narrow cleared path toward her. The low fence would never have kept him out if he'd truly wished to enter—he'd only to have swung his long legs over it to be inside—but she'd found comfort in the symbol of it, a barrier that he'd now crossed. "That is, I have many things to attend to this day, Mr. Crosbie, and have no time for entertaining company."

"But I am not company," he said, bowing before her with a flourish of his arm. "I am family. Which makes me Gerald, Serena dear, and not Mr. Crosbie. How dreadfully difficult that seems to be for you to do!"

From her step she looked down at him, smiling up at her as he held the bow a fraction longer. It *was* hard for her to call him by his given name. She wouldn't deny it. How could it be otherwise? Her family was her brothers, Joshua and Daniel and Samson, and, since last September, she'd come to include Anabelle in that family as well. But to extend that close-bound circle to the alarmingly charming, dangerous man before her was asking more than she could give.

Troubled, she rubbed her bare forearms for warmth, then self-consciously hid her scratched and scarred hands in the folds of her petticoat. Lord, but he had blue eyes, the bluest she'd ever seen on a man. Maybe they only seemed so blue because they also seemed perpetually close to laughter, as sunny and cloudless as the sky overhead. Or maybe it was no more than a trick of the light, reflecting up from the color he habitually wore.

"Now pray tell *me,* Serena," he said, "are you going to ask me into your house as decency requires, or am I still too terrifying a mortal to be let past your door?"

Her chin rose sharply, the way he'd expected it would, and for the first time since she'd noticed him by the fence she let her gaze square with his. It was one thing for her to admit that she'd felt intimidated by him, but quite another for a woman like her—at least the woman he'd kissed in an open boat in the fog—to stand by meekly and let him say the same.

"I never intended such a slander," she said warmly, brushing an errant strand of hair from her face. "You misspeak."

He smiled and spread his arms grandly to each side. "Then you have my apology for so doing," he said as he walked toward her, "and my gratitude for your hospitality. My walk from the village was a cold one, and farther than I recalled. If you've something warming in your kettle—"

"Come." Grudgingly she pulled the door open and stepped aside barely enough to let him pass before following him inside with Abel slipping in between them to return to his place by the hearth. Gerald tried not to smile; he might have won this much from her, but clearly she was going to make him earn every ounce of hospitality. Terrified, ha. *He* should be the one who was terrified, venturing into her dragon's—or would it be dragoness's?—lair like this.

She went to stand behind a spindle-backed armchair at the head of the trestle table, resting her hands on the bulbous finials. "If you're cold, you'll wish to sit here. 'Tis closest to the fire."

He bowed his thanks and took the seat she offered, smiling at her hurry to turn away and tend to the fire. He drew off his gloves and hat and unbuttoned his coat, looking curiously around the room as his eyes grew accustomed to the shadows.

Here within, the house was even smaller than he'd guessed from the outside, not much more than the single

63

room in which they sat. With its large open hearth, this one chamber seemed to serve as parlor and kitchen and bedchamber, too, for an old-fashioned bedstead, the curtains demurely drawn closed for day, was tucked into one corner where the roof dipped low. The walls were paneled with plain battens and boards darkened by age and smoke from the fire—he could well imagine how the northeastern wind whistled through them on a cold night. The four square windows held diamond-patterned casements that let in little light, even on as bright a day as this. Overhead the room was open clear to the eaves of the roof, save for a walled-off loft reached by a ladder.

Yet as humble as the house was, Serena still had filled it with countless small things that set it apart as hers: a branch of orange and gold bittersweet rising from a fat-bottomed bottle, an impromptu vase scavenged from the beach; a pewter bowl of lemons and oranges, their pebbled skin carefully knobbed with sweet-scented cloves; a parade of scallop shells, much like the ones in his pocket, all ordered by color and size along the narrow shelf over the fire. There were no fantastical monkeys capering in Chinese robes to be found here. Nor, decided Gerald, were they missed.

"What an agreeable little nook you have fashioned for yourself," he said, watching her back as she bent beside the hearth. It was an agreeable back, too, with a narrow waist he'd like to try spanning with his hands above the bowed strings of her apron. "How long have you lived here?"

"I was born here. Joshua, Danny, Sam—all of us." Without turning, she gave the coals beneath the wood another jab with the poker. "My father built most of this house by himself, before he wed my mother."

"All your life, then." He remembered what she'd said about her childhood last night, and he could almost hear the house echoing with the sounds of the four children.

"Hardly." She rose, dusting her hands on her apron, and busied herself before the cupboard, again without looking at him. "My father drowned when I was still a babe, and though my mother had loved him and depended on him to provide for her, he left her with nothing more than four children and his debts. Love did nothing for her then. Nothing. She saw this house and everything in it sold away from her. It took Joshua nigh fourteen years to earn enough to buy the house back, but he did. He did."

Gerald could sense how much more lay behind that simple telling and that stiff, straight back. "Your mother must have been proud of him," he said gently, "and of you, too, for keeping her house."

"She never knew. She died, too, before I'd reached my first birthday. I have no memory of her at all. As orphans of the parish, Joshua was sent to sea and the rest of us put out with whichever family had room and need of extra hands. I can brew you tea or coffee, if you wish, or pour you a cup of rum, or of the cider that's already hot."

"The cider would do handsomely," he murmured. This, then, was the hard truth, and her tales of a happy, boisterous childhood had been no more than that, meant to protect her stiff-backed brother who had done so much for her. "And I am sorry, lass, sorry for the rest."

Brusquely she set a pewter tankard filled with steaming cider before him. " 'Tis all old sorrows, long done."

Long done, perhaps, he thought, but from the careful set of her face the old sorrows and their pain lingered still, another fence she didn't want him to cross. No wonder she clung so fiercely to this house, her one connection to the parents she'd never known.

As he sipped the hot, sweet cider, she placed a plate of sliced cornbread and butter on the table and a small crock of red jelly beside it. "The bread's fresh this day," she said, "but you, Master Sparrow, must make your own crumbs of it."

He smiled, more at her obvious attempt to lighten the mood than at the jest itself. He understood the need to keep the past tucked away where it couldn't hurt. God knew he'd done it enough himself.

He rose long enough to pat the second chair. "You will join me?"

"Oh, I ate earlier," she said, but still came to perch on the edge of the chair across from his. She smoothed her hair back around her ears, watching with anxious anticipation as he spooned the red jelly onto a piece of the cornbread. "The cranberry quiddany is my own receipt. I add red rose water before I strain the berries—there, you know my secret—which explains the claret color. No one else in Appledore does it that way."

"Red rose water, you say." He held the bread up, letting the firelight shine through the glistening dollop of ruby quiddany, and gave it the same critical frown he'd show while tasting a prized brandy. "Paramount to the greatest secret of crown, I'd vow."

At last he bit into it, savoring the expression of mingled pride and dread on Serena's face as much as the quiddany. He couldn't remember the last time he'd sat to table with the same woman who'd cooked or baked the food before him. Perhaps he never had, a grievous oversight on his part that he resolved to end at once.

"The finest I've tasted in all the world," he declared with, for once, complete honesty. He took another bite, trying not to consider how blessedly fortunate that unknown suitor of hers would be. "And my first taste of cranberries, too. Are the canes found here on your land?"

She shook her head, relaxing enough to rest her arms on the table and lean closer to him. "Cranberries don't grow on canes, or bushes, or brambles. Rather they grow in marshes or bogs. They're a great bother to gather and they take more than their own weight in sugar to cure their tartness, but still they are a favorite of mine."

"And of mine now, too." He dipped the spoon again into the crock and held it out before her mouth, the quiddany red and glistening against the polished pewter. "The cook deserves a taste, doesn't she?"

He saw the uncertainty flicker in her eyes. Doubtless no one had fed her since she'd been a little child, and she'd no notion of how pleasurable—and different—it could be once grown.

"Come now, Serena dear," he coaxed, his voice low as he balanced the spoon before her. "You know how wonderfully sweet it is. Please yourself."

Still she hesitated, her lips parted a fraction from their own longing. He waited, his patience for such things endless, and from her eyes alone he knew the exact moment she decided to trust him. Slowly she leaned forward, her mouth opened, as obedient as a hatchling's. He held the tip of the spoon to her lips and slid the red jelly into her mouth, watching how it stained her lower lip a darker red, how her tongue licked the bowl of the spoon clean, how she smiled shyly at the quiddany's sweetness and at him, how she swallowed with her chin lifted, baring the whiteness of her throat.

God help him for a fool, but he wanted to taste the cranberry on her. He wanted to kiss her now, here, and with a degree of hungry urgency that startled him, and that he knew was unwise. He had serious matters to discuss with her, and there'd be nothing serious said if he pulled her onto his knee and kissed her charming self senseless, the way he was so strongly tempted to do.

Damnation, what was it about her that could reduce him to this miserable state?

Somehow he managed to break the wordless link between them, and with a sigh he dropped the wanton spoon back into the crock. "It is an honor to have such a cook in the family. Nan couldn't bring a kettle of water to boil, not if all eternity depended upon it."

To his regret, Serena's smile faded and she looked down at the table. "No. No, I don't suppose she could. But I do not believe Joshua cares. Anabelle has so many other . . . so many other ways to please him."

A sudden blush burned her cheeks as she continued rapidly, her clasped hands twisting before her. "You must think me disloyal, as well as terribly rude, to speak of Anabelle this way. She has become very dear to me, and I know she loves Joshua with all her heart, and has made him happier than I've ever seen him, and yet—and yet it is so hard for me sometimes, to see them so happy together while I—oh, pray forgive me, I did not mean to speak so!"

"There's nothing to forgive, Serena," he said gently. How could he ever fault her for such a confession?

"But you are also a better person than I am, Gerald," she said miserably, her head hanging low. "I'm being petty and selfish, while you are generous and forgiving even after I've insulted your sister."

"Ah, you're not so wicked as all that." He reached to stroke her cheek softly with the back of his finger. "Nor am I such an angel."

She had called him Gerald. She'd made it sound new on her tongue, twisted and turned into Massachusetts syllables that enchanted him because they were hers. He wished he could stop there, with cranberry quiddany and stolen kisses his one pleasurable goal, and without considering how and what to say next that would make her agree to help him. He would have to be clever if he were to persuade her. He would need a kind of cunning cleverness that he didn't much like, not in others and especially not in himself.

It was all for Anabelle's sake, he sternly reminded his faltering conscience. His sister's happiness mattered more than all the Fairbournes put together. He was doing this for Anabelle, for her good and the good of their family.

But any fool could see that by saving Anabelle, he would in turn hurt Serena's brother, and whatever else Serena Fairbourne might be, she was no fool.

He sighed heavily, still wishing there were another way. "Nan has asked me to stay here until the birth," he began, "and to be godfather to the baby."

Serena glanced up, her gold-flecked eyes shining though her smile was wobbly. "They have asked me to do the same. To be the godmother, that is. They know I'd no intention of journeying away."

"A rare honor for us both." His own smile felt wickedly false as he forced himself to continue. "But in these next months I intend to play the dutiful brother as well. Our grandmother in particular wishes assurance that Nan is content in her, ah, new situation."

The happiness vanished from Serena's eyes. "You won't try to steal her away and back to England, would you? Though he would never say it aloud, that is what my brother fears the most—that with you here, Anabelle will recall all she gave up to marry him, and change her mind, and leave. You wouldn't do that to Joshua, would you?"

That was precisely what Gerald intended. To hear it from Serena was disquieting indeed.

"You can't make Anabelle do anything against her will," he said with finality, for that much at least was true. "I never have been able to, anyway."

Serena sighed. "You are right. No one can. Not even Joshua."

"Then might I ask you to help me see as much as I can of Nan's new life here?" he asked. "To show me the bad as well as the good, so that I can set things to rights for her, as much as is in my power?"

That was also true, in a way. He wished to know Anabelle's dislikes so he could play upon them and make her realize how much happier she'd be back in London, where she belonged. Where they *both* belonged.

So why, then, with so much at stake, did he despise himself for smiling at Serena Fairbourne?

"You *are* a good brother, to have come all this way for her sake," said Serena softly. What more could she wish than to see Anabelle happy and content, and Joshua with her? If Gerald Crosbie wanted to accomplish that, then there'd be no question but that she'd help him.

"You shall show me all the glories of Appledore, sweet," he said lightly, teasing again, as he brushed her cheek again with his fingers. Such a light touch for so large a man! "You shall be my own *cicerone.*"

She frowned at the unfamiliar word. "I will not agree until I know what is expected of a sissa—a sissa—"

"A *cicerone.* That's what they're called in Rome,

lurking about the ruins." His dark brows framed the amusement in his eyes. "'Tis but a guide, Serena dear, with no other improper duties expected. But a true *cicerone* must be a most excellent sort of guide, one familiar with not only the interesting landmarks of a place, but with the customs and histories as well."

"You and I alone?" she asked doubtfully. "No one else?"

He nodded, winking with mock canniness. "Ah, but that is the advantage of a *cicerone.* No coarse, jostling crowds of idlers to spoil the vista."

"I see." And indeed she did, though her view had nothing to do with crowds of idlers. It was, as he'd said, just the two of them, his handsome face already so near to hers that she could see how tidily he'd shaved the little cleft upon his chin, and close enough to make her heart beat painfully within her breast and her palms grow moist where they pressed together.

She looked down at those traitorous hands now, struggling to regain her composure. She'd never felt like this with a man before, and she couldn't guess why this one would affect her so. But oh, dear Lord, how he *did* affect her! When she'd said he frightened her, she had not been entirely truthful. What she'd meant was that he could make her fear herself.

"There is not a great deal of history to Appledore, and our customs are simple enough," she said quickly. "I can tell you all you wish in an afternoon."

"Ah, but I have four months to devote to my education," he countered easily. "Perhaps five. But then you may not feel such thoroughness is necessary. You may believe—and you may well be correct—that Nan's love for your brother alone is strong enough to occupy her, entirely and endlessly, and my attempts to ease her way here won't be necessary."

"Love is never enough," she said wistfully, remembering the sorrows of her parents. She owed so much to Joshua. To spend this time with Gerald Crosbie would complicate her life immeasurably and make her visits to

Denniman's Cove all the more difficult to keep secret. There was also, too, the uncomfortable suspicion that she might be the one who'd be learning more, more than was good for her, and she glanced guiltily at the quiddany spoon. But if this would help preserve her brother's happiness, then she would do it.

Even if, she thought with sad foreboding, by doing so she destroyed any chance of her own.

He sighed, lightly tracing the grain of the table's top. "Or perhaps, Serena dear, your reluctance is less complicated. Perhaps it is simply that you find me a bore, my company distasteful."

Her gaze started upward. "Oh, no, never that! 'Tis not that at all!"

"Then you agree," he said with satisfaction, the deep, rich timbre of his voice suggesting she was agreeing to far more. "You agree. Ah, Mistress Mermaid, what a splendid guide you shall make for me! We'll make a grand tour of your Appledore that will make me forget everything I've ever seen in Rome. And for you, too, Serena. I give you my word that you won't regret this in the least."

But in her heart, Serena already did.

Five

Though Gerald would never confess such to his sister, he was in fact every bit her match in greeting the day at a leisurely pace. It was not so much the actual hour of his rising that he guarded with such vigilance—unless he'd returned exceptionally late the night before, he awoke as a rule not long after dawn—but the ritual that surrounded it.

First came coffee, blended with chocolate and without even a breath of sugar or milk, and served in a special oversized teacup he'd found years ago in Vienna. Three cups generally served to see him through the earliest of the day's newspapers and gossip sheets and fortified him for an hour of reading and letter writing, both to friends and to his men of business. Then he'd be shaved by Rourke, letting his thoughts wander pleasantly, planning his day, as the razor scraped warm suds and whiskers from his jaw.

Last came breakfast: four fresh hen's eggs, cooked and coddled in a skillet so the yolks were still soft, and fried ham and a decent fish, sautéed crisp, if any could be had;

a dish of the same boiled Dublin oats he'd been eating since he was a child, and served the same way, with molasses treacle and a decent-sized dollop of butter; and a half-dozen pieces of bread, sliced thick and toasted to be browned but not burned, and spread with raspberry marmalade.

This, too, was Rourke's domain, and Gerald was most grateful for the care his servant took in overseeing his breakfast, alternately cajoling and threatening the cook and kitchen staff as was necessary. The long voyage from London had tested Rourke's abilities most sorely; there had been days when the seas were so rough that galley fires were forbidden, and while fresh fish were always in supply, after the first weeks the same could not be said of butter or bread.

But now that Gerald had settled here at the White Swan, Rourke could once again provide suitably for his master, and with glowing anticipation Gerald surveyed his much-loved breakfast arranged on the table before him. He could, if pressed, do without letters and scandal sheets—here in remote Appledore he'd have no choice—but to be forced to sacrifice his eggs and ham and toast was a sadly different matter altogether.

He sat in the armchair nearest to the hearth, the heavy silk of his banyan settling around him as he breathed in the rich, mingled fragrances. He couldn't imagine a more fortuitous beginning to the day, and with a happy sigh he reached for his fork, just as the first pounding began at the door to his chamber.

The fork went down, his anticipation ruined and his sigh now markedly unhappy. It was too early in the morning for such thumping. Pounding on a door for entrance, instead of a less obtrusive scratching, seemed to be the custom here in the colonies, just as it had been at sea.

"Rourke," he grumbled. No other order was necessary as the servant hurried to the door.

"There be a lady below t' see Mr. Crosbie," boomed the host, a ruddy-cheeked man with a checked shirt beneath his leather apron. Likely he'd been a sailor, too, decided Gerald; from what he'd seen, there didn't seem to be a man in this whole blessed town who didn't boast of having gills.

"A lady?" repeated Rourke with perfect lack of emotion. Despite being a smallish, freckled man born on the wrong side of the blanket in County Kildare, Rourke could still rival an archduke for bland-faced arrogance. It was one of his many invaluable talents. "Pray, sir, what lady might that be?"

"The lady what's waiting below," said the keep, impatience spurring his urgency as he peered around Rourke and the half-open door to look for Gerald, who was sitting at the table near the fire where he could watch them a good deal better than they could see him. "Captain Fairbourne's sister."

Gerald sipped his coffee and swallowed his surprise. Not that he'd complain, however, considering how Serena had already spent most of the morning as the sole occupant of his thoughts.

"I believe," he said, raising his voice just loud enough to be heard, "that the lady has a name of her own, doesn't she?"

The carelessness of the man's shrug proved to Gerald exactly how little Serena's name meant compared to her relationship to her brother.

"Best not to keep the captain's sister waiting, sir," he advised, sagely tapping the side of his nose. "Captain Fairbourne, you know he don't—"

"Mr. Crosbie is not available at present," said Rourke firmly. "You shall tell the lady—"

"You shall tell me whatever you please to my face," said Serena, suddenly there in the doorway beside the innkeeper. "Mr. May, I do believe I hear another customer calling for you downstairs."

Reluctantly the innkeeper craned his head over his shoulder, listening. "I can't be leaving you here alone, Miss Fairbourne, indeed I cannot," he said almost petulantly. "What would Captain Fairbourne say to that, eh? Captain Fairbourne wouldn't have it, and that's the honest truth. I can't have a lady upstairs in a gentleman's room. It's not respectable for the establishment, nor for you nor Captain Fairbourne, neither."

"Captain Fairbourne would have absolutely nothing to say, Mr. May." Serena smiled at the innkeeper, warmly enough to make Gerald wish she'd turned toward him instead. At least he could tell she'd dressed for his benefit. He recognized the red cardinal cloak as her best and, beneath a ruffled cap, she'd dressed her hair more becomingly, in soft, loose waves that begged to be touched. "My brother, you see, is married to Mr. Crosbie's sister, which makes Mr. Crosbie a member of our family. What could be more respectable?"

"Off with you now, man," called Gerald. One watchdog wasn't enough for poor Serena; she seemed to have an entire town minding her welfare. "You have my word that Miss Fairbourne's virtue will leave this room as untouched as when it, and she, entered."

Now it was Serena's turn to try to peek past Rourke and into the room. "Is that you, Mr. Cro—er, that is, Gerald?" she called. "Faith, you've been so quiet I didn't realize you were actually here."

"Oh, I'm here," said Gerald, "though it seems that entirely too many others are here, too. Mr. May, your attentions are no longer needed. Go. Rourke—this is Rourke, sweet, in the event you hadn't guessed the little rascal's identity—see that our good host does as I've asked."

Serena hesitated, standing in the doorway while the two other men left. She would not miss Mr. May. He had wanted to stay only to be able to add to his abundant store of gossip, and besides, he smelled of the raw onions he ate to cover the habitual rum on his breath. But she rather wished that Mr. Rourke was here still, bustling about and doing whatever he did in the room for his master.

She rather wished it even more as soon as she closed the door and saw Gerald.

"Good day, Serena dear," he said as he rose to his feet, managing a welcoming bow despite a full cup in one hand and a crumpled napkin in the other. "And how much improved the day is now, too, with you here to share it with me. Pray, come, join me, won't you?"

Yet still she hung back, wishing desperately that she could control the warm flush she felt creeping up her throat and cheeks. She never would have followed Mr. May upstairs if she'd known she'd find Gerald like, well, like *this*.

Though he was properly dressed as for breeches and stockings and shoes, he seemed to have forgotten his shirt altogether. Instead he wore some sort of long, loose, flowing coat—she'd no notion of what the proper word might be for such a garment—of heavy gold silk brocaille, without any buttons or laces to close the front. Inexorably her gaze was drawn to what the gold silk framed, the dark hair that curled across his bare muscled chest and down his lean, flat belly to trail intriguingly into the top of his low-slung breeches.

She gulped and, as swiftly as she could, raised her eyes once again to his face, yet the image was already indelibly carved into her guilty memory. Appledore men were more modest and seemly than this, and even with three brothers Serena had never seen a man as carelessly confident in his appearance as Gerald Crosbie. With his hair still untied and falling sleek and loose over his shoulders, he looked for all the world like her notion of an exotic, pagan pasha, or at least he would if he weren't holding an outsized porcelain teacup.

"You will join me?" he asked again, coaxing. He drew back his chair, offering it to her. "Alas, I've none of your excellent quiddany, but Rourke can fetch you whatever else you please."

She wished he wouldn't remind her of the quiddany, or the odd feelings he'd managed to rouse when he'd slipped the spoon between her lips two nights ago—the same odd feelings that simply trying not to look at him was causing now.

"You would have eaten all this yourself?" she asked, striving to turn the conversation in a safer direction. Although there was but the one chair, the table before him was laden with an astounding quantity of breakfast for a single person. "You alone?"

"Well, yes." He reached for the coffeepot to refill his cup, the gold silk sliding open further across his chest. "You will have noticed that I am not a small man."

"Not at all," she murmured faintly, her gaze wandering again where it shouldn't. "That is, no, thank you. I have already breakfasted."

"Doubtless hours and hours ago, too, before the cock's crow," he said, bringing another chair closer for her. "Don't deny it. I can see the truth plain on your face. You are thinking that I am the worst variety of London-bred sloth you have ever encountered."

"I am thinking no such thing," she declared, a patent lie if ever she'd told one. She perched on the very edge of her chair, ready to flee if she had to, her hands clasped primly in her lap. She'd never watched any man other than her brothers eat breakfast, and never, ever in an upstairs room at the White Swan, and her conscience was fair shrieking with outrage. "I was wondering what you would call that—that coat you are wearing."

"A banyan. A sort of gentleman's dressing gown." He held his arms out with a flourish to show off the banyan, before he, too, sat and began to eat. "I believe they were first worn by planters in the West Indies, where it is too deuced hot to wear much else. Not a problem in these northern colonies, I'll grant you, but this way Rourke can't fuss at me for growing absent-minded and spilling marmalade upon a fresh shirt. Nags worse than a wife, does Rourke."

She had an alarming vision of that spilled marmalade upon his chest, and she herself offering to remove it for him. She would lean close to him and shove the heavy silk aside to keep it from getting spoiled, too, and she'd lay a hand upon his chest for balance while she dabbed away the marmalade with a cloth. Only to spare him Rourke's wrath, of course.

"It makes you look like a heathen pasha," she said, trying to control her thoughts and remember why she'd come in the first place. "The banyan, I mean. You do not look like a decent Christian gentleman."

"Perhaps because I'm not." He drew his brows together, making his face as stern and fearsome as he could over a plate of coddled eggs. "Perhaps I truly am an evil heathen pasha, come all the way from China to carry you away."

"Oh, bother, you are no such thing," she scoffed, trying not to notice how wickedly merry his eyes were when he pretended to be fearsome. He had extravagant lashes for a man, black like his brows, that could veil his eyes with lazy charm. "You come from the same place in Ireland as Anabelle, and though Ireland *is* Romish, that's not exactly the same as being heathen. Besides, if there are no nymphs in Appledore, then there certainly can't be any evil pashas, either."

"And what, pray, of my mermaids?"

"Mermaids live only in the pretty tales invented by sailors who've taken too much rum," she said severely. "You know that, too."

"Pretty tales and rum, and so die my fondest dreams. Ah, Serena, you have smoked me again." He sighed, waving his fork gently in her direction. "Whatever am I to do with you, eh?"

A score of possibilities sprang unbidden to Serena's mind, only two of them involving quiddany and marmalade and all of which shamed her for their boldness. What was it about this man that made her think such sinful nonsense?

She sighed, too, though more from despair at her own weaknesses. She'd purposefully kept from his path yesterday, hoping that solitude would help, but it hadn't, not in the least.

"I must speak to you, Gerald," she began, her tongue

taking a slight stumble on his name. "That is why I've come, you see."

"I do have my excuse for rising late this morning, if you're requiring one," he said, bemused, as he shook his untied hair back from his forehead. "I was at Nan's house playing loo well into the small hours. I missed you there at supper, sweet."

"I don't dine with them every evening," she said swiftly, but it still pleased her more than it should to have had him miss her. "I don't wish to test Anabelle's good will that way, the tedious spinster sister always on the doorstep at suppertime."

"Ah, Serena, Serena," he said, reaching out to brush his hand lightly along the inside of her wrist, one of the few parts of her not swaddled away beneath the cloak. "You could appear on my doorstep every night in creation, and I'd not once complain, nor call you tedious, either."

Swiftly she drew away from his hand, choosing to ignore the compliment and whatever else he was offering with it. "You and Anabelle were gaming?"

"Oh, aye, Nan is ever mad for it," he said, his smile wry at her rejection as he leaned back in his chair. "Even your brother, stout-hearted as he is, abandoned us for his bed sometime after midnight. And I managed to come away even, no insignificant accomplishment with my darling sister. She remains the greatest cheat at cards I've ever played, man or woman."

He shook his head sadly as he tore a piece of toast in half to soak up the puddle of yellow yolk on his plate. "Poor little Nan. Cheat or not, there is nothing she enjoys more than card-playing, but she claims there's not a soul in Appledore who knows how."

"No one *does* play," admitted Serena. Cards and wagering were the devil's pastimes, or so she'd always been taught by Dr. Townsend from the pulpit, and a great squandering of time and money, too. "In the taverns or on the ships I suppose there might be games of draughts and dice and such, but 'tis not common."

"Then I shall teach you," he declared. "You're more than clever enough. I can make you as great a sharp as Nan."

She stared at him, genuinely scandalized. "I could never do such a thing."

"Of course you could," he countered with easy assurance. "If it were difficult, then you wouldn't find every apprentice and stableboy tallying jacks and kings. Or Nan either, for that matter. And I promise, Serena dear, that I'd be a most agreeable tutor."

She didn't doubt that for a moment. "It is not that I cannot learn. It's that I do not wish to."

"Even if it would make Nan happy, and therefore your brother as well? If no one else in the town plays, then no one else would know, would they?"

"*I* would know," she said stubbornly.

"Oh, aye, and the sun and the moon and the stars as well." He finished the last of his coffee, letting his smile curl with amusement as he watched her over the rim of the cup. "And, of course, *I* would know, too."

He was certain she'd not the faintest notion of how lovely, and how eminently desirable, she was at this moment, her eyes wide and her whole body nigh quivering with indignation. He had always considered himself a man of subtleties, delighting in viewing life from many sides, yet Serena's unshakable, constant sense of right and wrong was one of the things that intrigued him most about her.

Or perhaps *intrigued* wasn't exactly the proper word. *Challenged* might be more apt. As much as he might wish it, seducing Serena Fairbourne into his bed was out of the question. He was not such a reckless fool as to go poaching on another man's property, nor such a notorious rakehell, either. He was here to rescue his sister, and he could not afford to let himself be distracted even by so lovely a distraction as his special mermaid.

But despite all these good, noble intentions, there might still be some compensation to be found. He might not be a fool or a rakehell, but he wasn't a saint, either.

He was sure he could find other, more ingenuous paths
to be taken, little games of pleasurable risk between a
man and a woman with which he might entertain
himself, and Serena, too, if she proved willing.

He smiled as he studied the bright patches of color on
her cheeks, the stiff set of her back as she sat with her
hands clasped in her lap. He dearly loved to coax and
cosset a good woman into doing things she believed she
shouldn't. He remembered how she'd swayed gently into
his kiss in the boat, and he remembered how her lips had
parted for the quiddany.

Strange to think he'd known Serena less than three
days. In an odd way he felt as if she'd been here with him
forever.

And four months in Appledore might not be so very
long at that.

She frowned to herself and gave her head a little toss,
almost as if to shake away his smile.

"I didn't come here to speak of gaming, Mr. Cro—
that is, Gerald," she said, clearly striving to be stern in a
way he found charming. "It is this idea of me as your—
your guide."

"Ah, forgive me!" He swept to his feet and flung open
the door. "Rourke! At once, man, at once!"

He turned back toward Serena, gold silk swirling
around his legs like a banner. "How selfish I am,
dawdling over my toast while my dear *cicerone* waits!"

"Nay, that was not my intention!" she exclaimed. "I
wished rather that—"

"Rourke, you scoundrel, here you are at last," he said
impatiently. "I must dress directly. I've been most
barbarously ill-mannered, and I cannot keep Miss Fairbourne waiting a fraction of a moment longer. Make
haste, make haste!"

Quickly Serena began to rise to her feet. "I shall wait
for you below, while you—"

But it was already too late. To her horror Rourke
reached up and stripped the banyan from his master's
broad shoulders and back, leaving him entirely un-

clothed from his hips upward, standing there before her in exceptionally shameless glory. She knew she should look away, yet she couldn't. She *couldn't.*

"Sit, Serena, please," said Gerald, either unaware or ignoring—she couldn't tell which—her discomfiture. "Now pray tell me all. What grand sights have you ordered for me this day? I am entirely yours, however you wish."

What she wished was that Rourke would not be so slow in bringing Gerald his shirt and covering the grand sight of his nearly naked splendor. For a man who dressed in velvet and who ate such enormous breakfasts, he was remarkably lean, muscular, and hard where he should be, and altogether fascinating. No wonder she was standing there as frozen as a deer before a lantern. He'd have that effect on any woman, even one who'd spent her entire life in a place like Appledore.

But she didn't want him to mistake her for a hopeless spinster from a backward colony, the way Anabelle already had. She wasn't like the clever, elegant ladies he knew in London, and she never would be. But when he'd first kissed her in the little boat, she hadn't been Captain Fairbourne's sister, either. She'd simply been his mermaid, and she wanted very much to be simply that again.

No, she wanted more, or less, than that. She wanted to be herself.

"Serena?" asked Gerald when she didn't answer. "Serena, are you unwell?"

From long practice he automatically lifted his arms out toward the shirt that Rourke held for him, ducking his head to vanish into the yards of pressed holland. With one easy motion Rourke tugged the shirt down and Gerald reappeared, or at least his head and hands did, with the unsettling remainder of him covered at last.

And, at last, Serena once again found her voice. "So are all the London gentry like you," she asked, "needing to be dressed like a little child?"

"A *little* child?" he asked, while Rourke fastened the

thread buttons on his cuffs. "I thought it had already been established that there was nothing *little* about me."

"Excepting, perhaps, your ability to button your own waistcoat? That seems very slight indeed."

He frowned down at Rourke, who was in fact at that moment nimbly closing the long row of cut-steel buttons up the front of his waistcoat.

"I *choose* not to button them," he said. "It is not because I can't. Rather like you not wishing to play loo. Choice balanced against ability. There is a world of fine difference between the two, you know."

"That I did not," she said solemnly. "But how fortunate for me to have you to explain it to me."

How fortunate for himself as well that he did not believe it for a moment. Her face was angelic in its innocence, holding true even in the clear winter light from the window beside her. And no wonder he'd been unable to forget her since that afternoon in the fog.

"I am ever willing to oblige," he said, easing his shoulders into the coat that Rourke held for him. "Is there any other matter you wish, ah, explained?"

"Aye, there is," she said slowly.

He watched her warily as she let her glance wander around the room, as if drawing her thoughts together. He didn't believe that, either. She knew exactly what she wished to say. She always did.

"There is one question," she began. "Is it the custom in London for ladies and gentlemen to receive company in this way, in their shifts and their banyons and their nightshirts, or perhaps, no nightshirt at all?"

He raised his jaw to allow Rourke to wrap and tie his neckcloth. "Do you ask this as a general question, or as a specific one, having to do with the London lady and the gentleman who miraculously are both at present in your colony, nay, within your own family?"

She smoothed her hair behind one ear, a gesture more of tidying than coquetry. "You and Anabelle *are* the only

London lady and gentleman I know, so any simpleton could guess I meant you."

"'Any simpleton.'" He sighed, tugging his shirt cuffs through the sleeves of his jacket. "You shall turn my head with your flattery, Miss Fairbourne."

"You are no more a simpleton than you are little," she declared soundly. "But both you and Anabelle do seem to be a great more . . . *familiar* in the morning than anyone else I've known."

He lifted one brow. Serena Fairbourne might have this entire infernal town watching after her, but she didn't need a chaperone half as much as he did. "Ah, lass, but you've missed the greatest difference between us two Crosbies."

"Another fine difference to be explained?"

"Oh, yes." He paused, waiting for Rourke to give his cocked hat one final swipe of the brush before he took it. "When you join me here for breakfast, Serena dear, you have me entirely to yourself. You have shared me with no one, excepting Rourke, and he doesn't signify. But Nan, the randy little stoat, makes it wretchedly clear that while you may have her company with morning tea, she in turn has already had your brother. Now shall we go, *ma bella cicerone?*"

Serena's cheeks grew hot as she realized his meaning. He was right about Anabelle, of course, horribly right, but at least Anabelle and Joshua were married. Allowances could be made. Newly married people were expected to behave in that fashion.

What flustered her more was how Gerald's reasoning turned upon some sort of analogy that she couldn't quite grasp, one that linked her to him in the same way that Anabelle and Joshua were, and not by marriage, either.

It was entirely her own fault. If she hadn't fallen into the same easy pattern of conversation with him—if she hadn't teased him about not dressing himself—then she wouldn't be blushing so furiously now. Calling on Gerald Crosbie had seemed innocent enough, even necessary, considering her reasons. But that had been before the gold silk banyan. Her heart sank as she remembered Mr. May peeking around the door, and imagined the version of her visit to this upstairs chamber that the innkeeper was probably telling in the taproom even now.

Dear Lord (and Joshua) forgive her, whatever *had* she done to her good name by coming here to the White Swan this morning?

Purposefully she rose to her feet. "Yes, we shall go," she said, shaking out her petticoats so she could pretend not to see how he was offering her arm to her. "But I cannot grant you the entire day, as you proposed."

"No?" Somehow he managed to sound simultaneously surprised and wounded, and amused, too. "Dare I ask why?"

"Because I have other responsibilities that demand my attention," she answered promptly, the rehearsed words serving her well. "I shall help you learn to make Anabelle content, as I promised. That is a worthy task. But I cannot do it to the exclusion of the rest of my life."

He sighed heavily. "One landmark, then, my *cicerone?* One little one?"

She retied the ribbons at her throat, trying hard to be firm with him. "I thought that 'little' was not a word that delighted you."

"It is not," he declared with another sigh, drawn so deep as to have come clear from China. "But I resolve not to belittle myself into having no guide at all."

Her smile flickered in spite of her resolution. "One *small* landmark, then."

"One small landmark," he agreed. "And you must also promise to come to Nan's house this evening."

"Not for dinner." She couldn't agree to that. She doubted she would be back from Denniman's Cove in time, and she couldn't risk the questions from Joshua if she were late.

"Afterward, then." He reached out and took her hand and she let him, and let him tuck it neatly into the crook of his arm, too. "I shall depend upon it."

She looked down at her hand on his arm, remembering how he'd done the same when he'd taken her home that first night. "I won't play your wicked games, you know."

He turned his head and cocked one brow, letting the other meaning hover in the air between them before he smiled. "You won't have to, sweet. Nan will be too occupied in fleecing away my last few humble groats to notice. Now say you will come."

"Say you will be content with that and one smallish landmark."

"Agreed." He settled his hat upon his head, his smile blossoming into a full grin. "But what a devilish hard bargain you drive, Miss Fairbourne!"

He liked the sound of her laughter as they went down the stairs together, almost as much as he liked having her hand upon his sleeve. He'd wager a hundred guineas that she wasn't a woman who granted such favors lightly, which made that light, tentative touch all the more special.

He valued it further the moment they stepped from the inn's door, where Abel had been waiting patiently, and together into the street. Despite his resolution to devote the next four months to discovering Appledore, he doubted the town could offer enough to hold his interest for four hours.

Like all places that depended on the sea, Appledore's few streets either lay parallel to the waterfront, or, running crossways, ended in a dock or warehouse. Houses and shops and taverns were jumbled together as if they'd been scattered along the narrow, unpaved streets by a careless child and without any of the order that Gerald admired. Everything was covered with the same monotonous clapboarding, some of it whitewashed or painted in drab shades of red or green, but most left to weather into a silvery gray. From the bare, shivering trees to the small, sad displays in the shop windows, he could not imagine a more cheerless town, or one less likely to become home to a merry creature like his sister.

Yet as unwelcoming as the town itself appeared, the

people who lived within it seemed worse. It was nearly noontime, and the streets were full of people picking their way through the dirty snow and ice-filled ruts, from apprentices on their masters' errands to housewives with market baskets and yowling babies to young women dawdling on their way to the well to paid-off sailors unsteadily seeking another rum shop. Most recognized Serena by sight and by name, dipping a respectful curtsey or tugging on the front of a knitted cap, but for Gerald there was nothing but the blackest of looks, ranging from unfriendly suspicion to out-and-out hatred. Even his warmest, most winning smiles, liberally dispensed, failed to earn him a jot of goodwill in return.

"Charming folk, your neighbors," he murmured to Serena after an elderly woman pointedly drew her skirts away from him to pass on Serena's side instead. "I have the distinct impression that were I not in your company, they'd set their dogs upon me."

"Abel would see that they wouldn't," said Serena, and with great understanding the dog reached up to thrust his damp nose against Gerald's palm.

"Ha," he said, rubbing the back of Abel's neck above the collar. "Has it come to such a sorrowful pass as this, that I must depend upon a dog to defend my good name?"

"You must not take it to heart," said Serena, patting his arm in commiseration. "They're wary of you only because you're a stranger and a foreigner."

"I'm as British as they are," he said defensively. "Father is Irish, I'll grant you that, but I defy any of these ill-bred tradesmen or mechanics to quibble over that."

"But you're not from Appledore," she explained patiently, "or even from Barnstable County, and no one cares a farthing for your father because he's not from here, either."

He glared at a pair of boys he was certain were bent on mischief, specifically of a muddy kind directed at his coat. "By God, if they treat Nan like this—"

"They don't because she married Joshua. If you wed an Appledore woman—that is, if you could find one willing to have you—then they might accept you, too, in ten years' time or so."

He glanced at her suspiciously to see if she was smiling at his expense, but with her face in profile within her hood it was impossible to tell. "Ten years' penance and contrition seems rather steep."

"Oh, you would need at least that much," she said blithely, hopping over a frozen puddle. "If Mr. May's done his usual work on your behalf, then he has already told the entire town the hour you returned last night and the hour you breakfasted this morning, and that you wear gold silk whilst you eat it. He's also likely informed them that you keep yourself fine as a lord, with a servant just for yourself and your clothes, and that you seem to have no honest trade or craft to speak of. Considering the circumstances, I'd say ten years would be the absolute minimum needed to overcome such grievous deficiencies."

"I am a gentleman," he said, wondering why, even to his ears, such an honest declaration sounded so pompous here in Appledore. "I have no need of a trade, honest or otherwise."

She turned to look at him curiously, the gold flecks in her eyes more noticeable in the sunlight. "What do you do, then? How do you pass your days?"

"Oh, the world answers well enough for that," he said with an off-handed shrug for emphasis. "I'm fortunate to be a wanderer by nature."

She shook her head and frowned. "But all men must have some gainful way to occupy their days, to leave their mark upon the world."

"Not if they've the inestimable good fortune to be born a younger son of a good family," he explained, oddly reassured by that frown of hers. If she frowned, then she wasn't laughing at him after all, and he needn't be serious in return. "I have not one blessed reason for being on this earth except to please myself. I like to journey, to find new places, new things to amuse me. Paris, Naples, Augsburg, Vienna, and now your Appledore."

"I see," she said, though it was clear she didn't. "Yet you are not as selfish as all that. You came here for Anabelle's sake, didn't you?"

"An unconscionable lapse," he said with wry cheerfulness. "I shall resolve to do better next time."

But to his surprise she didn't laugh or even smile. Instead she stopped in the shelter of a listing stone wall, drawing him to a halt before her as she searched his face, her own confused.

"You make no sense to me, Gerald Crosbie," she said softly. "You can call yourself a wanderer, but wandering is no more than running away. I know; I've two other brothers besides Joshua who contrive every reason under heaven to sail to one more port, over one more sea, to any place other than to come back here."

"I told you before, I'm no sailor." He grinned, hoping to break her seriousness.

But Serena only shook her head, her eyes inexplicably sad. "I know why Danny and Sam ran away, and why they keep running still. Who could blame them, when our life here was so unkind? But you, Gerald. You were born a gentleman, the son of a lord, in a grand, fine house with clean beds that you didn't have to share and warm clothes and plenty to eat. What reasons could you—and Anabelle, too—ever have to run away from home?"

He stared at her, both unable and unwilling to answer her. How could he, really? How to explain that there was so much more to a child's happiness than clothes and food and beds? She had been born in a house smaller than the buttery at Kilmarsh. How, then, could he describe to her the awful echoing, emptiness of a home so vast that he could go for days without seeing either of his parents? How could he tell someone whose whole life had been circumscribed by a single county that he found more comfort in the faces of strangers than he ever had in the aching loneliness of his own family?

With a great effort he forced himself to smile, swallowing back the bitter taste of the memories she'd roused.

"It was Nan who skipped away," he said as lightly as he could. "I have merely followed. She will have your reason, not I."

Abruptly Serena looked down. "I have offended you, haven't I?" she said. "I spoke too plain, didn't I, and asked of things that were not mine by rights to know, and now, oh, now, I must ask your forgiveness."

"No, sweet, you must not," he said gently, slipping his hand beneath her chin to turn her face back toward his. "No regrets, no apologies. I believe I've told you that before as well. If I continue like this, I shall need a secretary to take note of my words and warn me if I begin to repeat myself into debilitating tedium."

She smiled then, wistfully, even as she shook her chin free of his hand. "No regrets, no apologies, and no more explanations either, Mr. Crosbie?"

"No tedium," he said firmly. "I should never wish to be thought a bore, especially by you. Now come, tell me, my fair guide, what is that great hole dug in the ground before us?"

"A great hole?" With obvious relief she turned away from him to look toward where he was pointing. "Ah, that. That is our largish landmark, or shall be, once it is done. Our new markethouse, to shelter the farmers come to town to sell their goods."

She crossed the street to look down into the square-cornered pit, half-filled with dingy snow drifted into the corners of the foundation. Gerald followed, coming to stand beside her.

"The last one burned in the summer, after Lady-Day," said Serena. "To be more truthful, I suppose this must seem a smallish landmark rather than largish, but I do believe it shall soon rise to be quite large and grand. The subscription for the funds has already been completed; Joshua is, of course, in charge of seeing it done. It will be among the first buildings to be seen from the water, a true landmark to ships. Leastways that is what is planned."

"Then why is no one working this day?" Looking down into the unfinished cellar, Gerald had the uncomfortable sensation of peering down into an open grave, and it took considerable control not to remove his hat in respect to the dead. "Surely the weather is fine enough."

"Surely it is," agreed Serena. "The problem lies with the men, not the weather. No one can agree on a design beyond this start, and so they do nothing beyond squabbling. Joshua says that in England there are men whose sole occupation is to draw plans for grand buildings— that is where the meetinghouse spire came from—but here we must depend upon a pack of ill-tempered shipwrights and carpenters, each convinced he is better suited to the task than his fellow. 'Tis always the same with men."

"Now, now, do not be so harsh on us hapless creatures." He gazed down into the unfinished hole where Abel was nosing through damp piles of last autumn's leaves and tried to envision the grand public building that Serena was describing. "We're not all so alike to be tossed into the same basket."

"Not you, perhaps," she admitted, more grudgingly than he might have wished. "No. You could hardly be included in any sort of basket that also contains Mr. Gardiner. He's the master carpenter, and the master grumbler, too, says Joshua. Joshua says Mr. Gardiner's like a good, sturdy man at the helm who can hold to a set course but can't navigate a new one without proper charts. Which, of course, he's too blessed proud to admit."

But Gerald wasn't listening. Instead he was imagining a markethouse that would rival every other building he'd yet seen in the colonies, one that truly was fit to become a landmark in the town. He thought pleasantly of markets he'd seen in his travels, humble structures ennobled by graceful arches and well-conceived proportions, Vitruvius filtered through Palladio with a nod to what Christopher Wren was doing with London.

He thought, too, and with even greater pleasure, of the turmoil and mixed feelings such a building would bring to these ill-humored citizens of Appledore. *That* they would deserve. What was it that Serena had said, that every man must leave his mark? Perhaps his was meant to be left here, on this bit of frozen mud, and he nearly laughed aloud at the sheer, brilliant lunacy of it. He might be here to steal back the captain's bride, but he could still leave Fairbourne—damnation, he'd leave them *all*—with a *memento* they'd never be able to overlook.

Unaware of his thoughts, Serena sighed deeply beside him. "You are disappointed, I can tell," she said, her own disappointment keen in her voice. "You expected more, even though I'd warned you not to. Appledore is not your Rome, any more than I am your *bella cicerone.*"

It was the first time he'd heard her say such words, his words, the unfamiliar Italian sliding off her Massachusetts tongue so easily that he doubted she'd noticed herself. But he did, and he grinned in return. He could not help it. Her hood had slipped back from her head, her hair was coming undone in enchanting wisps around her face, and her mouth, that charming little mouth that had already betrayed itself by speaking Italian, reminded him again of the sweet-tasting quiddany. Before she could object he took her hand from the folds of her cloak and slipped it free of the shaggy mitten before he raised it briefly to his lips.

"You have not disappointed me, Serena dear," he said with cheerful gallantry, "nor do I believe you ever could."

But as she looked back at him, her gold-flecked eyes at

once solemn and confused, he felt the first ripple of doubt, of unfamiliar uncertainty, shake his good humor. There was no question that he'd already left his mark on Serena Fairbourne. That was clear enough.

But could it be, the devil claim him for a fool, that she'd done the same to him?

Six

The tall case clock chimed nine times, and Gerald tossed his cards down on the baize-covered table.

"She's late," he said. "Damnation, Nan, she should have been here an hour ago."

Anabelle sighed and let her own cards flutter one by one to the table. "And I say, Duckie, that Serena's not late because she was never expected in the first place. I do wish you'd mind our game. I had a most excellent hand that you've quite spoiled by being so petulant."

"I'm not being petulant, Nan. I'm being concerned." He shoved his chair back from the table and went to stand at the window, parting the curtains to look out into the night. "Serena promised me she'd come here this evening, after we'd dined."

"La, so she's making promises to you already," said Anabelle with fresh interest, nestling her plump chin in her hand as she rested her elbows on the table. "I did not realize such an attachment had grown between you two. That is fast work among the maidens, even for you."

"There is no attachment, Nan," said Gerald irritably

94

without turning from the window, "and there has been no 'work', as you so charmingly phrase it."

Anabelle's eyes narrowed with wicked glee, like a cat ready to pounce. "You are right, Duckie. I should have chosen my words with more care. Your assignations with ladies—even quick-witted Massachusetts ladies such as Serena—would never be work or toil for you, but rather the greatest pleasure imaginable."

"What's my sister done now, eh?" asked Joshua. "What kind of lady's mischief have the two of you plotted?"

Gerald turned to find Captain Fairbourne standing in the parlor doorway, his tone more indulgent than stern as he gazed at his wife. He had spent most of the evening across the hall, discussing some sort of tedious mariner's business with another Appledore captain, but Gerald had noted that no matter how heated their discussion had become, Joshua had always kept the two doors open and, suspected Gerald, his ears wide open as well. He didn't trust Gerald, not where Anabelle was concerned, and he tried his best not to leave them alone together. His jealousy was so blatant that it might have amused Gerald if Anabelle hadn't been the prize at stake between them.

Right now that prize had dipped her chin and was pouting, twisting the ribbon from the front of her bodice around and around her finger with the same graceful ease as she did her husband.

"I vow Serena and I have never planned any mischief whatsoever," she protested so meekly that Gerald almost laughed aloud. "Ask Duckie if you dare not believe me."

Immediately Joshua's attention shifted toward Gerald, his gaze hardening perceptibly.

"For once I fear Nan is telling the truth," said Gerald. "I was the one who was speaking of your sister. It is a quarter past nine, yet she hasn't arrived."

Joshua frowned. "I did not expect Serena here, not this night. She often prefers to keep her own company."

"She told *me* she was coming," said Gerald, unable to resist that extra proprietary emphasis. No wonder Serena felt she was an unwanted guest with encouragement like that from her brother. "Considering how far her house is from here, I was concerned that some misfortune might have fallen her way."

Joshua's frown blackened to a full scowl. "Why the devil would Serena have told you anything, Crosbie?"

"Oh, my love, please," interrupted Anabelle, pleading anxiously. "Please, I beg you, please, no harsh words, not with my brother, not in our home."

But Joshua only shook his head angrily, shaking her plea away as well. "You heard him, Anabelle. You heard what he claimed about Serena."

"That is hardly the issue," said Gerald, mastering his temper for Serena's sake. "Shouldn't you be caring more about your sister's welfare than the messenger who brings news of it?"

"Blast your impertinence," growled Joshua, but he couldn't keep the wave of concern from his face. "My sister is safe at home where she belongs, with Abel there to guard her door."

Gerald shook his head, incredulous. "You would trust Serena's well-being entirely to a dog's keeping?"

"Aye, Crosbie, I do," he thundered back, "for this is Appledore, my town and my people, and not your hellhole of London!"

Suddenly Anabelle was at Joshua's side, her hand resting lightly upon his sleeve, as much restraint as she dared. Both her pout and her winsomeness had vanished, swept clear away, and in their place she looked pale and unhappy.

"Please, love, do not do this," she whispered miserably to Joshua as she held her other hand tight across her belly. "Please, oh, please, can you not behave as you swore to me you would?"

It was that palpable misery that halted Gerald like a wall of stone. He had wanted to make Anabelle happy, and instead he'd done this. One look at her pale, taut face, and he knew what she was remembering, what she was hearing, for the sounds of their parents' nightmarish battles were echoing through his thoughts as well. Now, by goading Joshua, he had made them both remember, and his disgust at his own behavior rose bitter in his throat. He thought of what Serena had said earlier, about how both he and Anabelle were running away from the past. How wise she'd been to see that, and how wrong he'd been to drag that same past here to Anabelle. Why would she ever wish to return to London if such memories were there waiting?

His head and his heart reeled with the impact of what he'd done. Silently he bowed to Anabelle, and then did the only thing he could: he left, left them and their parlor and their house.

And ran away again.

Serena skidded on a patch of ice, caught herself, then stepped on the hem of her petticoat, the sound of ripping linen unmistakable. In exasperation she swore, one of her brother's lesser oaths but more than sufficient for the moment. She didn't often swear, but then she wasn't often as late as she was now.

She should never have told Gerald that she'd see him this evening at Joshua's house. He wouldn't forget, she was certain of that, and worse, he would just as certainly have told her brother to expect her, too. She might be able to talk her way clear with Gerald, but she'd never survive Joshua's interrogation if she didn't hurry.

She looked up at the new moon sliding higher over the rooftops and tried to guess the hour. The way would be shorter along Water Street, past the warehouses, a path she wouldn't ordinarily take after dark, at least not without Abel, but she could trim at least ten minutes from her walk, and ten minutes could make a world of difference. She was already sure there wasn't time to go back to her own house to change. They'd simply have to take her as she was, dressed for day, and overlook the damp places on her skirts from the sea and the snow.

She sighed, wondering what Anabelle would make of her friend Mary Sears. She already knew what Joshua thought of Mary, or rather of Mary's husband Robert. Robert Sears was a thief and a drunkard, declared Joshua harshly, a man whose carelessness had brought great sorrow to others, and any woman who'd wed him could scarcely be better. Serena's opinion of Robert was less severe, for she remembered him as a gawky boy, painfully shy with everyone except Mary. But Joshua judged all men that way, as unequivocally as he judged himself. At least Mary's only sin had been to fall in love with Robert, coupled with a fierce loyalty that blinded her to all his faults, and for that she would pay for the rest of her life.

Serena shivered, more from sadness than the cold. She remembered the disbelief on Gerald Crosbie's face when she'd said that love alone could never be enough. For a man life held so much more promise, so many more possibilities. But for a woman life was a perilous journey at best, and she thought not only of poor Mary in her lonely house at Denniman's Cove, but of her own mother as well. How could Gerald—effortlessly secure with his servant and his velvet coats and his unquestionable place in the world—ever understand?

She bowed her head, pulling the hood of her cloak higher. The wind had come around during the afternoon, blowing harder off the water now, funneled through the narrow streets, biting hard through the wool of her cloak. A fur-lined coat might not be such a self-indulgence after all, not on such a night, and she smiled at the idea of herself in such a garment, and what Gerald would say if—

"There she be, th' prideful strumpet!" Though slurred with drink, the man's voice echoed back and forth against the shuttered warehouse walls that lined the narrow street. "I would know th' creature anywhere!"

With an indignant gasp Serena spun around to face the direction in which the voice had come.

"I won't have you calling me such names, Job Pinkham!" she called back fiercely, straining to see into the shadows. The nasal whine in the man's voice was unmistakable; she'd known Job Pinkham since they'd both been children, and even though he'd moved to the less civilized town of Truro years ago, his cod fishing still brought him to Appledore often enough that Serena would be hard pressed to forget him. "I know your voice, so there's no use in hiding your face like the mean little coward you are!"

"Oh, aye, an' how brave *you* be, Miss Serena High-and-Mighty Fairbourne!" the man jeered, still hidden. "If'n you want t' be treated fine like a lady, then you shouldn't go parading like a royal strumpet with that fancy Londoner, playing patty-hand with him in the street for all t' see!"

"Oh! *Oh!* Now you have gone too far, Job, truly you have!" cried Serena furiously. She didn't know which was worse: being called names by a worthless scrap of cod-fishing rubbish like Job Pinkham or having her name linked so publicly, and so intimately, with Gerald Crosbie. Swiftly she reconsidered her walk with him earlier that day. She had linked her arm with Gerald's—no sin in that—and as they'd stood beside the market he'd kissed her hand. That was all, she was sure of it. But who knew what had been said of her this evening in the taproom of the White Swan, what invented tales Mr. May might be repeating even now for the amusement of his patrons?

The idea made Serena angrier, and braver, still, and she dropped her basket to settle her hands on her hips beneath her cloak and took another step in the direction of Pinkham's voice.

"You would not dare say such things to my face, would you?" she shouted down the narrow, empty street. "Come show yourself, Job Pinkham, show yourself directly or leave off your blustery raving!"

"Always been too proud for us Appledore men, wasn't you?" said Job as he lurched from between two buildings. "Didn't I tell you how she was, lads? Didn't I?"

"'Lads'?" repeated Serena crossly. "Faith, Job, you make even less sense now than you did as a pimple-faced—"

But as two other, much larger shadows followed Job into the street and the shifting moonlight, she suddenly realized what kind of sense he did make, and what kind of trouble she'd stumbled into now, too. From their knitted caps she guessed them to be Truro fishermen like Job, men who'd no notion of who she was, nor fear of Joshua, either.

Swiftly she glanced over her shoulder, up the empty street. She'd find no help so far from any houses or friends, and she knew better than to try to outrun the men, not uphill and in heeled shoes and stays. She'd learned the futility of *that* from her brothers, too. No, she'd have to depend on her wits if she'd any hope at all of escaping.

Slowly she bent to retrieve her basket. Beneath the cloth on top was an empty stoneware butter crock she'd brought back from Mary's house, and while it wasn't much of a weapon, it might be heavy enough to cause a bruise or two if she swung the basket hard. Not, of course, that she intended to let them get that close to her. The ten feet or so that separated them now was scant as it was.

She lifted her head, trying to regain the assurance of the anger that had landed her here in the first place. But as the three men loomed before her, her heart pounded painfully in her breast and her mouth turned dry as sand, and the only assurance she felt was that of being the most careless woman in Appledore.

"I told you she be a pretty-lookin' chit, lads, didn't I?" whined Job eagerly, seeking the approval of the other two. "I told you she'd be worth your trouble an' time, didn't I?"

"And what will you be telling your grandmam, Job?" said Serena quickly, working hard to keep her voice clear and strong and without the fear she felt so keenly. "Did you go see her this day at your brother's house before you went to the rum shop, Job?"

"My grandmam?" repeated Job, shuffling his feet uncomfortably. "What business of yours be my grandmam?"

"None at all," said Serena firmly, "save that she's a good, fine woman deserving of only the best from her grandson."

"Aye, that be true enough," said Job with a moist, morose sniff of regret. "She be a good, fine woman, my grandmam."

Serena's fingers tightened on the handle of the basket, ready to flee the first moment she dared to trust that waver in his conscience.

"Then will you call on her tomorrow, Job, before you sail?" she asked more gently. "Or will you let her hear from others how you spent your night, traipsing about with your head full of drink and shouting in the streets after decent women?"

"Ye talk too much, hussy," growled the taller man behind Job, "an' Bill an' me be tired o' waiting. Now get yourself here, an' be willing about it."

Before Serena could answer he'd closed the gap between them. He stank of rum and of fish, old fish, and his grasp was like iron on her arm, his fingers digging tight to drag her back into his embrace. With a frightened gasp, Serena swung her basket upward as hard as she could, catching his jaw with the heavy butter crock inside the rough splints. He staggered back with an outraged roar of surprise and pain, clutching at his chin.

"Ye teasing little strumpet!" he said, lunging for her again. "Ye have made me mad now, ye have!"

Serena tried to scramble back out of his reach, but this time she was the one caught off balance, and when he grabbed her arm now the basket jerked from her hand and tumbled to the street. She gave a terrified yelp, twisting and turning to free herself as the man tried to pull her close to his chest. She was ruined, destroyed; there'd be no hope of saving herself now.

But just as she felt her feet sliding out from under her, the man's grip tightening further, she caught sight of a flash of blue from the corner of her eye. Abruptly the man's expression altered from greedy anticipation to stunned surprise before his face and his hand disappeared altogether. Without his support she toppled forward, landing hard on her hands and knees on the frozen ground.

Breathing hard, she stared at the basket on its side on the ground before her nose. It had been a most unusual shade of blue, a peculiar shade for a gentleman's coat that she'd recognized as surely as Rourke would himself when he brushed it clean. But whatever would a fine gentleman like Gerald Crosbie be doing here, on this street, at this moment?

The second man was bending over her now, silhouetted against the night sky with his long queue flopping over his shoulder. Without time to think she grabbed the stoneware crock from the basket, rolled over onto her back, and with both hands thumped the crock as hard as she could against the man's forehead. He let out a long rasping sigh, foully redolent of rum and tobacco, then folded over onto the ground in a sprawling heap beside her.

Awkwardly she rolled away from him and to her knees, her breath coming in short, painful shudders. She heard a crash behind her, and turned swiftly to find two men grappling and swearing and swinging their fists at each other against a wall. The one on the outside she recognized as the tall man who'd come after her first, while the other, with his back to the wall, could only, impossibly, be Gerald.

That tall, half-drunken fisherman would kill him, kill him dead here while she knelt in the street, and it would be entirely her fault. The devil watch over his own, didn't Gerald know he'd no place here?

She clambered to her feet and ran stumbling toward them, the crock still clutched in her hands. She hated seeing men fight like this, grunting and thrashing away like huge, mindless animals determined to destroy each other. They'd nearly succeeded, too, both of them blowing hard, their clothes torn and their faces bruised and bloody. But at least Gerald was still alive, even if it meant he was still able to fight as well.

"Stop this!" she shouted, the same way she would have with her brothers. "Stop this *now!*"

They did not even hear her, let alone stop, neither one willing to give up his grasp on the other for a moment, and with a muttered oath of her own, she struck the tall fisherman on the back of his head with her butter crock. The man's head jerked backward as the pot finally cracked into pieces in her hands. Gerald's fist shot forward and clipped the fisherman under his jaw and, with a final grunt, the fisherman's legs melted away beneath him and he slipped to the street and into loose-limbed unconsciousness.

Her heart still pounding, Serena raised her gaze to meet Gerald's over the fisherman's body. Even by moonlight Gerald looked dreadful, his neckcloth torn away and the front of his shirt ripped and dappled with blood, his hair straggling loose around his face. True, he'd given worse than he'd gotten, but in the process he'd managed to earn a bleeding lip and his brow was already beginning to swell and purple, and he winced as he lifted his battered hand to smooth his hair back from his face.

"Look at you, Gerald Crosbie," said Serena at last. She did not want to consider the danger he'd been in, or how phenomenally lucky he'd been that the fisherman hadn't drawn a knife. She especially didn't want to remember how terrified she'd been for his sake, worse than anything she'd felt for her own foolish skin. Long ago she'd learned to turn her back on fear like that, the fear of losing someone she cared for; it was the only way she'd survived herself.

"Look at yourself," she said again, unable to think of anything else to say.

Not that Gerald noticed. "All things being equal," he

said, his words slurry and tasting salty with blood, "I'd rather look at you."

She didn't answer at first, staring down at the broken crockery in her hands as if all the answers lay somewhere within the shards. Then she dropped the pieces and covered her eyes with her hands, her careful composure shattering as readily as the butter crock.

"Ah, Serena, don't weep, please," said Gerald unhappily. All he wanted to do now was to take her into his arms, to comfort himself as well as her, but he wasn't sure he could do it. While all of him felt as if he'd been squeezed and battered through a laundry mangle, his left knee was the one part of him where the pain centered and throbbed—he remembered the exact moment when he'd felt it wrench the wrong way—and without the wall at his back he feared he'd collapse in an unheroic heap at her feet. "Please, sweet, don't."

"I can't help it, Gerald," she said, her words muffled by her sleeves. "I don't want to, but I—I thought you were *different*. I thought that with you being a London gentleman and all, you wouldn't be like my brothers and every other man here, always ready for brawling with the cod fishermen or cracking heads with whalermen in a tavern."

"I didn't do it for the *sport,* you infernal ninny," he said thickly, his mouth not working exactly as it should. "Did they harm you?"

"No," she sobbed. "Of course they didn't."

She certainly didn't seem unharmed to Gerald, not with her cap gone and her kerchief trailing from around her neck and her petticoat drooping forlornly with a long rip near the hem and the way she kept hiding her face with her hands. He'd wager he wasn't the only one pretending to be much more brave and better off than he actually was. But he'd take her word for it; he didn't really have much choice.

"I am glad," he said thickly. "I don't know what I would have told your brother if it were otherwise."

"Oh, aye, and what am *I* to say to Anabelle?" she

cried, at last dropping her hands from her eyes to let him see the mixture of fear and anger and relief and the tears that she was trying so hard not to shed. "You might have been truly hurt, or even killed outright! Look at yourself, Gerald! Just look!"

"I don't see what the state of my clothes has to do with this," he said as gallantly as he could. "What matters is that you're safe."

"I didn't mean your *clothes.* Look at your poor, battered face." She snuffled loudly and tugged her handkerchief from her pocket, bundling it into a little ball to dab at his split lip instead of using it on the tears on her cheeks.

This was, he realized suddenly, her way of coping, fussing about as if he were a naughty child to hide her own fears. To his surprise, he found he rather liked it, too.

"Serena," he began, wincing as his lip rubbed against the handkerchief. "Serena, I——"

"Hush," she ordered. "Please don't tell me you came here with the intention of rescuing me. I don't think I could bear having you as my savior again."

Gently he pushed aside her hand so he could talk, keeping his fingers against the soft skin of her wrist. "You were late, Serena. And I suspected that if you'd been out in the boat again, you wouldn't have Abel with you."

"How did you know I'd be in the boat?" she asked quickly.

Too quickly.

"Because if you'd been anywhere other than visiting that infernal sweetheart of yours, you wouldn't have been so damned mysterious this morning," he said with a sigh that was more of a groan. It was hard for him to put this many words together. "I should have let him come defend your honor, and saved myself the trouble and a good deal of my own blood, too."

"Oh, Gerald," she said softly. "What a foolish thing for you to say."

"As foolish a thing as it was to say, Serena, I believe it was even more foolish to have done." He did not understand why the mention of her sweetheart had softened her to *him,* but it had, and he wasn't up to questioning the result.

"Foolish for you, but wise for me. And so I thank you, Gerald. I thank you indeed." Self-consciously she curved her hair behind her ears, her smile in the moonlight sudden and shy as she stepped back. "Come, I shall return the favor and see you back to the White Swan before these other two awaken. Besides, I don't believe we'd be welcomed into Anabelle's parlor now, not a sorry pair of ragamuffins like us."

He smiled, and that alone made him wince. She was, God help him, waiting for him to join her. He took one tentative step, trying his weight on the left knee, and slumped back against the wall with an oath as the pain ricocheted through his leg.

"You *are* hurt," she said with fresh concern, "and worse than you wished me to believe, too."

"Left knee," he said tersely. He'd no idea the pain would strike him so hard, enough to make him sweat on this cold night and his heart to pound in his ears, and he prayed that if there were any mercy that he would not faint before her.

"Then let me help you," she said, gently slipping her shoulder beneath his arm to take his weight. "I'll send for Anabelle as soon as we reach the inn."

"No," he said as he struggled to keep the stars in the sky overhead where they belonged, and the street beneath his feet. "No."

"But Anabelle will know what to do to help you!"

"No," he said again, his voice echoing inside his own skull. "All I want is you."

She was there when he woke.

Not *there,* beside him in the bed where he'd been dreaming she so pleasantly was, but there in the ladder-back chair pulled close to the bed, and for now that was enough.

"You're here," he said, still laboring to bring the bed and the candlestand and her bending over him into sharper focus. "You're here."

"Well, yes," she said, her voice soft as silk velvet. "And so are you. I couldn't have abandoned you on the step last night the way Abel would with a dead rabbit, could I?"

"You could have," he said thickly. "I wouldn't have known the difference, rabbit-wise."

"At least your wit seems undamaged. Rabbit-wise, that is," she said, and he heard the smile in her voice even if drowsily he couldn't quite make it out. "How does the rest of you fare?"

He didn't want to move to find out, and when at last he tried, he heartily, and vocally, wished he hadn't.

"Answer enough," she said, laying a cloth over his forehead that was cold enough to make him squirm. "Clearly your store of blasphemy is untouched as well. You'd be feeling a great deal worse if your Mr. Rourke hadn't poured half a bottle of whiskey down your throat."

"I told you Rourke was a marvel." The drowsy, good-natured haze made sense now; Rourke's idea of phys-icking was simple but effective. Encouraged, he tried bending his knee beneath the coverlet, and the good-natured haze exploded in an instant.

"You shouldn't have done that," she scolded, pushing him gently back against the pillows with her palm light against his chest. "I have your poor knee wrapped with ice—snow, actually—to keep the swelling down, but beyond that there's nothing much to be done except for you to rest."

"My 'poor knee' will be right as rain in a few days," he rasped, his throat dry, and he wondered if Rourke had conveniently left the bottle anywhere within reach. "It always is."

She sat back in the chair, her hands folded in her lap. She was once again neatly dressed, her hair tidy beneath her cap, and he wondered how long he'd been lying here—evidently long enough for her to go home and come back. With the windows shuttered, he couldn't tell. By the time they'd half-dragged him up the stairs, he'd been as dead to the world as an old log, but still he liked knowing she'd chosen to return. With idle, wicked curiosity he found himself wondering if she'd been the one to undress him for bed, or Rourke. Gerald knew which one he'd have preferred.

"Mr. Rourke told me all about your knee," she said. "How you hurt it the first time, years ago, falling from a horse whilst hunting on Lord Somebody-or-Other's land. How it grieves you most when the weather turns damp, and how the voyage here was a constant trial to you. How it will give way beneath you at the most inopportune moments, and that none of the learned surgeons and physicians that you've consulted have been able to offer any more sage advice than my own."

He winced again, this time not entirely from pain. She and Rourke had made quite a night of it over his sorry carcass. "Did Rourke leave me any secrets at all?"

She smiled shyly. "You told me Rourke fussed over you like an old wife, and he does. But like the best of wives, young or old, he never betrays you, either."

"That is gratifying." Gerald grimaced, trying to find a more comfortable position in the bed. "Tell me, sweet, did that good bewhiskered wife of mine leave me any more of his, ah, physick?"

"He did." She disappeared from his sight long enough to collect a squat brown bottle and pour from it into a tavern tumbler. "But he made me promise to give you just a little bit and no more, and I agreed."

He could have managed the tumbler well enough himself, but it seemed a humble deceit to let her help him, watching her frown with pretty concentration as she tipped the glass for him to drink. While he was in general a man who disliked cosseting, from her such tending seemed agreeable, even exceptionally pleasant. He smiled as the whiskey warmed his blood, nearly as much as did her nearness as she bent to smooth his pillow bier.

"Ah, Serena dear," he said as the whiskey's drowsy well-being began to reclaim him, "you are as worthy of battle and blood-letting as fair Helen herself."

She nodded solemnly, turning the empty tumbler in her fingers. "This Helen," she began. "She is a lady among your London acquaintance?"

He grinned sleepily. "This Helen was a very beautiful but rather slatternly queen who caused no end of mischief, and she lived so long ago, hundreds and hundreds of years, as to be no . . . no . . . oh, lass, forgive me, but I . . . I seem to misremember."

"You need to sleep," said Serena softly, beginning to rise. She and Rourke had agreed that what Gerald needed most was rest, and there'd been a sleeping draught mixed into the whiskey and water. No wonder he was drifting off now. After that last tumbler, he'd likely sleep the day through. "My foolish questions can keep."

"Not yet." He sought and seized her hand in his, swallowing up her slender fingers in his palm to hold her as his unwilling captive. "Stay, Serena. Don't go. Stay and talk to me."

Reluctantly she settled back into the chair. "I do not know what to say."

"Tell me anything," he ordered. "Tell me . . . tell me of your sweetheart. Aye, that will do. Tell me of *him.*"

Troubled, she looked down at her fingers clasped by his, his hand warm and oddly comforting despite its raw, bruised knuckles. She did not like to tell falsehoods, nor did she have a gift for it, as some people did. She'd always believed what she'd been taught, that one lie told would inevitably lead to another and another and another after that, building a whole unsteady construction of deceit.

And here, now, with Gerald, was the proof of that

wisdom. She had never in her life been graced with a
sweetheart's love, and she'd been wrong to let Gerald
believe otherwise. But what truth would she tell him
instead? What interest would a noble-born gentleman
like him have in the troubles of lowly Mary Sears, or
whether and when her missing husband would return to
her?

"Tell me," he whispered hoarsely. "Surely even you
can think of one thing to say for the poor man."

Her voice was scarcely louder. "I do not know where
to begin."

"One thing, Serena," he whispered, his half-closed
eyes with their long black lashes still managing to offer a
bemused challenge. "Every true-hearted lover can offer
that much."

"He is—he is tall," she began, praying he'd fall asleep
before she needed to invent more specifics. "He is a tall
man."

"More," murmured Gerald, "else I'll judge you
cruel."

She had never had a sweetheart, but if she did, she
knew she'd never be cruel to him. "He is tall," she said
again, more forcefully, "and he is most handsome."

"More," he whispered, his eyes slipping closed.
"More, Serena dear."

She felt his hand relax around hers, his breathing
growing more regular, and as he slept she felt the
wariness and tension wrapped up in herself begin to ease
as well, enough that she could study him with open,
unabashed concern.

He seemed pale to her, his dark hair tousled over the
pillow. Of all of his injuries, the strained knee was the
most serious, but his face had suffered, too, with his
upper lip swollen on one side with a cut and one brow
puffed and purple beneath the damp cloth she'd placed
over it. He'd have to wait a week or two before he'd
break any more tavern girls' hearts.

It was already too late for her. He'd fought for her
sake, and he'd suffered to protect her. From the way he

murmured in his sleep he was suffering still, despite the draught, and as gently as she could she brushed his hair back from his forehead. He was so quick to call himself selfish and shallow, unfeeling, absorbed by only his own pleasures, yet he'd cared enough for her to come to her defense without hesitation. He *must* care.

Yet what if he did? Such caring was meaningless. He was not part of her world, and he'd never pretended otherwise. He found Appledore tedious and backward, and by spring he'd be on his way back to London and Paris and all his other amusements, with scarcely an absent thought to spare in passing for a foolish, besotted spinster. It always happened that way with the people she cared for most. They would go, and she would be the one left behind, to cope with her loneliness as best she could.

She let her finger trail from his forehead down his cheek, along the strong, straight line of his jaw. No promises, he'd told her, and no regrets . . .

She had never had a sweetheart, and she wasn't going to have one now. But regrets, oh, those she'd have by the bushel.

"He is tall, my sweetheart," she began again in a wistful whisper meant only for herself, "and he is handsome, the most comely, well-made man I've ever seen, enough to make me wonder still if he were flesh and blood, or instead a perfect creature to be found only in dreams."

She leaned closer, smoothing the collar of his linen nightshirt away from his throat. "He is tall, my sweetheart, and he clothes himself like a prince, in gold silk or blue that matches his eyes. Though he pretends not to be, he is good and kind and loyal, things that Abel must have understood because Abel likes him, too."

She smiled as she remembered how her dog had bounded through the snow to greet him, how he'd only grinned when Abel had put his snow-covered paws on the front of his coat.

"He is a good man, my sweetheart. He makes me smile

and laugh, even when he twists words about in ways I cannot follow, and he makes me feel clever, and pretty, and good, and . . . and like a sweetheart. Aye, that is it: that is it. He makes me feel like I'm his sweetheart, too."

"Is he sleeping then, miss?" asked Rourke softly behind her, and Serena started with a little gasp.

"He awoke, took more of the whiskey, and then went back to sleep directly." Desperately she prayed that Rourke hadn't overheard her whispers. There seemed precious few secrets between master and servant, and she'd simply die if Rourke repeated any of what she'd whispered to Gerald while he slept. "He's been asleep ever since."

"That's how it should be," said Rourke with a nod of satisfaction as he bent to take the bottle and empty glass from the floor where Serena had put them. "He'll be well enough now. I thank you for sitting with him, miss, indeed I do. Might I send for a boy to see you home?"

"There's no need," she said quickly as she rose from the chair, glancing at the windows where thin bands of late afternoon sunlight edged the drawn curtains. She stood self-consciously while Rourke draped her cloak around her shoulders. "Please tell Ger—that is, Mr. Crosbie that I hope he recovers soon."

She tied the strings of her cloak beneath her chin herself and stole one last, lingering glance at Gerald. He'd turned on his side, the sleeves of his nightshirt shoved up over his forearms, one hand curled beside his cheek and his hair falling across his brow, and somehow, despite the bruises and the dark shadow of new beard along his jaw, he managed to look both very young and very wicked.

"I will tell him, miss. You may rely upon it," said Rourke. "Have you any other message for him when he wakes?"

She looked at him sharply, wondering again if he'd overheard her earlier, but his expression remained impassive, a perfect servant's face. Not that it mattered if he'd heard or not, or even if he repeated what she'd said to Gerald. All that she'd said had been nonsense, foolish, babbling nonsense.

"No, Mr. Rourke," she said softly. "There is no other message."

Nonsense, aye, every last word of it. But at least this time she hadn't lied.

Seven

"You had men fighting over you, Serena?" demanded Mary eagerly. "Fighting in the streets of *Appledore?*"

"They were not precisely fighting over me," said Serena, squirming as much from her friend's open-mouthed disbelief as from her questions. "It was rather more around me."

"Over, around, above, or beneath, it makes little difference, does it?" exclaimed Mary, pressing her palms to her cheeks with amazement. "Oh, Serena, I never would have dreamed such a thing would come to pass! Over you, and in Appledore, too!"

"Hush now, Mary, calm yourself," scolded Serena, "else you'll turn feverish and swoony, and I won't tell you another thing."

She was only half teasing. Mary was a fine-boned wisp of a woman with skin as ivory-pale as parchment and wideset eyes as changeable as the weather. While Mary's constitution had never been strong, Serena had watched her friend's elfin delicacy fade into frailness since Mary's husband, Robert, had disappeared at sea last winter.

Now the cold cut through sharp to Mary's bones, and she spent most days alone in her cottage, wrapped in a cocoon of woolen shawls with her back pressed close to the warmth of the chimney corner and her feet propped upon a tin foot warmer full of coals while she spun wool for a nearby merchant and knitted endless pairs of stockings for the husband only she was convinced would return.

"What else can you expect of me, when you come with such wild tales!" Mary laughed with delight, rare rosy patches of excitement showing on her cheeks. "Sweet Jupiter, Serena, I cannot fancy you in the middle of mischief such as that!"

"I was hardly standing idle, you know," said Serena, part of her already wishing she'd kept her escapades to herself. "I defended myself quite stoutly with my butter crock, the one with the blue stripe that I'd lent to you. It did well enough until I cracked it upon the rascal's thick-witted skull."

Mary gasped. "Oh, Serena, you are so brave!"

"I wasn't brave at all," she said as she poured herself another cup of tea. "I was foolish to begin with, going by that street after dark and without Abel, and then I was frightened nigh out of shift. I was the most cowardly excuse for a Fairbourne you'd ever hope to see."

"Bah, I do not believe it," scoffed Mary as she once again gathered up her knitting from her lap, wrapping the yarn deftly around her index finger to begin the next round. "You are the bravest, boldest creature I have ever known, and I won't hear you say otherwise."

"You'd not think so if you'd seen me skittering away with Job Pinkham at my heels!"

"Not Job Pinkham!" Mary's eyes filled with horrified delight. When they'd both been fatherless girls dependent on the mercy of the parish and the town, they'd spent five years together learning dairying and tending the milk cows on Mistress Cullen's farm, not far from the Pinkhams' house. "Did you know the others as well?"

"I'm not sure Job knew them himself, though they might sail from Truro, too."

Perplexed, Mary shook her head over the back and forth of her needles. "You were saved by a Truro cod fisherman you did not know? I cannot conceive of one of them coming to a woman's rescue, even yours, Serena."

Serena sighed, running her fingertip around the chipped edge of the tea dish. She should have known better than to expect Mary to be satisfied with only half the story.

"It was not a stranger," she said reluctantly. "That is, not entirely. It was Anabelle's brother."

The rhythmic clicking of Mary's needles stopped. "Lord Gerald Crosbie his own self?"

"I have told you before, Mary. He is only the youngest son of a lord, and has no title of his own, any more than does Anabelle."

Mary sniffed. "Your father was a Fairbourne, and that makes you one, so if his father was a lord, then I'd warrant he's a lord, too. Noble-bred folks like those niceties, Serena. Robert told me how the governor of Jamaica's so fine that no one's allowed to sit before him, not 'til he sits first. You should be calling Anabelle 'my lady', you know."

"Anabelle is not *my* lady, Mary," said Serena patiently. As dear a friend as Mary was, there were some topics on which they were bound never to agree, and this had become one of them. "She is my brother's wife."

"She is both," declared Mary, "and there's an end to it. Besides, I'd much rather hear of Lord Crosbie coming to rescue you, all glory like a hero in a ballad-ditty."

Serena sipped the last of her tea and sighed. She was glad she'd never told Mary about kissing Gerald, or the quiddany, or even the gold silk banyan. Already Mary seemed determined to paint Gerald as the greatest, most noble gentleman ever to grace the colony—which he most certainly wasn't—and she didn't need any more beguiling details to gild her fantasy, any more than Gerald needed another champion.

"He does not look so very glorious now," she said instead, "not all bloodied and battered from brawling. Though perhaps, being a man, he may believe he does."

Mary's needles began again, slipping one loop after another as she considered this. "I don't care what you say. It was most gallant of Lord Crosbie to rescue you. He must have taken a great liking to you."

Serena shifted uncomfortably in her chair. She didn't like keeping things from Mary, even if it was to protect her own heart.

"Gerald Crosbie takes a great liking to every woman he meets, Mary," she said, "and I've told you that before, too."

But Mary dismissed her pronouncement with a quick shake of her head. "You're far too quick to decide such things, Serena Fairbourne. You might have had your pick of the men in this county, fine men, too, if you hadn't been so swift to turn them away."

Serena sighed impatiently, wishing there were some way to make Mary understand without wounding her friend's feelings. Turning away the Appledore boys who'd come calling hadn't been difficult, particularly since most offered no more security for a shared future than a winning smile and the pay of a fo'c'sle hand. She'd only to look at the sorry state of Mary's life to see the folly in accepting the first charming young man who dared steal a kiss.

All around the tiny cottage were poignant reminders of Robert Sears's empty promises: the broken shutter he'd never found time to mend; the tottering stack of graying lobster pots abandoned outside the door; the corked bottle filled with sand from the beach on Martinique where he'd vowed to take Mary to escape the harsh winters of Massachusetts. Empty promises and remembered kisses might be enough for Mary Sears, but for Serena it seemed precious little indeed.

"'Tis one thing to have my pick," she said, "but 'tis quite another to decide what to do with the creatures afterward."

Mary jabbed one of her needles into the next loop of

yarn for emphasis. "You would have found out soon enough if only you'd been more kind to the poor lads. I do not like to say it, Serena, you being my friend and all, but sometimes you're too proud by half. Aye, you know you are, so don't say you're not."

"Pride and kindness have nothing to do with it," said Serena defensively. "'Tis the commonest of sense to wish for a happy, useful life."

Mary glanced at her slyly. "Then I wonder if one day you'll be finding a use for Lord Crosbie his own self."

"Oh, aye," scoffed Serena, "and on that day I'll find the path to my house paved with golden guineas, too."

She rose and went to rinse her tea dish in the wash kettle near the fire, hoping that Mary wouldn't notice the guilty flush that would betray her. By now she'd realized that that was why she'd kissed Gerald in the first place. It hadn't been like straying behind the dunes with one of the boys she'd known all her life, a fumbled embrace that the entire town would have known of and judged almost before it was done. But shrouded in the fog with a stranger, separate from her life and from Appledore, there'd seemed no possible consequence to that single, magical kiss.

Until, of course, the stranger had turned out to be Gerald Crosbie.

"Mayhaps it's not because you're proud," said Mary more softly behind her. "Mayhaps instead it's only that you do not know how a man's love can change your life."

"Oh, I know," said Serena, furiously wiping the worn checkered cloth around and around the dripping dish. Since Gerald had sailed into her life, she'd become confused and moody and not at all like herself, her stomach as fluttery as June butterflies and her heart filled with doubt and longing. "I *know*."

"You wouldn't speak that way if you did," said Mary wistfully. "If only you'd let yourself love, Serena. I don't care who the man might be. If only once you'd let yourself dare discover what I have with my Robert."

"Oh, Mary, forgive me," said Serena with instant

remorse, turning back to face her friend with the dish-cloth still clutched in her hands. "I didn't mean it that way, not about you and Robert."

"There's nothing to forgive." Mary's eyes were red with unshed tears, her mouth wobbling with a sham of a smile. "Nothing that you can mend, anyway."

"But I didn't want—"

"'Tis done." Mary blinked fiercely and tried to concentrate on her knitting instead. "How I should like to see true gentry like Lady Anabelle and Lord Gerald Crosbie with my own eyes. Such finery they must have! Mayhaps when they stepped out to meeting, in their Sabbath clothes. Aye, that would be a rare sight, wouldn't it?"

"Then leave with me," begged Serena, coming to kneel beside Mary's chair. "Now, today. The sun's bright and warm this afternoon, and we can bundle you into my boat all snug with coverlets. You can stay with me as long as you please, and you can take tea with Anabelle, as grand as any duchess. Oh, say yes, Mary. Say yes!"

But Mary shook her head sadly. "I cannot, Serena, as much as I'd wish to. Your brother would never—"

"Joshua cannot turn you out of my house, nor would he!"

"And whose pretty house was it first, I ask you?" asked Mary. "No. Your brother has never hidden his feelings about my Robert, and for that alone I'll not take charity from Joshua Fairbourne."

"It would hardly be charity, Mary, and you know Joshua would never—"

"Never what?" Mary's eyes flashed fever bright. "You haven't told Joshua you come here, have you? You swore you wouldn't, Serena, you swore it, and if you have—"

"No," said Serena, the weight of that oath still a burden she wished she didn't bear. She didn't like keeping such a secret from her brother, and only Mary could have asked her to. "He does not know."

"I am glad." Mary sighed with relief, or perhaps resignation, twisting the yarn in her lap with her fingers.

"You will not change me on this, Serena. Nay, you will not. Besides, I can't go traipsing about whenever I please. I must stay here, where Robert can find me. What would he say if he came home to find the hearth cold and me gone to sit in Captain Joshua Fairbourne's parlor, taking tea with Lady Anabelle?"

Unfortunately Serena could imagine all too well what poor Robert would say, or wouldn't say, under those circumstances. But much harder for Serena to hear was how her friend still had not given up hope in a hopeless situation. Miracles could, and did, happen where the sea was concerned, but not after more than a year, and not with a man as loyal to his wife as Robert had been to Mary.

"I understand," she said gently, and as she rose she wrapped her arms around Mary's narrow shoulders, an embrace meant to express all that words couldn't.

"There now, Serena, don't go teary," said Mary, even as she fumbled in her pocket for her own handkerchief. "I'll be waiting here for you, too, eager for whatever gossip tumbles into your ears."

"Tomorrow, then," said Serena, straightening. "In the afternoon."

"Again?" asked Mary with surprise. "Four days in a row?"

Serena paused, taken aback with surprise of her own. "You will not have me, then? You'd rather I didn't come?"

"Of course I'll have you, and welcome the company, too," said Mary quickly. "It's only that you never come so many days in a row."

The unspoken question rose large between them. "You seemed low, that was all," said Serena, wondering why she was feeling so defensive once again. "I thought as friends you'd wish it."

"If that *is* all, very well." Though Mary's eyes were feverishly bright in her pale face, her voice was firm. "But if it is otherwise, if you've come here to hide yourself away—oh, Serena, don't. For my sake, for Lord Gerald Crosbie's, but most of all, Serena, for your own."

With his ailing leg propped gingerly upon a footstool, Gerald sat at the long table he'd had brought upstairs from the taproom to his chambers in the White Swan. Sheets and sheets of paper covered the table and the floor around him like drifts of cream-colored snow, like snow, that is, that was covered with scribbles and blots and long sweeps and flourishes of ink, abandoned sketches of porches and porticos and pilasters, columns and ceilings and lowly cellar-plans, string courses and stairways. For inspiration he had only his old quarto-sized copy of the fourth volume of Vitruvius's *De architectura* propped on the windowsill before him, the pages wavy and a trifle mottled after a decade of voyages in his company, and the memories, more carefully preserved than the poor Vitruvius, of every city, every villa, every town or county house he'd ever visited.

Impatiently Gerald slashed his pen across one more drawing that had failed him, crumpled the sheet, and reached for another. His arm grazed the empty pewter coffee pot, sending it clanking to roll unevenly across the floorboards, but he barely spared it a glance. Once each day, in the morning, he permitted Rourke to clear away the empty plates and crumbs, but he'd strictly forbidden him to disturb any of the papers themselves, not until he was absolutely certain he'd wrestled his nebulous vision into ink-bound reality, and compliance.

And he was, at last and after four days, nearly there. He spread the latest set of drawings before him, absently scratching his cheek as he considered his work. He should have realized how the days and nights, too, had slipped past by how the swelling on his knuckles had faded, the bruises nearly gone. At least this time he had something more to show for his effort, and he studied the drawings with growing satisfaction.

The building he'd drawn itself was simple enough, a

first floor open on all sides through rows of arches, with a single enclosed story above. The roof was peaked, a necessity in a snowy climate, and punctuated with two dormers and a small cupola that could host a weather-vane and perhaps a clock. The colonnade was particularly fine, he thought, and the proportions between the—

"Mr. Crosbie, sir!" bellowed the innkeeper May as he pounded on the door. "Are you within, sir?"

With a sigh at being interrupted, Gerald dropped back into his chair. Of course the man knew perfectly well he was within; he hadn't left this room for days. But May had been more accommodating than most keeps would have been about the table, and besides, it would be in Gerald's own interest to have his scheme discussed among the patrons in the taproom downstairs.

"Enter, May, enter," he called, hastily running his fingers back through his hair. It was one thing to toil by the hour for a good reason, but altogether quite another to look as if he had. "Shouldn't be latched."

The door swung open, and May eagerly pushed his way in, bowing with his hands clasped together, while his gaze gathered in every detail he could to report to his other customers.

"You've a guest, Mr. Crosbie, sir," he said with the perpetual sly wink. Gerald still had not decided if it was intentional or merely a nervous twitch. "A most *important* guest, Mr. Crosbie, sir."

Serena, thought Gerald immediately: Serena.

He hadn't seen her since she'd had to practically drag him through the streets. He didn't have much memory of what had happened beyond her sitting by his bed the next day and holding his hand and scolding him in a charmingly stern whisper, and though what he remembered was quite pleasant, it was what he couldn't recall that worried him. What in blazes could he possibly have done or said to make her keep so completely away ever since? Over and over he'd tortured himself, imagining every manner of unforgivable horror and sin, but now it didn't matter. She'd come to him at last, and with great effort and an unmanly grimace he hauled himself up-right, using the back of the chair for support.

"Aye, Mr. Crosbie, sir," began May, dipping low in another bow, "a guest that you—"

"Enough of this nonsense, May," rumbled Joshua Fairbourne crossly as he pushed past the keep and into the room. "You grovel any lower and you'll have your nose on Crosbie's shoe."

"Ah, Fairbourne," murmured Gerald, hiding his disappointment and his dismay. This was not a guest; this was the enemy. But what was worst of all was that it was not Serena. "What an unexpected . . . *honor.*"

Joshua glared at him, not missing the unflattering emphasis, but not jumping to seize the bait it represented, either. He waved his arm once, like a man brushing away a horsefly. "Clear off, May. And no cocking your ear at the keyhole, mind?"

Though the smile on May's fleshy face collapsed with unhappiness, he didn't argue with Joshua—Gerald doubted anyone in Appledore did—but meekly backed his way from the room, closing the door with scarcely a squeak of a hinge.

Gerald's expression remained impassive as he met Joshua's gaze. His knee ached with even the slight weight he'd suddenly put upon it, and he wished he could sit again. But he'd be damned if he couldn't stand his ground, both figuratively and literally, before Anabelle's husband.

"Come for tea, brother?" he asked, his lips curving in the faintest of smiles.

"Blast it, man, don't begin," growled Joshua, going to warm his back at the fire. "I've come to make, ah, inquiries."

"Where's Nan?" asked Gerald, determined to make an inquiry or two of his own. Given his sister's taste for fussing over others, he'd been surprised and more wounded than he'd admit that she, too, had kept away. Kept away, or *been* kept away, which he suspected was closer to the truth. "Why didn't she come with you?"

Joshua smiled faintly, his teeth white against his weathered face. "She said you'd ask that. She knows you well, your sister."

Gerald nodded once in acknowledgment. He felt as if he didn't know Anabelle at all any more, but that was beside the point. "Thus if she'd known I'd ask, why didn't she know that I'd like to see her?"

"She did." Joshua sighed, and to Gerald's surprise it seemed as if a whole thick layer of hostility faded away from the man in that single hoarse breath. "'Tis the babe. Anabelle's been running through a patch of rough sea, puling into chamberpots again and weak as a new kitten for her trouble. She thought she was done with that, but the midwife says it's common enough. Nothing amiss, she says, and I pray she's right. You know how it is with woman's travail."

But Gerald didn't, not the way that Joshua so evidently did. The man might be an overbearing bully, yet not even Gerald could deny his concern for Anabelle. His broad shoulders were knotted beneath it, his black-browed face clouded with worry. It wasn't jealousy that made him so, or simple possessiveness, but love. Even Gerald, as purposefully blind as he'd made himself in such matters, could see that. The great oaf *loved* his sister, loved her with all his bluff, ox-sized heart.

It was a stunning realization. Anabelle might find herself bored to tears once her infatuation began to fade—which it was bound to do for her the way it did for all Crosbies—but Gerald was disturbingly certain that this man's feelings never would fade. Whatever other faults Joshua possessed, he'd never treat Anabelle with the same careless, genteel neglect that would have been her lot if she'd married the marquis' son in London who'd asked for her first.

But was that enough to condone such a lopsided marriage? Before Anabelle had run away, she'd been an heiress with a fortune of her own worth five thousand pounds a year. Could love erase the inequities between her station and Joshua's, or put aside all the differences between their families and expectations? Did love have the power to make low-born Joshua Fairbourne worthy of a lord's daughter?

And, strangely, the answer came to him not in Anabelle's voice, but in Serena's. *Love is never enough:* that is what Serena had said, what she believed, and, before this, Gerald would have agreed. But not now. Now life, and love, and his sister's situation and Serena's place in it, didn't seem nearly so uncomplicated.

"Nan will come through with banners flying," he said finally, and cleared his throat with an uncharacteristic heartiness that betrayed exactly how damned awkward he felt. "You'll see. She's a stout little creature beneath all the furbelows."

Joshua looked up at him from beneath the black thicket of his brows. "Aye," he said firmly, as if to convince himself, and Anabelle, too, if she'd been in hearing. "She will. She *will.*"

Joshua cleared his throat, too, a great rumbling that began deep beneath the horn buttons on his waistcoat, and grew loud enough to be marveled at by anyone in the room below.

Lord help them both, thought Gerald, they must sound like a wretched pair of consumptives. Not that he could think of much else to fill the yawning silence, either, and only at the last moment did he manage to turn another throat-clearing into a more discreet cough behind the back of his hand.

"Aye," said Joshua, agreeing to nothing in particular that Gerald could see. "Aye. Anabelle couldn't come see you herself. But she did wish me to ask after you and to determine the extent of your injuries and to inquire as to how you are pretending to treat them."

He spoke without hesitation, without any sign of having learned the sentence by rote, but Gerald's ear was quick to hear his sister's words coming from her husband's lips.

"You tell Nan not to worry," he said, warmed by her concern, even if it came secondhand. Rourke always did an admirable job of patching him back together after all manners of scrapes and mishaps, but there was nothing like a woman's solicitude and kindly touch, whether from Anabelle or Serena.

Especially Serena, and Gerald stifled the memory of her sitting beside his bed, her hand resting lightly upon his nightshirted chest as she'd pressed her breasts against his arm and whispered delightful foolishness into his ear. It was probably better not to indulge that particular daydream with her brother standing two paces away. Who could guess what sorts of powers the devil granted to Massachusetts sea-captains born in his own infernal image?

"Tell Nan not to worry," he began again, "and that the only part of me that's still somewhat awry is my knee. The old trouble again. Tell her that, and she'll understand, just as she'll understand that there's not a farthing worth of physick that will make it improve any faster. But tell her that I do thank her for asking."

"Your knee. Aye, I'll tell her that." Joshua nodded, sternly glancing down at Gerald's knee as if he could see through the leg of his breeches to the offending joint itself. "That is all?"

Gerald smiled benignly. "Are you disappointed?"

Joshua scowled, studying Gerald's face and hands. "Serena said you'd taken a pounding. Said you were all banged up and battered for all that you'd run the bastards off, and Serena would know. Mind she's seen her share of such to judge fair, too. And damnation, she was right. I'd say you won."

"You *are* disappointed." Gerald himself was not. Far from it. Serena might not have come calling, but she was still speaking his name. Better than that: she was singing his praises as a warrior upon the battlefield of honor, singing them to her sainted brother.

"Not disappointed," admitted Joshua grudgingly. "Surprised. Where the hell did an overbred poppycock like you learn to fight?"

Gerald shrugged. "Any of the better schools for young

gentlemen in Britain will do the job admirably. In England I was roundly thrashed by my noble young peers for daring to have an Irishman for a father. In Ireland, my English-born mother provided much the same offense. Both provided wonderful inspiration and training for taking a turn in the ring at Donnybrook Fair."

"Hah. One long crossing among the hands in the fo'c'sle would do much the same, and a sight less dear, too." Impatiently he swept his hand through the air. "Sit, man, sit! Don't stand on my account. If your knee pains you, then damnation, do something to ease it!"

"It's well enough as it is," said Gerald. As much as he'd rather be sitting with his leg propped up again, there was no way under heaven that he'd do so with Joshua's permission. "And you may tell that to Nan as well."

"What I'll tell her is that her brother's a stubborn ass." In two long strides he came back across the room, dropping heavily into the chair opposite Gerald's. "There. Will you sit now, you blasted fool?"

Staring down at the other man, Gerald did in fact feel like a blasted fool, and a stubborn ass in the bargain. How could he not? Gingerly he lowered himself back into his chair and swung his leg back up onto the footstool, working hard to keep the relief from his face.

"Better, isn't it?" said Joshua. "Even if you're too damned proud to admit it. And here's more to puff you up even further. You were right about Serena."

"Right?" repeated Gerald uneasily. There seemed far too much in that statement that could be open for lethal misinterpretation. "Right how?"

Joshua gave him a look that reaffirmed his earlier pronouncement of fooldom for Gerald. "Right that she'd meant to come to my house that night. Right that she was late a-coming. Right that she needed help."

"It was no great secret," said Gerald, relieved enough to be graciously modest. "She'd told me herself earlier in the day."

"Well, she's lucky you listened. Though why she chose to take that path at night among the warehouses, coming to my home from hers—and without Abel, too—still makes no sense to me. Not a lick."

He shook his head and sighed with disgusted resignation. Clearly Serena was now included in the same fool's paradise with Gerald. Gerald didn't mind the company.

"Not that it signifies now," continued Joshua gruffly. "What matters is that Serena's safe and has you to thank for it. And I shall thank you, too."

He thrust out his hand, a work-hardened, outsized offering of gratitude that Gerald could scarcely refuse. Nor, he realized suddenly, did he wish to.

"Defending younger sisters against themselves is a damnable trial," he said, commiserating, as he shook Joshua's hand. "I cannot tell you how many times I had to fish Nan out of the Kilmarsh duckpond, her petticoats dripping and her nose blubbering."

Joshua smiled fondly at the image. "I had to haul her out of Nantucket Sound in the middle of a nor'easter. She blubbered then, too."

"Some things never change," declared Gerald soundly. "Nan's weakness for deep water being one of them."

"Aye," said Joshua, his expression turning soft again, the way it seemed to do whenever Anabelle was mentioned. "She is a rare little creature, my wife."

But that "wife" stopped Gerald cold, a reminder he needed but didn't welcome. Wasn't Anabelle's marriage to this man—this man whose hand he'd just shaken with the greatest good feeling and camaraderie—wasn't this the latest pond that he'd come to rescue his sister from?

Fortunately unaware of Gerald's thoughts, Joshua had turned to look at the piles of drawings and notes scattered over the table. "What is this, eh?" he asked curiously. "The famous Kilmarsh?"

"Not exactly, no," said Gerald, imagining what his father would say to his seat at Kilmarsh being likened to a proposed public market in the colonies. "Something I've been amusing myself with, that is all."

Joshua rose to lean over the table for a better view.

"Damned fine sort of amusement. Anabelle never told me you'd an eye toward being a housewright."

Gerald choked back his first response. He himself wasn't a true architect, only an interested amateur, but he suspected that here in Massachusetts even the gloriously gifted Palladio would be no more than a housewright. "Serena told me there'd been difficulty finding suitable plans for a markethouse. While my knee kept me trapped here, I decided I'd try my hand at a few sketches of my own. They are not done, of course, but—"

"They're exactly what's needed," said Joshua with such open enthusiasm that it bordered on glee. "But do you think the men here can build it so?"

"If the work they did on your own house is any measure of their skills," said Gerald diplomatically, "then there's no question of it. And since I've told Nan I'll stay until she's brought to bed, there's time and more to see to a good beginning."

Joshua waved his large hands over the drawings, almost as if he could touch the finished building already. "All these gimcracks and furbelows—you've gotten them just so, haven't you?—and all in the best London taste. I can see that myself. You outdo any of those carpenter-hacks in Boston, and that's the honest truth. Why, there wouldn't be another market in all the colonies to hold a candle to this one here in Appledore!"

Gerald nodded in agreeable silence, while inwardly he was rocking with laughter. Anabelle's wild, rough sea-captain, the man their grandmother decried as no better than a pirate, was really at heart no better than any merchant prince from the city. At least he was where buildings were concerned. Joshua didn't give a tinker's dam for proportions or design: what mattered most was outdoing his neighbor, and the more decisively, the better.

Suddenly Joshua thumped his fist on the table. "Where's Serena?"

"Where's Serena?" repeated Gerald blankly. He

seemed to be doing that a great deal this morning, as often as a prating parrot. "Serena?"

"Aye, my sister," demanded Joshua. "Has she been here with you?"

Even though Gerald knew she hadn't been there in days and certainly not in the way his feverish imagination had wished, he very nearly turned to look at the bed for a telltale lady's stocking or garter peeping from beneath the coverlet.

"Not since the night I—ah, defended her honor." He reasoned it couldn't hurt to remind Joshua, especially not when his own conscience was overreacting to the point that he felt guilty for something he hadn't begun to do. "She hasn't been here, no."

"Then I'll see that she comes." Joshua thumped the table again for emphasis. "She must see this. Though you might not think it because she's a woman, Serena has an eye for such things. Trusted her enough to leave her to make the decisions for me on my house while I was at sea. Of course, now I leave such things to Anabelle, but Serena did well enough before I was wed."

Again the specter of that marriage filled the room, but this time it was Serena that Gerald considered, not Anabelle. How hard it must have been for her when Joshua brought home his new bride! She must have felt that she'd lost not only her brother's devotion, but her own larger place in the town as well. Yet, though her life could return to what it had been before if Anabelle left, Serena still loved her brother enough to wish him only happiness, even if that happiness made her wretched in the process.

Automatically Gerald's gaze shifted to the windowsill, and the scallop shells, Serena's shells, that he'd put there for the sort of inspiration that Vitruvius couldn't provide. He didn't need Joshua to tell him she had an eye for beauty. An eye, and a soul, which was infinitely more important. They were alike that way, and he'd sensed it about her in the first moments they'd been together, bobbing on the waves in her little boat.

Joshua pushed his chair away from the table and settled his hat more firmly upon his head. "I must be gone. But I'll send Serena to you at once."

"Don't," said Gerald quickly, pulling himself upright to face the other man. To his mind, Serena had had far too many orders in her life as it was, and she didn't need any more because of him. "Let her come when she chooses, on her own will."

"Wait upon a woman's will?" Joshua laughed as he opened the door to leave. "Then you shall have one long wait, Crosbie, a long wait indeed."

His laughter echoed in the stairs, seeming to linger after he'd gone. Gerald could see him from the window, the top of his black cocked hat so much higher than anyone else's as he walked down the street.

With a sigh Gerald began to stack the papers more neatly upon the table before him. He'd no doubt now that the markethouse would be built along his plans. When Captain Joshua Fairbourne made up his mind to something, the rest of Appledore listened and obeyed. All that was left for Gerald to do was to savor the private triumph.

But somehow, strangely, the satisfaction he'd expected wasn't there. Lord knows it should have been, and he'd be damned if he knew why.

He reached for the twin shells, lightly turning them over in his palm. He couldn't believe they'd survived the scuffle with the two fishermen in the street, but when he'd finally awakened, the shells were waiting on the table beside his bed, rescued from the pocket of his torn and tattered coat by the unquestioning Rourke. Or maybe Serena had done it herself; he'd like to think she had, and he smiled at his own foolishness.

He'd begun the designs for the markethouse on a whim, an impulse born from a certain vengeful gloating that, in retrospect, wasn't particularly noble-minded or especially admirable. But as he'd grown absorbed in his work, another, more appealing, more shameful motive, had pushed itself forward.

He wanted to impress Serena.

He winced as he admitted it to himself, feeling ten times the fool that Joshua had earlier judged him to be. He wasn't sixteen any more, urging his horse over the highest stone wall in the county to catch the eye of some giggling girl with pink ribbons and a wreath of daisies. Thank God, he was mercifully past that.

But he hadn't forgotten what Serena had said as they'd stood beside the snow-filled foundation of the market-house: "All men must have some gainful way to leave their mark upon the world." In return he'd told her that gentlemen didn't need any purpose except to be gentlemen, which was what he'd been raised to believe. He'd never questioned it before, anyway.

But the cold, sorry truth was that he did lead a remarkably ungainful life and always had. If he were to die today, struck dead by apoplexy or perhaps a more accomplished drunken fisherman, then the sum of his legacy would be his dog-eared collection of books, a handful of excellent *quattrocento* temperas by a forgotten Siennese master, and two Corregios that he suspected were forgeries. His small but comfortable income would revert to a nephew he'd never met. That, then, would be all.

And now, thanks to Serena, it didn't seem to be quite enough.

He glanced back down at the drawings, now only able to see the flaws in his work. The arches were clumsy and crowded, the pillars squat, the angle of the roof hopelessly wrong, all of it a misguided pastiche that any other roving dilettante could have pieced together in a spare hour's time. It was just as well she hadn't come, if these scribbles were the best he could muster. No wonder it would take a direct order from Joshua to make her climb the stairs if this was all that waited for her.

Roughly he shuffled the drawing together, the papers rustling against each other in protest. One slipped to the floor and, as he bent to retrieve it, he cursed its mean existence so soundly that he almost didn't hear the dog barking in the street below. He straightened, listening, the sheaf of papers clutched in his fist. He knew that bark; what was better, he knew the dog. A *black* dog. Swiftly he leaned across the table, searching the crowded street from one corner to another.

The red cloak swung behind her as she hurried his way, the hood shoved back and the nape of her neck a startling, vulnerable white above her kerchief and below her pinned-up hair.

She had come, of her own will. And the wait hadn't been so very long after all.

Eight

"Faith, look at you, Gerald," said Serena with surprise as she pushed open the door to his chamber, Abel at her side. "You're dressed."

Gerald spread his arms wide and bowed grandly from the waist in his best Italian-dancing-master manner. "Your servant, ma'am. I only live to please you, you know, and if you'd rather I were in some form of undress—"

"Oh, no, no, not at all," said Serena hurriedly, her cheeks turning hot at the prospect. What she had expected was an invalid, pale, weak, and, above all, safe, and the Gerald standing before her was absolutely none of those things. "It is only that I remembered that, ah, banyan, and I—"

"You *liked* the banyan, didn't you?" He grinned wickedly, running one hand back through his black hair. The mottled pattern of bruises that had marked his face had faded dramatically, and instead of disfiguring him, the small, healing cut over his eye lent a bit of rakish dash to his face.

"The silk was very beautiful, yes," she admitted stiffly. And that was as much as she would admit, especially since the silk had been the very least of what had captured her eye.

"I knew from the first you had excellent taste," said Gerald, beaming. "Isn't that so, Abel?"

After sitting in patient silence beside Serena, the dog ducked his head and made a happy little growl at finally being addressed, and thumped his heavy tail against the floor.

"Clever fellow," said Gerald, beaming with approval. "And I commend your choice of a mistress, too."

Swiftly Serena hooked her fingers into Abel's collar before he wriggled his way across the floor in joyful ecstasy to Gerald. He'd never behaved this way with any other man, but then, neither had she. She had come here to check on an invalid's progress, and instead she could feel herself slipping deep into one of his infernal, flirtatious word games.

"Gerald, please," she said as sternly as she could. "You must stop turning my words around and making it sound as if I were saying something entirely different from what I'd meant."

"*I* do that?" he asked, the picture of wide-eyed disingenuousness with the plate of cold bacon and toast left from his breakfast in one hand. "To you?"

"You do," she said, "and it's very troublesome to me. I never know what to—faith, can you not bend your knee more than that?"

He grimaced as he bent awkwardly to set the plate down on the floor.

"It's much improved," he said through gritted teeth. "Truly."

Abel whined at the scent of such an unexpected treat, pulling so hard at Serena that he tugged her with him a step closer to Gerald.

"If this is improvement, then I'm thankful I didn't see you before," she declared with concern, letting the dog go free to scramble to the plate. Perhaps she'd end up tending to an invalid after all. "Didn't Rourke put more of the snow on your knee to help the swelling, the way I told him?"

"Of course he did," said Gerald quickly. "If there's one thing that Rourke knows how to do, it's obey orders, even orders from ladies. Surely you must trust my word as to my own welfare."

She looked at him sideways, her eyes narrowed. She'd seen the same sort of panicking defensiveness in small boys refusing to take a dose of wormwood water. Was it really that important to him that he seem strong, manly, invulnerable before her? Yet she found the notion oddly endearing, for it meant that he cared enough about her to worry about her opinion.

"Do I trust your word?" she repeated. "Not in particular, no."

"And I tell you, Serena, that there's no reason." He glanced past her, his eyes brightening with sudden inspiration, and as quickly as he could he hobbled across the room to snatch up the walking stick that was leaning against a chair. "Here's proof enough, too. I've been planning to go for a walk, you see, planning to make this sorry old limb of mine earn its keep."

"If that is true, Gerald, then you are quite mad," she said. But the walking stick was genuine, no macaroni's affectation, with a sturdy hawthorn shaft and a crest polished smooth from use. "You belong in your bed, not parading about in the street."

He tapped the stick against the chair for emphasis, his knowing, confident grin returning, almost as if it, too, had needed the stick for support.

"That is kind of you to wish me to bed, another example of your infinite generosity," he said, reaching for his coat. "But this *is* my knee, and this *has* happened to me before, and I do know what will improve it. And that means a walk."

"You *are* mad," said Serena, shaking her head with dismay. "And therefore I cannot let you go, Gerald."

"You don't have to." He was surprisingly agile with

the aid of the stick, first retrieving his hat from the top of the chest of drawers and then one of the papers from the table, rolling it into a loose scroll and tucking it into his coat before he came to stand before Serena, holding his arm out to her in invitation. "You can come with me instead."

Abel scurried to join him, his dark eyes shifting expectantly from Serena to Gerald to Serena again, wordlessly pleading with her.

"What a vastly clever beast," said Gerald. "Will you be as agreeable, Serena, and join me?"

"Any dog will be agreeable if you feed him bacon and buttered toast." Serena knelt to scratch the traitorous Abel in his favorite spot, behind his ear. "Gerald, I don't know what you hope to prove by this—"

"I didn't realize any proof was necessary, not between us." His smile warmed, coaxing. "*Ma dolce cicerone.* Today I have something to show you instead, if only you'll come with me."

Serena sighed, her fingers stroking Abel's thick fur, shaggy and rough for winter.

Gerald reached down and took her hand from Abel's ruff, his fingers warm around hers. "I could bear watching, you know. To see that I don't fall into trouble again."

"Aye, you do." She smiled in spite of herself, letting him draw her back to her feet. "And I should warn you that my sight is most keen. It runs in our family, you know. Joshua says I would have made a splendid lookout."

"I'll remember that, Serena dear," he said as he settled his hat on his head with a flourish, "especially when I'm forced to post my white flag in surrender."

She laughed and linked her hand into the crook of his arm as they slowly began down the stairs, Abel bounding ahead before them. It was preposterous to imagine Gerald surrendering to anyone, especially to a woman, and most especially to a woman like her. She told herself fiercely that it was better that way, just as she told herself she'd no wish in turn to surrender to him, either. That was the honest truth, and nothing Mary could say would change her mind.

But Gerald *would* bear watching, and she wondered uneasily what he wished to show her. She always wondered when he began speaking in Italian; the uneasiness that likewise always followed seemed entirely understandable, even if the words he chose weren't.

At least today, she thought wryly, she'd be able to outrun him.

They made slow progress, the day gray and cheerless with a biting wind from the water that threatened snow. Even Abel seemed subdued by the weather, keeping close to Serena's petticoats with his head low against the wind. Though Serena tried to suggest that they keep their walk brief, Gerald insisted on continuing, intent upon reaching whatever secret goal it was that he'd set for himself, and he also refused to lean upon her for assistance. Such a show of determination took Serena by surprise. She hadn't believed a man who let himself be dressed by a servant would behave with so much, well, independence.

Nor had he been telling tales when he'd said this had happened to him before. She could tell by the way he knew how to compensate for the weakness in his knee that such exercise, and the little grimaces of pain that accompanied it, weren't new to him. Yet he'd willingly suffered like this for her sake, and the sacrifice troubled her almost as much as it secretly pleased her.

"Tell me, Serena dear," he said, his words coming out as little puffs of white in the chilly air. "Am I merely delirious, or are your good neighbors regarding me more cheerfully today, and less inclined to wish me drawn and skewered and straight to the devil?"

"You're not fancifying, no," said Serena reluctantly. Given the reason, she was almost sorry that he'd noticed. "There are few things this town loves more than a good fight, and in these last days news of ours has been common around every hearth."

"Is that so?" He stopped, unable to keep the happy

grin from his face. "But what of the other rascals, eh? Haven't they been telling their side of our little *contretemps?*"

"Most likely they are, but not here in Appledore," said Serena. "Once Joshua discovered their names, he had them sent back to Truro by the next boat, and made sure they knew they wouldn't be welcome to return, not the next night, not ever."

His grin faded. "That is all your brother did? After what those bastards did to you, that is *all?*"

"Well, yes," she said, puzzled. "What else did you expect?"

"Imprisonment at the very least," declared Gerald warmly, thinking of Anabelle in the same situation, and thinking, too, of the punishments suggested by his own family for Joshua Fairbourne after he'd eloped with her. "Deportation to New South Wales, or a term in His Majesty's navy, even a trip to the gallows, considering your suffering!"

She looked at him strangely. "Faith, have you forgotten how much you made *them* suffer already?"

"And have you and your infernal brother forgotten that I'm a gentleman?"

"What would matter most here would be that you are a foreigner, not of this colony," she explained with maddening patience. "Gerald, how you came to help me was very wonderful and noble, and Joshua is almost as proud of you as I am. He likes men who can take care of themselves because that's the way he is. He only wishes he'd been there, too. But if we'd taken those fishermen before the magistrate, then they could have sworn out complaints against us in turn. They wouldn't win, of course, but whyever should we wish the trouble? We won, and they lost, and let that be an end to it."

"But, damanation, this won't be the end." Angrily Gerald stabbed at the ground with his stick, thinking again of Anabelle. "There will be talk. Talk about *you.* Likely there already is."

"This isn't London, Gerald," she said. "People here aren't like that."

He shook his head, unconvinced. "People are much the same the world over, Serena. Even here. Don't fool yourself into believing otherwise."

But people in London *were* different from Appledore, she thought, her heart pounding wildly, and he was the proof. He cared about her, and what became of her. He *cared.* Lightly he cupped the side of her face in his palm, holding her gaze even with his own. His deerskin glove was soft against her cheek, the scent of the leather pungent, the linen ruffle on the cuff of his shirt tickling her throat: foolish things she realized afterward.

"You deserve better, that is all," he said with a gentle gruffness that seemed to Serena to speak more from his heart than all the elegantly phrased folderol he usually favored. "Remember that."

He paused, clearly deciding whether to speak more or not, and didn't. Instead he let his hand trail down across her cheek, his smile strangely bittersweet. "We're here now."

"Here?" she repeated blankly, struggling to haul her thoughts back down to earth where they belonged. They were standing once again before the unfinished market-house, or rather the rutted hole meant someday to become its cellar.

"Here here," said Gerald. "Where we are at present."

He reached into the front of his coat and fumbled with the paper he'd tucked inside, the chill in his fingers making him clumsy. Nearly as clumsy, he thought with despair, as his own tongue had been just now. No wonder Serena was regarding him as if his senses had fled from beneath his hat, straight away with the wind.

But he believed what he'd told her, that people everywhere loved a good scandal, and the smaller the town, the worse the gossip. There was none of the casual anonymity possible in a city; the little parish around Kilmarsh had been worse than the royal court at St. James. He was certain now that the tales being told here in Appledore of their scuffle were painting Serena in the most disreputable, disagreeable light possible. How could they not?

Whatever was Miss Serena doing in that part of town and at that hour in the company of four—four!—men? . . . . Crashing heads like a fishwife, they say, then off to pass the night in the Londoner's rooms at the White Swan, Mr. May told me his own self. . . . Always so fine and nice and kind, that Miss Serena Fairbourne, but look what came of it, her being no better than she ought to be, not in the end.

He could imagine it all, and Serena deserved none of it. She was a good woman, an honest woman, unlike any other, rich or poor, that he'd met in his travels, yet to describe her like that made her sound like some backward, stuffy spinster, when she was something altogether different. Not even her infernal brother seemed to realize how rare she was.

But Gerald had seen how Serena's face could light from within with happiness, brighter than any candle's flame, just as he'd heard the intoxicating merriment in the way she laughed when he teased her, and even more when she'd learned to tease him back. And that single stolen, wanton kiss from her, his mermaid in the fog, was an unforgettable memory that would warm him on cold nights the rest of his life. He'd known her only a handful of days, but in some ways it felt as if she'd always been hovering there in his thoughts like a practical angel in homespun linsey-woolsey with a magic recipe for cranberry quiddany.

She *did* deserve better than the life she had here. He glanced at her now as she bent to scratch her dog's ears, her back a graceful curve, her profile clean against the red wool of her hood, as perfect as an ancient goddess on a Roman coin. He smiled to himself, thinking how charmingly she'd frown at such a compliment, and frown, too, at the notion that she needed a white knight of her own.

Strange to realize that he'd come here, rather unwillingly, to defend Anabelle, who didn't appear to need or want any defending whatsoever. But instead of his chivalrous impulses lapsing back into the genteel disuse where they'd been languishing for the previous twenty-odd years, they seemed bent on leaping into full-flowered outrage on behalf of this low-bred sailor's daughter. He could think of no other excuse for him to have gone flailing away into the middle of a drunken brawl in a seaport town.

Not that excuses were of much value at this point. Rationally speaking, his actions of late were better suited to a confirmed Bedlamite than a gentleman and would bound to be the subject of endless laughter and ridicule among his London and Dublin friends, if they ever learned of it. He was clear-sighted enough to see that. Knights on white horses seldom earned the sort of respect they deserved, even from the damsels they sought to rescue.

That much he could accept. But worrying him no end was the final fate of the damsel once he packed away his lance and silver armour for good. What indeed would become of Serena when he sailed back to England in the spring?

He looked down at the rolled drawing in his hand, a flattened scroll that now seemed no more than a mis-guided conceit. In some way he'd intended the market-house design as a kind of offering for her, proof that he wasn't the idle, fashionable dunderhead she believed. At least not entirely, anyway. But in this way, too, Serena deserved better, better than anything he'd ever be able to give.

"What is that you're holding?" she asked curiously, moving closer to see. "Is this what you mean to show me?"

"Ah, 'tis nothing." He began to shove the drawing back into his coat, not caring now if he crumpled it or not. "It would seem instead that I've taken you all this way upon an empty whim."

"I don't believe you, Gerald," she said with firm

conviction. "You've worked far too hard walking here to dismiss it as a whim. Now won't you please show me that paper?"

He frowned down at her, trying to look forbidding, an impossible task when she was angling her gaze up at him through her lashes with her chin tipped to one side. Damnation, where had she learned *that* beguiling little trick?

She edged closer still, her hand in its thick mitten coming to rest lightly on his sleeve as her voice turned playfully wheedling. "Please, please, Gerald. Won't you show me? Please?"

He rather liked it when she begged like that. He wished rather more she were begging for something more pleasurably worthwhile in his power to grant, but a cold, windy street wasn't the place for nurturing such fantasies. Instead he merely sighed, and unrolled the drawing without any of the flourish or fanfare he'd once planned.

"It's a design I made for a markethouse," he said as he held it outstretched between his hands for her to see. "You'd told me there wasn't one. Some scribblings while my knee was healing, that is all, idle marks to pass the time, of no account nor—"

"Oh, hush, Gerald," she said as she leaned over his arm to see better. "Just hush, and let me look."

He let her, and she did, in a lengthening silence that was excruciating.

"You needn't labor so to think of something creditable to say," he said at last, swiftly beginning to recurl the paper with his thumbs. "I warned you the drawings were worthless, didn't I?"

"Oh, aye, you did, you great dunderhead." She put her hand over his, forcing him to keep the drawings open. "I cannot believe you can draw like this, Gerald. These are better than any of the plans the others made up, far better, and far from anything I'd expect from a—from a—"

"Dunderhead?" he supplied helpfully.

"That will do, aye." Her interest growing visibly, she leaned forward again, studying the drawing. "It is beautiful, you know, perhaps the most beautiful market I've ever seen, with all those columns and that fancy part beneath the roof."

Almost lovingly he traced the line with his fingertip. "The stringcourse, Serena. This fancy part beneath the roof is called the stringcourse."

"The stringcourse, then." She was nearly hopping with excitement beside him, her face glowing with it in a marvelous way that mirrored and magnified his own. "Oh, if it could be built to look like this!"

"It could," he said, striving now to seem offhanded, as if he did such things on a daily basis, as if her approval didn't matter more than his own life. "It will. Even your grim-faced brother approved."

"You've shown this to Joshua already?" she asked, her eyes rounding with surprise. "He has agreed to see that it is built, here in Appledore?"

Gerald smiled, joy and pride sweeping over him with a fierceness he hadn't anticipated. "Here in Appledore, on this very spot, too. And it's all your doing, *ma cher cicerone,* for you were the one who brought me here in the first place. You were my muse."

She glanced up at him sideways again, narrowing her eyes just a fraction more. "I believe you would wish me to thank you for the compliment now, Gerald, but I'm not going to do it, not until you tell me exactly what the duties of a 'muse' might be. Mind, you never did explain what a 'nymph' was, either, and I have the greatest suspicion that a muse isn't much more respectable."

"Ah, but a muse *is* infinitely more respectable, you see," he said with as much seriousness as he could muster, which was precious little indeed, given the winsome way she was looking at him. "Muses are a sort of goddess who drops out of the clouds at opportune moments to inspire pitiful mortal men to achieve great things. Their duties are entirely cerebral, while nymphs occupy themselves mainly by frolicking with satyrs and such."

"Satyrs." She twisted her mouth wryly as a little gust of wind swirled her hood away from her head. "Dare I ask what those are?"

"Wicked, licentious male creatures," he said, wondering what she'd do if he kissed her, "who occupy themselves by frolicking with the nymphs."

"Rather like you, then."

"Not exactly, no." He would wager a hundred guineas that no other man and woman in the history of Appledore—perhaps in the entire colony—had ever stood in the street at mid-day and discussed the pastimes of satyrs and nymphs. It was, he decided, an intriguing achievement for them both, and certainly one meriting a kiss in celebration.

He leaned closer, letting one side of the drawing flutter free in the wind so he'd be ready to circle her waist with his arm. "Satyrs are infinitely more wicked than I, Serena, and besides, they have the nether-regions of a goat. I'd say I'm more deserving of a muse."

"A *goat!*" She tipped back her head and laughed, enchanting and tempting. "A goat! Faith, I cannot fathom what—oh, blast, look, it's raining!"

As soon as she spoke a large, wet drop splattered on her cheek, and as she squinched up her eye and wrinkled her nose and hurried to tug her hood back over her head, Gerald realized that the moment of enchantment and temptation had slipped away, and with it his celebratory kiss.

And it wasn't raining. It was sleeting, immense, icy blobs that combined all the worst qualities of rain and snow as it pelted down upon them.

Just in time, too, thought Gerald glumly. First he'd let himself become thoroughly outraged about Joshua's behavior toward Serena, then had nearly outdone him by kissing her there for all the world to see, or at least as much of it as cared to watch. Apparently not all satyrs had goatly nether-regions; this particular one wore breeches from the best tailor in Dublin.

"Your drawing, Gerald!" cried Serena, grabbing the loose end. "Oh, no, look what has happened to it!"

Already the sleet had struck one of the columns, the inks smearing into a purplish blotch, and as they watched another met the same fate, and then another.

"Hurry, roll it up, oh, please!" Frantically Serena tried to shield the paper with the side of her cloak, heedless of how her skirts whirled around her ankles. "Hurry, Gerald, don't let it be ruined! Oh, Joshua will have my head if there's no new markethouse because of my carelessness!"

"It doesn't matter," said Gerald, barely reaching up in time to jam his hat more firmly on his head before the wind carried it away. "There's a cartload of others in my rooms."

"Not like this one, I'm sure! Now come with me, here, so you can roll it properly. Abel! Abel, come!"

She seized Gerald's arm, hurrying him toward a small, rough shed that stood on the edge of the site. The shed had been built to shelter the last disgruntled overseer—before he'd quit—and his plans from the glare of the summer's sun, and so had neither door nor window nor floor beyond earth. But the shed did have a sturdy batten roof that would protect them from the sleet, and gratefully Gerald ducked inside, drawing Serena in with him.

Anxiously she looked over his shoulder as he blotted at the drawing with the sleeve of his coat. "Will it be all right?"

"Well enough," he said, touched by her unnecessary concern as he pulled off his gloves and began rolling the paper to put it back into his coat. "I told you I've drawn them by the score, and I can make others, too, if need be."

"Yes, but they won't be the same as this one," she said, her voice a little breathy from running. "Because *this* is the one you showed me first."

"Then you may have it," he declared. Awkwardly he twisted himself around so they faced one another, and handed her the paper. "A gift from the artist."

"Oh, my, Gerald!" She tugged off her mittens and took the drawing gingerly in both hands. Droplets of melting sleet clung to the front of her hair like little jewels, and her face was rosy with the cold, and happiness, too. "I don't know what—that is, thank you, Gerald. Thank you so much."

"You are most welcome, sweet," he said. "My only wish is that it were ten times finer, and so nearer to be worthy of you."

The shed had been made for the overseer to stand by himself at the narrow blank desk pegged to the wall, and he and Serena and her petticoats made for a crowded fit as they tried to keep clear from the sleet. She was close enough that he was aware of the warmth from her body, melting the snow on the shoulders of her cape, close enough that he was aware of the violet scent she always wore.

Not that Gerald objected. No man with half a breath of life left in his carcass would. But such unexpected proximity was testing his newly honorable intentions again, and reluctantly Gerald eased himself back as far as he could against the raw wood of the wall. In her company he'd almost forgotten the nagging ache in his knee, and he still couldn't tell if the drumming he heard in his ears came from the sleet driving against the roof overhead, or from the reckless pounding of the blood in his own veins.

She ran her fingertip along the edge of the rolled paper, concentrating so intently on it rather than him that Gerald realized that she, too, was hearing that same rhythm of the sleet.

"You say such foolish things, Gerald," she began. "As if I am—oh, Abel, *no!*"

The large, wet dog hurled himself into the shed with a happy bark to announce his arrival, wriggling so close to the back of Serena's knees that she lost her balance and

147

began to tumble backward, over Abel's back. Instinctively Gerald caught her by her forearms, pulling her upright, then slightly forward against his chest to steady her.

Or so he told himself.

"Bad dog, Abel!" said Serena sternly, wriggling herself as she tried simultaneously to scold Abel and untangle her two feet from his four as his paws scrambled wet, muddy blotches over the skirts of her petticoats and the backs of her stockings. "You're very, very bad, Abel!"

"Don't listen to her, Abel," said Gerald, slipping an arm around her waist to draw her closer as the dog settled, panting happily, on the floor behind her. "You're an exceptionally good dog, and don't let her tell you otherwise."

"He is not!" said Serena indignantly, though Gerald noted that the indignation wasn't strong enough to make her push away from him. "He is a very bad dog, and refuses to mind me."

"Ah, and what of it?" said Gerald as he guided her arms over his shoulders. "I've never been much for minding orders, either."

"I'm not giving any to you." She glanced nervously over her shoulder, through the open door, trying to see if they'd be seen in return. "Not yet, anyway."

"Don't begin, Serena," he murmured, tracing his finger along the pink, sleet-dampened bridge of her nose. "I'd rather we kept this mutually agreeable, with orders neither given nor taken."

"But Gerald," she protested weakly, "I do not believe that we should be—that is, that I—should be here, in this way, with you."

"Believe it," he said, slanting his face over hers, "because you should be nowhere else."

He told himself that he couldn't help it, that she welcomed his attentions, that under such circumstances he'd had no choice but to kiss her. But the moment his lips touched hers, the lightest of grazing kisses of enticement, of invitation, he realized how empty these kinds of excuses were. He wanted to kiss her, and worse, or better, he *needed* to kiss her, and no excuses in the world could change that impossible truth.

Her mouth opened to his with a little gasp of protest, letting him taste again the incalculable sweetness that he remembered. Here with the sleet drumming overhead, she tasted fresh as the faraway springtime, of places and times he'd long forgotten, and in her kiss she offered a kind of haven that he hadn't known he sought.

A haven, yes, but not a particularly saintly one, not from the eagerness with which she was returning his kiss. He'd begun with the tenderness she deserved, but tenderness couldn't last, washed away before the urgency racing through his body now. If it had been lust alone that drove him, he could have stayed in control of himself. He was a gentleman of the world, no inexperienced boy with women. But what he felt for Serena ran deeper than mere physical desire, deep into places in his soul that he'd never ventured, and the newness of it was as terrifying as it was intoxicating.

He could feel how she curved into him, her cape falling open as she curled her hands around the back of his neck. It took him longer to realize that the faint rustling sound behind his ear was the drawing—*his* drawing—still clutched tightly in her hand.

Deftly he unfastened the hook on her cloak, his lips following the line of her jaw, lower to kiss the hollow of her throat. Her skin was cool, tasting slightly of salt from the wind off the sea and fragrant with the scent of violets. He whispered her name, so softly against her throat that he doubted she'd heard him, as he slipped his hand beneath the linen kerchief she wore around her shoulders and tucked in the front of her bodice. He loved this contradiction in women's dress, the way the stiff, boned stays lifted and offered the velvety bounty of her breasts, so soft beneath his fingertips that he could feel her heartbeat racing as fast as his own. His hand drifted lower, and he heard her gasp as the peak of her breast hardened against his palm.

"Hush now, sweet," he murmured as he brushed his lips over hers in reassurance. "You must know by now I'd never hurt you."

Her eyes closed, her breath ragged, she shook her head, and he smiled to think that was all the answer she could volunteer. He doubted he could do much better himself, anyway, and instead kissed her again, tumbling deeper into all she promised.

"Once you said I frightened you," he whispered, the words another caress against that softest place beneath her ear. "But you're not frightened of me now, are you?"

"Oh, no," she murmured. "Not now."

"Not now, not ever," he whispered as he kissed the shell of her ear. "Promise me that, Serena."

"Not now, not ever," she said with a broken little sigh. "Oh, how right my friend was about you, Gerald!"

"Your friend." He froze, more surely than the sleet itself. God help him, there was but one friend she'd ever mentioned in Appledore, only one that she spoke of in that way. He drew back, his heart pounding now with dread, not desire. She had tried to tell him, and he hadn't listened. He had wanted so badly to be her hero, her savior, her only true friend, that he'd ignored what she'd never bothered to hide. He longed to remain in ignorance, to return to the extraordinary, unthinking bliss he'd just abandoned, but he couldn't do it. His hideous conscience wouldn't let him.

"Your *friend,*" he said again, the extra emphasis his, not hers. "Is this your friend across the water who has warned you about me?"

She opened her eyes with obvious reluctance at the change in his voice, and nodded slowly. "Though I wouldn't call it a warning, not exactly."

"But you would say this friend is concerned for your happiness?" He didn't mean to interrogate her like this, as cruelly as if she stood on the dock, but the keenness of his own disappointment drove him to it. As if their embrace was melting away like a snowflake, he let his arms drop away from her and took the single step backward, away from her, that was possible in the tiny shed. "An old and familiar friend, then, Miss Fairbourne, to venture such opinions upon your acquaintance?"

Serena stared at him in growing confusion. She had done exactly what Mary had recommended, and had given herself over to Gerald, and for those briefest of moments she'd thought she'd found happiness in his embrace, joy, maybe even love. But inexplicably the warm, teasing man she'd kissed had abruptly vanished, leaving in his place this formal stranger who was addressing her with such icy politeness. Why hadn't Mary warned her this could happen?

"We were children together, aye," she said, her fingers unconsciously tightened on the drawing, crumpling the fragile roll of paper. "But Gerald, I do not see—"

"You do not have to see, Miss Fairbourne," he said as he bent to retrieve the walking stick from where he'd let it fall. "For I believe I've finally seen enough to suit us both."

Self-consciously she tucked her kerchief back into place and rehooked the front of her cape. If he had seen enough, he certainly wasn't going to see any more of her, and the shame she felt over what she'd let him do—no, what she'd done, too—was bitter indeed.

She swallowed hard, and raised her chin in one last, fragile show of independence. "Perhaps this sort of spleeny, contrary behavior shows well with your London ladies. Maybe your nymphs and—and your muses find it tolerable. But I don't, Gerald, nor will I, not without hearing the reasons behind it."

He set one hand atop the other on the head of the stick as he studied her, an elegant mannered pose fit for a gentleman's portrait. But no matter how hard he tried to keep the pose, she still had come to know him well enough to see the weaknesses in it, a sad regret in his eyes that was like the fine crack in the mortar of a stone wall.

"Tell me, Gerald," she said, striving to keep the trembling from her voice. That stone wall might be flawed, but she doubted it would yield to her without a fight. "Can you not grant me that much?"

He didn't answer at first, the wet rattle of the sleet overhead the only sound between them. But even before he spoke, Serena could see the tiny change in his expression as he decided against her, that little chink in the stone wall holding firm.

"Better to ask your *friend*, Miss Fairbourne," he said softly. "He should be the one to advise you, not I. No doubt he can explain far better the differing natures of men and women, and with considerably more intimacy as well. Good day."

He eased around her and stepped over Abel, hunching his shoulders against the driving sleet.

She stared after him, stunned by what he'd said. No wonder he'd looked so sorrowful, and no wonder, too, he'd needed a wall of granite to bolster his pride. Lord help her, how had she so completely forgotten that he believed the friend she visited was a man, and her lover at that? If it weren't so horrifyingly wrong, the woeful result of half-truths, she might have laughed at the silliness of it. *She* might have laughed, but not Gerald, not with that grim, wounded face. She knew enough about a man's pride to recognize how infinitely fragile it could be, and how infinitely pig-headed, too.

She ran after him, heedless of the sleet, and grabbed him by the arm. "You great dunderhead, listen to me! My friend is exactly that, a friend, my oldest and dearest in the world, and *she* is a woman named Mary, Mary Sears!"

He frowned. "Serena, I am not a fool. I'd rather not be treated as one."

"You *are* a fool, Gerald Crosbie," she cried, shielding her face with the flat of her hand as she looked up at him, "and worse than that, too, if you listen to your pride instead of to me! Mary has fallen upon sad days, but she is still my friend, and always will be, and she alone is the one I visit at Denniman's Cove. I have no hidden sweetheart, not there, not anywhere."

"No?" he asked, his disbelief shockingly, scornfully clear in that single word.

"No!" she cried, driven by pride of her own. "How can you believe that I would—would kiss you if it were otherwise?"

"Would your brother tell me the same thing if I were to ask him?"

"About Mary?" she asked, her anger and her pride faltering together. How could they not, torn between the truth and her loyalty to Mary, between being branded a faithless slattern in Gerald's eyes or destroying what remained of her friend's life? "You would ask Joshua about—about her?"

"No." In an instant his face shuttered against her. He shook his arm free of her hand, and turned away. "Now I don't have to."

Mary drew her shawl more tightly around her shoulders against the wind, watching her brother-in-law as he hauled the basket of new-spun wool into the back of his cart.

"You done more'n usual this week, Mary," said Ezra, squinting down at her as he wiped his nose with a grimy handkerchief. "More'n double, from the look of it."

"I spin what you bring me," said Mary. She was shivering despite the shawl, but she would rather stay here on the step in wind ten times worse before she asked Ezra into her house. It was wrong of her, of course, and she knew to her sorrow that she should be more charitable toward Robert's brother, but Ezra was such a mean, hard man—and so very unlike Robert—that charity withered to nothingness in his presence. "You bring me more fleece, and I'll see that it's carded and spun."

"Likely then you'd be expecting more from me in return," said Ezra sourly. "I'm not made of gold guineas, you know."

Mary lifted her chin and tried to look as brave and capable as Serena always did. No one would ever take advantage of Serena, not the way that Ezra managed to do again and again with her. "I never said you were, Ezra. But I know Master Coombs at the mill in Marston is said to be a fair, Christian man. When he pays you, I should be paid, too."

"Oh, aye, Mistress High-and-Haughty," mimicked Ezra. "And how would you be familiar with the likes of Master Coombs?"

"Serena Fairbourne told me," answered Mary promptly, and just as promptly wished she hadn't.

"Miss Serena Fairbourne told you, did she." Ezra blew his nose with disparaging vigor. "Then mayhaps *Miss* Serena Fairbourne can tell you how to pay for your food and firewood without me to see that it be done."

Mary's head drooped forlornly. "I didn't wish to seem ungrateful, Ezra, you know that. 'Tis just that I see so little in return for my work."

"Times be hard, Mary." Ezra sniffed contemptuously, not bothering with the handkerchief. "Less'n you be a thieving Fairbourne chit, anyway, with cream for your tea and a silver spoon to stir it."

"Serena Fairbourne is my friend," said Mary with daring, tremulous defiance, "and I won't listen to you speak ill of her!"

Ezra spat on the ground beside the doorstep, close enough to Mary's toes that she automatically stepped back.

"I'll warrant she speaks plenty ill of Robert, don't she? Her and her lying bastard of a brother both, to hell with the whole lot of 'em! Or have you forgotten that Robert'd be here with us still if it weren't for Joshua Fairbourne?"

"Upon my word, Ezra, I've never once taken Joshua's side against Robert, nor have I ever accepted one farthing of charity from him! Not once!"

"Then you keep on swearing to it, sister," said Ezra as he unlashed the reins on the horse's harness, "and you start believing it, too. If Robert had any spine, he'd thrash you dumb just for letting that Fairbourne bitch into his house."

"But Serena is my friend!" cried Mary plaintively.

"What Joshua did to Robert—that doesn't matter one whit to Serena and me!"

Ezra paused. "Maybe it should, Mary," he said slowly. "Cap'n Fairbourne's a rich man. Maybe, if you played him right, he'd pay us for what he done to Robert—pay you handsome."

Mary drew back, appalled he'd even suggest such a thing. "Nay, Ezra Sears, I'll never sink so low! I'll not take a penny in blood money from Joshua, not one farthing!"

"Pride won't keep you warm come winter, Mary," said Ezra, wiping his nose with a dirty bandana. "How can you believe that Robert would want it that way, with you shivering and suffering on account of your being too prideful to ask for what's yours by rights? If you will not speak for yourself, then I shall. A word to your fine friend Serena, and—"

"Not Serena, Ezra, not Serena!" pleaded Mary. "You would not dare poison our friendship, I beg of you! She has no power with Joshua, not in this, for she has not even told him she comes to me. She swears to it, Ezra, swears it to me! Cannot you see that she is all the comfort I have while my Robert is away? Oh, he would never wish you to do such a thing to me!"

As Ezra climbed onto the cart's bench, gathering the reins in his hands, Mary thought he'd ignore her now that he'd decided she'd taken enough of his time. That was how he usually took his leave, without squandering a farewell.

But not this time. This time she wouldn't be so fortunate.

"What Robert would see is how his wife has snugged in tight to them that ruined him," he said harshly. "Mind, I'll say nothing for now. But you have to choose between the Fairbournes and us, Mary. And the devil take you straight to hell if you choose wrong."

Nine

Anabelle rested one hand upon her ever-increasing bosom and gasped dramatically. "Pray tell me, brother dear, is it truly you, come at last?"

"And good afternoon to you, too, Nan," said Gerald as he bent to give his sister a dutiful kiss. "When you tire of the colonies, there might well be a place for you upon the boards in Drury Lane."

"Hah, wouldn't Grandmother fancy that?" She grinned wickedly at him over a dish of peppermint tea. "But you have kept to yourself of late, Duckie. I can't remember the last time you came to keep company with your round old sow of a sister."

"You're hardly a sow, Anabelle," he said gallantly, but his gallantry stopped short of denying her roundness. She seemed well enough, but since he'd seen her last—it could not have been more than a fortnight, could it?— she seemed to have swelled nearly as wide in front as she was tall, and in his cautious inexperience he wondered if such prodigality was normal.

"You'll say otherwise when I'm finally brought to pig,"

she said cheerfully. "Now tell me what you've been doing to amuse yourself instead of calling upon me. Is she vastly pretty?"

"'She' is the new markethouse, as you'd know perfectly well if you ever listened to your husband," said Gerald as he warmed his hands over the fire. "Which, you being you, I doubt."

"Which shows *you* are most grievously insulting. Of course Joshua has told me of your interest in the building, but I didn't know how much to credit. I still do not." She leaned forward as far as she could over the mound of her belly. "But la, Gerald, look at your poor hands! Whatever have you done to yourself?"

Self-consciously he did look down at his hands, frowning as he spread the fingers for consideration. "I suppose they are a bit nicked here and there, but that's no reason to—"

"You *are* working," accused Anabelle with gleeful amazement. "Joshua told me the drawings were only the beginning, that you clambered in amongst the others as if you were born to it, but faith, I never believed him! You, of all the gentlemen I know!"

"It is not so inexplicable, Nan," he said, defensively banishing his guilty hands behind his back. "I have always taken an interest in architecture and such. Likely you were too young to recall it, but when Father put the new wing to the west of the house, I thought it was the best adventure in the world. The carpenters let me hammer away as much as I pleased, and the masons even allowed me to crawl up the scaffolding with them."

"You *did?*" she gasped. "I cannot conceive of Father permitting such a thing!"

Gerald shrugged. "He didn't."

"I should say not, Duckie!" she said, her eyes round with stunned delight. The dalliance with the barkeep's daughter that she'd expected would never have provided such a titillating scandal.

Gerald turned a sigh of resignation into a slightly more

polite yawn. Anabelle herself might have courted scandal on the grandest of scales, but there were still many things about him that she couldn't understand, or wouldn't even bother to, really.

But Serena would, and unbidden she appeared once again in his thoughts. If he had seen little of his sister these last weeks, then he'd seen even less of Serena, as he'd purposefully attempted to lose himself in the construction of the markethouse and forget about her. He'd taken to rising before daybreak to be there when the laborers arrived, and he was often the last to leave at dusk, returning to the White Swan so exhausted that Rourke could scarcely tumble him into bed before he fell asleep.

Yet even pure exhaustion hadn't worked the way he'd hoped, any more than the singularly unsatisfying knowledge that he'd been the one to turn his back and walk away. He might have stopped carrying the twin scallop shells in his pocket—they now graced the mantel in his rooms at the inn—but she stayed firmly in his thoughts even without such reminders.

Making it harder still had been the glimpses he'd caught of her, from a window or ahead of him in the street, her head high and her red cloak swinging as she walked with Abel trotting at her side. Appledore was small; it would have been impossible to avoid seeing her that way even if he'd wished to. Like everyone else in the town, she, too, had stopped by to watch the building, and he'd seen her there as well, standing beyond the piles of timbers. One day he'd been trying so hard to ignore her presence that he'd nearly lost a finger to a carpenter's hammer. He couldn't stop wondering if she approved of what she saw, and if she'd kept the drawing he'd given her.

And if, the devil take him for a hopeless fool, she still thought of *him* as much as he did of her.

Reluctantly he dragged his thoughts back to his sister and her question, tapping his knuckles lightly on the mantel. "Once Father learned of my disreputable interests, my tutor was dismissed and I was shipped off to Wandsworth after Johnny and George."

She nodded sadly. "I recall the row, but I knew not the reason."

"Too dishonorable for Father to mention, I'm sure," he said with more bitterness than he'd realized. "Doubtless my departure came earlier than he'd expected—no use squandering too much costly education on a third son—but the school's expense was worth saving me from such barbarously low company."

It hadn't been nearly as tidy as that, not at all, but with Anabelle there was no need to explain the details of their father's fury or the cruelty of his punishment. But being banished from the green fields and sunny schoolroom of Kilmarsh to the cheerless world of a public school had very nearly broken Gerald's nine-year-old heart, as his father had predicted it would. In some ways, their father had known his children all too well.

"Poor, poor Duckie," said Anabelle softly. "Sometimes I do believe that we would all of us have been vastly better off in a little thatched cottage with a milch cow on the common, and forced to make our own ways in the world like most other people."

"Heresy, goose-girl, sheer heresy," he said lightly. "Whatever would Grandmother say?"

But Anabelle shook her head. "I am in perfect earnest, Gerald. Who knows what grand things you might have done if you hadn't been born one of us? You might have been another Christopher Wren!"

"And I might just as well have been another Dick Turpin, born to dance on the wind at Tyburn."

Anabelle pouted. "You never will treat me with any seriousness, Duckie."

"About such things, no," he admitted. Speculation in this vein could only lead to discontent, and Gerald was discontented enough without it. "We are what we are born, Nan, and not likely to change. I'm not, at any rate. But you, it seems, have become alarmingly productive."

She stared at him blankly at first while she rested her hand on her belly, believing he'd meant that sort of productiveness. Then she followed his glance to the bed, to the neat piles of clothing for the baby that she'd been sorting when he'd arrived, and she laughed.

"Oh, how vastly mistaken you are!" she said, reaching for one of the tiny gowns. "I'm still all knots and tangles with a needle and thimble, and ever shall be. That certainly won't change. Serena made all these, every last dear little shirt and neckcloth. Here, look at this work, even hollie-point inserts at the seams. You won't find any finer stitches from a convent."

Reluctantly Gerald took the gown she offered, his hands dwarfing the tiny white linen garment. It was not merely his inexperience that made him uncomfortable holding an infant's gown, but the fact that Serena had worked so long and with such care to produce it. There was something infinitely sad to him that she had; she often made jests about being a spinster, but to him the endless care that she'd lavished upon these clothes only proved how much she longed for a child of her own to fuss over and to love.

She'd be very good at mothering, too. At least he'd enjoyed having her fuss over *him,* not that it was likely to happen at any time in the reasonable future.

"Serena is well?" he asked with what he hoped was offhanded politeness instead of burning curiosity.

Anabelle glanced at him again as she took the little gown back. "Tolerably well, I suppose, though Serena can be so silent about herself that I cannot say for certain. Yet I wonder that you ask. She would seem to hold you in as little esteem as you do her."

"Ah." That was all he could manage as his sister's careless, murderous bolt shot through his heart.

"Ah, indeed," said Anabelle blithely. "She cannot bear to have your name mentioned. Not because she's said so, of course, but because I noticed, and tested her, and she nearly leaps from the room if I venture one word about you. It's quite amusing, really."

But it wasn't amusing to Gerald, not in the least. "Does she seem, ah, happy?"

Anabelle frowned, clearly unaccustomed to linking happiness and Serena. "As happy as Serena ever does, I suppose. To my mind, she spends entirely too much time alone."

Then she brightened, and winked slyly. "But that will change, and this very evening, too. Joshua has invited one of his captain friends to stay with us for a few days. Joshua swears that Captain Parrish has been most attentive to Serena in the past, and that this time he won't let the man leave Appledore until they've made a match of it."

"A match?" he repeated, knowing he sounded like some infernal echo. "For Serena?"

"Whosoever else? Upon my word, Duckie, you are acting very dense and queerish this morning. Perhaps all this common work has put calluses upon your wit as well as your hands."

"This has nothing at all to do with my hands, Anabelle," he said, and he saw how her face grew instantly solemn once he'd used her entire given name. A good thing, too; perhaps for once she'd listen to reason. "You cannot go about playing Cupid with Serena and some rogue of a sailor, merely because it amuses you."

"I'm not doing it because it amuses me," she said defensively. "And besides, I'm not the one doing it at all. It's Joshua's idea entirely, and no one could wish better for Serena than her own brother. He's quite convinced they'll be rapturously happy."

"Nan, please, I—"

"No, no, you must listen," she interrupted stubbornly. "The match does have merits on both sides. I cannot pretend otherwise. Joshua says Captain Parrish is a good man with a decent living, the most desirable of bachelors in this colony, and of course Joshua will settle a suitable dowry upon Serena. If Captain Parrish can be brought to offer for Serena, why, then, of course Joshua shall give his blessing."

"But what of Serena?" demanded Gerald. "Have either of you thought to ask her opinion of this plot of yours? Have her wishes even been considered once?"

Anabelle had grown very serious indeed, her round little face drained of its usual merriment. Slowly she pushed herself up from her chair, brushing away Gerald's hurried offer of help.

"Come, Duckie," she said softly. "There's something I must show you."

Slowly she led him to the far side of the large curtained bed. There in the corner of the room, below the window, sat an oversized cradle, already lined with a soft woolen coverlet for the coming baby, with two or three more laid by to be handy, if necessary.

But though the baby would be new, the cradle most certainly wasn't; it was fashioned from oak that had darkened and grown scarred and marked through years of use. The bulbous turnings on the railings and the emphatic sweep of the rockers were done in the heavy style of the last century. Yet it was the cherub's face carved into the cradle's overhanging bonnet that drew Gerald's eye, a sweet-faced cherub that would smile down upon any sleeping baby with the same boundless tenderness as the child's mother, as Gerald's own mother had done to him.

"Do you remember, Duckie?" asked Anabelle, running her fingers over the cradle's bonnet. "How this always sat on Mama's side of the bed?"

"How could I forget such a monstrosity?" he answered gruffly, burying his emotions where they belonged. "Lord, it's even uglier than I recalled."

She smiled, not fooled by his bluffery. "Grandmother made sure to take it from Kilmarsh for me when I was going to wed Henry Branbrook, and even though I didn't, I would not leave England without this cradle. Joshua will tell you the trials I put him through on its account, but I insisted. I can't guess how many babies have slept in it. You and me, for two."

"Slept and wept and wet and puked, most likely, in the manner of all wretchedly selfish babies," declared Gerald. "But I don't see what the cradle has to do with Serena."

"You don't?" Her smile wobbled, and he worried that he'd have to offer her his handkerchief. "Then you must suffer through my telling, you great oaf. I know you think I was little more than one of those selfish babies when Mama died, but I remember her, and I remember how unhappy she was with Father. And though Grandmother tried to make me believe that that was for the best, that love wasn't necessary in a marriage, I couldn't do it. I tried, Duckie, truly, but I couldn't. And how could I possibly now wish the same for Serena?"

"Silly goose-girl," said Gerald gently. He was uncomfortably close to needing that handkerchief himself if she kept on like this. "I'm sure Grandmother didn't mean her advice quite like that."

"No?" She searched his face, her eyes swimming with tears. "Perhaps not for you as a gentleman, but for me there could be no other meaning. Seeing the cradle again was one of the things that decided me. I wanted—no, I *needed*—to love the father of my children, and in my heart I knew that if I married Harry Branbrook the way Grandmother wanted, I'd never, ever love him even a tiny bit as much as I love Joshua."

He frowned, concentrating on being stoic by studying the carved cherub instead of his sister. He had never expected to find himself in this predicament, having this conversation with her. Not expected to, nor wanted to. What in blazes was he supposed to *say?*

But he didn't have to say anything. To his horror, Anabelle said it instead.

"I know that's why you came after me, Duckie," she said sadly. "To haul me back to London and try to marry me off to someone more suitable, damaged goods though I might be. No, please, don't lie to me. I don't believe I could bear that, not from you, not when I realized the truth the moment I found you stumbling about amongst my apple trees. What I'd rather think upon is how you came because you love me. Which *is* true, isn't it?"

"Of course it is, pet." He sighed heavily and closed his eyes. He wouldn't insult either of them with denials. What would be the point? Besides, his punishment had already begun: his head ached and he hurt all over, worse than when he'd fought those men in the street and with a recovery that was going to take a good deal longer, too. *Truth, true, truly:* he never wanted to hear any of those words again. Truth might very well be held in great esteem by society, but for the life of him he couldn't fathom why it should be so blessed painful.

"The reason, Nan," he began slowly, "the reason that you can't force this damned Captain Parrish onto Serena is that she already loves another man."

"Serena?" Anabelle gasped with astonishment. "Faith, who is it?"

"I don't know the fellow's name," he admitted, wishing he were saying his own instead. "But she goes to him in secret almost every day. I'd wager he's some fisherman or other sailor, living in a place called Denniman's Cove. But whatever the man's trade, Serena's convinced her brother would not approve."

Anabelle gasped again. "Denniman's Cove! Oh, Duckie, you've no notion of how grievous this is! Denniman's Cove is home to the lowest form of scoundrels, cheats, and drunkards and Heaven only knows what else! Joshua has had no end of trouble with one man there who used to sail for him. However could Serena have fallen in love with anyone from *there?"*

Gerald smiled bitterly. "Grandmother says much the same thing about you."

"This is different, vastly different, and you cannot conceive of—no, no, *no!"* Anabelle pressed her palms to her temples, sucking in her breath as sharply as if she'd just been burned. "Whatever am I saying? You are right, Gerald, and I am wrong, most barbarously wrong. If

Serena loves this man and he loves her, that should be enough. That *will* be enough!"

"Hush now, Nan," said Gerald uneasily. He'd never seen his sister so agitated, and he'd no wish to be the reason for harm to her or her baby. "Here, sit, and be calm. It's not worth you troubling yourself like this."

"But it *is,* Duckie!" she cried. "You must go to Serena now, at once. You must find her and her sweetheart and make them listen and warn them about Captain Parrish coming and tell them that I—that you, too—shall do everything we can to help them!"

"I'm going to wish them all to the devil unless you sit, and quietly at that." He took her firmly by the arms and guided her back to the edge of the bed. Before she could protest again, he eased her gently back against the pillows, swinging her little feet up onto the bed and drawing the coverlet over the furbelow-covered hill of her belly. "You rest, and we'll discuss this later."

"Oh, please, please don't leave me yet, Duckie," she said mournfully, her hand seeking his to hold him back. "I will behave, I swear it."

"An oath I expect you to keep." Clumsily he patted her hand, wondering what else one did under the circumstances. She still looked flushed to him, her eyes too bright, even for Anabelle. "I'm always on uneasy ground with your husband, and I've no wish to vex him further by bringing ill to you. He's a fearsome man, your husband."

"Bother my husband," she said with a prodigious sigh as she twisted her fingers around his. "You must know by now that Joshua is mostly bark anyway. But Serena—I'd never want Serena to suffer the way I did, or to feel she'd no choice in whom she married. She needs to hear that, Gerald, and you must be my messenger."

Once again he glanced back at the old cradle, his emotions waging a fierce battle with his conscience. He couldn't deny that their mother had been wretchedly unhappy in her marriage, any more than he could blind himself to how blissfully happy Anabelle was in hers. Before now he'd always subscribed to the accepted view that love had no place in marriages between men and women of his station; love was the stuff of mawkish tavern ballads and Italian operas, and the only marriages founded upon its shaky base were between milkmaids and soldiers, and even then it was probably more lust than love.

But the feelings between Anabelle and Joshua were harder to discount, harder to dismiss. Though he'd made this journey to find his sister out of duty to his family, he'd also come because he'd wished her to be happy. That hadn't changed, but somehow his definition of happiness—and love—most decidedly had.

And complicating it further was Serena.

There was absolutely nothing he'd like less than to pay a call on Serena and her mystery lover. He told himself he shouldn't care, but like the world's most besotted fool, he did. He cared a great deal. It had been bad enough to imagine her with another man, kissing him, smiling for him, even letting him pet her blasted dog. But to see them actually together, to be forced to watch this other man occupy the place that he'd so like for himself—that was far too much to be asked to do, even by Anabelle.

He shook his head unhappily, raking his fingers back through his hair as he tried to think of a plausible way to refuse his sister. The sooner he returned to London, the sooner he put aside this nonsensical attachment to an oblivious, unsuitable woman, the better for them all. He could build markethouses from now to judgment day, and it wouldn't make one whit of difference to Serena or any of the rest of this infernal town. He didn't belong here. He never would.

"My dear, darling Duckie," murmured Anabelle, running one finger back and forth along the braid on the cuff of his coat. "I don't care what bold claims you make about being as unfeelingly constant as a block of granite.

You've changed since you've come here, haven't you? I can see it in your face, your manner, and most certainly in your hands."

"Have I now?" he asked with forced lightness. "I wonder then that you even recognize me."

"You *have* changed, Gerald," she said seriously, refusing to be distracted, "oh, how very much, and I believe for the better, too."

He sighed heavily, wondering when his little sister had become so all-seeing and wise, certainly a good deal wiser than he felt himself.

"Hah, you've caught me out again, goose-girl," he said softly, and his smile was bittersweet with resignation, and regret. "Now let me go, or I'll never be able to find Serena."

"Someone's coming!" whispered Mary fearfully. "Harken there, Serena, on the path outside!"

"You're daft, Mary," scoffed Serena, balancing on a chair as she tried to mend the broken hinge on the window's casement. "You know well as I that no one's likely to come here today besides me. You said so yourself."

Yet Mary still stood in the center of the room, frozen in place with her head cocked to one side like a robin listening for an earthworm. "It's not you that's making me worrisome," she whispered ominously. "And it's the others I fear."

"What you fear is stuff and nonsense," declared Serena firmly. She scowled down at the broken hinge, trying to wiggle what was left of the pin back into place to hold the frame steady for now. She was accustomed to making her own repairs and improvements at home, but Mary was absolutely hopeless at such tasks, and always had been. "What you should be wishing for is that lazy creature Ezra to come and fix this wretched window properly. You'd think for Robert's sake alone, he'd be willing to do more for his brother's wife."

"You'd best hope Ezra doesn't come," said Mary anxiously. "Not when you're here, anyway. You know how much he dislikes you."

Serena clicked her tongue dismissively. "And I dislike him in return. What of it?"

"But he doesn't want you here, not with me. Oh, Serena, what if that *is* Ezra outside?"

"It's naught but the wind, you silly ninny. Now come, hold this steady for me so that I can—"

But the knock on the door interrupted her, a loud, rattling knock that had to come from a man. Mary's hand fluttered to her mouth to stifle her gasp.

"Hush, Serena, hush!" she ordered in a shrill whisper. "Pretend we're not here!"

Serena twisted about on the chair, bracing the heavy casement with her shoulder. "How can we?" she asked, though she, too, dropped her voice to a whisper. "Even if he hasn't heard us talking, then he's likely seen my boat tied up at the bottom of your path, or remarked the smoke from your chimney. Why else would he have come, anyway?"

The visitor at the door knocked again, harder this time, and with an unmistakable masculine impatience.

Mary shrunk back. "We still don't have to answer it, Serena! Maybe then he'll go away, and leave us alone. Oh, dear Lord deliver me if it's Ezra!"

Yet even as she spoke the long end of the latch string twitched upward and the door groaned on its hinge as the man began to push it open.

"If you don't want company, Mary," said Serena with considerably more bravado than she felt, "then next time don't leave your door unbolted."

The door swung slowly open, the sunlight slanting in around the man's broad-shouldered silhouette. But it wasn't Ezra Sears. It wasn't anyone from Denniman's Cove, yet still Mary recognized him at once and sank to as sweeping a curtsey as she could muster.

Gerald lingered in the doorway, blinking as his eyes accustomed themselves to the dimness within. The house was dark and small, too small, really, to be even called a cottage, a single, murky, crowded room redolent with long-ago cook-smoke and chowder and an appalling, close animal smell that he recognized as sheep.

Good God, could Serena really be trysting with a man so low that he kept his field animals inside his own *house?*

He blinked again, pushing the door more widely ajar so that the sunlight filtered past him and onto an elfin young woman swathed in layers of knitted shawls and homespun petticoats that she held out to either side in her hands. An outlandish idea of a curtsey, he decided, but the openness of the woman's thin little face softened any misgivings he might have.

"My Lord Crosbie," she said with an overstated and, in Gerald's opinion, completely misplaced, awe. "Good day to you, my lord, and welcome."

"Up on your feet, lass," he said gallantly, holding his hand out to her. "I've no right to such homage, any more than you should be calling me lord anything. That's my father, and will be my older brother, and thankfully shall never be me. Mr. Crosbie does well enough by me. Mr. Gerald Crosbie, lass, your servant."

He smiled as charmingly as he dared, and she melted into dreamy-eyed homage. He didn't really want to know how this odd little creature had come to know his name, just as he was rather desperately clinging to the hope that he'd somehow come to the wrong house. That must be it: a misjudgment, an unfortunate error. After all, he'd had only the sailboat tied at the makeshift wharf to go by. In his unhappy haste, he could easily have mistaken someone else's boat for Serena's.

"'My servant'," repeated the woman in a swoony murmur. "Jupiter, my lord, how you talk! You're even finer than Serena said you were, and that's the truth!"

"You are acquainted with Serena?" he asked quickly. "Miss Serena Fairbourne? If you can tell me where I might find her, then I'd be much obliged if you—"

"For heaven's sake, Gerald," interrupted Serena from the gloom, "you of all people needn't be obliged to anyone."

How had he missed her, even in the gloom? She was standing on a chair against the far wall, holding a warped, smoke-blackened casement in both hands as carefully as if it were the greatest treasure in the world. She had her skirts looped up through their pocket-slits to keep the hems clean while she worked, high enough that he had an exceptionally unencumbered view of her ankles and the sweet curve of her calves in white thread stockings. Her sleeves were pushed up high upon her arms, too, and with an apron pinned to the front of her bodice she seemed the most delightful portrait of huswifely industry that he could imagine.

Except, that is, for the expression on her face, where his view of her feelings was equally unencumbered. Unencumbered, and unmistakable.

She was not happy to see him.

"Serena," he began, abruptly leaving off his customary *dear* as unwise. She wasn't going to make this easy for either of them, and he cleared his throat to beggar another moment of time to gather his words. "Serena. I am glad to see you looking so, ah, so well, Serena."

She wrinkled her nose. "I did not realize that my health was so much in doubt as to deserve comment."

"It's not," he said hastily. "Neither in doubt nor deserving of comment."

Belatedly he let his gaze flicker around her, praying that her errant sweetheart wasn't lurking somewhere in the gloom, ready to thump him over the head for untoward foolishness.

"Lord Crosbie, sir," said the elfin woman shyly, wiggling another peculiar curtsey as she steadfastly refused to abandon that improper lordly title. "Might I fetch you a dish of tea, my lord?"

"Be chary with such offers, Mary," said Serena. "If you give him tea he'll never leave."

The elfin woman turned to look plaintively up toward

Serena on the chair. "But I would wish him to stay, Serena. I've never had a true gentleman beneath my roof."

"I'm not sure you do now." Serena sighed with impatient resignation. "*Mr.* Crosbie. May I introduce to you my dear friend Mrs. Mary Sears?"

"Mrs. Sears." Gerald bowed, and as he did the woman's name echoed ominously in his conscience, like a stone tossed into a black well. Mary Sears: hadn't that been the name she'd shouted at him on that black, blasted day in the sleet? "I am honored, ma'am."

"You should be," said Serena, "for Mary's far more genteel than you'll ever hope to be."

"*Serena!*" said Mary, shocked. "What a cross-tempered, spleeny thing for you to say to Lord Crosbie!"

Serena glared over Mary's head, directly at Gerald. "He is neither a lord, Mary, nor is he a gentleman, not a true one. A gentleman would never have doubted my word, and he certainly wouldn't have followed me here in the vainglorious hope of proving his stubbornness right!"

With a determined effort to have the final word, she pointedly began mending the window once again, turning so swiftly on the chair that she nearly toppled from it. She just caught her balance as the chair's legs wobbled precariously beneath her, and the oath she muttered, though low, was quite audible and worthy of any of her brothers, and not entirely directed toward the unsteady chair, either.

"Ooh, my lord, you must forgive her!" cried Mary anxiously, twisting the sides of her skirts in her fists. "Serena is by nature a kind woman, and does not mean such cruel things, sir. Oh, she cannot!"

"Of course she can," said Gerald. "She can, and she does. Frequently."

The frequency was not what rankled him. But knowing she was right did, nearly as much as knowing he should admit it to her, and grovel for whatever forgiveness she might deign to scatter before him.

Knowing, however, wasn't the same as doing. There were still some small mercies to be found in his life.

He circled around Mary Sears to come to stand behind Serena, while she bowed her head closer to the frame as if concentrating, steadfastly bent on ignoring him.

Slowly he reached around her to steady the frame in her hands. "From the look of it," he said, "I'd say the pin in that hinge is beyond redemption."

"And what of it?" she said crossly, without meeting his gaze over her shoulder. "I'll make do. New ones don't drop from the trees like acorns, you know."

"Not from the trees, perhaps, no." This was easy: this was something he *could* do. He reached into his coat pocket, his fingers searching through the contents. While he'd stopped carrying the scallop shells with him, he had begun carrying a great many other things from the markethouse site instead, iron nails and wooden pegs and bits of wire and string, much to Rourke's consternation. From such a magpie's collection it didn't take Gerald long now to find a replacement for the missing pin. Gently he took the frame from Serena's unwilling hands, replaced the old pin, and rehung the casement.

"There now," he said proudly, giving the window a final, testing swing before he latched it shut. "That should do, shouldn't it?"

He hardly expected praise, especially not from Serena, but a word or two of gratitude didn't seem unwarranted.

At least it didn't to him.

"Oh, my lord, no, not at all!" cried Mary Sears, scandalized. She snatched up a cloth from the back of a chair and rushed forward to grab his hand and wipe a smudge of oil from his fingers. "Mending windows, covering yourself with grime and filth like this—it's below your station, sir, indeed it is!"

"Don't be fooled by his cleverness, Mary." Serena hopped down from the chair, ignoring Gerald's offered arm. "He'll say or do anything to earn a woman's favor. 'Tis a pity you don't keep a horse, else you could ask him to muck out the stable."

"Yes, indeed," said Gerald. If she wished to battle with words, then she'd have to do far better than that. "Though I'm better with dogs. You might ask Abel, if you've any doubts. He and I get along famously."

"You leave Abel out of this!" With fingers clumsy from anger, Serena jerked the pins from the front of her apron and tore the bowed ties free from around her waist. Then, for the first time, she squarely met Gerald's eye, just long enough to be sure of her aim as she hurled the apron into his face.

He caught it easily with one hand. Lord knows she'd given him warning enough. "Does this mean you're ready to leave, Serena?"

"It means whatever you wish." She turned her back to him, hugging her bewildered friend close. "I'm sorry, Mary. You can see why I cannot stay any longer today, not the way things are. You know I'd never willingly bring such—such *offal* into your house."

" 'Offal'?" said Gerald with mock horror. "Not *offal*! Oh, deary, deary, dear. Such strong language for ladies!"

He saw how her shoulders twitched defensively, almost as if he'd tossed the bundled apron back at her. Perhaps that was what she expected. But instead of answering him in return, she grabbed her cloak from the peg on the wall and fled, not even pausing to close the door after her.

"You must forgive my hasty farewell, ma'am," said Gerald with a bow to Mary Sears. "But it seems Miss Fairbourne has decided our visit is at an end."

Serena's cloak made her easy to spot, a red patch bobbing ahead among the scrubby pines and tall, dry grass that lined the path to the water. Yet his boot heels sank into the sand, slowing him as he ran after her, and she'd nearly reached the beach by the time he caught her arm to stop her.

"Serena, wait," he said, more breathless than he wished. He'd have trouble enough finding the words without having to fight to bring them out. "Wait."

"You would give orders, too?" She turned swiftly to

face him, and to his surprise there were tears on her cheeks, tears that she didn't bother to hide from him. "It isn't enough that you distrusted me, or that you hunted me down here with the same persistence that Abel would a rabbit through the marshes?"

"No," he said, shaking his head, at a loss to explain. From past experience he'd learned to shy from the complete truth where ladies were concerned, but with Serena, he wasn't so sure it would work. "No, Serena, not like that."

"Then how?" she demanded. "How did you come here, anyway?"

He waved vaguely toward the water. "I hired a man with a boat who knew these waters. And I didn't need Abel's skill to find you. You'd told me about Denniman's Cove yourself, you know."

"Faith," she said bitterly, "and here I thought you never listened to a word I said!"

"I didn't listen to what you said about Mary Sears because I didn't believe it. You'd told me yourself you had a lover here."

"I never told you that, not really," she said defensively. "I didn't lie. It was you who chose to believe it."

"Just as you chose to let me." His grip on her arm gentled, sliding into a kind of caress. "Of course a woman as charming, as beautiful as you are would have a lover. How could it be otherwise?"

"Well, it *is.*" Blinking hard, she looked down at his hand on her arm. "I have told you before that I've never had a sweetheart, yet you refused to believe me then, too. And I am not charming, or beautiful, so don't pretend that I am."

"I'm not pretending."

"Then—then you should be." Bright patches of color had appeared on her cheeks, but that could be from the tears, or from the wind. "But such foolishness doesn't explain why you're here. Even if you believed I was keeping company with a man instead of with Mary, then what would you have gained by pounding your way through the door like that? What did you mean to do next?"

"I suppose I could have behaved like any good knight-errant, and challenged the rascal to a joust," he said lightly, hoping to make her laugh. "You could have decided which of us would wear your favor on his lance. Then once I'd triumphed on your behalf, I'd be off on other well-intentioned adventures. Slaying dragons, perhaps."

But she didn't laugh. She didn't even smile, and belatedly he wondered if knights-errant found much occupation defending Massachusetts damsels. He sighed, and lightly brushed the windblown strands of hair away from her forehead. Her hair was always a little mussed like that, a little disheveled, and whether it was the wind from the sea that did it or only the innate unruliness of her hair, it was one of the things he remembered, and liked, about her.

"I don't know, Serena," he said softly. "I never actually thought that far ahead. All I cared about was finding you."

She raised her chin bravely, prepared to hear the worst. "Why?"

"Because I missed you, Serena," he said, the words neatly slipping out of his mouth to betray him before he'd realized it. "I—I missed you."

"Oh," she said, her expression unchanged. "Oh."

That single, unemotional syllable that was scarcely the response he'd wished for, and he felt his brows drawing together in a black scowl. If he'd sworn on a mountain of scriptures he couldn't have meant it any more. Why the devil didn't she understand? Couldn't she tell that a confession of this magnitude and rarity deserved more from her in return than a blank face and one word?

"Damnation, Serena, I missed you," he growled. "I'm sorry I was such a bloody idiot, and I missed you, and I wanted to see you again."

She'd begun by being dumbstruck. Now she was completely stunned. She could not believe he'd say such a thing. For him to apologize, to admit that he was wrong, to tell her he'd missed her when their estrangement had been totally his doing—she'd never known any man who'd admit so much in so few words. Certainly none of her brothers were capable of such an act. But then Gerald was always behaving in unexpected ways, saying unexpected things, and she realized that if she'd any wits left at all she should stop worrying about it and begin accepting him as the great, unexpected gift to her life that he was.

"Well," she said after a pause that nearly destroyed him, "if that is true, Gerald, then you needn't swear about it."

Suddenly she smiled, though from the way her mouth twisted, wavering up and down, he feared she'd begin weeping again. He wasn't sure he'd survive that, and so he did the one thing certain to stop her crying before she began.

He drew her into his arms and kissed her.

He'd intended it to be a quick, distracting kiss, nothing more, but by now he should have known that such a thing wasn't possible with Serena, and especially not since he now knew she belonged to no one else. The instant his mouth found hers and she sought him in return, he felt that familiar urgency rising in his blood, and the rest of his body, too. A moment only, he sternly ordered his slavering animal self, one moment only. Any longer and that animal self would win and he'd be tossing her onto the dunes, there among the tall, dry grasses, and with a frustrated groan he broke away.

She shouldn't have smiled, not like that, or touched her fingers to the lips he longed to kiss again. But at least she seemed to have forgotten about crying.

"You did miss me?" she asked shyly, daring to slip her hand into his. "Truly?"

"Truly, yes." He'd heard that confession was good for the soul, but it didn't seem to be offering much solace to the more worldly portions of his being. "And I've missed kissing you, too. I won't deny it."

"I'm glad." She *was* blushing now, and delightfully, too. "Not the denying part, I mean, but the other. I'm glad because I missed you as well. And the kissing. As much as I tried to tell myself it was wicked and wrong of me, I couldn't forget it."

He sucked in his breath hard, and it seemed that even the gulls mewing in the air were taunting him. "Do not tempt me, Serena. You're wise to reckon wickedness and me in the same thought, for I'm a bad man. A bad, bad man."

She laughed, offering more unwitting temptation as the tip of her tongue flicked across her lips. "Bad, aye, but in a good sort of way."

"No, bad as in very bad." Which, considering the wildfire path of his thoughts, was very, very bad indeed. Purposefully he looked past her, toward the water. The afternoon sun was dropping and the tide was coming in, the boat that he'd hired now moored beside Serena's at the very end of the two-plank wharf.

He pointed to the two boats, and she turned to look. "I'll give that man an extra shilling for his trouble," he said, "and return with you instead, the better to discuss this prodigious badness of mine."

She frowned sternly, though they both knew she didn't mean it. "Oh, aye, as if that needed more discussion."

"It rather thinks it does."

"*It* doesn't think, and if you continue like this, I'll doubt that you do, either. Now let me go back to Mary and reassure her before we leave," she said, wavering as her conscience jabbed at her. Her friend's life was uncertain enough without her adding more strain and stress to it. "I didn't leave with a proper farewell."

"But I did," said Gerald. "For us both."

"Oh, I'll wager you did." She narrowed her eyes, looking up at him through her lashes. "Mary was already half beguiled by you the moment you blundered into her house. My Lord Crosbie, indeed."

"Then you know she's fine if Lord Crosbie told her so."

"You *are* bad." But she grinned and began down the path toward the boats, tugging him to follow. "I'll come back tomorrow to make sure. Besides, I must be back in time to dine with Josh and Anabelle."

"Hell." He stopped, drawing her up abruptly with him. "How the devil could I have forgotten? One of the other reasons I came was on Nan's behalf. She wanted me to tell you—to warn you, to be honest, though not that it matters any longer—that a certain Captain Parrish was expected as a guest, perhaps as soon as this evening."

He took great care to mention Parrish's name without any extra emphasis or even the faintest whiff of jealousy. He'd learned the error of doing otherwise, but damnation, how much he wanted to know her feelings toward this man, too.

And Serena, bless her, didn't make him wait.

"Captain *Parrish?*" she cried with undisguised dismay. "Coming here, tonight? Oh, however could Joshua have done this to me?"

"You are not pleased by this news?" Gerald asked as lightly as he could, working hard not to gloat. "He is not good company?"

"Oh, he is good enough *company,*" she said, her dismay now larded with a healthy indignation. "Oliver Parrish is one of Joshua's oldest friends, another shipmaster, and like Joshua he is handsome and respectable and most successful in his trading. He can be very charming, too, very gentlemanly in a serious sort of way. No *reasonable* woman could hope for more in a husband."

Gerald only nodded, his need to gloat much diminished before such a paragon. It had been one thing to hear a catalogue of Oliver's virtues from Anabelle, but quite another from Serena herself.

She swept her hands impatiently through the air. "But I am *not* reasonable, at least about this, and I do not know why Joshua refuses to accept it! I do *not* want

Oliver Parrish as a husband. I don't want any husband at all!"

"None?" he asked with surprise. He thought of the tidy little house on Cranberry Point, the neat piles of tiny clothes sewn for his sister's baby, of Serena's wit and the way she jested and laughed, of her beauty and warmth, all more than enough to bring joy to some fortunate man. It wasn't as if he'd intended to ask for her himself, not in any permanent arrangement, but to picture her alone for the rest of her life disturbed him far more than he wished to admit. "None whatsoever?"

"None," she declared fiercely. "I'd have thought you'd understand, Gerald, even if Joshua refuses to. Look at all the sorrow marriage brought to my mother, and yours, too, if Anabelle's to be believed."

"That was long ago, in different circumstances," he said swiftly, wishing she hadn't mentioned his own family. His mother's misery had been one of the reasons he'd always been wary of marriage himself, but he'd never expected to hear the same argument used to him by a woman. "And you'd never wed a man like my father."

"Very well, then," her eyes flashing, finding an insult where he hadn't intended one. "No Irish lords. But what if I were to marry some wetched Massachusetts man, like my poor friend Mary? She gave her heart away to such a one who has not only left her a widow, to pine and to weep, but has also destroyed her character and good name simply by giving her his own. For love, Gerald. All for love, and for what?"

"But it needn't always be so," he protested. "Consider Nan and your brother. They seem happy enough."

"And consider when Joshua goes to sea again, as he must, and what would happen to her if he were lost and did not return, the way that happens to more Appledore men than not."

"Serena, I don't see what good this—"

"It would kill her, Gerald," she said softly, her fierceness abruptly swept away before the infinite sorrow of the truth. "It would kill Anabelle outright. If I were in her place, it would kill me, too. And I won't dare take that risk, Gerald. I cannot. I can *not*."

She turned away, and bowed her head wearily, pressing her fingertips to her forehead. She hadn't meant to speak like this to Gerald Crosbie, and she certainly hadn't intended to reveal as much as she had. They'd shared a handful of kisses, that was all, and if he'd never promised more, she'd known better than to expect it. It was her fault if she'd let herself feel more: her own foolish fault.

Now, when he left Massachusetts to return to England, Gerald would remember her like that, Captain Fairbourne's addlepated sister, the way everyone else in Appledore did, the way she sometimes did herself. Why else would she choose not to wed and question the laws of both God and man? Women were supposed to marry, to be good wives to their husbands and good mothers to their children. But how could she accept such a role when her earliest memories had shown her how easily— and disastrously—all those tidy, good hopes and dreams could collapse?

"Forgive me, Gerald," she said unhappily. "I've no right to burden you this way. For men perhaps it is different, but a woman's heart and life are such fragile things, and God help me, I am such a mortal coward!"

She felt his hands rest on her shoulders, not with a lover's touch, but with the gentle understanding of a friend, and she could have wept from the bittersweet comfort she found in such a simple gesture.

"Never a coward, sweetheart," he said softly. "You're many things, Serena Fairbourne, but never that. Now come, back to Appledore, and prove it to me, and to yourself."

Ten

It was, hands down, the worst supper that Serena could ever remember.

Not that the food was ill prepared or the table ineptly laid for guests. She'd never be able to fault Anabelle as a hostess, and this night the silver gleamed by the light of more spermaceti candles than most Appledore families used in a year. The linen was bleached white as new snow and pressed to geometric perfection, and the gold-tipped French porcelain that Anabelle had newly coaxed from Joshua was nearly too fine to cover with food.

But there as well Anabelle had done splendidly, or, more accurately, she'd cajoled her cook to splendidly wondrous achievements: planked scrod with shallots, a sorrel tansey, savory rice, a roast turkey set out among roasted sweet potatoes, dried apples simmered with bacon, winter cheeses, a savory marrow pie, and even a twelve-egg Shrowsbury cake, no mean accomplishment with spring some weeks away and the hens not predisposed to laying their customary quota. The house had been filled with the wafting aromas of baking spices and roasting meat, enough, declared Joshua with a happy groan of anticipation, to tempt a saint to break his fast. Even Abel, blissfully worrying the mutton bones left from the marrow pie, recognized the bounty of such a feast.

Everyone, that is, except for Serena. With her stays laced tightly enough for her best blue satin, she alone sat in silence, pushing the food around and around the elegant porcelain plate and praying for the evening to end. At one end of the long mahogany table her brother was serving as captain as much as host, benignly ordering his guests to eat and drink more, while at the other end sat Anabelle, a queen with her back cushioned with pillows and her belly between her and the edge of the table, endlessly bantering and teasing and bestowing sly winks or merry laughs with an ease that amazed Serena.

But why shouldn't Anabelle be merry? *She* wasn't the one trapped here deep in a morass of her own making, and crossly Serena jabbed her fork into the piped hillock of sweet potato on her plate.

"An excellent meal, Miss Fairbourne, you would agree?" said Captain Parrish heartily, bending toward her from his chair to her left. "I cannot recall a better one, especially in regard to the company."

Reluctantly Serena glanced his way. His smile was warm, his gray eyes full of unmistakable interest. She'd never denied that Oliver Parrish was an attractive man. With his strong, weather-beaten features and a shock of gold-blond hair, his bluff good humor, he would turn women's heads wherever he went. The problem was that he didn't turn *hers*.

"Anabelle has schooled her cook well," she said, carefully ignoring his heavy-handed compliment to the company. She wished he'd stop hovering over her, too, but she couldn't think of a way to retreat that the others wouldn't notice. "She brought her mother's book of cookery with her from England, and thus now my brother dines as well as any gentleman in London."

"Then you must have a copy of this cookery book, Miss Fairbourne," said Parrish, rapping his knuckles on the tablecloth as if to summon the book immediately. "Which is not to say that your own skills are lacking. No, no! Your brother has assured me you're a first-rate cook."

"My brother is very loyal," said Serena, edging her arm away from where his pressed too closely into hers. "Truly, Captain Parrish, I'm a modest cook at best."

Parrish's smile widened, perhaps a shade wider than he'd intended since his grin now showed where he'd lost a tooth.

"I like a modest woman, Miss Fairbourne," he said with conviction. "That I do. But I know you looked after Josh in his bachelor days, and he never seemed underfed to me."

"But that doesn't mean I'm a good cook," protested Serena. "Joshua would eat a whale in its entirety if it could be convinced to remain on his plate."

"Simply crook your little finger and beckon, Serena dear," said Gerald cheerfully from the other side of the table, "and Leviathan himself would leap from the waves. You have that power over males, you know."

Serena set down her fork, her cheeks flushing the way they had all evening whenever Gerald had spoken to her. It wasn't as if he'd made himself disagreeable or behaved churlishly. Far from it. After their short sail back from Denniman's Cove, in near silence, Gerald had again become his usual charming self. But he'd also begun some sort of personal battle of extreme politeness and double-meanings with Captain Parrish on her behalf, a battle that would put her smack in the crossfire. She didn't want to be there, and she most certainly didn't want them at each others' throats at Anabelle's supper. Yet with every word the tension between the two men grew, and so did Serena's hapless misery.

"Captain Parrish and I were discussing cookery, Gerald," she said with as much stern dignity as she could muster. "As you know perfectly well."

"I did know it, yes," he said without a trace of remorse for interrupting what had clearly been a private conversation. But then Serena had never known Gerald to be quick to feel remorse and, besides, he'd been interrupting her and Captain Parrish all evening long, partly because to Gerald's right sat the remarkably unstimulating Mrs. Maghee, a widowed merchant's wife who'd been invited to even out the table.

"I knew it because I'd heard it," he continued, "yet I had not quite believed what I'd heard. You do yourself an injustice, sweet. You're a fine cook. Pray don't try to beguile poor Captain Parrish into believing otherwise."

"She's not beguiling me, Crosbie," said Parrish irritably. "And I'll thank you not to be muddling Miss Fairbourne's good name with your gimcrack endearments, y' hear?"

"She's family to me, Parrish. Gimcrack endearments are part of my due." Gerald's smile was lazy, and suggestive enough that Serena could feel the man beside her practically bristle. "Serena's my darling sister's sister though marriage, which makes her sister to me, too, in a roundabout way. Which also makes me familiar with her culinary gifts, served *en famille* beside her own hearth. A most delightful experience, Parrish. She makes a cranberry quiddany that could make a man tumble to his knees with gratitude for the honor."

"Is this true, Serena?" asked Joshua, his expression an odd mixture of surprise, confusion, and outright horror. "You've had Crosbie to dine at your house? Alone?"

"It wasn't like that, Josh," said Serena defensively. "Truly! Gerald called while I was finishing my own dinner, and I shared what I had."

"Oh, Joshua," scoffed Anabelle, "and what if Serena had invited my brother to sit with her? Duckie is right. They *are* family, brother and sister, sister and brother, and all because of us. I should rather think you'd be pleased they'd found each other agreeable."

"Agreeable," repeated Joshua unhappily. His black-browed glance traveled pointedly from Parrish to Gerald to Parrish again, while Serena would have given whatever was necessary to have the floorboards yawn open and swallow her up. "Agreeable, hell. Damnation *and* hell."

"Joshua, love, remember yourself," said Anabelle now, her voice too purring to be a real reprimand, though close enough to make everyone else look self-consciously, and swiftly, down at their plates. "Mind that my table is not your quarterdeck."

Serena rushed to try to ease the awkwardness that she'd unwittingly caused.

"I'm certain, Captain Parrish, that in your voyages you must have tasted a great many rare dishes," she said swiftly. "Pray might you tell me of your favorite?"

Parrish beamed and preened, but before he could answer, Gerald did.

"You'll find nothing more rare than Serena's quiddany," he said. "It is a gift from the heavens. Or more precisely from the bogs. That was the peculiar term for the cranberry's nascent spot, wasn't it, Serena dear? Bogs?"

"Of course it's bogs, Crosbie," snapped Parrish. "Any idiot knows that. Now if you can keep your—"

"Gentlemen, I beg you, another topic!" Anabelle held up her hands for silence, her lace cuffs dropping back over her elbows. "This one quite bores me to distraction. Bogs! Dear Heavens above! Is there anything more inelegant?"

"Perhaps Captain Parrish can tell us what was in his last cargo," said Serena quickly. "That is always of interest."

Parrish drummed his fingers beside his plate, his gaze still locked with Gerald's across the table. "I fear you'd find little to amuse yourself on my bills of lading, Miss Fairbourne. My hold was filled with sailcloth and iron goods, with a smattering of tin and coarse creamware fit for tavern use. But you, Crosbie, you and Joshua: you would, I think, take interest in some custom pieces I brought back from London."

"The pistols, Oliver?" asked Joshua, leaning forward

with excitement. "The ones you'd bespoke from Gro-shick were ready?"

Parrish nodded. "Aye, and well worth the wait, too. You've never seen another pair that shoots so straight and true."

"Pistols," murmured Mrs. Maghee sagely as she dabbed her napkin to her lips. "Pistols are always of interest to gentlemen."

"No wiser words were ever said, ma'am," said Gerald, and indeed it seemed to Serena that his eyes had taken on a fierce new glow that made her decidedly uneasy. "A pair from Antoine Groshick! You are to be congratu-lated, Parrish!"

"You've brought them with you, Oliver, haven't you?" demanded Joshua eagerly. "Ah, can you picture the damage we could have done among the French off Martinique with such guns!"

"You did damage enough, Josh," said Serena, wishing her brother wouldn't refer to his old privateering days. She knew he hadn't been a saint, but she wanted to believe that those bloodthirsty—albeit very profitable—days were long done and in the past. "What use would you have for pistols now?"

"Not mere pistols, Serena," said Gerald with an expansive sweep of his hand. "You might as well speak of mere gold or mere diamonds. Herr Groshick is a verita-ble wizard among gunsmiths, a genius of blackpowder magic. His guns are so close to perfection that you could hand one, loaded and primed, to a wild ape, and the creature could outshoot any man."

But Parrish seized the insult for what it was and thumped his fist down hard. "The devil take your savage ape, Crosbie! A steady hand, a practiced eye—that's what makes a decent shot, not some blasted gunsmith. I say a gun, even a Groshick, is only as sure as the hand that aims it!"

"Indeed." Gerald's smile was slow and vaguely pity-ing. "And I say you're wrong."

Parrish was on his feet in an instant, so fast that his chair toppled backward with a thump. "Damn your impertinence, Crosbie! I'll lay ten guineas to prove it!"

"Ten guineas." Gerald glanced toward the ceiling for divine guidance. "I am shocked, sir."

Parrish smiled, sensing blood. "Ten guineas says your shot's no better than that ape's. Your choice of pistol, mine of target. Though God knows the ape wouldn't cover himself in a coat fit for a mountebank."

"Thirty guineas," said Gerald as he brushed an infinitesimal speck of dust from his velvet sleeve. "To make the point stick, that is."

Parrish didn't hesitate. "Thirty it is, Crosbie."

Unconsciously Serena's hand covered her mouth, stifling her gasp at the size of the wager. Thirty guineas was an enormous amount of money, an unconscionable sum to squander on a wager like this.

"And," continued Gerald as if the other man hadn't spoken, "to make the contest more interesting, a crock of Serena's divine quiddany and a silver spoon to eat it."

Serena flushed. No one else would understand the significance of that silver spoon, but she did, and so, of course, did Gerald.

Gerald smiled, the same memory so obviously in his thoughts, too, and her face grew hotter still.

"You'll agree, Serena dear?" he said softly. "To, ah, sweeten the contest for the contestants?"

He was only amusing himself. He would be gone in the spring. He'd promised her nothing.

Dear Lord, why was he doing this to her?

"Oh, go ahead, Serena," ordered Joshua. "Agree. 'Tis only a crock of jam."

But it wasn't; it wasn't at all.

"You'll lose, Gerald," she said, her voice brittle. How could he possibly win? He was a gentleman. He'd known nothing of Caribbean privateers, of the desperate battles her brother and Captain Parrish had fought against French pirates. "Captain Parrish is the best shot in the colony."

Anabelle laughed merrily. "La, Serena, such drama! One would think this a duel, an affair of honor!"

But Serena wasn't convinced it wasn't, not when she saw the determined expressions on the faces of the two men. "The quiddany is yours, then. For the sake of the contest."

"Good!" Swiftly Parrish turned toward Joshua. "I'll send for the pistols. The beach beyond to the east should do; the tide must be nearly out. A dozen flambeaux should be light enough. You'll rouse the necessary men?"

"The work of a moment." Joshua was on his feet now, too, downing the last of his wine before he clapped his friend on the shoulder. "How I love a good contest!"

"But now, Joshua?" asked Anabelle. "*Now?* Why not wait until morning, and not spoil my supper?"

"Hang supper," he said, then sighed contritely as he realized how that must sound. "I'm sorry, love, but 'tis the sport of it. Now, by firelight, on the beach, before anyone can change their mind or weasel on the stakes."

They all knew he meant Gerald, but Gerald only smiled across the table at Serena.

"You are mad to agree to such foolishness," she whispered fiercely at him as Anabelle and Mrs. Maghee left the table to see the other men off to make their preparations. "Entirely mad!"

"I'm half Irish," he said, his eyes shadowed in the candlelight. "I can't help it."

"But you're also half English, and so you *should.*"

"Perhaps you should speak to your brother and his friend instead. They're entirely English and might see reason more clearly."

"Very well. Then you're all mad to do this." She sighed with exasperation. "Especially for thirty guineas. Thirty guineas!"

"'Tis nothing," he said with a shrug. "I've squandered ten times that on a hand of cards."

"You cannot be serious about this, can you?" She shook her head in disbelief, searching for a way to make him understand. "Can't you see that they'll make a fool of you, there for the whole town to watch and laugh?"

"And what is new about that?" he asked lightly. "Besides, sweet, you should have more faith in my abilities. Being half Irish also means I was brought into this world with a pistol clasped in my baby hand. Do you think I would have agreed so willingly to slay your dragons for you if it were otherwise?"

"I don't know what you would agree to do," she said unhappily. "I don't know why you're doing any of this."

"Then have a bit of faith in me, too," he said softly. "Your knight-errant is no coward, either."

Eleven

In the course of his travels, Gerald had tried many unusual things, and seen a great many more. But this night, on this beach, rivaled everything else in his memory for its peculiar mixture of grand spectacle and sheer, determined lunacy.

Gerald smoothed back his hair and resettled his hat, striving to remain the one sane figure in a landscape filled with lunatics. *Lunacy* was the word that best described it, for with the tide at full ebb the broad beach gleamed white in the moonlight, the same moonlight that seemed to have maddened everyone else.

The proof was all around him. Lanterns bobbed here and there along the beach in the gray half-light, their owners darker shadows behind them, and more spectators' shadows lined the tops of the dunes. Tiny glowing pinpricks marked the bowls of sheltered pipes, and even over the unending *shush* of the waves he could hear the dull clink of bottles being passed among friends and the excited, muffled laughter that followed. Most of the town must have tumbled from their beds—or from their tavern benches—to be here at this hour, and Gerald smiled wryly to think of what passed for great entertainment here in Appledore.

Certainly the company of players would make it diverting enough. First on any program would have to be Anabelle as the *grande dame,* swaddled in a fur-lined cloak and chatting merrily to anyone who came close as she sat in the armchair brought specially from the house for her. A serving girl hovered alongside with a teapot, wrapped to keep the contents hot, ready to refill the dish in Anabelle's gloved hand. Joshua was every bit her equal, a veritable pirate king as he stood nearby, bareheaded so that his long black hair tossed gently in the breeze, laughing and calling and accepting wagers—wagers that, Gerald noted, seemed entirely against himself.

Finding the heroine was easy, too, and as he did Gerald felt a quick jab of bittersweet joy. Serena stood alone, a punched tin lantern in the sand at her feet, and studiously away from Joshua and Anabelle and their crowd of acquaintances. She did not look happy. Pressed close to her skirts was Abel and, if his presence kept others away, she did not seem to notice, or mind, either.

But if Serena was the heroine, then where on this beach was her hero?

Certainly the role couldn't fall to that lunk-headed Parrish. Even now he stood in his shirtsleeves and waistcoat, loudly describing his talents as a marksman to a small circle of admirers. No, Serena deserved more in a hero than that.

He'd offer himself, imperfect as he was, before it came to that. Though God knows it wouldn't, for as a heroine, Serena had her flaws, too. More specifically, she had only one, and an enormous, improper, and unheroinelike one it was: Serena Fairbourne didn't *want* a hero.

"I believe they're nearly ready to begin, sir," said Rourke. "Shall I take your coat?"

"I'd rather keep it," said Gerald. "Let that clod-pate Parrish's arm shiver and quake with the cold."

"Would serve him right," said Rourke with a sniff of supreme contempt. "He's not worth your trouble, sir. Neither yours nor the young lady's."

Gerald didn't answer beyond a minuscule nod. Better not to think of Serena now. Tonight what she wanted instead of a hero—and what she very much needed—was a level-headed knight-errant, and that was one role he could fill with ease. Or could, anyway, if he set his mind to it instead of mooning after what she wasn't about to grant.

He forced himself to concentrate on the upcoming contest. A dozen flambeaux, held by sailors drafted from Joshua's and Parrish's ships, lit a long, bright path over the sand. At the far end of the path stood two barrels on their ends, with a dark plank stretched across them like the mantelpiece on a fireplace and, arranged like chalkware figurines on that mantelpiece, were white scallop shells that would serve as the makeshift targets.

They'd agreed on seven shots apiece. Neither of them had mentioned a tie, for each was determined to win outright. The stakes seemed outwardly simple enough—thirty guineas to the victor, along with a healthy dose of respect—but Gerald understood how much else was at risk, too. To outshoot Parrish would be to humble him so grievously that he'd leave Appledore without Serena. That, then, was the dragon Gerald had come to slay. In return his prize would not be to claim Serena for himself, but to keep her unattached, the way she swore would make her happiest.

He'd never done anything half so noble in all his life.

He glanced back at Rourke, who was carefully measuring the powder from a flask—because of the damp, he'd waited until the last possible moment for loading—into the barrel of the pistol Gerald had chosen from Parrish's pair. They *were* beautiful guns, perfectly balanced and long-barreled enough to be holster pistols, with silver butt caps and side plates to match, engraved with ships and waves.

With a small bow, Rourke held the loaded pistol out to

him. Gerald's fingers curled around the polished walnut with easy familiarity. He hadn't been exaggerating when he'd spoken so confidently to Serena. Exploring the more exciting ways of destruction was a male Crosbie weakness. He'd scarcely been breeched when he and his brothers had begun experimenting with blackpowder and flintlocks, and even an old matchlock musket they'd found in the stables. In Gerald's opinion, pistols would never replace smallswords for a visit to Tothill Fields to face an aggrieved husband, the way some predicted, but they were useful weapons nonetheless, and gunsmiths like Groshick were improving their accuracy all the time. Which, of course, he now meant to prove.

"Are you ready then, Crosbie?" called Joshua. "Since Captain Parrish is the challenger, you'll go first."

Silently Gerald stepped to the line someone had marked in the sand. The air was surprisingly still; he wouldn't have to compensate for a breeze from the water. The uneven light from the torches was going to be challenge enough. Slowly, effortlessly, he raised his arm until the barrel, and the white shell in the distance beyond, were both level with his eye.

He didn't like shooting at the scallop shells. They reminded him too much of Serena and of that special pair of shells he'd superstitiously once again tucked into his pocket this night. He wondered what she'd say if he confessed that to her. Someday perhaps he would; perhaps she'd laugh.

Jesus, he had to concentrate . . .

Beneath Serena's cloak her hands were clasped into tight fists, and her heart pounded at a furious rate. Among all the people here on this beach, she felt sure that she was the only one who truly cared for the man standing in the flickering light of the flambeaux. She'd seen the raucous way other men were betting against him; the odds had grown so lopsided she wondered that anyone could be found to accept the wagers. Even Anabelle must have chosen to side against Gerald, else she wouldn't be laughing now at something Captain Parrish had said as he bent over her chair.

Serena frowned at Anabelle's disloyalty. It didn't matter that this ridiculous contest was Gerald's own doing. Men were often backing themselves into such situations, trapped by their own pride and honor, and in that way he was no different from the rest. But how isolated he must feel at this moment, how horribly alone against the whole town! Belatedly she remembered what he'd said about being her knight and wearing her favor, and now she wished she'd thought to give him a ribbon or some other small token to carry for luck.

She watched him standing there at the mark, his right hand raised to hold the pistol, the other curled gracefully behind his waist. There wasn't a shade of nervousness or tension about him, only a level of concentration that was almost palpable in the night air. She'd never seen a man stand so still, as if carved from wood or stone, and when the crack of the pistol's fire finally came, she gasped, startled by the suddenness of it. But as the drifting cloud of gunpowder cleared, there was no mistaking the result: the white shell was gone, shattered, and Gerald had won his first shot.

Amidst the excited murmuring from the crowd, Parrish quickly took his place at the mark, and just as quickly raised his pistol and fired. The shell that had been his target burst apart, his shot true, and the spectators cheered, doubtless relieved their wagers were, so far, still safe.

Two more times the men took their turns, and two more times they found their targets. After Gerald's third, perfect shot, Parrish turned to glower at him.

"How fortunate you are, Crosbie," he said curtly, his tone no match for the civility of his words. "Luck smiles upon you."

Gerald smiled and gave a slight bow of acknowledgment. He was surprised to see how unsettled Parrish had become. By the light of the flambeaux the sheen of nervous sweat glistened on the man's forehead, and the sleeves of his shirt clung damply to his arms. A nervous man was a man prone to mistakes, exactly the kind of man Gerald wanted to face in a contest like this.

"Luck is a fickle mistress, sir," he said lightly as he took the reloaded pistol from Rourke. "I fear I prefer the more tedious constancy of skill."

"Damn your skill," muttered Parrish. "You wouldn't know true skill if it bit you on the ass."

Gerald didn't answer, partly because he saw no reason to do so, and partly because he'd already begun to concentrate on the white shell in the distance. He squeezed the trigger, felt the recoil of the polished butt against his palm, and looked through the acrid cloud of burned powder to where the shell had been. Four for four: he'd learned the feel of the gun, the infinitesimal pull of the barrel balanced by the breeze from the water, and slipped into the rhythm of the contest. Now he felt he could shoot until dawn without faltering, if he had to, and almost wished he did.

With another oath Parrish raised his gun, barely pausing to aim, and fired. When the gunsmoke cleared, the shell remained, and the excitement rippling through the crowd swelled to a wave. Before it died away, Gerald shot again, and with the same dry, percussive pop, the white shell shattered.

Five for five. He couldn't help turning, glancing over his shoulder to try to see Serena's reaction.

"Give me that damned gun," ordered Parrish, flushed with embarrassment, as he wrenched it from Gerald's hand and tossed the pistol he'd been using to Rourke instead. "You knew which one was the better, didn't you?"

Again Gerald didn't answer.

Parrish raised the new pistol, aimed, and fired. And missed.

By a trick of the breeze, Parrish's words had reached the people gathered on the dune, their sudden silence proof enough of their feelings. A good-natured contest was one thing; this was becoming something else altogether, and Gerald knew it. No wonder Serena didn't want this man beside her for the rest of her life.

As soon as Rourke had readied the second gun and put it into his hand, Gerald turned and fired it, swiftly and easily and without any doubt in the pistol's merit.

Six for six.

He heard his name as part of a ragged cheer and recognized the voices of men he was working with on the markethouse. He smiled, more pleased by their support than they'd ever know.

Parrish muttered something to himself as he fired next. And missed again.

Gerald could have quit then. He'd already won, and there'd be nothing tangible to be gained by continuing. But the pistol was already in his hand, and he could not resist the opportunity that his seventh shot offered. A chance at pure heroic perfection like that seldom came to any man. In one last, easy motion, he raised his arm and fired.

Seven for seven, and his smile widened to a grin of unrestrained pleasure. Even Serena would have to be impressed by that.

"I'd say, sir, that Herr Groshick has acquitted himself admirably," he said as he held the now-empty pistol out to Parrish, "and I thank you for the chance to prove it."

Someone among the spectators laughed, a laugh that was quickly smothered. The one that followed next wasn't, nor was the jeering, anonymous catcall that came from the next dune.

Parrish's face grew rigid. He grabbed the still-smoking pistol from Gerald's hand and in disgust flung the two guns into the sand behind him.

"You win, sir," he said stiffly, handing Gerald a little bag with the coins. "This night, I must concede."

Gerald nodded as he took the wager. The elation of winning that he'd expected hadn't come, and instead he felt curiously drained, and worse, almost sorry for the dragon he'd just slain.

Suddenly Joshua was there, clapping his hand on his

friend's shoulder. "A good contest," he said with a show of heartiness that fooled no one. "Fair shooting by you both. Now back to the house before Anabelle takes my head."

But Parrish didn't seem to hear him, his expression both pained and glum. "Tell me, Crosbie," he said. "Did you really want Serena so badly for yourself that you'd do this to me?"

Slowly Gerald shook his head. An hour before, he thought he'd known the answer to that question. Now he wasn't in the least sure.

A score of images was shifting before him, like canvases in a gallery: Anabelle, silent for once, coming to tuck her little hands into the crook of Joshua's arm; the sailors who'd held the flambeaux going to douse them in the sea, their flames disappearing with a serpent's hiss; the workmen who'd cheered him nodding and doffing their hats and caps with respectful awe from a distance but coming no closer.

And in the middle stood Serena with Abel, so painfully alone and forgotten that she might have been invisible.

But not to him. Lord help them both, never now to him.

"It doesn't matter whether I want her or not, Parrish," he said softly, his gaze still on Serena. "The sad truth is that she doesn't want either one of us."

He left them then, without waiting for a reply, and walked across the sand to where Serena waited.

"You won," she said, but she did not smile, and neither did he. "You said you would, and you did."

"I did," he said softly, "and thank God for once I was speaking the truth. Now come, sweetheart, let me see you home."

They walked in silence to Cranberry Point, a silence that Serena had no wish to break. Gerald was a man to whom words came easily and in great, amusing volume, and though she liked that about him, she also liked how he'd come to trust her enough to say nothing. From him silence could be far more intimate, linking them together in the chilly night as surely as their twined fingers.

She unlatched the gate and let Abel push ahead, his tail drooping with weariness as he went to stand expectantly on the doorstep.

"Poor puppy," she said as she followed the dog. "All he wants now is his place by the fire where he can chase rabbits all night in his dreams. Isn't that so, Abel?"

"It sounds agreeable enough to me," said Gerald behind her. "The part about a warm place near the fire to sleep all night, anyway. I cannot vouch as convincingly about the rabbit chasing."

She smiled, trying to imagine Gerald bounding through the marshes with Abel's enthusiasm, heedless of muck and mud. As far-fetched a picture as it was, it was infinitely preferable to the memory of him standing before Oliver Parrish's raised pistol.

She bent to stroke Abel's head, and to hide the emotions that must surely be playing across her face. "I don't know for certain, either. I've only guessed he's dreaming of rabbits when he growls and twitches his legs in his sleep."

"I doubt I'll dream of anything tonight," said Gerald with an extravagant yawn. "Not even rabbits."

"Of course not." Serena knew she should thank him for his trouble and then bid him good night. She'd no reason to keep him longer, and besides, he was tired and so was she. But part of her wasn't ready to be alone yet, especially since her own dreams would not be nearly as untroubled.

She glanced at him as she straightened, forcing herself to meet his eye. "Have you forgotten the other part of the wager?" she asked, striving to sound lighthearted instead of merely bold. "About the quiddany? You can come inside and claim it now, if you wish."

"Now?" Gerald knew he should refuse, especially after all she'd told him at Denniman's Cove. She didn't want to be hurt, and he didn't want to be the man that hurt her by leaving. It was as simple, and as complicated, as that, but he could accept it. For her sake, he had to. He didn't have a choice, not when he meant to sail from her life altogether in two months' time. Wasn't that foolish contest proof enough?

Yet nothing had changed, unless perhaps for the worse. The more time he spent with her, the more he found he, too, dreaded the day he'd leave for home. Besides, he still couldn't trust himself to be alone with her, not when the one thing he wished most to do was to forget himself and this wretched night in the soft welcome of her kiss and her body.

And she *would* mention the quiddany, blast his own wicked impulses.

Swiftly she looked away, hiding the hurt of his rejection beneath the curve of her hood. "You don't have to. You're tired now, I know. I can leave the quiddany with Rourke tomorrow instead."

"Now is fine," he said quickly. It was his own baseness that was the problem, not her, and he didn't want her believing otherwise. To banish that wounded look from her eyes he'd agree to anything. He reached out to pull the latch string, pushing the door open. "Better than fine."

But still he didn't bolt the door after them once they'd entered, and neither did she. It was better this way, he told himself sternly, with both of them silently acknowledging his visit would be brief. An unbolted door could be a most useful reminder, even here on Cranberry Point.

While Abel immediately went to the worn braided mat that marked his special spot before the hearth, there was little warmth to be found from the banked fire. Serena crouched down without pausing to take off her cloak and began to prod and fan the fire back to life.

"Here," said Gerald, hunkering down beside her with a fresh piece of firewood. "I'll do that for you."

She glanced at him, surprised to find him there. "You don't have to."

"I know that," he said patiently, the corners of his mouth twitching as she repeated herself. "I don't have to do any of these things if I don't choose to, but I do, because they're for you."

The expression in her eyes was so full of doubt that he laughed.

"I do know how to tend a fire, Serena, since that's what you're so clearly thinking. I'm not half the incompetent fool you seem to believe me to be."

"I didn't say that!"

"Not with your lips, perhaps, no, but everything else spoke clearly enough," he said, and gently smoothed a stray lock of her hair back behind her ear, as she so often did herself. "I'd have thought after tonight you'd begin to take me more at my word."

But to his surprise Serena didn't answer. Instead she rose in silence, dusting her palms as she yielded the fireplace to him, and retreated to the far side of the kitchen. Slowly he fanned the coals until they glowed bright again, wondering why it wasn't as easy to warm her toward him. On this day when his life had seemed so disturbingly unpredictable and fragile, too, he longed for one constant to hold on to, and he wished she'd spoken up to defend herself the way he'd expected, the way he'd come to like so much.

He jabbed the poker hard with frustration at the burning wood. He'd had so little experience putting his own desires second, and it didn't come easily.

"There you are," he said with a false cheerfulness as the fire began to burn in earnest. "I cannot promise you all the heat of the tropics, but in a few minutes we should be warmer here inside than out."

While he'd worked on the fire, she'd lit the candles on the table, and by their glow he noticed she'd pinned his drawing of the new markethouse in a place of honor on the wall. She hadn't quite been able to smooth away the ripples that the sleet had left on the paper, and he wondered if those ripples brought back to her the same memories of finding shelter—and a few other things— in the tiny workman's shed that they did for him.

Damnation, he hoped they did. It wasn't fair that he should be the only one to suffer like this.

She came back to stand before the fire, beside him. "I suppose you are not entirely useless," she said with a game attempt at her usual familiarity. "Your Mr. Rourke himself couldn't have done better."

He realized it was only an attempt, but he seized at it anyway. As long as he could remember he'd been able to fall back on his wit to ease his way, and he'd never needed that gift as much as he did now.

"My Mr. Rourke wouldn't approve at all," he said with a solemn shake of his head that was worthy of Rourke himself. "First he'd find fault with the fire, then fuss at the soot on my coat."

"Would he?" She peered at the smudge on his sleeve. "Then I warrant I'm much more easily pleased than your Mr. Rourke."

Jesus, he didn't even want to consider that. "Yes," he said, his voice sounding faintly strangled. "I'd say you are."

With considerable faith in his fire, she'd taken off her cloak and, as she lifted the kettle for tea onto the hook over the fire, she was careful to keep the silk skirts of her best gown from the ashes and sparks, bunching the costly fabric back with one hand. It may have saved her skirts, but it didn't save him, not the way she'd unwittingly pulled the gleaming blue silk taut over her hips and thighs, their curves so evident by the firelight that he nearly groaned aloud.

"I've tarried here long enough, Serena," he said swiftly, before he had a chance to toss his hard-earned nobility to the winds. "I'm too tired for good company, and unless you wish to see me curl up on your hearth beside Abel, I'd best claim my quiddany and be on my way."

"I don't think Abel would agree to that," she said, striving to keep her voice, and her heart, light. "He's not very good about sharing."

But she was. Wistfully she knew she would have

shared anything in her house if he'd but asked, if it would make him linger even five minutes longer. She'd lived so much of her life alone that she'd thought she'd come to prefer it that way, but not tonight. Lord, what had happened to her careful, proud defenses?

She turned and hurried to the cupboard, and away from Gerald. She had to stand on the stool to reach the highest shelf where she kept her jams and pickles and other preserves, and she surreptitiously brushed away the dust that had collected on the top of the last little crock. Perhaps she did in fact have a small amount of pride left, albeit for her huswifery.

"Here you are," she said, returning with the crock cradled in her hands. "This is the last of it for the year, you know, so treasure it. Quiddanies don't keep well— the color grows wan, and the flavor spoils—so I only make as much as I'll use in time."

He frowned and shook his head. "I didn't mean to take your last."

"No, you must," she said firmly. "I want you to have it, and enjoy it, and—what is that in your hand?"

His smile was crooked, almost sheepish, as he held his hand out to her, his palm open to reveal the pair of rose-colored scallop shells.

"Do you remember these?" he asked softly. "A certain mermaid gave them to me, and I've kept them ever since to remember her by."

She stared at the shells, blinking hard. "You kept them?" she whispered with disbelief. "All this time, you kept those shells to remind yourself of—of—oh, damn, Gerald, I didn't want to cry!"

"Go ahead, Serena," he said fondly. "Cry all you wish. 'Tis better than trying to keep it locked up inside."

"Oh, don't be so bloody gallant about it!" She thumped the crock down onto the table in frustration, her voice squeaking upward. "I know you don't like teary women—some men do, but not you, so stop pretending otherwise!"

"As a rule, you're right, I don't like teary women," he said, setting the shells down on the table so he could reach for her hand instead. "But teary mermaids are an entirely different thing. In fact I seem to have developed quite a weakness for them."

She edged away from him, furiously shaking her head as the tears streamed down her cheeks. "It's not as if I'm crying for no—no good reason. It's just that—oh, how I hated to see you with that gun in your hand!"

"I wasn't as if Parrish was going to shoot *me*, you silly goose," said Gerald. "He wouldn't have dared, not for a mere thirty guineas. Even the third son of an Irish lord is worth more than that."

"Will you never be serious?" She turned her back to him, struggling to control her emotions as she paced across the room. "Or perhaps that is to be my punishment for weeping, that the more I cry, the more you'll jest and tease and refuse to grant any value to what I say."

"Serena, please, I never—"

"No, you never, and I never, and that should be an end to it," she said miserably through her tears. "But I cannot bear to even imagine the world without you in it!"

"But you don't have to," he said, his hands on her shoulders, gently turning her around to face him. "I'm here, Serena. I'm here tonight, and I'm not going anywhere else."

When his arms circled around her waist, it seemed to be the most natural thing in the world to be there, his heart beating against hers and his fingertip wiping the tears from her cheek. Here was proof enough that he was *here,* and joyfully she seized it, and forgot everything else.

She did not know exactly how they'd come to be kissing, but that, too, seemed blissfully right. How could it be otherwise with Gerald? This was the one sure way he could speak to her from his heart, without the witty mask of words to hide behind. She loved him for risking that much with her. No, she thought, it was more than that. She loved *him,* pure and simple.

Yet that was wrong, too. Loving Gerald wasn't simple and never would be, and it certainly wasn't pure, but she wouldn't dare find fault on either account. How could she? No other man could steal her breath away like this, or turn her limbs so butter-soft that she'd no choice but to press closer to him for support, for more of the sweet, heady touch of his mouth and his body.

More, and more again, and when he toppled her backward onto the bed she only gasped with surprise before she pulled him closer, sliding her hands inside his coat to hold him, to steady herself. He seemed so much bigger like this, so much stronger and so very male, and it did not help that he seemed to know far better than she what would come next. He tugged the front of her gown lower, enough to free her breasts from the tight-laced bodice. She gasped as the cold air puckered the tender skin of her nipple, then gasped again and arched into the wet warmth of his mouth.

He was easing himself on top of her, pressing her deep into the mattress, the linsey-woolsey of the coverlet rough against the back of her thighs where he'd pulled her skirts high over her legs. His breathing was ragged, too, hot against the pulse of her throat, and she closed her eyes, giving herself over to the rush of new sensations. He rasped her name, half a groan, half a plea, begging her for something she didn't know how to grant, and as she tried to tell him she heard the other sound from across the room, the unmistakable thump of the door being shoved open and the sound of her name being called.

With a startled cry she tried to twist around beneath Gerald's weight, and heard Abel scuffle to his feet, growling a warning that died as soon as it began once he'd heard the voice on the other side of the door. Gerald heard it, too, swearing as he rolled to one side and sat, shielding her with his shoulder as she frantically tried to pull her gown back into place.

And for yet one more time that night Gerald Crosbie heard the oiled scrape of a flintlock pistol being cocked to fire.

"I can't fathom why any woman would wish to wed a bastard like you, Crosbie," said Joshua Fairbourne slowly, his expression black with fury, "but now it seems my sister does. She *must*. And God help you if you don't make her the happiest bride alive."

Twelve

Gerald shoved the tray with his uneaten supper to one side and stared out the window at the rain as it pelted steadily against the glass. According to Mr. May, it was the experienced opinion of the rest of the White Swan's customers in the taproom downstairs that the rain was a fair omen of an early spring, coming as it did instead of sleet or snow.

The skies could have been dropping purple turnips for all that Gerald cared, for neither rain, snow, sleet, nor turnips was going to improve his humor. But still he swore at the weather, tossing in a fervent wish for eternal damnation for all male Fairbournes, living and dead. Even that didn't help. By this time tomorrow night, he'd be married to Serena Fairbourne, and all the oaths in Christendom wouldn't be able to rescue him then.

He took another long swallow from the tankard of rum. If he chose to lean a bit to the left, he'd see the two men hired to make sure he didn't escape, his own private pair of brutish nannies thanks to his dear, trusting brother-in-law. At least the men were getting soaked to the skin, standing in the street in the rain. Gerald could, and did, take some small solace in that. For these past two weeks the two had been his constant shadows, following him from the White Swan to the site of the markethouse, even to dine with his sister.

For Serena, there'd been even less freedom. According to Anabelle, Serena had become a prisoner in her brother's home, shut away upstairs in belated safety from the man who'd ruined her, the man who'd soon be her husband. Most likely even Abel was somehow being punished, too, banished to some low kennel to ponder his sins against the great name of Fairbourne.

With another bitter oath, Gerald kicked at the leg of the table. He supposed things could have been worse. If Joshua had had his way, he and Serena would have been hauled before the minister the morning after he'd caught them together. Only Anabelle had earned him this fortnight's reprieve, and that simply because she swore she could not stage a decent wedding in less time. *Decent.* Gerald's lips curled contemptuously as he remembered the word. There was nothing, absolutely nothing, decent about this sham of a wedding, and he gave the table leg another kick in purposeless frustration.

"You've eaten none of your supper, sir," scolded Rourke. "That chicken was spit-roasted, just as you like best, and fit for His Majesty himself."

"Then his royal blessed majesty is welcome to it," said Gerald sourly. "You'll take care that he gets it, won't you, Rourke? You see, I am quite otherwise engaged for the rest of my life."

Rourke gave an indignant little huff. "Most humorous, sir, I'm sure. But you must eat. To keep up your strength for tomorrow, sir. You wouldn't wish to disappoint your lady bride, would you?"

"It will take far more than a lowly chicken to appease her and her brother, doubtless the Massachusetts branch of the Borgia tree. They're altogether beyond you, Rourke." He emptied the tankard and clanked it onto the table. "Would you have May refill this for me? You recall how melancholia stimulates my thirst."

"Melancholia isn't the half of it, sir," declared Rourke as he took the tankard from Gerald. "Now no more rum, or you won't come close to performing your bridegroom's duties tomorrow."

"Hang my duties," growled Gerald. Caged animals growled, and that was exactly how he felt. Or maybe a prize Newmarket stallion, what with Rourke carrying on about his "duties" as if he'd been sold to stud. "Don't know why they didn't just hang me."

"No more rum, sir," said Rourke stoutly. "If it's your thirst that's aggravating you this way, then I'll bring you water. But no more rum."

"No more rum," repeated Gerald morosely. "And no more anything else, either, once I'm married. I don't want to be married, Rourke. Haven't I told you that?"

"Aye, sir, you have." Rourke set the empty tankard on the tray with the uneaten chicken and gave the wet rings left on the table an extra swipe with the napkin. "Now, sir, I've brushed your dark blue coat and breeches as being most suitable for the ceremony tomorrow, and laid out the rose-colored waistcoat with them, as you wished."

Gerald scowled. He had dearly wanted that rum. It had been the one thing that had made these last two weeks bearable. "Not my wish, Rourke. Yours. Mind the difference."

"Aye, sir. As you say." Rourke nodded with annoying patience. "If you'll give it to me, I'll slip the bride's ring into our pocket so you won't forget it in the bustle of tomorrow."

"I can't give it to you because I don't have one," said Gerald, growling again. Growling seemed highly appropriate, considering. "No ring, nor gift, nor other costly trinkets. If Fairbourne wants such rubbish for his sister, then he can damned well buy them himself, just as he's bought me."

"Now that's unkind, sir, deuced unkind, even from

you." Rourke put his fists to his waist like a stern, freckled schoolmistress. "You can't go lumping Miss Fairbourne into that particular kettle. Whatever mischief her brother's done, I'll wager she hasn't had any part of it. She's a good lady, sir, and she cares for you."

"Mind your tongue, Rourke," grumbled Gerald. "You're speaking of your betters a great deal more freely than you should."

He didn't want to admit even the possibility that Rourke might be right. He'd been too angry with Serena and her brother this past fortnight for that. His hard-won shell of bitterness was the only protection he had left.

How could it be otherwise? He had believed she was different from all the other women he'd known, more honest, more generous, more innocent and guileless. He'd even believed her when she'd said she'd rather remain a spinster. He'd kept on believing even after her brother had burst in upon them.

But then the truth had come bursting in, too, and all the rum in Appledore wouldn't ease the pain that had come along with it. Not one word had Serena offered in his defense, nor had she murmured a single syllable of explanation to her brother or let her hand touch Gerald's for reassurance. Once Joshua had come and the trap had been sprung, she hadn't even bothered to meet Gerald's eye.

Instead she'd dressed and gone silently to her brother's side, choosing her family over him with an ease and speed that cut Gerald straight to the place he supposed his heart must have been. It certainly wasn't there now. Now all he had inside that hollow place in his chest was a wealth of bitterness and a paucity of regret, and the memory of Serena standing in her brother's shadow, her face pale and expressionless and without any of the special rare joy he'd come to treasure.

And he'd been so damned close to telling her he loved her.

"Miss Fairbourne *is* my better," said Rourke stoutly.

"I'm not shamed to say it, sir. She's your better, too, leastways in this. She'd never say half the wicked things about you that you've said about her. Nary would even think them, the dear creature."

"Don't be so blasted familiar," ordered Gerald, though his spirit wasn't in it. He and Rourke had been together for so long that the boundaries between them did occasionally blur. "And how the devil would you know, anyway?"

"Oh, aye, sir, I know." Rourke nodded sagely and tapped his forefinger against the side of his nose. "So should you, sir, seeing as she's bound to be your wife. Though maybe you do already. If you was truly of a mind to run, we could have gotten past those two outside, sleek as silk. But I'd wager you wasn't, else we'd be long past off and gone."

"You believe I'd let myself be married off if I had a choice in the matter?" scoffed Gerald scornfully.

Emphatically Rourke nodded again. "Aye, sir, I do. If you wanted out, you'd be gone. You and I've dodged villains worse than a dozen of those puddingheads. What about that old Venetian fellow who thought you'd dallied with his wife, and wanted to see you a-floating in those wretched canals? And that low pair of thieving cheats you bested in cards in Bologna? And think on the press gang in Portsmouth, and how we outplayed them, too."

In spite of his mood, Gerald smiled at the memories. His life *had* been full of adventures. It was the way he'd always kept his ennui—and his family—agreeably at bay. "We've showed the rogues a pretty chase in our time, haven't we, Rourke, eh? God willing, there'll be another hand or two left in the game ahead of us."

"Not with me, sir." Rourke was standing very straight, his back like a musket's ramrod, and it seemed to Gerald that he was concentrating intently on the air to the left of Gerald's ear. "That's the other thing I have to say tonight, sir. I'm leaving your service, sir."

"Leaving?" Gerald stared at him in disbelief. "Damnation, you can't do that, Rourke! You cannot simply leave me! I'm your master!"

"Aye, you *were*," said Rourke. "But begging pardon, sir, I'm still a free Irishman, no bondsman nor heathen slave, and I've as much right to choose my life as Prince George himself. Maybe more."

"But to leave me?" Gerald shook his head, unable to comprehend such a disaster. Rourke had been with him forever, or at least since he'd left school. He'd spent more time in his company than in that of his own brothers. Hell, he was closer to Rourke than to any of his brothers, too. "Where would you go?"

"Down the same tidy path as yourself, sir," said Rourke, seeming to swell with pride and happiness before Gerald's eyes. "Mrs. Hannah Weldon is the finest-looking widow in this town, and she keeps the best rum shop, too. When I asked her to wed me, she agreed, as easy as that. I've a mind to make the rum shop into a public house, and Hannah, bless her, has a mind to let me."

"Does she now." Gerald's disbelief was giving way to a deep sorrow and a disturbing sense of being abandoned. First Anabelle and now Rourke. What the devil was it about Appledore that made them prefer this wretched little town to London?

Yet even as he blustered about it to himself, deep down he already knew the answer. It wasn't the town that held them here. It was love. He thought of the blissful, balmy look in Anabelle's eyes whenever she mentioned her husband, and how Rourke had that same look when he spoke of his widow, and then, before he could help it, he was thinking of Serena, the way her smile came quickly, how she tipped her head back when she laughed so the sunlight would tangle in her hair, how she'd learned to tease him nearly as much as he teased her.

And he'd never felt more alone, or more lonely, in his life.

"I give you much joy, Rourke, of course," he said

glumly, "and health to the bride and all the rest of it—
I'll settle a bit upon you, too—but when I consider my
own loss, I am bereft. Absolutely bereft. I would wager
my good name that there's not another on this side of the
ocean who has your touch with a goffering iron on a fresh
shirt. You've spoiled me, Rourke, ruined me entirely for
anyone else. I don't know how I'll survive."

Rourke nodded solemnly, as if he, too, doubted his
master's chances, and picked up the supper tray. "You
might begin, sir, by trusting your own new wife."

"Miss Fairbourne?" Gerald balked at calling her his
wife. "I don't trust her not to poison me the first chance
she gets, let alone trust her with my shirts."

"As you say, sir." He bowed slightly over the tray in
his hands before he turned to leave the room, his half-
smile of parting colored with more pity than Gerald
might have wished. "But you needn't worry over your
linen with Miss Fairbourne. Not one bit."

"There, Serena," said Anabelle with satisfied triumph
as she plucked one last ribbon into place. "You are
without question the most beautiful bride imaginable,
and anyone who dares not agree with all his heart—for
of course it is only the male hearts that matter to us, isn't
it?—then *he* must answer to me."

Serena stood before the tall mirror in her brother's
bedchamber and tried to find herself in the fashionable
image that stared back at her. No wonder Abel kept a
little to one side with his head cocked uncertainly, wary
of this new and strange version of her. She'd had no say
whatsoever in choosing this gown, the Lyons silk brocade having been rushed from Boston in one of Joshua's
sloops, and the cutting and stitching accomplished by
Appledore's two seamstresses toiling feverishly under
Anabelle's direction. It was all so much their creation
that the reflection in the mirror seemed to Serena to be a
taller, thinner, image of Anabelle rather than of herself.

Even the way that Anabelle described the gown was
foreign to Serena, confusing words that defied her own

tongue to speak them. The soft, heavy pleats that fell from the back neckline to the hem marked it as a *robe à la française,* and the dark green brocade, dappled with pink roses, was a color—or was it a pattern?—called *verte de chasse-royale.* The stomacher that added another unyielding layer of whalebone to force her breasts higher was decorated with a ladder of frothy loops of pink ribbons called *echelles,* and the three layers of embroidered ruffles that fell softly around her elbows weren't mere flounces, but *engageantes.* Even her hair, drawn severely back from her forehead into tight little curls and crowned by a cluster of silk roses, was dressed *à la belle d'Aiguirandes.* Anabelle declared the *ensemble* made Serena now fit to enter any parlor in London (though only, confided Anabelle, between the hours of two and six), but secretly Serena felt as false as the white paste and pinchbeck buckles on her brocade shoes, as false as this entire sad mockery of a wedding.

In the reflection beside her, Anabelle frowned. "Near perfection, yes, but upon my word, your throat does look very bare and needy. Hasn't Gerald sent over some sort of little bauble to you yet?"

Serena flushed with unhappiness and shook her head. Her last memory of Gerald had been of his handsome face turned as hard and unforgiving as granite, convinced that she had somehow betrayed him. She'd thought that, of anyone, Gerald would have understood the depth of her shame. Joshua had always trusted her to be a credit to the Fairbourne name, even when he'd been gone at sea for months at a time, and for him to discover her as he had had broken that trust forever. Nothing she could have said or done would have changed that; she'd had no choice but to accept her disgrace and go as meekly as she could with her brother.

But by losing Joshua's trust, she somehow seemed to have lost Gerald's as well, and she never would have guessed how much it hurt. Gerald hadn't spoken another word to her that night, and she hadn't seen or heard from him since, not even so much as a scribbled note smuggled in through one of the maidservants. Why, then, should she expect him to send her a gift on a wedding day that neither of them wanted?

"Well, he should send you *something*," said Anabelle indignantly. "It's vastly rude of him not to. A length of pearls on a ribbon should be the very least. Gerald knows what's proper. He shall hear from me if he doesn't, the wretched old tight-purse."

"Oh, please don't," said Serena swiftly, imagining all too well Gerald's response. "Pray do not say a word! He'll think I asked you to do it!"

"Hah, he'd know it was me," said Anabelle, wrinkling her nose. "What else are sisters for? But I won't meddle if you don't wish it. Shall I give you my garnets to wear instead? The red would show handsomely against your skin."

Serena's hands fluttered up to touch her throat, almost as if to guard it from the weight of the elaborate garnet necklace that Anabelle was offering to lend her. "I don't want—that is, you have already been generous enough to me, and I don't—"

"You don't wish to wear the necklace. Fair enough." Anabelle smiled impishly. "You needn't be so polite about it, Serena. We'll just wait and see if Gerald does as he should."

Suddenly she winced, and cradled her belly with her arm. "Do you mind if I sit? I vow that Joshua's son is already practicing his skylarking, with me as the rigging."

Hastily Serena guided her to the armchair nearest the fire, and Anabelle sank into it with a grateful sigh, propping her tiny slippered feet onto the footstool before her.

"Is there anything I can fetch you?" asked Serena with concern. "Some tea or a glass of the cordial?"

"Oh, no, I shall be well enough, or so the midwives tell me." She took Serena's hand in hers and winked, gently tugging her downward to a more confidential level in a rustle of silk damask. "Of course, you shall soon be in the way to discover that for yourself, won't you? Our two families together seem to be most prodigiously accomplished in that area."

Serena looked down at the floorboards, wishing her wicked thoughts hadn't so readily supplied an image to go with Anabelle's words. She had tried hard to forget the wanton way she'd behaved with Gerald; there seemed so little point now in remembering it.

"You speak for Joshua and yourself," she said stiffly. "There is no assurance that matters would be—be the same with anyone else."

"Nonsense. The Crosbies are as randy and fertile as stoats in a hedgerow, and from what Joshua has told me I doubt the Fairbournes are much better. Or would that be worse?" Anabelle's laughter bubbled merrily. "But at least all this brings me neatly to what Joshua tells me I must say next. You will probably think me meddling again, especially considering the circumstances of this wedding, yet since you have no mother or grandmother, I fear that the task has dropped into my lap by default. Or rather where my lap would be if I still had one."

She patted Serena's hand, her own plump fingers heavy with rings. "I'm not sure what the custom is here in the colonies, and though I am very certain that Gerald will be an affectionate and inventive—*most* inventive, from what I've gathered—husband, I know there might be certain questions you might wish explained, or—or—oh, folderol, Serena, is there anything you don't understand about what women and men do to amuse one other?"

Mortified, Serena could only manage a muffled noise that passed for no. She'd spent her childhood on a farm, and if the bull and his cows hadn't provided example enough, then Mistress Cullen had been ready to fill in the details through her unflagging speculation into her neighbors' lives. But it was quite another thing altogether to hear of such private matters discussed as lighthearted fact by Anabelle, who was not only four years younger than Serena, but also Gerald's sister and Joshua's wife.

"Ah, so I *was* right," said Anabelle with satisfaction. "I told Joshua you weren't a complete noddy about men. I don't believe women are even a quarter as dullwitted that way as gentlemen wish them to be. *They* may call it innocence, but it really is a kind of unobservant stupidity. And with Gerald as your lover, why, that certainly won't—"

"He's not my lover," said Serena, her voice still muffled. "He never has been."

Anabelle paused, and blinked. "Well, he most certainly will be after tonight. One's husband can be one's lover, you know, just as one's lover can be one's husband. Yes. And most fortunate it is, too, considering—"

"He's not my lover because he doesn't love me," said Serena as she bowed her head, curling into her own misery. Without Mary, she'd had no one to confide in except for Abel, and though he was an excellent listener, he wasn't able to offer much advice in return. She didn't know why she was telling this to Anabelle now, when nothing could be changed, but once she'd begun she felt the unhappiness spilling out of her as fast as she could find the words.

"He never has loved me," she said in a rush, "or even pretended to, and—oh, Anabelle, this is all so *wrong!*"

"Oh, my poor Serena," said Anabelle softly. "This may not be what you expected your lot to be, but things are not so very bad as they might seem. Do you believe that Joshua and I did not have our share of misunderstandings before we wed? La, the tales I could tell you! But sometimes, you know, wrongs can be turned and refashioned into a very fine right."

"What can possibly be right about being forced to marry a man who hates me?"

"Oh, pish." Anabelle clucked her tongue. "Gerald doesn't hate you, not in the least. In fact I believe he cares for you rather a great deal, else I would not have let

Joshua take things this far. I do not know how I was so blind as not to see it from the beginning, but when I consider how often he has come to your defense, why, I believe he has always had an admiration for you."

"Admiration isn't love," said Serena, her voice taut with all the emotions she'd kept bound up these last weeks, "and even if he once thought—thought kindly of me, he doesn't any longer. Now he only blames me for this—this foolish wedding."

"The only foolish part of it is Gerald himself," said Anabelle. "How can he believe that you'd go through all this simply to trap him into marriage? He is hardly such a wondrous catch himself."

"But he is!" cried Serena. "Gerald is charming and brave and handsome and kind and clever and—and he makes me laugh!"

"Does he now?" Anabelle smiled, but without any of her usual merriment. "Then there is a certain *attraction* on your part as well. I am glad; you both deserve that much. But no man likes to have his hand forced, and Gerald believes himself most barbarously ill used. You'll have to be strong if you're to persuade him that—oh, Joshua, is it time already?"

Serena rose quickly to her feet, self-consciously smoothing her skirts before she turned to face her brother where he stood in the doorway. He, too, was elegantly dressed for the wedding in a brass-buttoned coat of dark green superfine with waistcoat and breeches to match, his black hair sleeked back into an oversized bow. In any other circumstances Serena would have gazed at him with considerable pride, a collective pride in their family that would have pleased him nearly as much as it did her. But today he was focusing only on Anabelle, almost as if Serena weren't there at all.

"You're needed below, Anabelle," he said gruffly. "Some desperate riddle about the punch that only you can solve. Come, give me your arm and I'll see you there."

"If only I can solve this riddle," said Anabelle as she

brushed aside his hand and instead struggled clumsily to her feet by herself, "then only I shall go. Oh, stop fussing, sweetheart, I can manage perfectly well. Better you stay here and tell your sister how lovely she looks before you bring her downstairs."

She sailed from the room with surprising grace, leaving Joshua behind with Serena. With a deep sigh and obvious reluctance, he forced himself finally to look at her, beginning with the hem of her gown and slowly rising upward until at last he reached her face. Though his face revealed nothing, he nodded once with curt approval.

"Anabelle's done well by you, Serena," he said, the first words he'd spoken to her in two weeks. "She's managed to make you look like a lady, even if you can't behave like one. At least you won't shame me today."

"I never meant to shame you before, either," said Serena, her bitterness giving her the backbone she needed. "It's you who have made things so much worse by insisting upon this feather-brained wedding."

"Oh, aye," he countered, bristling defensively, "and I'll warrant I was the one rolling about on the bed with my petticoat rucked up like some common harlot?"

At his tone, Abel growled a low warning and came to stand close beside Serena.

"See now, you've upset Abel," she said, bending to rest her hand on the dog's head. "Isn't that so, pup?"

"I've half a mind to upset his wretched carcass down the stairs! Why in blazes didn't he growl like that at Crosbie, eh?"

She flushed, but stood her ground. "I know I erred, Joshua, but do I have to pay for one mistake for the rest of my life? Is that what you wish for me?"

"I wish you'd never behaved like such a damned slattern." He sighed uncomfortably and raked his fingers back through his hair. "It was bad enough to watch what Crosbie did to poor Oliver, cutting him out that way for sport, but damnation, Serena, you were the one who left me no choice. The damage is done, and now you must marry him. And I'm damned sorry about it, too. Crosbie's hardly the man I would have chosen for you."

"You chose his sister quickly enough!"

He frowned, clearly taken aback. Serena had never once spoken against Anabelle, and it was a measure of her desperation that she'd dare do it now.

"Then let me ask you the same thing I asked myself before I wed Anabelle," he said, so clearly searching for the right words. "Do you love him, lass? Oh, aye, love can grow between married folk—I've learned that well with my little wife—but there must be something there to start, or no more will follow."

Serena swallowed hard. She'd never doubted that Joshua loved Anabelle with all his heart, but to hear him say so now was enough to make her weep. "Oh, Josh, I don't—"

"Do you love Gerald Crosbie?" he asked again, more urgently. "Anabelle swears you do, but I would hear it from you myself. Do you love him, Serena?"

"I do," she whispered sadly. "God help me, Josh, but I do."

"I am glad." He reached out to take her hand, patting it self-consciously. "Then it will be up to me to see that Gerald's brought in line, eh? The two men I've had watching him will remain as long as you—"

"You've had Gerald *watched?*" Serena stared at her brother, aghast that he'd made Gerald as much his prisoner as she'd been herself. How could he speak of love in the same breath?

But Joshua's frown only deepened. "Aye, and why shouldn't I? You know as well as I that otherwise he would have run the first chance he had."

"No," she said softly. "I didn't."

And she hadn't. Somehow she'd managed to nourish a last tiny hope that Gerald, though pushed at first, had ultimately agreed to marry her of his own free will. It had been an exceptionally tiny hope, and an irrational one at that, but it wasn't until now that she realized how important that tiny hope had been to her during these last, long nights and days alone.

She stared down at her hands, at the thin silk ribbons that Anabelle had tied in bows so charmingly around her wrists. Silk bows and broken dreams: was that all that fate had set before her? Or was this what Anabelle had meant about trying to make right from wrongs? Though she'd tried so very hard to deny it, she still cared for Gerald, cared for him more than she'd ever cared for another man, and before her brother had blundered in between them, she'd dared to hope that Gerald might care for her in return. It wasn't much to build a marriage upon, especially one that neither of them had sought, but what else, really, did she have?

She took a deep breath and lifted her gaze to meet her brother's. "You must send them away," she said, her voice trembling only a bit. "Those two men, Joshua. You must send them away."

"Why the devil would I—"

"Because if I must marry Gerald, I want him to stay from choice," she said carefully, "and not from force."

"But I don't see how—"

"Because I asked, Josh." She reached out to rest her hand upon his arm. "All my life you've taken care of me. Nowhere under heaven is there a better brother, and I thank you for it, Joshua—I thank you, oh, so much! But it's past time that I began looking after myself, and if I don't start now I may never learn how."

"You shouldn't have to look after yourself," said Joshua gruffly. "You're a woman, and you're my sister. You're my responsibility until you're wed, and then the task falls to your husband."

"And what a trial I've been, haven't I?" she asked forlornly. She wished there were some way to make him understand what she meant, but Joshua being Joshua, she doubted such a way existed. "I've never asked for much from you, but this—this I will ask. Please take your men away, and let Gerald and me begin by ourselves."

Joshua looked at her hard, considering, then let out a long sigh of capitulation. "Very well, lass," he said as he gave her fingers a final squeeze. "If you wish that much to be alone with the rascal, then alone you shall be. But I warn you, if he bolts, I'll have him hauled back to Appledore in chains, and nothing you or Anabelle could say would make me do otherwise."

"You won't have to." Serena smiled, and wished she didn't feel so close to weeping as he began to lead her toward the stairs. "And thank you, Josh. For everything."

"Hah." He fumbled uncomfortably with his neckcloth. "Crosbie don't deserve you, Serena."

"Oh, no, Joshua," she said softly. "I rather hope he does."

"Doesn't put you much in mind of our dear brother Johnny's wedding, does it?" said Gerald as he bent to kiss his sister's cheek. "No carriage drawn by snow-white steeds, nor scores of bridesmaids and pages to trip over, nor hothouse flowers covering every inch of the chapel. No chapel at all, in fact."

"Oh, hush, Gerald," scolded Anabelle over her fan, "don't fluster me any more than I already am. Third sons don't merit white horses and pages, especially third sons who can't keep their breeches buttoned around respectable virgin ladies. Besides, my front parlor is a great deal less drafty than the chapel at Kilmarsh, and your bride is a great deal more comely. Think of that plain, wheezing creature that poor John had to wed, simply because she was a duke's daughter."

"Don't pity him, Nan," said Gerald absently. "As I recall, he found consolation enough in her dowry."

He straightened and looked around the room. True, there were no hothouse flowers, but Anabelle had managed to make the parlor surprisingly festive with swags of evergreen and white bows across the doorways. Across the hall in the dining room the table was covered with porcelain dishes of sweetmeats and biscuits, and crowned by the wedding cake itself, sitting high on a throne of tiered silver platters that was draped with white paper chains. Though it was still afternoon, Anabelle had ordered the candles lit, too—a great extravagance—to make all the silver sparkle more and fill the air with the sweet smell of beeswax.

"Besides, I didn't mean to fluster you, Nan," he said as he linked his hands behind his waist. "You've managed to make things quite properly festive, even without snow-white steeds."

"I shall take that as praise, even if I'm not certain it was so intended." She jabbed him with her fan. "But considering the circumstances, a parlor wedding is much more suitable than one in the meetinghouse, and this way Dr. Townsend was willing to overlook crying the banns and such. And, of course, because it was Joshua doing the asking."

Gerald nodded. He was glad the ceremony wasn't in a church, too, but for entirely different reasons.

She pursed her lips, studying him. "You're vastly cheerful this day, Duckie," she said suspiciously. "It's not like you, or rather it's like the way you used to be, but not how you've been lately."

He smiled benignly. "It's a cheerful occasion, Nan. I am merely doing my best to rise to the appropriate level of cheerfulness."

She was going to be furious with him. That much was certain. So furious, in fact, that he wondered if he'd be leaving Appledore before her baby was born, perhaps even in time to reach Naples in July.

He gazed out among the well-dressed guests who were arriving in pairs and in groups, his smile still firmly in place. They were all going to be furious with him, but there wasn't any other way around that. The idea had come to him this morning, while Rourke had dressed him for the final time, and the simple logic of it nearly stunned him.

If he didn't *want* to be married—which he most assuredly didn't—all he had to do was say so. When the minister asked him, he would refuse, politely, but firmly. Not even Joshua Fairbourne could make him do otherwise, not before a whole crowd of guests. If Fairbourne had been less intent on playing the genteel country squire, then he might have simply had his two seafaring henchmen beat Gerald to a near-senseless point of acquiescence, but Appledore's most successful sea captain couldn't do that, not and keep his hard-won position in this priggish little community. The look on Joshua's face when he realized he'd lost would be a sight Gerald intended to savor, and one he was anticipating, too.

But he didn't feel quite the same sense of justice served where Serena was concerned. No matter how hard he tried to argue with himself that she'd betrayed him, that she'd shown her loyalty lay with her brother and not with him, that every spinster's goal was to trap a man into marrying her, and no matter how rich and indignant his outrage became, he still couldn't make himself blame Serena the way he should in order to escape cleanly.

Lord knows he was trying. But instead in his mind he kept seeing her face and hearing her laughter and touching her skin and kissing her again and again and again, and the blame he needed to rationalize his actions evaporated like mist in the morning. He sighed, shaking his head at his own weakness. He would just have to keep reminding himself of the consequences, that was all. Summer in Appledore couldn't possibly compare to the warm-weather delights of Naples. Concentrate on the sorry state of perpetual bondage and misery that was matrimony for a man, and ignore how much—how appallingly much—he'd miss Serena Fairbourne.

"There, now that looks more like the familiar gloom

and grump we've been favored with lately," said Anabelle. "Faith, Duckie, I was beginning to worry."

"Never on my account," murmured Gerald, striving to recompose his features so that his thoughts might follow. "But who are all these persons, Nan? Some I've met at your table, I know, but there's a good many new faces, too. Don't tell me the bride has such a vast acquaintance."

"Hardly that." Anabelle craned her neck to better see around the room. "We've guests from the entire county. Most of these belong to Joshua, though perhaps a few of Serena's are scattered about."

"There's one in particular I don't see," he said, scanning the faces to be sure. For himself it didn't matter, but for Serena's sake, he'd hoped she have at least one friend here. "A young widow named Mary Sears. Considering how close she and Serena are, I'm surprised she's not among the party."

"Well, you shouldn't be!" said Anabelle, scandalized. "I don't care how close Serena may be to Mary Sears. She wouldn't set foot in this house, not even for Serena's sake."

"I'll grant that she seemed a bit common, true," said Gerald, remembering Mary's dingy existence in the house that smelled like sheep, "but that's not reason to—"

"No, no, no!" exclaimed Anabelle. "It's her choice, not ours, on account of what her husband did to Joshua! Oh, I disremember his name now—this all happened before I arrived, you see—but the man was one of Joshua's privateering officers back during the last war. Joshua trusted him enough that he made him master of a prize crew on one of the ships they'd captured, with orders to take it into port."

"No sin in that," said Gerald mildly. This was good; privateering tales were a first-rate diversion from his own misadventures. "Unless you take offense to having privateers in your family, which I suppose you, Nan, by practice, do not."

Anabelle swatted him again with her fan. "Will you let me finish? Mr. Sears behaved very badly. He and his crew became so roaring drunk on the brandy in the hold that they let the ship run up on the rocks, a total loss, and most of the prisoners dead, too, trapped and drowned where they'd been chained below. It was a great scandal for Joshua, and though he still will not have Mr. Sears mentioned in his hearing, he has tried his best to make things comfortable for his widow. But Mary has refused it all from sheer, stubborn pride, and so she would never come here, even if we begged. Faith, Duckie, how completely out of breath I am!"

"No sin in that, either," said Gerald, this time prepared to dodge the jabbing fan. "Nor remarkable, considering how you—"

"Hush, hush!" exclaimed Anabelle excitedly, pushing herself up to her feet to see better. "Quickly now, you must go stand over there, near the window, beside Dr. Townsend! Here comes Joshua with Serena!"

Obediently he turned to join the minister, going against the sea of faces eager for their first glimpse of the bride. Dr. Townsend was a small, gaunt man dressed in black below an over-large snuff wig, and though he bowed solemnly to Gerald, he, too, quickly turned his interest to the others coming through the doorway. Gerald sighed weightily, accepting his lot as the far less interesting groom, twitched at his cuffs one last time with more nervousness than he'd ever admit, and then, finally, turned to face Serena.

The last time he'd seen her she'd been at her brother's side, too, but there was nothing else in her appearance today to remind him of that night. She scarcely looked like Serena at all, at least Serena the way he thought she should look. Instead she was the very model of a fine London lady, a paragon of enticing perfection from the pointed tips of her satin slippers to the wired flowers in her sugar-stiffened hair. Like a butterfly from a cocoon, she'd wrapped herself in spun silk and emerged a fashionable beauty. Dressed like this, she would have turned the heads—no, more likely she would have snapped them clear around—of every blade and lecher at court, and left them panting in her wake. He knew, because six months ago, had she appeared like this in London, he would have been first among her admirers. He saw Anabelle's touch in every ruffle and furbelow, every pat of masklike face powder, and he would have to admire how expertly she'd managed to coax such a stylish effect from colonial seamstresses and mantua makers, especially in such a short time.

And he hated every last wretched stitch and ribbon and bit of whalebone stay. Serena belonged in linsey-woolsey petticoats and simple bodices she'd sewn for herself, the hems bedraggled with seawater and sand and sprinkled with a good measure of black dog hairs. He wanted to see her again with her red cloak over her shoulders, the hood slipping back, her hair tousled and tugging against her hairpins and dotted with snowflakes like tiny sparkling diamonds. He longed for the healthy rose that the wind from water brought to her cheeks, and the glow that came to her lips after he'd kissed her. That was the way he'd always see her, his Serena, and not this stiff, laced fashion-doll of a woman.

The only problem was that she wasn't *his* Serena any more. Maybe she never had been. Now she was Miss Serena Fairbourne, and in another quarter of an hour, unless he said otherwise, she would also be his wife.

He was vaguely aware of Dr. Townsend speaking, his voice as dry and distant as if he stood on a hillside instead of three feet before him. Joshua Fairbourne had become nothing more than the man who passed Serena's hand to his own, and then vanished from this curious unreality. Someone asked Gerald questions and he answered, though he had no more notion than an automaton might as to what he'd been asked or what he'd replied. All that mattered to him now was Serena beside him, her fingers chilly and damp in his hand, with as little life to them as her profile. He had never seen her this pale, as if she'd no blood left within her, and he prayed it was only Anabelle's powder. So pale, and so still; only the silk flowers on their wires in her hair trembled and quivered.

Damnation, what had they done to her?

"Serena?" he whispered, heedless of Townsend's grave, portentous drone, and so softly that only she could hear. "Serena dear?"

And at last she turned to him, her eyes so wide that he felt himself tumbling head-first into her gaze. She *was* still there, his Serena, and the realization swept through him with a wild joy. But the joy was short-lived, for in her eyes he discovered something else, too: that the woman who'd shouted at him in the fog, who'd challenged drunken sailors in the street, and who'd even dared to face down Rourke, was now frightened.

Very, very frightened.

"The ring, sir," said Dr. Townsend, with enough emphasis to make Gerald suspect he'd already asked at least once. "You have a ring for the lady?"

"The ring," repeated Gerald blankly. There was no ring, and the flippant remark about its absence that he'd made to Rourke last night echoed in his ears with unfortunate clarity. He looked again at Serena. There was no way he could abandon her the way he'd planned, not now, and he didn't stop to wonder why his feelings had changed so abruptly. Instead he pulled off the gold signet ring with the Crosbie crest that he'd worn since he was fourteen and slipped it carefully over Serena's finger. It didn't come close to fitting, the heavier part with the crest swinging downward on her extended finger, glinting in the sunlight from the window behind her.

Dr. Townsend cleared his throat. "If you please, sir," he said. "With this ring . . ."

"With this ring," repeated Gerald with dutiful haste. He curled Serena's fingers toward her palm to keep the ring from dropping off, and let his hand linger over hers. Her hand seemed warmer now, and he was glad of it.

"I thee wed."

"I thee . . . wed." The awful finality of what he'd just done came sweeping over him like a wave born of a hurricane. He had only wanted to take the fear from Serena's eyes, to bring back the Serena he'd grown so fond of, and now God help him, he was *married*.

She was squeezing his hand, drawing him closer, her eyes bright as she lifted her lips to his to be kissed. "Oh, Gerald," she whispered as she hugged him close. "I was so afraid you wouldn't have me."

Thirteen

Serena rested her head against Gerald's shoulder and stared dreamily up at the stars and the curving sliver of new moon. It felt strange indeed to be riding in Anabelle's two-wheeled gig along the path to home that she always walked, nearly as strange as to be doing it in the company of her new husband. The gig bumped and rocked, the horse and the driver together struggling gamely with the rutted path, but Serena didn't care. There wasn't a single cloud in the night sky, and already her marriage was succeeding far, far better than she'd ever dared hope.

She curled her fingers more tightly into Gerald's simply for the pleasure of feeling him squeeze hers in return. It had been his idea for her to leave off her customary mitten on her right hand, and to keep it warm he'd tucked hers linked with his into the pocket of his coat. True, it was a simple gesture, but exactly the kind of small, thoughtful notion that made Gerald so easy for her to love.

And she did love him. Not until she'd seen him again,

standing there so gravely beside Dr. Townsend, had she understood how much that love had become a part of her. It had been one thing to tell Joshua and Anabelle that she would do all she could to make this marriage work, but it had been quite another to see Gerald again, and to realize the precarious reality of her challenge. He *was* a proud man, one who'd been ill-used. She hadn't needed Anabelle to tell her that, especially not after she'd seen the stern set to his handsome face. She'd been terrified she'd do or say the wrong thing and drive him away, that he'd drop her hand and walk through the door and take away forever the promise of love from her life.

But to her great wonder, Gerald hadn't. He'd taken her hand as if he'd wanted nothing else more in the world, and he'd given her his own ring to seal his vows. What more could she want? If he'd been unusually quiet during the long party after the ceremony, why, that was understandable. There'd been an endless succession of toasts, enough to make most of the male guests exceptionally warm and loud in their good wishes while the women passed her from one to another with whispered advice on everything from the best way to whiten linen to how to keep a new husband from wandering among the Water Street doxies. A fiddler brought from one of Joshua's ships to play reels and jigs had raised everyone's spirits, and their voices with them, even higher, the revelry going far into the night.

No wonder Gerald had been quiet, for she'd been quiet, too, overwhelmed by everything that was happening to her. No, to *them*. That was how she must think now, not of herself, but of Gerald as her husband and herself as his wife, and she grinned to herself again in amazement.

"Are you cold?" he asked, his voice low so that they wouldn't be overheard by the driver.

"No, not at all." She laughed softly. "I suppose if I'm shivering against you it's from being so happy. I don't seem to be able to hold myself still."

"I won't argue with that," he said, though he pulled

the fur-lined carriage robe higher over her knees. She was still wearing her wedding gown, and silk brocade was seldom chosen for its warmth against an early spring night. "A wife that moves is to be preferred to one that resembles a corpse."

"I should hope so," she said, giggling a bit. Though she'd been alone with him many times before, this was different, and if she were honest she'd admit that her shivering, and her giggling, came from nervousness as well. "But do you feel that way, too, Gerald, or is it only me?"

"Only you how?"

She couldn't make out his expression in the dark, nor did his voice betray his feelings. "Only me nothing. I wanted to know—that is, I was wondering if you were happy, too?"

"Ah, so it's my happiness that worries you," he said lightly, the same lightness she knew he often used to hide behind. "What kind of sorry excuse for a bridegroom would ever admit to being unhappy on his wedding day?"

"I don't know," she said, suddenly finding it all too easy to sit still. "My experience with any kind of bridegroom is limited to you."

"And a good thing it is, too. I hadn't fancied you to be the merry widow with a score of cast-off husbands mouldering in your past. Here we are, pet, away from the crush and home at last."

He jumped down as soon as the gig had come to a stop, holding his arms up to lift her to the ground. The sureness of his hands around her waist and the gallant flourish with which he swung her through the air, her petticoats fluttering over the hoops, made her gasp, and nearly made her forget her uneasiness.

Nearly, but not quite.

He kept his hand at her waist as he guided her through the little gate and up the path of crushed clam shells to her house while the driver turned the gig around to return to town. It felt odd, too, not to have Abel bounding ahead of them, but for tonight he'd been left behind with Joshua and Anabelle. The ground was at last beginning to thaw, and the heels of Serena's shoes sank slightly in the crushed shells.

"Spring's almost here," she said, striving for a bit of lightness herself as Gerald unlocked the house. "I can smell it in the air. You will not believe the difference that spring makes on Cranberry Point, Gerald. Almost overnight everything will turn the brightest green you've ever seen. Even the sea seems to turn a brighter blue."

"The same thing happens in Ireland," he said as he pushed the door open for her. "I've always maintained that Kilmarsh is the grandest place on earth for springtime, so you must offer your best to convince me otherwise."

"You'll see for yourself when—oh! *Oh!*"

Though she hadn't been home in two weeks, someone else had visited the house, and recently, too. A well-laid fire crackled in the hearth, taking the chill from the air, with a neat pile of split wood beside it to keep it burning the night through. More of the same white paper chains that had decorated Joshua's and Anabelle's house were festooned across the tops of the windows, and twin porcelain bowls of fresh-rubbed potpourri on the mantelpiece made the room redolent of last summer's roses. The table had been set for two with a light supper— sliced ham, bread with butter, oranges, and more of the little white-iced wedding cakes—with a bottle of brandy ready to be poured and the candles waiting to be lit.

"My dear sister Nan," said Gerald softly as he brushed his fingertips across one of the white paper chains. "For such a small and foolish creature, she can be most remarkably busy, can't she?"

"I won't hear a single word spoken against her, not tonight," said Serena as she draped her cloak over the back of a chair. She sifted the potpourri through her fingers, realizing how much the scent, with its undercurrents of jasmine orange, reminded her of Anabelle herself, and once again today she found her eyes glazed with tears. She might not have been blessed with a sister of her own, but surely there could never be another to rival the one that Joshua had brought her through marriage. "I cannot believe all she's done."

"You've done your share of good deeds on her behalf, Serena," he said, hanging his coat and hat upon the peg near the door with an offhanded familiarity that renewed Serena's hopes. Would he let himself be so comfortable in her home—no, *their* home; she must be sure to remember that—if there were any problems?

"Mind, I'm not saying Nan doesn't deserve it," he continued as he used a twig from the kindling barrel to light the candles on the table, "but she showed me that veritable mountain of baby things you'd sewn for her."

"Oh, 'twas nothing," said Serena quickly as she turned away from him, almost ashamed that he'd seen her handiwork. If Anabelle was any example, few fine ladies in his world bothered with such mundane things as sewing swaddling bands for infants. "Anabelle has so much else to do, while I—oh, Gerald, *look!*"

The candlelight had reached into the corners of the room and over her bedstead, and now she could see what Anabelle's orders had done there, too. Gone were Serena's well-worn—and frugally well-mended—bed sheets, and in their place were new linens bleached as white as fresh snow, with wide ribbons to tie the biers closed on the bolsters and the pillows. As white as snow, and as deep as a snow drift, too, on account of the new featherbed that was piled high upon the mattress. The coverlet had been turned down in invitation, with a bouquet of dried lavender placed carefully in the center. Laid across the edge of the featherbed was the final gift, the most beautiful bed gown Serena had ever seen. The white linen was so fine as to be nearly sheer, with pale pink ribbons threaded through the casings at the neck and the wrists and a froth of lace on the cuffs. With a little cry of delight Serena swept it up from the bed, and only then did she see the tiny monogram cross-stitched at the neckline in pink: SFC.

"Have you ever seen anything so lovely?" she said, holding the gown close to her body to show Gerald. "Do you know I've never had a gown just for sleeping?"

"No?" He paused with the brandy bottle in his hand. "Nary a one?"

She flushed. "I mean that I've always slept in my shift, not that I went to bed in—in nothing."

"Ah, well." He poured the brandy into the two glasses. "But I would guess that from the appearance of that particular gown, Anabelle has no expectations of you *sleeping* in it, either. And you must have noticed she provided not even the hint of a nightshirt for me, doubtless assuming that I, too, shall have found some more entertaining way to keep warm."

Serena's flush deepened, her fingers tightening into the fine linen. She told herself that such talk was entirely proper now that they were wed, but from Gerald it still sounded far more wicked than proper, and she felt her heart begin to beat faster in a way that surely wasn't proper at all.

"Would you like me to change?" she asked shyly. " 'Tis very late, you know."

"Must be nearly ten by the clock," he said slowly, his gaze lingering upon the bed gown in her hands as he sipped the brandy. "At the very least."

She decided he meant yes, and modestly turned away from him to begin unfastening her gown. This was one of the things she should have asked Anabelle: were wives supposed to undress in the plain sight of their husbands, or would it have been more seemly for her to retreat up the ladder to the sleeping loft and return when she'd changed? But the loft would be very cold at this time of night, and the climb up the narrow ladder almost impossible in hoops, and so she stayed where she was, beside the bed, and painfully aware of Gerald sitting at the table behind her.

Anabelle and one of her maidservants had helped her dress earlier, and now, on her own in the half-light, she found her fingers stumbling over the unfamiliar rows of hooks down the front of the bodice. It didn't help that she was nervous as well, and she felt that by the time she'd finally unfastened the ribbons that held the skirts to her bodice and let the gown drop with a silken *woosh* to her feet, another hour must have passed. Carefully she stepped from the brocade puddle, laying the gown across a chest, and then untied the tapes that held the whalebone cage of her hoops, letting them, too, drop to the floor. She was glad to have the hoops off; she'd felt wide and clumsy as a barrel in them, and with a sigh of relief she now reached around her back to unlace her stays.

These stays had been bought specially for the gown, the neat rows of whalebone beneath the brocade cover fashionably and painfully unyielding to give Serena's body the correct flat front with her breasts forced high, a narrow back, and a tiny waist. Unlike the plain linen stays she wore for everyday, these laced up the back instead of the front, the assumption being that any lady who wore them had a maid to help her dress.

And to undress, realized Serena unhappily as she twisted and wriggled to try to untie the knot that Anabelle had used for securing the lacing cord through the top eyelet. How wretchedly foolish she must look to Gerald as she writhed about, unable to free herself from her own clothes! With a final, exasperated effort, she muttered one of Joshua's best oaths, and came to stand before Gerald, her cheeks bright with exertion and embarrassment.

"Difficulties, pet?" he asked solicitously, though his smile proved he was amused enough by her struggles.

"You don't have to laugh," she said indignantly. "I know how I must look, wriggling about like a fish on a hook. Except that instead of a hook, I'm trapped in these infernal stays, standing here like a ninny in my shift and shoes."

" 'Ninny' is not the word I would have chosen, no," he said softly, his eyes shadowed in the firelight. "Enticing, perhaps. Engaging, definitely. Altogether very . . . charming."

"You will not help me then?" she asked rebelliously, not sure if he were teasing or not. "You would rather watch me dangle on my whalebone hook?"

"Oh, hush, of course I'll help you," he said with a monumental sigh. "I am not so purposelessly cruel as all that. But I was enjoying myself in the meantime. I won't lie and deny it. You have very pretty legs for a fish. Now come, my pretty little codfish, and let's see how thoroughly trapped you are."

She took a single step closer. "I believe I should rather be called a mermaid again than a codfish."

"Then mermaid it shall be." She was still not near enough to please him, and he reached for both her hands to draw her forward to where he sat, holding her close between his knees. "Now turn about, Mistress Mermaid, and we'll see how best to rescue you from your distress."

He smiled up at her, but his voice was strangely hoarse, without any of the lazy invitation he'd always shown with her before. Gently his hands slid from her wrists to settle on her hips, below the stiffened tabs of her stays. Through the thin linen of her shift she could feel the warmth of his palms, of his fingers spreading to caress her ever so slightly, and her heart quickened with excitement mingled with uncertainty. This was the first time he'd touched her since they'd been alone together in the house, and with that first caress came the reality of what being married to him might mean.

"You're trembling again," he asked softly, looking up to meet her gaze, his eyes so dark they seemed nearly black. He wasn't smiling any longer.

"I can't help it." Her own smile wobbled; she was in uncharted waters now, and he was her only guide. "I told you before. You do that to me."

"Ah, so I'm guilty once more." He turned her then, her back now toward him to better reach her stays.

His hands left her hips to untangle the knotted cord, and she sighed softly, though whether from relief or from loss she didn't know. She wondered if she knew anything, really, where Gerald was concerned. She'd thought her discomfiture would be easier to bear this way, not having to meet his gaze, but instead she found her mind all too willing to provide the images her eyes didn't see. Even the lightest brush of his fingertips across her shoulder blades was enough to send a fresh shiver of sensation down her spine, and unconsciously she closed her eyes to shut out everything else.

"There," he said after a moment, and she felt the knot tug and slip apart. "No challenge to that."

But though the knot was gone, he didn't continue to loosen the cord down through all the eyelets so she could slip the stays over her head, the way it was usually done. Instead he pulled the cord completely through the top eyelet, and then the next, and the next, with slow and infinite care. With each eyelet, she felt her body freed from the rigid whalebone, growing softer and more responsive, until, at last, he'd drawn the cord through the last eyelet and the unlaced stays hung loosely over her shift from the shoulder straps alone. She didn't move; she wasn't sure she could, waiting in tantalizing anticipation for whatever he'd do next.

Yet still when he reached up to pull the first pin from her hair she caught her breath with surprise. One by one he drew out first the pins, and then the silk flowers and their wires, until the heavy weight of her perfumed hair tumbled freely over her shoulders. He ran his fingers through the thick waves, and she let her head tip back in response, swaying back into his arms, against his chest. She heard him groan as he pulled her closer, sliding his hands between her stays and her shift and burying his face in her hair.

"Oh, Serena," he murmured, his cheek rough against her bare shoulder. "You shouldn't be letting me do this."

"I'm not *letting* you do anything," she said with breathless distraction. "You are—*ahhh*—simply helping me undress."

"Then *we* should not be doing this."

She smiled to herself, touched by his consideration for her inexperience, and she thought again of how endlessly lucky she was to have him for a husband. *"We* haven't done much of anything, Gerald," she said shyly. "You haven't even kissed me yet."

"Lord, if it were only that simple." To her surprise he gently pushed her away, letting his hands drop to his sides. "Look at me, Serena. The game we're playing now is as dangerous as the one your friend Captain Parrish was playing with his new pistols. If we continue like this, we'll both be ruined."

She turned to stare at him, bewildered. "But how can I—how can *we*—be ruined? We're married, husband and wife."

"And so we'll be forever doomed to remain if I carry you over to that bed and ravish you the way I want to." He closed his eyes for a moment and shook his head, clearly struggling with himself. "Damnation, Serena, do you think this is easy for me?"

She folded her arms tightly over the front of her stays to cover her breasts. "Gerald, you're making no sense."

"Then I'm not explaining it as well as I might." He sighed wearily, his face bleak. "I am flattered that you would worry so about my happiness, and you are very dear to try to put the best face on this whole ridiculous marriage, but we both know the truth of it, don't we? You've no more wish to be wed than I do."

"How can you say that after we've just—after we've almost—" She broke off unable to say more as her shame and misery grew.

"I still desire you, sweet," he said softly. "I always have, from the first. But if I do not leave you your maidenhead, then there'll be no question of an annulment."

"An annulment?" Like so many of Gerald's words, this one was unfamiliar, but she could guess its hard, hateful meaning. "But we are married, Gerald. We made vows before witnesses, before Dr. Townsend."

"Nothing that a clever lawyer or two in London

cannot undo, especially with the deed itself done by a country parson in the colonies."

"Dr. Townsend is not some 'country parson.' He is a good and wise gentleman, and he's the minister who baptized me when I was little, and now—now—oh, *damn* your annulment, Gerald Crosbie!"

"But I wouldn't suit you, Serena, not as a husband," said Gerald hurriedly, flinging his arms out in supplication as he rose to his feet. "I am selfish and shallow and far too easily beguiled by novelty, and I am very much set in my own habits. You're too good a woman to deserve a sorry rascal like me."

"That's a wretched coward's answer, and you know it!" she cried. "If I am brave enough to risk my life and my happiness on you, then you can at least be brave enough to give me an honest answer in return!"

She held out her hand with the heavy gold ring on her finger, kept there by the thread Anabelle had hastily wrapped around the band until a jeweler could size it. She had believed that with his ring he had given himself to her as well; now she found he'd given her nothing.

"You will want this back," she said, furiously trying to tug it from her finger. Her finger had swelled in the warmer room, and the ring stubbornly refused to yield. "It's no use to me now."

"No, Serena, you must keep it." He reached out to stop her from taking off the ring by covering her hand with his, but she jerked her hand free, still pulling at the ring as she backed away. "I want you to wear it."

"Why?" she demanded bitterly, her brother's predictions of Gerald's faithlessness echoing loud in her memory. "So that when you've vanished tomorrow, I can still prove to everyone who asked that you truly did exist?"

"I'm not leaving tomorrow," he said, so clearly surprised by her reaction that it hurt her all the more. "I've promised Anabelle that I'd stay until her babe is born, and I mean to do it."

"What of the promises you made to me, to be my husband?"

"I never meant for it to go so far, Serena," he said defensively. "It was your blasted brother that I wanted to show up for the overbearing idiot that he is. And when you told me that you wished never to marry, just as I had decided for myself, I believed you. How was I to know you'd changed your mind?"

Her mouth worked hard as she fought back her tears. "You changed my mind for me, Gerald. You were different from any other man I'd known, and because of that I'd dared hope we could be happy together. But I was wrong about you, wasn't I? Oh, God, how *wrong!*"

"Serena dear, please," he said, his expression as stunned as if she'd struck him with her hand. "I never wished to hurt you, never."

"But you did, Gerald," she whispered. "You *did.*"

She didn't know if it pleased her or not that he could not meet her gaze. Instead he sank back into the chair, letting his head drop forward into his hands with a groan.

"I swear by all that's holy that I meant to stop this foolishness earlier," he said, each word dragged from deep within him, "to free us both, the way we each wanted. But when I saw you again this day, and how frightened you were, I could not do it. I nigh lost all my wits, and I couldn't do it."

She didn't answer because she didn't understand. How could he have done what he had and believed he wouldn't hurt her? Her heart and her pride and her whole body hurt so much that she doubted she'd ever feel well again. She would never trust him, that was certain. How could she?

Yet the worst part of all was knowing that she loved him still, and, perhaps, that he loved her as well. Her pride told her she was a fool to even consider it, but the miserably confused proof was sitting there before her, his head cradled in his hands with a despair that matched her own.

If he really were the wicked, spoiled gentleman he

wanted her to believe him, he would have taken what she'd so innocently offered and used her the night through and left in the morning. He could have done it. There would have been no one to stop him, and a man with money could always disappear when he pleased, especially in the colonies. He would not have bothered with her feelings or felt as much remorse and guilt as he so clearly did. He wouldn't have cared about promises made to his sister. For that matter, he wouldn't have come clear to Massachusetts after her in the first place. He would have cared only about himself, and his own pleasures in Venice or Paris or whatever other foreign place he'd be instead.

But Gerald wasn't that wicked, not by half. She wouldn't have fallen in love with him in the first place if he had been. He'd hurt her, true, but he'd been hurt and betrayed first by Joshua and, though wrongly, by her, his pride as wounded as her own was now. In a roundabout way he *was* behaving honorably. He might protest that he didn't wish to be married, but he wanted her to keep wearing his ring and to stay here and to let the world believe it was so, at least for the last month or so before his sister was brought to childbed. For that time, at least, he was willing to be hers.

She sighed, and stopped pulling at the ring. Perhaps this was what Anabelle had meant about making him understand that he loved her. A month was not very long to try to heal all the wounds that they'd given each other, but the alternative was losing him completely and forever. And what was a month compared to that?

"You cannot go back to town," she said, her voice wooden. "If my brother hears of this, he will kill you outright."

Slowly Gerald raised his head to look at her, his eyes empty. She had never seen a man's face change so completely, or drain so entirely of any life, any animation, and if her own heart hadn't ached so badly she might have pitied him.

But not tonight. "You can sleep in one of my brothers' beds, in the loft. We can—we can talk more tomorrow, if you wish it."

"Tomorrow, then." He nodded and rose, taking the bottle of brandy with him. "You must believe me, Serena. I never wished to hurt you."

But as she lay curled alone in the cold, new sheets of her bed, crying herself to sleep, she wondered how much worse it could have been if he had.

Gerald woke slowly and with great unwillingness. His first recollection was of brandy: an ill-considered amount of brandy. His mouth felt as if he'd swallowed Appledore's entire north beach including all the wrack-weed and other random unsavory flotsam, and his head throbbed so grievously that it took all his concerted concentration to muster the effort to open his eyes. He squinted upward, groping unhappily toward that second recollection that would tell him where he was.

He was alone in the bed, which showed slight good judgment, but the bed itself was both unfamiliar and unfriendly, a coarse mattress filled with dry rushes that rustled most alarmingly beneath him and a pillow seemingly stuffed with the same sand that clogged his tongue. He had slept in his clothes, clothes that were now thoroughly rumpled and disreputable, though he had at some point removed his shoes and untied the queue in his hair.

More good judgment, he thought wryly. Given this morning's circumstances so far, he had the distinct feeling he should grasp at any goodness he could.

The low bedstead had neither a frame nor curtains, but the rough-hewn beams of a roof slanted upward not far above his face. Was he in some sort of garret, then, or attic? The space was musty and chilly and mercifully dim, without windows or a candle to offer any clues, but when he listened beyond the thumping in his head he could just make out the mewing cries of gulls on the other side of the roof, and closer, below him, the sound of a woman singing softly to herself.

Not just a woman, but Serena.

His *wife* Serena.

And the memory of where he was, and how he'd come to be there, and every other hideous detail of yesterday came crashing back upon him.

With a groan he covered his eyes with his forearm. The plan had all made so much sense when he'd first thought of it: causing an uproar at the wedding he didn't want, refusing to be married, walking out on all the Fairbournes—except his sister.

But one look at Serena's poor, frightened, and very dear face, and he'd had to scramble for a new plan to salvage his bachelorhood: a marriage in name only, abstinence, and an annulment would be his path back to London. Not as tidy, perhaps, but the result would be the same. He did not want a wife, and Serena did not want a husband. This way they'd both get their wish, and the only one to suffer would be her stiff-backed bully of a brother.

But again he hadn't counted upon Serena herself. Who would have guessed a woman like her would actually *want* to be married to someone like him? He certainly wouldn't have; nor would he have predicted that he'd behave like such an unspeakable idiot when she told him. He had rejected her outright, her love and her body and all her other wifely attributes. He'd discounted her marriage vows, something she clearly took most seriously, and he'd tried to make a fool of her brother. His only salvation would have been to grovel at her feet for forgiveness, and instead he'd stumbled off to this bed with a bottle of brandy for company.

He *was* an idiot. Who would argue? His one goal in all of this mess had been to leave Serena unharmed and unencumbered. And on both counts he had failed, failed so dismally that he hadn't the remotest idea of what to do next.

This was not altogether a bad thing, he decided grimly. Given how his other two plans had disintegrated, it was in fact perhaps something of a blessing.

He could not make out the words of the song she was singing, but the tune was sad, some lonely sailor's lament. On the day after her wedding she should have been singing a much merrier tune, but then that, too, was his fault.

He sighed wearily, remembering how happy and excited she'd been during their ride in the gig, and how pleased she'd been by the little niceties that Anabelle had arranged. He remembered, too, how she'd undressed before him, how innocently unaware she'd been of her effect upon him. All she would have had to do was to glance down at the front of his breeches, but she hadn't even known enough to do that. It was just as well he *hadn't* kissed her. Once she'd shed that overwrought gown she'd become breathtakingly seductive, her face aglow with eagerness and her satiny, scented body his for the taking. He couldn't name a woman he'd desired more, not in his entire life, or another whose company he enjoyed more. That is, though he didn't want a wife, he did want Serena.

And now, of course, he'd broken her heart.

High holy hell, but his head hurt.

With a muttered oath he forced himself to sit upright, swinging his legs over the side of the bed and staying there until the floorboards stopped spinning like a Catherine wheel beneath his feet. He fumbled for his watch in his waistcoat pocket, flipping it open with his thumb and tipping the face toward the small amount of light that filtered up from the ladder opening in the floor. Half-past nine, not nearly as bad as it might have been.

He rubbed his palm over his stubbled jaw, wishing he had Rourke standing ready with a razor and a basin of hot, soapy water, not to mention a steaming pot of coffee. Those things would have gone far to improve his day. But there was no hot water and no Rourke, either, and the best he could do was to swear halfheartedly again. He stuffed his feet into his shoes, brushed and straightened his coat as best he could, and headed backward down the narrow ladder, praying he wouldn't crash off the rungs in a wretched heap at Serena's feet.

"You're awake," she said with the Appledorian habit of observing the obvious. "And just in time, too."

"In time for what?" he asked warily, that sand beneath his tongue turning his voice to a rattling rasp. "And pray stop bustling about, Serena. So much motion is not natural at this hour."

She went instantly still, standing beside the table. Her face was pale and her eyes were red-rimmed from crying and ringed with gray circles of sleeplessness, and he despised himself all over again for having brought her to this.

"In time for breakfast, of course," she said, her sharpness a match for his. Sleeplessness hadn't improved her temper any more than it had his. "Whatever else would I mean?"

She was dressed once again in her everyday clothes, a woolen petticoat and a close-fitting linen shortgown with an apron pinned to the front, her hair braided neatly in a single coiled plait. He was glad. Not only did he find the tidy predictability of it comforting, but also because he'd come to associate such dress so much with her, he found it infinitely more seductive than the silk gown she'd worn yesterday.

Not that he was in any condition to act upon it this morning, even if his conscience would have let him.

She took a single step aside, turning the chair toward him with a thump so he could sit. It was the same high-backed armchair that he'd sat in last night when he'd unlaced her stays, and he wondered if her thoughts were turning down the same unruly path as his.

"Serena," he began, not sure what he'd say next. "Serena, perhaps we should—"

"I have ordered everything exactly to your liking," she said tartly, cutting him off before he could say something she wasn't ready to hear. "The four coddled eggs beside the ham, six thick slices of bread, toasted brown but not burned, and slathered with butter. I had to make do with my quiddany, not having any raspberry marmelade, and I've had my trials keeping the lumps from the Dublin oats—more fit for a horse than a gentleman, those oats—but I did put the treacle and the butter exactly in the center, in a little dip, if you'll but look."

He stared down with dismay at the enormous breakfast—*his* breakfast—arrayed before him. "Rourke?"

She nodded. "He told me you were most particular, and that if I wished—oh, blast, the coffee!"

She scurried to the hearth, coming back with the heavy pewter pot carefully wrapped to keep it hot but not boiling. "No milk nor cream nor sugar, only a bit of chocolate grated and melted."

She poured with a surprisingly elegant flair, arching the dark liquid into his own favorite Viennese porcelain cup; Rourke *had* tutored her well. The rich, steamy fragrance of the mingled coffee and chocolate rose into the air, joining those of the coddled eggs and fried ham, the remaining fat still sizzling in the spider skillet on the hearth.

His uneasy stomach lurched ominously, his palms moist and his forehead icy. This was not a good beginning.

She sniffed defensively, misinterpreting his silence. "It has been a while, since Joshua left and wed, that I have cooked for a man. I know I've not Mr. Rourke's touch, not yet, but I won't learn what to change until you try it and tell me."

"True enough," he said with a heartiness he didn't come close to feeling. "Though from here everything looks vastly splendid."

For the first time she smiled, albeit grudgingly, and he realized he *had* to eat this breakfast. He had no choice. To reject it now would be to reject her all over again. Besides, given her mood this morning, she'd likely dump the entire table onto him.

"Then don't let it grow cold," she ordered. "Come,

there's nothing worse than eggs that have chilled so that the whites turn all stiff and greasy and the yolks stare up at you from the plate like dismal eyes."

He could not disagree. Quickly, before she explained in more queasy detail, he sat in the offered chair, and let her fuss over him, setting the plate with the eggs closer, tipping the coffee from the cup to the saucer to cool. Then she sat at the other end of the table, her hands in her lap, waiting expectantly for him to begin.

"You won't join me?" he asked with more hope than hospitality.

"Oh, no," she said. "Mr. Rourke has told me how you must eat enough for two men each morning or you're not fit to greet the day."

"Indeed," he said weakly, and reached for a slice of toast. Toast would be the best way to begin, and with a silent prayer he took his first bite. He chewed slowly and methodically, concentrating on her face rather than the food before him. Next came a gulp of coffee, its bitter heat burning into all the aching corners of his stomach.

"Now the eggs," she urged, blissfully unaware of his misery. "I am monstrously proud of those eggs. I drizzled the last of the ham's fat over the yolks for flavor, the way Rourke suggested."

Gerald raised his fork and silently wished Rourke to the devil, and with each successive bite and chew and hapless swallow he wished him farther and deeper into the hottest flames in Hades. Even that would be too easy, considering the extent of the punishment Gerald himself was now suffering.

He was going to die. Here, now, on Serena's well-swept floor. His last wish would be that she realize the manful penance he'd done for her.

"You are very quiet this morning, Gerald," she said. "I'd rather hoped that we—that is, that we might—"

"I must be gone," he announced, rising so abruptly that the chair tipped backward to the floor with a crash behind him.

"Now?" she asked, confused. "Where?"

"Where?" Frantically he searched for an acceptable answer, fighting to keep his stomach at bay just a moment longer. "Outside. To the—ah, to the market-house. To help. With the carpenters."

He bolted then, throwing open the door and stumbling around to the back of the house, his head and his stomach spinning in opposing circles. Somehow he managed to reach the privy, and there, without any further noble gestures or sacrifices, was miserably, thoroughly sick.

Afterward he leaned his forehead against the rough boards of the privy wall, feeling weak but much improved. Long ago he'd learned that was the way with him; he'd also thought that he'd learned long ago to keep from drinking so much in the first place, but no matter. What was most important now was that he hadn't hurt Serena's feelings any further. He wiped his face with his handkerchief, pulled his shirt and coat back into place as best he could, and swung open the privy door, prepared once again to face the day.

"You should have told me, Gerald," said Serena. She was standing not five paces away, her hair gold in the morning sun and her petticoats tossing lightly in the breeze, and the empty brandy bottle hanging neck-down from her hand. "I would have understood, you know. You recall I have three older brothers, and all of them sailors, and I have, I am sorry to admit, seen far sadder and more bedraggled creatures than even yourself."

He stared at her, at a complete loss for words. He could not imagine mortification of this degree. He didn't want to be either sad or bedraggled in her eyes. It was humiliating enough for her to discover the reason for his swift departure, but to layer upon that humiliation a large serving of shame from her seeing him like this— staggering from a privy in yesterday's soiled clothes, unshaven and stinking like the worst sort of brothel *habitué*—was more this morning than he could, quite literally, stomach.

"I could have fixed you a draught to settle your

stomach properly," she said with something unbearably close to pity in her eyes, "instead of forcing that hideously outsized breakfast upon you. I still can, if you'll come back into the house."

"That shall not be necessary," he said, his words more frosty than he realized as he scrambled to retrieve whatever dignity he could. "There is no need to trouble yourself."

He saw the doubt flicker through her eyes, the hesitancy growing. "It's no trouble," she said, her cheeks flushing. "How could it be?"

"I told you, it's not necessary." He ran his fingers back through his hair, striving to bolster his sorry appearance with at least the air of a gentleman. Before he could talk to Serena in any decent fashion, he'd need to stop at his sister's house, to wash and shave and change his clothes and make himself presentable once again. "I find I'm no longer—ah, indisposed. The walk to town will improve me further."

She nodded, her gaze dropping to the grass at her feet. "Oh, yes," she murmured. "The carpenters are expecting you."

Damnation, he'd done it again. She had pride, too, but the sad little slope to her back betrayed her. He remembered how easy it had once been to talk and laugh with her, perhaps the easiest he'd ever found it with any woman. So why was it that now whenever he tried to improve things between them, he only succeeded in making them infinitely worse? He cleared his throat and bowed low to her to cover his own unhappy ineptitude.

"I wasn't following you," she said, her words in a defensive rush, "and I don't want you thinking I was. Truly. But I did want to give this back to you, before—before you left."

She dug her hand into her pocket and pulled it out quickly again, hurrying forward to press the object into his own fingers before she turned and ran back toward the house, her skirts flying and her neatly braided hair coming undone over her shoulders. As she slammed the heavy door, he swore softly to himself, expecting that she'd returned his ring.

But when he looked into his hand, he realized how wrong, wrong about everything, he'd been.

For there in his palm lay the twin rose-pink scallop shells.

Fourteen

Gerald sat high in the markethouse scaffolding, his back pressed against one of the tall brick chimneys, and turned his face to the warmth of the noontime sun. He'd worked hard beside the others this morning, trying to forget his troubles with Serena in the simpler challenge of fitting pegs and posts and beams together. Like the others, too, he'd shed his coat and waistcoat to work in his shirt and breeches, welcoming not only the freedom of it, but also the privacy. While none of the other men would dare ask why he'd appeared in the same clothes he'd been married in the day before (though there'd been a certain amount of leering and jesting behind his back), at least this way, without the embroidered waistcoat, he'd be less remarkable.

He wiped his sleeve across his forehead, gazing out over the shingled rooftops to the water. From this height the handful of boats in the harbor looked like children's playthings, bobbing on the glittering waves with their sails dipping triangles in the bright sun, a pretty enough scene to make him long for a painter's gifts. It would be easy to sit here with his legs splayed over a wide beam and forget the rest of the world, to think of no more than the warm brick pressing against his back, the sun on his skin, and how gently the breeze swept up from the water to flick at his hair and the full sleeves of the shirt Anabelle had borrowed from Joshua's chest for him.

It was easy, yes, but it wasn't going to be possible. As seductively peaceful as the scene was before him, he found his gaze shifting eastward, beyond the curve of the harbor's embrace, to the long, low point of land, the palest of greens now that the grasses were turning with the spring, that jutted out farther into the sea. That was Cranberry Point, and though the rise of the hill hid the house on the other side, Gerald still could not look there without thinking of Serena, imagining what she'd be doing at this time of the day and wishing, too, that he were there to do it with her.

In all honesty, he wasn't sure what that might be. In some ways he felt he knew Serena very well—for example he could predict instantly what would make her laugh, just as he could describe with absolute accuracy the way she blushed, from south to north, like a sunset blossoming across her cheek—but as for the details of how she passed her day, he was rather at a loss.

He squinted hard at the hill, as if he could see through it. He hoped she wasn't tossing all his clothes out the window in disgust. He'd had one volatile mistress, a French dancer, who'd done that, heaving shirts and breeches and neckclothes into the muck of an inn's courtyard on the road to Bath. There were, of course, sizable differences between that lady and Serena: Serena was neither volatile, nor French, nor inclined to dirty so much as a garter ribbon, but Serena, alas, also had considerably more justification.

With a sigh Gerald remembered the scallop shells, now once again hidden away in his coat pocket for safekeeping, and for luck, too. He'd wondered what had become of the shells, left behind that night when Joshua had surprised them. If she hadn't thrown the shells away by now, then Gerald's clothes were probably safe as well. But as for what she'd do with his own particular person—that was something else altogether. He could have used a few more useful ideas for the future himself.

He did not want to lose her. He was perilously close already. The more he thought about what he'd done and said to her last night, the less likely it seemed that she'd ever forgive him. As it was, he doubted he could ever forgive himself. He'd always believed that he'd never marry, that there was no one woman in the world who would be able to amuse him sufficiently for the rest of his life. But mere amusement couldn't hold a candle to love, and with Serena he'd learned the difference. He only hoped now that he hadn't learned it too late.

He heard a woman's saucy laughter, and he looked down over the beam to the ground below. While some of the unmarried men would troop to a nearby tavern for their noontime meal, most of the others had wives or sweethearts or daughters who'd bring them dinner and a jug of small beer or cider in a basket. He watched them meet and go off now, in couples or in small groups, to find a place in the shade to eat and talk. When he'd been a boy, he'd often managed to appear around the harvest workers at Kilmarsh when they, too, had been brought their lunch, the smallest boy from the big house blatantly hoping for an invitation to share a meal in the field. Nowadays he'd too much pride to go begging for scraps from dinner baskets, but it didn't stop him from still wishing to be included, or better yet, to have his wife bring him dinner as well.

His *wife:* sweet Jesus, who would have dreamed that Fitzgerald James Rockingham Crosbie, of Kilmarsh and so many other places he'd lost count, could long for such a thing as a wife with a dinner basket?

With a sigh he settled back against the sun-warmed bricks, concentrating instead on the gulls that hovered in the breeze, only the tips of their wings wobbling. How did they do it, he wondered idly, hanging there in the air without any effort that—

"Damnation!" he howled as he grabbed his shoulder, nearly toppling from the beam. The sudden stinging pain was so sharp that he thought first that he'd been shot. But his fingers found no wound, no blood: a thrown rock, then, and he glared down at the ground to find the culprit.

"Don't fall," called Serena with a cheerful wave of her hand. "But if you don't wish to come down, why, then I shall have to come up to you."

Somehow Gerald didn't doubt that she would, and he swiftly swung himself down through the scaffolding before she could prove her skill. She'd already showed herself an accurate enough hand with a stone, doubtless more of the work of those three infernal brothers of hers again.

"I nearly fell, you know," he said indignantly. "A simple 'halloo' would have served just as well as a rock."

"It wasn't a rock. It was a walnut," she said, not in the least contrite. "And I tried calling to you, but you ignored me."

"Ignored you, hah," he said sternly, slipping effortlessly into their old pattern of bantering. "As if any man with a breath left inside him could ignore a deadly creature like yourself, Serena."

He meant it as a jest, though he wouldn't have objected if she'd taken it as a compliment. But though she'd begun it by throwing the walnut at him, she chose not to answer now. Her face instead had gone curiously blank, and with a sigh he began to curse himself again as a thoughtless boor. God help him, how had he wounded her *now?* Then he noticed the way Serena's eyes had glided to one side, indicating without words that they weren't alone. Too late Gerald became aware of their audience, every laborer and his wife lingering within earshot as long as they dared. Hell, they might as well put themselves upon the stage and charge admission.

He drew himself up straight and smoothed his hair back as best he could, striving to make a better impression. It didn't take a genius to guess why they were all smirking and sniggering behind their hands. He and Serena were newlyweds. But while he looked haggard and spent, she'd somehow managed to dispel the dark circles beneath her own eyes. Her cheeks fair glowed beneath her wide-brimmed straw hat, her eyes bright and her smile as warm as the bricks he'd just abandoned. Lord, if he'd been on the other side of the picture alongside the carpenters, he would have been laughing out loud himself.

Poor old Crosbie, one night with our Miss Serena as his bonnie bride and he's used up and spavined and ready for pasture.

Abel bounded forward, and Gerald bent to scratch beneath the dog's collar, thankful for the distraction. Abel whimpered with gratitude, shoving his shaggy head against Gerald's leg for more.

At least he still had one eternal friend in Appledore.

"I've brought you dinner, Gerald," said Serena, shifting the basket from one arm to the other.

"Have you?" asked Gerald, standing upright again, as he winced at how patently stupid such a question must sound.

"Yes," she said loudly, as aware of their audience as he was. "I have. I am your wife, and it's now my responsibility to see you don't go hungry."

Behind them someone guffawed and was promptly shushed. Serena flushed but kept her head high. What with her pegging walnuts and all, he'd overlooked how much courage it must have taken for her to come to him here, especially considering how they'd parted last. This wouldn't be easy for him, either, but now that she'd made the first step, he could damned well take the second. And seeing her there, dressed in rough homespun with the old willow basket on her arm, had given him a splendidly inspired idea, his own first step toward redeeming himself in her eyes. Thank God he'd learned a few things about women over the years.

"I'm glad you came, sweetheart," he said as he took the basket from her. "And I'm glad you brought dinner, too. You'll save me from the Swan's fish pie. Come, we can sit here."

He led her to the side of the pile of stacked timbers, a shady, dry spot that was usually one of the first to be taken but, now that Serena had come, seemed to have magically emptied for them. Silently Gerald thanked whoever had moved. Here at least they'd have a chance at not being overheard.

He pulled out his handkerchief and gallantly draped it across one of the timbers for her to sit upon. She misunderstood, sitting carefully beside the spread hand-kerchief and using it instead as a tablecloth, lifting bundles from her basket while Abel settled in the grass, his head still raised expectantly to be ready to catch whatever might tumble his way from the basket.

"I'm thankful you've given me another chance," said Serena, then blushed all over again. "My cookery, I mean. After that dreadful breakfast."

Gerald was sorry he made her so nervous, but he didn't regret the blushing.

"No apologies, sweet. It was hardly your fault," he said, watching her unpack the basket. A half-round of cheese, a loaf of bread crusty with cornmeal, a crock of potage that smelled deliciously of onions, and he real-ized his appetite was now fully recovered. He uncorked the earthenware jug and tipped it back, gratefully letting the chilled, sweet cider slip down his throat. "Blame it upon Anabelle's brandy instead."

"But I—that is, you wouldn't have drunk the brandy in the first place if it weren't for me." Self-consciously she looked down at her lap, the bread knife clutched tight in her hand. "I'm not a complete fool, Gerald. I do know something of men's weaknesses."

"What you know is your infernal brothers," he said, wanting to hear not another word more of the marvelous Fairbourne brothers. "You don't know much of anything about my particular weaknesses."

"That is true," she said defensively. "And if I do not know much of you, then you, in turn, know little of me, else you never would have—oh, it doesn't signify now, does it?"

He set the cider jug on his knee. "It *might* signify a great deal."

She shook her head unhappily, concentrating instead on cutting the bread into neat slices.

"Tell me, Serena," he said softly. "What other way am I to learn?"

But she shook her head again, refusing now even to meet his gaze as she handed him a thick slice of the bread topped with a slab of cheese.

"I think you shall find this more agreeable than those horrid coddled eggs," she said, a tremor in her voice that had nothing to do with bread. "Careful now, the crust crumbles."

Gerald sighed, taking the food from her. His fingers brushed over the back of her hand, and he was stunned by how much that slight touch made him long to pull her into his lap, to feel her bottom atop his thighs, to kiss her and make her laugh and push her petticoats up over her legs and—damnation, *no*. He wasn't some greenhorn youth from the country. He had to get rein over himself, or he'd never find the chance to tell her he loved her, at least a chance that she'd believe. Right now he doubted she'd believe him if he said the sky was blue.

"If you won't tell me," he began slowly, still wrestling with his more unmanageable inclinations toward her, "then I shall tell you. I've been considering this well, Serena. I know you don't give me much credit for consideration at all, but I am capable of it, especially where you are concerned. No, where *we* are concerned, since it's hardly fair to consider you alone at this point."

She looked up warily, waiting, her face dappled with the tiny pinpricks of sunlight that filtered through the straw brim of her hat.

"But that's what you wish, isn't it?" she asked with surprising bluntness. "To be—to be alone, by yourself whenever you finally chose?"

"Well now, I did say that," he admitted uncomfortably. "I won't lie and say otherwise, not to you. But damnation, Serena, we can't go on acting like Darby and Joan here without making certain, ah, changes to this arrangement. At least I'm prepared to make them. You don't have to if you don't wish it."

"But I do!" she cried, then quickly lowered her voice when she saw that others had turned their way from curiosity. "For you, Gerald, I—I do. I will."

Serena couldn't believe he was actually saying these things, and worse, that she was agreeing to them so quickly. What had happened to her pride, or even her common sense? Was her memory really so woefully weak that she'd already forgotten how she'd cried herself to sleep only last night? To come here with his dinner was her wifely duty; instant forgiveness shouldn't have been packed in her basket as well.

But the moment she'd spotted Gerald there on the crossbeam, his long legs swinging gently back and forth like a boy hiding in a favorite tree and his handsome face turned toward the sun, she'd known she could have done nothing else. How could she? Rourke would have suffered an apoplexy on the spot if he'd seen his master so ill-kept, but to Serena's eyes Gerald had never looked more wickedly appealing, because she loved him. Aye, that was the truth of it. She *loved* him. Gerald was her husband, no matter what he thought otherwise, and she loved him. She must remember that.

"I will," she repeated, more firmly. "I will do that."

"Well, then, good," he said, clearing his throat with a rumble. "At least we are in agreement so far. As I said, I've been considering things. In the eyes of the world, you are my wife, and as my wife you should be entitled to certain, ah, benefits."

She nodded slowly. This was something she could understand. She'd heard that marriage should bring gain for both husband and wife, and though she had her doubts if such a thing were truly possible, she would be willing to put her misgivings aside for Gerald's sake.

"Hear me out, Serena. I won't have you agreeing before you know what you're agreeing to." Gerald frowned solemnly, waving his arm in warning. The shirt, and the shirt's sleeves, were too big for him, the cuffs flopping a bit over his wrists, and from the darns she recognized it as one of Joshua's.

"I'll agree to seeing you not have to go about in borrowed clothes," she said promptly. "You shouldn't have to go begging ancient shirts from my brother, especially one that's more full of darns and threads than a cobweb. It's not seemly, Gerald."

"Seemly," he repeated, seizing upon the word. "That's exactly it. I want this marriage of ours to be, ah, *seemly.*"

She nodded again, her heart jumping with fresh hope. Perhaps he'd reconsidered; perhaps, after all, he was going to stay; perhaps he'd come back home—to *their* home—to make her his wife in the one way that truly mattered.

"I'm only a third son," he continued, "and though I can't set you up grand as a duchess, you won't have to live like a pauper, either."

She smiled shyly, the first time she'd let herself do so. "I don't live like a pauper now, you dunderhead. You've seen my house for yourself. As for 'setting me up' like a duchess—Appledore needs only one Anabelle."

"Doubtless Anabelle would agree, too." He grinned, reaching into his pocket. "I must admit I've no notion of what things cost here—that was one of Rourke's tasks— but I'll wager they don't come for free."

She frowned down at the gold coins glinting in his outstretched hand, enough guineas to keep an entire Appledore family fed and clothed and housed for the better part of a year.

"Nothing's free," she said uncertainly. "That's true enough. But what could I want that would be so costly?"

"Ah, Serena, you needn't be so coy with me." His grin widened, and he winked. "I know what pleasure you ladies find in fripperies and foolishness, and what pleasure I'll find, too, in seeing you in them. And that will be all, you know. I promise not to repeat last night's misadventure again."

"You won't?" she asked, that new sprig of hope beginning to wither.

"I will not," he said firmly, though he seemed to be looking somewhere past her shoulder, avoiding her eyes. "I won't let my—ah, my baser nature shame you like that again. You have my word. And a new pair of buckles for your shoes, ribbons or feathers for your hair, whatever you please. Or if you'd rather buy a new looking-glass or chocolate pot, that's well enough, too. I won't have it said that I'll pay your market bills with nothing to spare for yourself."

"But I've no need of a chocolate pot," she protested unhappily. "That is, unless you wish me to have one. But I should not know what to do with one if I had it."

"Then find yourself some other trinket or two," he said warmly. "My point is, Serena, that I don't want you living on your brother's *largesse* any longer. You must come to me. This should be enough for the first week or so, yes?"

The coins sat there still in his hand, the old queen's profile bright in the sunlight. He was being generous, aye, most generous. Yet Serena wouldn't take them. She had given him the shells to show how she'd felt, that she'd remembered what had brought them together in the first place, and in turn all he offered was money, cold and hard.

"That is what you meant?" she asked softly. "A pocketful of guineas? That is all?"

"If it's not enough, I can certainly come by more," he said quickly. "I may not be my father's heir, but my income should be sufficient to meet your wants, at least for now."

She told herself that this was what most women would want from a husband. He was indeed meeting her wants, her material wants, anyway. Certainly her own mother, left widowed and in debt, would have given a great deal for such—what had Gerald called it?—such *largesse,* and Mary Sears, too, would have welcomed it.

But still Serena could not make herself feel grateful. How could shoe buckles and chocolate pots replace the kind of love she'd thought they shared? Was it really so different in the world he'd come from? Of course money was necessary, but for Gerald to offer it like this to her made her feel more like his mistress than his wife, a woman bought for a night's amusement and no more. Though if she were his mistress, she thought forlornly, at least she would be sharing his bed, and maybe, just maybe, his heart as well.

He reached out and slipped the coins into the pocket that hung around her waist, where she could feel their weight against her hip, and gave the pocket a knowing little pat that made her feel cheaper still and even less like the wife she longed to be.

And beneath its golden weight, that fragile little twig of hope snapped and broke.

"There, Serena dear," he said with satisfaction. "I told you I could be considerate, eh?"

"Oh, aye," she said wistfully as she watched him eat. "What woman, really, could ask for anything more?"

Serena climbed the winding path over the dunes to Mary's house. Her shoes sank deep into the dry sand, nearly as deep as her spirits were now. She'd scarcely know where to begin her story, so much had happened since she'd come here last. But she needed her friend's ear more than ever before, and though she doubted Mary would be able to offer any real solutions to her foundering misery, perhaps sharing her problems with Gerald might ease her heartache.

At least today she'd no need to keep her visit secret. She didn't have to worry any longer about Joshua finding her here, or how she'd explain herself if he did. Now that she was married, the only man she'd have to answer to was her husband.

Her *husband.* She kicked her toe unhappily into the

sand. Gerald had done exactly as he'd promised, giving her all of the freedom of a married woman with none of the responsibility. If that freedom was all she was to have, she thought bitterly, then at least she should make use of it and come visit her friend.

She quickened her steps through the last stand of windswept scrub pines, eager to see Mary again. But to her surprise her friend's house offered none of its usual welcome: the shutters were barred shut over the windows, the door was shut with the latch string drawn, and the chimney was cold and without smoke from the hearth below. On a warm day like this one Serena had expected to find Mary sitting out-of-doors with her basket of wool and spindle, but even her bench was missing from its customary place beside the door.

"Mary?" called Serena, refusing to believe her friend could have vanished so completely. She pounded her fist first on the door and then the shutter as her uneasiness rose. "Mary, it's Serena, and if you're within I'd be obliged if you'd open the door. Mary? Maa-ry!"

No answer came, and Serena turned, searching the tiny yard for any clues. This wasn't like Mary, not at all. Since Robert had brought her to this cottage as a bride, she'd always refused to leave it, even for a day. But clearly she'd been gone longer than that—the sand drifted across the doorstep was testimony enough—and Serena hugged her shawl around her shoulders, her fear for her missing friend increasing as her imagination raced ahead.

What if Mary had fallen grievously ill? She'd always been frail, and this winter had been especially hard on her. She'd never mentioned any friends beyond Serena herself, nor neighbors who'd wish any goodwill toward Robert Sears's widow. Or what if some of Robert's wicked companions had returned? Mary's cottage was as remote as her own on Cranberry Point. Who would have heard her if she'd cried out for help?

She shaded her eyes with her hand, searching for smoke from any neighboring chimney. There, over that hill, she saw it, and the tip of the shingled roof as well, and as fast as she could she began to run. The cottage was much like Mary's, though in better repair, with a russet cow thoughtfully chewing its cud beneath a line of wet laundry. Breathlessly Serena rapped on the door, her heart thumping nearly as loudly.

The woman who answered studied her suspiciously with no greeting, her face unyielding and her hands folded beneath her worn apron as she waited for Serena to speak first. Not that Serena was surprised; Mary had often complained of her neighbors as being ill-mannered and unfriendly, backwater folks who kept to themselves.

"Good day to you, mistress," she began, out of breath from running and fear. "Forgive me for disturbing you, but I wish to know if you've any word from Mistress Mary Sears. I've been to her cottage, and—"

"Gone," said the woman succinctly. "And well rid we are of her, too."

"Gone?" repeated Serena with disbelief. "But when? Where did she go?"

The woman sniffed with contempt. "'Tis naught of my concern as t' where a creature like that would take herself. But when she left a se' night ago, there wasn't none o' us there t' stop her."

She began to close the door, but Serena pushed forward, blocking the door with her shoulder. "Did she leave with anyone else?"

"With the devil himself, I'm liking t' say," said the woman with an emphatic toss of her head. "'Twas her husband's brother Ezra Sears what came for her, a low man, an evil man, an' she quick enough t' go with him. She said she was going t' find her husband, but I say she'd have t' go straight t' Hell itself t' find him, the devil burn his wicked soul forever in fires o' righteousness."

Serena listened, stunned. Though Mary defended Ezra because he was Robert's brother, she had always seemed more than a little afraid of him, too. Ezra must have been able to show her some sort of very definite proof that Robert was still alive for her to agree to leave Denniman's Cove with him.

But Robert alive . . . Serena could scarce believe it herself. He'd been gone so long, and without any word home to Mary, that even the possibility seemed unlikely at best. And if he were, what next? There was no question of Robert returning here to live, for Joshua had sworn to see him tried and hung as a traitor and a pirate. There was no question, either, of Mary continuing to live here while Robert was elsewhere. Quite simply, she loved Robert too much for her to be apart from him even a day more than she had to.

Serena glanced back over her shoulder to where the black tip of Mary's chimney peeked over the hill. To her sorrow she realized she might well have seen the last of her friend, and she hated to remember how abruptly they'd parted, especially since Gerald had been the cause. Mary had been her friend since they'd been children; to have her gone would leave a hole in her life no one else could fill.

But as unhappy as that made her, Serena understood. How could she not? There'd been a time, and not long ago, either, when she would have shaken her head with dismay over Mary's blind devotion to Robert. She would have wished that Mary could be more reasonable, her judgment less clouded by love for her Robert. But now all Serena had to do was think of her own hopeless feelings for Gerald, and she understood. Lord help them both, she understood, and she could forgive.

"You're Cap'n Fairbourne's sister, aren't you?" asked the woman. "I didn't con the likeness at first, but with you turned like that, I could not miss it."

Serena nodded, and belatedly held out her hand. "I am Serena Fairbourne, aye, and Joshua is my brother."

But the woman didn't take her offered hand, instead staring coldly at Serena. "Then he should take a lash t' you for how you've shamed him, coming here over an' over after that low woman like you do."

"Mary Sears is my friend," said Serena sharply, "and

whatever happened between her husband and my brother will not change that friendship."

"Oh, aye, and does Cap'n Fairbourne believe that, too?" she said scornfully. "I'll warrant he does not, a fine gentleman such as that, nor never has. Mary Sears is a wicked, faithless slattern t' cozen you into betraying your own kin."

"That is not true!" said Serena vehemently. "My brother has never blamed Mary for her husband's crimes!"

"Then I ask you, what other reason would you have to come here so secret, other'n being daft? Leastways Mary Sears must obey her husband."

"I have a husband, too," said Serena without thinking, "and he doesn't mind me looking after Mary."

"Oh, aye, so you have a husband, do you?" jeered the woman, her sudden laughter raucous. "Then you hie yourself home t' that husband o' yours, mistress, and beg him t' take better care o' you than t' let you go traipsing about with the likes o' Mary Sears."

Serena flushed. "My husband takes most excellent care of me."

The woman laughed again. "'Most excellent care,' oh, aye, that's how you gentry are," she said as she shut the door. "But if he don't care more'n that, why, then, mistress, he don't love you enough, not by half. And that, mistress, that be the good Lord's honest truth."

He don't love you enough, not by half.

It didn't matter how desperately Serena tried to tell herself that those were the words of a spiteful, mean woman, a woman who knew nothing of her and less of Gerald: the words echoed over and over in her head, and worse, in her heart as well. If she'd been able to talk to Mary, then perhaps the words wouldn't have hurt so much, but by the time she'd reached Appledore, they'd become an inescapable tattoo, matching every step she took with grim regularity, and matching, too, the heavy thump of the hateful guineas against her thigh.

On Water Street she hesitated, torn between humbling herself further and returning to the markethouse to see if Gerald wished company on his walk back to Cranberry Point—which he might very well not—or going home directly so that she'd be sure to have supper ready when he arrived. Feeding him seemed to be one of the few things she did successfully, at least when he wasn't rattling with yesterday's brandy. Besides, if he'd wished her to walk home with him, the way most wives did, he would have asked, wouldn't he?

The thought sunk her spirits even farther, as low as a pebble tossed into a well. But as she trudged toward the lane to home, another possibility came to her, and another ally: Anabelle. Anabelle understood Gerald. She could likely tell Serena what she'd done wrong with him, or what she could try to do right. Of course that might mean having to confess her great shame, that she'd yet to make any use of that beautiful bed gown. But Anabelle's was the one voice Serena knew that might be able to drown out the spiteful voice ringing in her ears, and, with a sigh, she headed up the hill to her brother's house.

She paused at the door to smooth her skirts and straighten her cap. The formal paneled door of her brother's house with the brass lock and knocker always made her feel vaguely disreputable, as if she'd be more welcome coming around to the kitchen door instead. But this time, before she knocked, she heard Anabelle's laughter rippling from the back garden, where she must have gone to enjoy the warm afternoon, and with relief Serena hurried around the corner of the house and through the gate in the stone wall.

She ducked her way beneath the overhanging holly trees—Joshua would have to have those trimmed—ready to call to Anabelle. But as she held aside one of the branches, she could see Anabelle, and Joshua, too. The garden was tiny and surrounded by low stone walls and fruit trees, and while Anabelle had great plans to turn it into a paradise of flowers this summer, now only a few hardy shoots of green poked from the bare beds. One of the dining chairs, softened with an extra cushion, had been brought outside for Anabelle to sit upon, and on the wall beside the chair was a pewter tray with tea and a plate of biscuits, and the novel she'd been reading lay there, too, the pages turned open to the sunshine.

But Anabelle wasn't reading now. Instead she was sitting across Joshua's lap, her swollen ankles crossed and her mules on the grass where they'd dropped from her feet. Her cheek rested against Joshua's chest, her eyes closed, and a little smile of complete peace and contentment curved her lips. Joshua's eyes, too, were closed, his head bent over his wife's, one hand protectively around her hips and the swell of their unborn child, while with the other he gently rubbed Anabelle's lower back.

As quietly as she could, Serena let the branch slip and backed away. She couldn't disturb them, not now. It wasn't only that she feared she'd be an unwelcome interruption to such an intimate moment. She was also an intruder in this private world of love, a world that could turn her great, blustering brother into the most tender man imaginable, a world that gave Mary Sears endless hope where none should be.

A world that held no place for her.

By the time she reached home, the sun had slipped low on the horizon, taking with it the early spring warmth. The wind had shifted, too, coming now from the water, and the air was chill and heavy with the scent of the sea. As she unlatched her gate, Abel came bounding joyfully toward her, and this time when he jumped up with his wet, sandy paws on the front of her petticoats, she didn't scold him, but knelt instead to bury her face in his rough black fur.

"Oh, Abel," she whispered miserably as he licked her hand in wordless sympathy. "Whatever did I do wrong?"

As briskly as she could she tried to lose herself in the day-ending tasks. She rinsed the beans she'd put to soak in the morning, and she chopped the onions and the bacon to put in the skillet with them. As they began to simmer, she sat on the floor beside Abel and used his steel-toothed comb to work out all the nettles and burrs and sand that he'd acquired during the day. He was not by nature a tidy dog, but he had learned to keep his protests over particularly bad snarls to few low whines, and as a reward she gave him a piece of the bacon that should have gone into the beans, and, thought Serena with a certain satisfaction, into Gerald as well.

Next she ground the cornmeal for the bread with a mortar and sifted out the bits of dry kernel, to make the crumbs fine the way she preferred, and she scraped the last of the black molasses from the jug, reminding herself to buy more the next time she went to market. She put one of the last of her strings of dried apples into an apple cake, setting the kettle to one side of the fire and piling coals on top of the lid so the cake would brown slowly, without burning, as the apples cooked and plumped. She sang to herself as she worked, from long habit and to help keep her worst thoughts at bay.

But keeping Gerald away in the same way became impossible as she turned to his chest. Rourke had had his master's clothes delivered to the house the day of the wedding, and though Serena did not quite have the nerve to shift them all from the brass-studded traveling chests to her own cupboards, she told herself that she'd best have at least one shirt ready for him to wear tomorrow, especially after she'd made such a fuss over the sorry state of the one he'd borrowed.

Regarding shirts Rourke's instructions had been most explicit, for Gerald, apparently, was most explicitly particular about his linen. Serena could understand; one of the things she'd noticed first about him on that first foggy day had been the snowy perfection of his shirt. It was a perfection she was determined to maintain, for pride's sake if no other. She put a pair of irons to the fire to heat, set her flannel-covered pressing-board onto the table, and then opened the trunk that Rourke had marked for linen.

Yet though she wanted to be briskly efficient, she still

wasn't prepared for the overwhelming associations that came when she tipped back the trunk's top. It wasn't only that the shirts were so unmistakably Gerald's by the quality of the linen and the workmanship. What struck her almost like a blow was how much of him seemed to linger in them as well, his very scent a part of the fine linen. With no one else to see, she pressed her face into the cloth, her eyes closed, remembering when she'd touched her fingers to this same cloth and felt his heart beating beneath it. She'd had such hopes then; now she had only his wretched guineas and his ring and little else.

But she wasn't completely alone. With a rumbling growl of interest Abel thrust his head into the trunk, his black nose twitching as he snuffled at the shirts.

"Stop it, Abel, stop it now!" scolded Serena as she shoved him swiftly aside before his curiosity left its inevitable mark. "It's Gerald's things, that is all, and not some silly rabbit you've chased into the marsh."

Yet the image of Gerald in his fine London clothes hopping through the tall grasses and wet, muddy sand of the marshes did make her smile, and in spite of Abel's snuffling nose, she patted him fondly.

"You are quite right, my old pup, to chide me for feeling sorry for myself like this," she said softly. "I was a Fairbourne long before I became a Crosbie, and we Fairbournes are not supposed to turn into a weepy mess. Leastways Joshua never would, nor would Danny nor Sam, and I can hardly let my brothers better me, can I?"

She stood up, taking the topmost shirt from the trunk and slamming the lid shut with a satisfying little kick of her shoe. "Beside, Abel, it certainly wouldn't do to have Gerald find me like this, grieving over his trunk as if it were his coffin."

The dog thumped his tail against the floorboards in eager sympathy as Serena carried the shirt to her pressing-board. One shirt was enough for now, just as with Gerald himself she must be willing to go day by day. Swiftly she pressed the fold-line from the soft linen, taking special care with the ruffles on the cuffs, and then carried it gingerly up the ladder to lay it across the low bed in the loft. While she hoped that Gerald wouldn't retreat up here again, this was the one place in her house where she was sure that Abel—and his damp, inquisitive nose—could not go.

She took a peek at her kettles, pinned on a clean apron, and stood on the doorstep, gazing down the land toward town. The sun had long ago set, the night sky sprinkled with early stars and the sliver of a new moon. But there was no sign of Gerald, and with a shiver she closed the door.

Perhaps he'd lingered in town with Mr. Gardiner, the master carpenter, or decided to share a pot or two of ale with the workmen. Such things were common enough. But the next time she went to the door, the moon had risen nearly twice as high in the sky and the hour was far later than a pot of ale merited. When she stepped back inside she smelled the sugary smoke of the burning apple cake, and as soon as she yanked it from the fire she knew it was ruined, burned to blackened ruin. Those had been her last apples; there would be no more until fall, and with an oath that Joshua had no idea she'd learned from him, she scooped out the top of the apple cake into Abel's dish. Certainly Abel was more deserving than Gerald, and impulsively she dumped the beans and bacon into the dish, too.

Impulse felt good, very good, and so, to her surprise, did her growing anger. When Gerald had chosen to spend their wedding night alone, she'd been able to keep the humiliating truth to herself. But if tonight he stayed from her house as well as her bed—whether returning to his bachelor quarters at the White Swan, or sprawled on one of the benches in a tavern, or, most shameful of all, sharing the flearidden bed of one of the doxies who catered to sailors—the whole town would know of it by morning. She would be pitied and clucked over, whispered about and laughed at, and it would all be Gerald's fault.

But she *was* a Fairbourne, and she had had enough.

He had given her his name and advised her to make the most of her new status as a married woman. He'd also given her a small fortune in guineas, and had told her to find her own enjoyment with it. Nay, he'd nearly ordered her to do so.

Perhaps it was time to become more obedient.

The weekly packet for Boston would sail when the tide turned next, in the morning, in the last hour before daybreak. Married women were entitled to travel unattended, particularly when they paid their passage in hard money. In Boston, gold guineas would be most welcome, too, with milliners and mantua makers and innkeepers, and so, therefore, would she.

While Abel slurped and gobbled his way through Gerald's dinner, she returned to the small studded trunk that held Gerald's shirts. But this time she scooped up the fine linen in both arms with determined lack of ceremony and dropped it in a heap onto the floor beside the woodpile. If the floorboards had been in need of sweeping there, and if a few ashy cinders happened to drift from the coals onto the shirts, well, such accidents happened in even the most well-ordered households.

Swiftly she filled the trunk with her own belongings, the things she'd need for the short voyage until she'd buy new, better ones to replace them. She latched the trunk shut with a satisfying click, lightly running her fingers across the polished nailheads that spelled out Gerald's initials, a monogram that she had every right to use as her own as well.

Serena's smile was as complicated as her feelings, mixing satisfaction with sorrow and wistfulness. But she'd only be doing what he'd sworn he'd wished. He wanted his freedom from her, and she was going to give it to him.

Except that she would be the one who left Appledore behind, and not him.

She was sorry—*very* sorry—that she wouldn't be able to see his face when he learned that she'd gone.

Fifteen

"Where the hell is Serena?"

"I suppose wherever you left her, Gerald," said Ana-
belle as she nibbled delicately at her breakfast toast.
"Truly, you shouldn't be so careless as to mislay poor
Serena like this, and only two days after you wed, too."

"I am serious, Nan!" Gerald thumped his fist onto the
edge of her tea table. "I do not know where she is!
Damnation, you can at least look at me!"

"And you, Duckie, can stop laying waste to my
furnishings." She looked up at him, her eyes still heavy
with sleep beneath her nightcap. "Do you realize how
monstrously rude it is of you to call upon me at this
hour?"

Gerald turned on his heel and swore as he impatiently
charged across the room and back again. How could he
be still when the memory of Serena's empty house was so
keen? At first he'd feared she'd come to some harm, there
alone on Cranberry Point, but then he'd seen his shirts
deliberately tumbled into the ashes near the hearth, and

272

he'd come to another, less-flattering conclusion, one that did little to improve his temper.

"What in blazes," he demanded, "must I do to make you understand that Serena is missing?"

Anabelle sighed with resignation. "You could begin by telling me where you have been to come to this unfortunate state. This is the second morning in a row that you've come here looking like you've slept in a hedgerow. I asked for no explanation yesterday, but today I vow I must."

"It's not my doing, I swear it." He shook his head and raked his fingers through his unkempt hair, scowling down at the shambles of his clothing as if noticing them for the first time. He *did* look like hell, true enough, but then this morning he felt like it, too. "I have spent the last fifteen hours in the company of a cross-eyed thief of a Frenchman bent upon emptying every last farthing from my purse in exchange for his craft. I have done this for Serena, Nan, every wretched moment, and then she confounds me completely by vanishing!"

"Oh, my, my, a cross-eyed thief of a Frenchman." Anabelle's eyes lost their sleepy disinterest with remarkable speed. "But whatever can such a rascal have to do with Serena?"

"Because of this." With a miserable pretense of nonchalance he dropped the little reason for his hideous night onto the table.

"Oh, Duckie," breathed Anabelle, slowly lifting the ring to see it better. "So you have discovered the magic of our dear Monsieur Levoire. A Huguenot, you know, from Bordeaux, and most skilled. No wonder this is so beautiful."

And it was. Even after all his suffering on the ring's behalf, Gerald couldn't deny that much. The slender band was buffed and polished so the gold gleamed in the light through the window. But the real measure of the old goldsmith's skill lay in the twin gold scallop shells that he'd fashioned as the band's centerpiece, minutely detailed to sit upon the finger in place of the more customary gem. In London such a piece, and made on such a timetable, would have cost very dearly indeed; here in Massachusetts, Gerald had learned that the price of a transplanted master's art was magnified by colonial shrewdness, and he'd considered himself fortunate to escape with his grubby shirt still to his name.

He'd paid it willingly, imagining Serena's delight when he slipped it onto her finger. Only now Serena, and her finger, were nowhere to be found.

"I wanted her to have a proper wedding ring, you see." He leaned his elbows on the table, staring forlornly at the ring in Anabelle's hand. "She deserves that much. And the cockle shells—that's between us, Nan, but Serena would have understood."

Anabelle frowned. "Perhaps Serena will understand, but I do not, not in the least."

"I'm not sure I do myself, either." He shook his head again. "You see, Nan, things have not been precisely as they should between Serena and me."

"Well, how could they," reasoned Anabelle, "with Joshua insisting on being there in the thick of it?"

Gerald took a deep breath. He hadn't intended to confess his trials with Serena, but if his sister could help him find her, then it would be worth it.

"It is not entirely Joshua's fault," he began, hedging. The truth was not going to come easily. "I'd never intended to marry her in the first place, no more than she wished to wed me. Don't squint at me like that, Nan. Serena told me herself she didn't want to be any man's wife."

"You're not any man," said Anabelle. "You're you, and she most certainly wished to be your wife. Almost as much as you wished to be her husband. La, I've never seen a more smitten couple at a wedding! It was almost as if you'd forgotten all the rest of us were even there, you were so lost in Serena."

Gerald shifted uncomfortably in his seat. "That was

the problem, yes. But the result was that I—we—found ourselves married."

Anabelle nodded impatiently. "That is generally the result of a wedding between two people who are so head over heels in love as you two."

"But it didn't seem—ah, that *agreeable* at the time," he said uneasily. "To either of us, or so I thought, else I'd never have suggested that folderol about an annulment."

"An *annulment?*" Anabelle gasped. "You truly said that to Serena? On her wedding night?"

"I thought it was what she wanted, too," he repeated defensively. "But after I'd spent the night in her garret, I'd begun to wonder if I'd made a mistake, and then when I saw her the next noon—"

Anabelle's gasp deepened with real shock. "You've yet to share her bed? She's still a maid?"

"I've told you I've since changed my mind, Nan," he said, his face turning hot for the first time in memory. "That's why I've had the ring made, so that we could have a new start."

"Then you've told her you love her after all?"

He shook his head dolefully. "After everything else, I didn't think she'd believe me. But I did the next best thing. I told her I wanted the world to begin treating her as my wife, and I gave her thirty guineas to spend as she pleased."

For a long time Anabelle said nothing, a silence that made Gerald more and more uneasy with each second. Nothing silenced his sister into nothingness, at least nothing until now.

"My God, Gerald," she said finally, her voice low with disbelief. "You refused her bed and her love, but you gave her thirty guineas. Can't you even begin to comprehend what that must have done to Serena? She's your *wife,* you great ass, not another one of your greedy little dancers!"

He didn't need her to tell him he was a great ass. He

was already discerning that painful knowledge himself, his chin sinking against his chest with the weight of it. He had treated Serena like he'd treated all the other women who'd passed through his life, never stopping to realize how very different—and how very rare—she was.

Anabelle sighed, and she, too, looked down at the table between them.

"You know, Duckie, I'd rather thought Appledore had changed you, too," she said sadly. "The way you've been so attentive to me, and then designing and building our new markethouse, and, of course, falling in love with Serena and marrying her. It was most exciting to watch, you know. But now I see how wrong I was, that it was all just a show, and that you're exactly the same charming, selfish rascal you've always been. And I'm sorry for it, Gerald. Sorry for Serena, of course, but most of all sorry for you."

But he *had* changed. He'd changed more than he'd dreamed possible, and it was all Serena's doing. No, that wasn't quite right. What she'd been able to do was to take him back to being the boy he'd once been long ago at Kilmarsh, when his mother had still lived and his own life had seemed so full of possibilities. With Serena he'd come to believe that again, to look for more for, and from, himself than the next amusement, the next entertainment. He'd also begun to like himself a good deal better as well. Until this morning, anyway. Now he could think of no one he liked less, and though it pained him mightily, he could understand all too well why Serena had left.

"But I love her, Nan," he said, his voice no more than a hoarse whisper drawn from his despair. "Damnation, I *love* Serena."

"Then go tell her, not me." Gently Anabelle pressed the ring with the scallop shells into his palm. "This colony's not such a vastly large place for hiding, especially not for a woman as lovesick as Serena must be. Go find her now, and tell her. And I'll pray for your sake that she listens."

"Ah, Mistress Crosbie, there you are!" The innkeeper's portly wife sailed toward Serena to stop her at the bottom of the stairs. "Have you had success in the shops?"

Serena smiled wearily. It still sounded odd to be called by Gerald's name instead of what used to be her own, but after a day of shopkeepers bowing and fawning over her, she'd at least learned to respond to "Mistress Crosbie." "I suppose I've been successful, aye. There is so much to choose from here that sometimes my head fair spins from deciding."

Mrs. Whatman chuckled with delight. "Ah, that's the charm of our Boston shops. All the riches of the world are gathered here through our merchantmen, and what can't be brought, our good craftsmen make. It's a wonder, ma'am, a rare wonder and a rare temptation, too, eh?"

"Indeed," murmured Serena politely. "A rare wonder."

In truth she'd discovered that visiting shops held little of the charm that it seemed to for Anabelle, even when she'd been doing her level best to spend Gerald's money. But instead of distracting her, it seemed that every porcelain dish or length of kerseymere held out for her admiration reminded her of her lackless husband himself, and again and again she'd caught herself imagining how Gerald would like this particular shade of blue silk, or how he'd laugh at the foolishness of that chalkware spaniel. It was as if he'd come along with her, and her heart sank wearily at how hard it was going to be to forget him.

"Now if you'll excuse me, Mrs. Whatman," she said as she barely stifled a yawn. "I'd like to go to my room and rest."

"Of course you do, mistress, and here me letting my

mouth run like the stream beneath the bridge!" The
woman clucked her tongue at her own rudeness and
ducked a breathless curtsey of apology. "Let me show
how sorry I am by having the lass fetch you a pot of tea
directly. And perhaps Cook might find a bone for the
hound, too, eh?"

She beamed at Abel, who refused to be persuaded,
keeping his place at Serena's side. Serena wondered if
Mrs. Whatman knew enough about dogs to recognize the
wariness about Abel now, the little ruffle of bristling fur
at the back of his collar that meant he was not feeling
particularly friendly.

Abel was not enjoying Boston any more than Serena was. He had spent the entire crossing from Appledore shivering with his tail between his legs, as sick as
a dog can be, and once they'd reached Boston, he'd been
frantic trying to protect Serena from so many strangers
and unfamiliar scents. Serena could see how tired poor
Abel was now, his paws sore from the city's streets
instead of the soft sand and grasses around Cranberry
Point, but she knew he wouldn't relax until they were
once again safe alone together. He was unfailingly loyal
in a way that, she was quite sure, no man would ever be.

Especially that particular no-man who was pretending
to be her husband.

"That would be kind of you, Mrs. Whatman," she
said. "And now I truly must—"

"Before you go, ma'am, a word, I beg you." The
landlady hurried forward, glancing from side to side to
make sure they wouldn't be overheard. "'Tis none of my
business, I know, especially since your brother the
captain's been such a good customer—a fine gentleman,
your brother—but I would know if you'll be expecting
your husband to join you?"

Serena hesitated, not sure of what response she should
give. It wasn't that she was expecting Gerald herself—
she'd firmly put aside that particular fancy before she'd
left Appledore—but if Mrs. Whatman objected to unat-

tached ladies among the inn's company, then not even her brother's gentlemanliness would save her from having to find other lodgings.

"I cannot say for certain," she answered finally, and truthfully, too. "My husband's travels are not precise."

Mrs. Whatman nodded vigorously, eager to coax more details. "Ah, then he is another shipmaster like your brother?"

"Mr. Crosbie is a gentleman," said Serena severely. Whatever else Gerald might be or might not be, he *was* a gentleman. "He is the youngest son of a viscount, and he is also Mrs. Fairbourne's brother."

Mrs. Whatman rocked back on her heels, her mouth circling into round, impressed surprise. "I did not doubt it, ma'am, not for a moment," she declared, which proved exactly the opposite. "'Tis only the questions I've heard in the taproom, ma'am, hints that set me to worrying on your behalf. You know how men can be about a lady on her own."

"Men?" asked Serena more anxiously than she realized. "Whyever would any men be asking about me?"

"For no good reason at all, I'll warrant," huffed Mrs. Whatman. "Low rogues from the water, latecomers, tumbled too far into their cups to observe the niceties of decent company."

"Mariners, then." Of course it would be sailors; in a seaport, what other kind of man would it be? Serena disliked Boston's crowded, narrow streets nearly as much as did Abel, and if the harbor here was ten times as busy as the one in Appledore, then there were ten times the dangers for a lone woman, too, and the idea that she'd been noticed, even watched, by strangers made her intensely uncomfortable.

"Ah, ma'am, I did not keep them about long enough to ask their trade," said Mrs. Whatman, her indignation warming. "But you can be sure I scolded them soundly for their impertinence and sent them along. I should never have bothered you with such rubbish in the first place, ma'am, excepting that Mr. Whatman wished it of me, in the interfering way of men. 'Tis of no account, nor worry, either. Now you go along upstairs, and I'll send the lass with your tea directly."

Serena nodded, but her smile was forced, and she hooked her fingers into Abel's collar for reassurance. What had seemed like such a bold and satisfying adventure in Appledore was rapidly becoming something considerably less appealing. She felt foolish and impulsive, and all the more lonely for it. As she and Abel made their way up the stairs, she wondered wistfully when, if ever, luck and happiness would smile upon her again. But until it did, she'd sleep with the casement bolted shut and a chair shoved up against the door.

And try, again, not to dream of Gerald.

"It *was* her, Robert, no mistake!" said Ezra in a fierce hiss of a whisper. "I spied her myself!"

"But the landlady said—"

"To the devil with the landlady! That be Joshua Fairbourne's little sister at that house, or the devil can come for me, too!"

"None o' that kind o' talk, Ezra, none o' that." Robert glanced about uneasily, making sure the devil hadn't heard and decided to claim his quick-tempered brother anyway. He took another gulp of the rum in the battered tankard before him. The spirits were watered, no better than they should be in a six-bench rum shop that stank of old tobacco and vomit and the low tide outside, but Robert didn't care. Weak or strong, watered or neat, rum was more important to him than his own bone and blood. Perhaps it *was* his blood by now. He didn't know, and he didn't wonder enough to split his own skin to find out. There were enough others here in this colony willing to do it for him, and nervously he wiped his fingers over and over across his mouth.

Ezra leaned closer across the table, lowering his voice. "Where else d'you think Mary would have gone, eh? Off to the Fairbourne woman and her fancy ways, that's where. Why else would Mary have run off from me like she did?"

"I cannot blame Mary for running," said Robert sorrowfully. "Not after what I've done to her, poor, dear lass. Why would she want to see me, anyway?"

"Because she *must,* Robert!" answered Ezra sharply. "Mary's your wife, your property. She has no choice but to do her duty toward you!"

The anger in his voice was so obvious that not even the rum could let Robert overlook it. He had a right to be angry—according to Ezra, he'd suffered from Robert's infamy, too, blamed for it simply because they'd been brothers—but still Robert wished his brother had directed his resentment toward him, where it belonged, instead of toward Mary.

"Is there something amiss between you and my Mary, Ezra?" he asked reluctantly. "You are my brother, true enough, but Mary is my wife, and I do not wish t' hear you speak so harshly of her."

"Then perhaps you should speak to her first, if you can find the deceitful little baggage." Ezra spat contemptuously over his shoulder and into the fire. "I told you how she's been so thick with them Fairbournes ever since you went missing, taking their side against you. 'Tis no different now. She didn't want to come to Boston with me anyways, no matter that you were here a-waiting for her, and soon as she sees that Fairbourne woman here, off she goes to her. I'm nigh certain of it, Robert. Why else would she've run from me?"

Unhappily Robert stared down at the table, digging his thumbnail into the rutted grooves in the wood. In all the time he'd been away, taking one miserable berth after another as he hid himself and his shame away in the Caribbean, he'd prayed that Mary would understand, that she'd love him still.

Yet how could he fault her if she didn't? He wasn't the same man she'd married. Then his future had been promising. He hadn't needed to hide in a tankard then. England had been at war with France, and Robert had earned his rank as second mate on Appledore's most successful privateer, with hopes of prize money, maybe even a command of his own.

But instead he'd betrayed the trust of Captain Fairbourne, he'd caused the deaths of friends and the loss of the first vessel he'd ever captained, he'd become a homeless wastrel whose only comfort came with the oblivion of rum, and more rum. What woman—especially a woman as fine as his Mary—would squander her love on such a man?

Yet he loved her still, loved her in spite of his own cowardice and his disgrace. Her love given in return would mean infinitely more to him than all of Ezra's sour-sounding duty. Even the hope of it had been enough to make him finally come crawling back to Boston, as close as he'd dare get to Appledore, begging for one last chance with her. And it would be the last; he'd been a desperate man far too long not to recognize a last chance when it came.

"Are you certain you're telling me all, Ezra?" he asked slowly. "About Mary leaving you? She's a sensible woman, my Mary, and I cannot think why she'd come clear to Boston with you if she never meant to see me."

Ezra thumped his fist on the table, hard enough to make the rum slip back and forth in tiny waves in the tankards. "And who would you be doubting now, Robert Sears?"

Robert looked back down at his thumb, seeing how it and the rest of his hand was trembling like an old man's. The sad truth was that he didn't know who to doubt anymore or who to trust, either.

But Mary would. Serena Fairbourne had been Mary's friend since they were girls, the one other woman she could always turn to with her problems or sorrows.

"Mary would only have gone t' Serena if she were in trouble," he said. "They're friends, Robert, thicker than most sisters. If we went to Serena and asked her—"

"Why not go put your own neck through the hangman's rope?" cried Ezra. "Where are your wits, Robert Sears? She'd call the constable to put you in irons and then summon her brother t' come swear his crooked lies against you, and that would be the end o' you, my brother. Blood is blood, Robert, and Fairbournes will be loyal to Fairbournes, just as I am to you. Why, by now they may be holding Mary to get you, hoping to trap you that way!"

Robert shook his head. He'd earned Captain Fairbourne's wrath, there was no question of that, but for Mary's sake he hoped Serena hadn't turned against her, too. He remembered Serena that way, a kind, fair girl that had grown into a rare beauty, a woman who made him tongue-tied with awe when she'd come to their cottage to visit.

"I don't believe it, Ezra," he said. "The cap'n, aye, but not Serena."

Ezra swore, and struck the table again. "Then you listen to me, Robert, and you listen hard. Those Fairbournes will do anything to see you hung. The only way we'll get Mary back is to follow their path in trickery."

"Trickery?" repeated Robert uneasily, and took another long swallow of rum.

"Aye, aye, whatever you choose to call it," said Ezra impatiently. He narrowed his eyes, his voice low and confidential despite his excitement. "We know where Serena Fairbourne's lodging, and you heard the landlady say she was staying alone. We could take her next time she goes out, and keep her locked up tight until they give us back Mary. Maybe until they give you a pardon, too."

"Kidnapping, you mean." Robert shook his head again, struggling to find sense in what his brother proposed. They were born sailors, not criminals. What did they know of such things? "For us to play that kind o' game with Cap'n Fairbourne—I don't think it's wise, Ezra. He's a clever man, the cap'n is, and he thinks the world of his sister. If he thinks we've harmed her—"

"Did I say we'd do that?" said Ezra indignantly. "No man in our family's ever hurt a woman, and I'm not the one to start. We'll keep her cozy and nice, and just until her brother does what we say."

"But Ezra—"

"Do you want your wife back or not?"

Robert closed his eyes and emptied his tankard, letting the last of the rum trickle down his throat. He'd dreamed of Mary and her forgiveness, of the touch of her hand on his cheek and the way her eyes crinkled at the corners when she said his name; he'd dreamed of a new life for them both, another little cottage, but this time on Barbados or Martinique, where Mary would never need feel the keening bitterness of a New England winter again. He still couldn't understand how that dream had twisted about to include kidnapping Serena Fairbourne before Mary would come back to him. He knew he must have missed something; it was one of the bad things that the rum did to him, and his head ached from trying to think more clearly.

But this alone he knew for certain: that in every sense this would be his last chance, and slowly, before he thought the better of it, he nodded at his brother, and agreed.

Serena woke with a gasp, her heart pounding with blind terror as the edges of the nightmare fled with her sleep. Frantically she shoved herself upright, kicking her legs free of the tangled sheets. Disoriented, she could recall nothing beyond the fear that still gripped her, nor how she'd come to be here, in a bed that wasn't her own.

With shaking fingers she fumbled for the striker and flint on the shadowy table beside the bed, and barely caught the candlestick after she'd knocked it sideways. Somehow she managed to make a spark and light the wick, and, with the first glow of candlelight, her panic began to fade. A nightmare, that was all, a bad dream brought on by Mrs. Whatman's over-sugared trifle. Mrs. Whatman: so that was where Serena was, too, in Boston, in the second-best room in Whatman's inn, and with a shuddering sigh she let herself drop back against the bolster.

"Abel?" she called softly, leaning over the edge of the bed to where the dog usually slept. "Here, Abel. Are you awake?"

She heard a low snuffle of acknowledgment, but from near the door to the room. She lifted the candlestick, holding it before her so the light shone faintly across the room. There was Abel, staring at the locked door with the same steadfast intensity that he usually reserved for waiting out rabbits in their burrows. It seemed odd that he wasn't growling or grumbling the way he'd done at every other strange noise since they'd arrived here, but then at this hour the inn was quiet, the other guests asleep, the taproom shuttered for the night, and the Whatmans themselves finally abed. Perhaps some brave mouse had ventured into the hallway; certainly Abel would recognize an unthreatening sound such as that, and with a sigh Serena turned to put the candlestick back onto the table.

But that, there. That wasn't a mouse at her door. That slow scraping of metal against metal was the sound of a key turning in a lock. *Her* lock, to *her* door.

Swiftly she flew from the bed, glancing around the room for a makeshift weapon. At home she kept an old musket tucked beside the cupboard, but now she'd settle for anything heavy enough to swing across the head of the intruder. The best she could find was the earthenware chamberpot from beneath the bed, and holding it firmly by the handles, she hurried in her bare feet to stand beside the door.

Whoever stood on the other side was still fidgeting with the key as if it didn't quite fit, and Serena's heart thumped with sick anticipation as she remembered Mrs. Whatman's "low rogues" asking after her. Perhaps it wasn't a true key, but one of the false kind that she'd once heard Joshua describe, a pass key, made to open many doors. She should never have been so free with her money, paying for everything with Gerald's gold as she had. Thieves would take note of that and seek her out. Maybe they already had.

She lifted the chamberpot over her head and prodded Abel with her toe. "Fat lot of good you are as a watchdog," she whispered, but the dog only thumped his tail good-naturedly against the floor.

Finally the lock clicked open, and the intruder began to shoulder open the door. To Serena's horror, the chair that she'd wedged beneath the knob began to give way, too, the legs skidding across the floor.

"You there, stop at once!" she ordered as firmly as she could, which wasn't really very firmly at all. "Stop now, and go away!"

"Serena?" asked the owner of the shoulder.

"Gerald?"

At her voice he gently pushed the door open the rest of the way. No intruder could look less threatening, at least not to her. He was once again beautifully dressed, wearing the same dark blue coat from the first day he'd dropped into her boat and her life; a most genteel and elegant gentleman, never to be mistaken for one of Mrs. Whatman's low rogues, especially not with the huge bouquet of daffodils in the crook of one arm.

Unconsciously Serena took a step backward, away from him. He might not be threatening her physically, true, but the danger to the rest of her well-being, and especially to her heart, was grave indeed. And daffodils—*daffodils!*—how could he have possibly guessed they were her favorite flower?

"Serena, dear," he said with a gravity at odds with the cheerful yellow flowers. "God only knows I deserve it, but to be crowned by a thunderpot would be the most ignominious greeting, even from you, that I can imagine."

Hastily she lowered the chamberpot and set it on the floor behind her. "It *was* empty," she said defensively, already feeling that he'd won a point against her. "And I would not have struck you."

He blinked once, at once both skeptical and charming, and bent to give Abel a welcome scratch behind the ears. "Oh, I rather think you would have, Serena. Any other woman, you know, would have merely screamed for assistance, but not you."

"I am accustomed to being alone," she said, and inwardly winced at how hopelessly prim and spinsterish that sounded. It didn't help that her dog was rolling about with joy on Gerald's boots. "Who would have come rescue me if I'd screamed on Cranberry Point?"

"A most excellent point," he agreed. "And reason enough for you to have company, in case you need rescuing. The better to save your crockery, too."

She prayed that by the candlelight he wouldn't see how furiously she was blushing. At least he'd made no attempt to come any further into the room, just as she'd made no invitation for him to do so. And if she'd any pride left at all, she wouldn't.

She lifted her chin, trying to look resolute. "How did you come by the key to my room?"

"Your good landlady believes that husbands should not be kept apart from their wives." His smile faded, his expression guarded. "A belief, however, that not all women seem to share."

"Nor do all gentlemen." Appalled by her own boldness, she swiftly looked down at her bare toes, while her fingers began to play out her nervousness by smoothing her hair over her ears.

"Don't," he said softly. "I like your hair the way it is."

Her hands dropped to her sides and balled on their own into tight fists. The heady scent of so many daffodils threatened to overwhelm her, to swallow her up in this same soft, sweet world that his words promised.

"Oh, Gerald," she whispered hoarsely, still not daring to lift her gaze. "Why have you come to do this to me?"

"To begin again," he said carefully. "To make you forget, sweetheart, to make you remember. And, God help me, to pray you'll forgive."

She wanted to believe him, wanted more than she'd

ever wanted anything else. But before she could find the words to answer, she heard the door shut gently behind him. Too late she looked, and found him gone, and with a little cry of anguish she grabbed for the doorknob to follow. But as her finger closed around it, she heard a light knock on the other side, and she stopped. At her feet Abel whined impatiently, his nose pressed to the edge of the closed door.

"He's back, Abel," she whispered. "He's back."

She took a deep breath and opened the door.

"Good day to you, Miss Fairbourne." Gerald swept a low bow over his outstretched leg, deftly keeping the flowers to one side to avoid crushing them. "I trust I find you well."

She hesitated only a moment. "Very well, Ger—ah, Mr. Crosbie. And I thank you for your inquiry. Would you care to join me, Mr. Crosbie?"

She stepped aside to let him pass, close enough that his sleeve brushed against her bare arm, reminding her how she was dressed, or undressed, in nothing more than her shift, and she shivered.

"For you, Miss Fairbourne," he said as he handed her the daffodils. "In honor of the inestimable regard in which I hold you dear."

She nodded solemnly as she took the oversized bouquet in both arms, unsure exactly what was proper to say next. She'd never been given flowers of any sort before, especially not in honor of anything. And she wished he'd stop calling her "Miss Fairbourne." They *were* married, or at least they were as far as she knew. He said he'd wanted a second chance, and so, truly, did she. He couldn't possibly have had it undone—annulled, that's what he'd called it—in three days' time.

Could he?

"You don't have to keep holding the damned things, Serena," he said. "You can put them down, you know."

"Oh—oh, yes." She nodded again, and hurried away across the room to shove the flowers into the pitcher on the washstand. When she turned back, Gerald had tossed aside his hat and was crouching down to unwrap a flat package for an eager Abel.

"Bacon," he explained almost apologetically as he wiped the grease from his fingers with his handkerchief. "I recalled how much Abel liked it."

"He *is* very fond of bacon." She came and knelt beside Abel, thankful for something to discuss other than themselves. She patted the dog's broad back as she watched him gobble the bacon in greedy gulps. "No wonder he didn't bark when you came. Joshua says he is a wretched watchdog, and after this I would have to—"

"Serena." Gerald rested his hand over hers, on top of the dog's back as he ate. "Look at me, sweet."

Reluctantly she did, though without lifting her chin. "I can tell you are about to scold me, Gerald," she began, before he could, "but faith, I only did what you told me to do."

He frowned, his dark brows curving down over the bridge of his nose. "You did?"

She nodded vigorously. It wasn't much of an argument, but it was all she had, and she was determined to make the most of it.

"Aye. You wished me to spend money on myself, and I have. If you hadn't given me so very much, then I wouldn't have had to come clear to Boston. There aren't enough shopkeepers in Appledore to support such— such *generosity* as yours. And I do most certainly still consider myself to be your wife, no matter how you wish otherwise, so you can't scold me about that, either."

"Then I won't," he said, slipping his fingers more intimately in between hers. "Not that it was ever my intention to do so."

"It wasn't?" she asked with surprise. She didn't know which was warmer: Abel's rough fur beneath her hand, or Gerald's fingers on top of it.

"How could I possibly scold *you?*" he asked with no small surprise himself. "I have spent the better part of my life running away whenever things or people became disagreeable, and this is the first time that anyone has ever beaten me to the draw. It has not been a pleasurable experience, I can assure you of that. But as for considering yourself to be my wife, however: that is an entirely different matter indeed."

The bare floor suddenly felt cold beneath her. "It is?"

"It is. Quite." He turned her hand in his. "Ah, I see you have taken excellent care of my ring for me, Miss Fairbourne. I thank you for that. I've had that ring since I was a boy, and I would hate to see it lost now."

Before she realized it, he'd slipped the heavy signet ring from her finger and back onto his.

"Oh, no, Gerald, please!" she cried forlornly as he curled his fingers protectively to keep the ring safely back where he believed it belonged. Was this the first step toward his wretched annulment, then, to take back her wedding ring? She'd only worn the ring for three days, but without it her finger felt bare and exposed. "That is, I know it was yours, but I'd thought—I'd believed—"

"Hush, sweetheart, hush," he ordered gently. "I told you I followed you here to begin again, didn't I?"

"But how cruel of you to do it this way!" cried Serena as she bunched the loose linen of her shift in one hand to rise to her feet.

But before she could escape he'd taken her by the wrist, keeping her there with him. "No, lass, please, I beg you'll grant me my small indulgence. If afterward you call me cruel, well enough, but pray hear me first. Now away with you, Abel. Your part in this is done."

He gave the dog a firm pat on the back leg to encourage him along. Abel turned to give them a doleful look, his muzzle glistening with bacon grease, yawned, then padded dutifully away to find a warm spot before the banked coals in the hearth.

Serena tugged at his hand, trying to pull free. "I'll warrant my part is done, too, if only you'll let me go!"

"Not yet, it isn't," he said, struggling to hold her from where he still was crouching awkwardly at her feet. "Damnation, Serena, but you're making this diffi—oh, *hell!*"

She hadn't meant to pull him over onto his knees, or more specifically, his bad knee, but from the grimace that now twisted his face to the oaths that fought their way through his gritted teeth, she realized she'd done exactly that.

"Oh, Gerald, I am sorry!" Swiftly she knelt beside him, slipping her arm around his shoulders to steady him. "Here, let me help you over to the bed."

He looked at her fiercely from under his brows. "It's not that bad," he said, though to Serena it certainly seemed that it was. "Now you stand there—*there*—and let me finish. I'm supposed to be on my knees anyway, though the devil knows this wasn't how I'd intended to get there."

"But Gerald—"

"Do it." He took a deep breath, forcing his face to twist into a smile. "Please."

"If I must," she said as she finally retreated the one step away that he'd indicated. "But mind, I judge you a great stubborn dunderhead for insisting."

"Thank you." He closed his eyes for a moment, his extravagant lashes sweeping down over his cheekbones, as he took another breath to compose himself. When he opened his eyes again, he'd managed to make his smile look almost at ease, though not to someone who knew him as well as did Serena.

Foolish man, she thought: dear, handsome, under-brained, foolish man that she had the infinite good fortune to love. He said he'd belonged on his knees. There could be but one explanation for that, and she felt relief, and joy, begin to wash over her like the waves on her beach at home.

"You *are* stubborn," she said.

"And so, thank God, are you," he said, "else we'd never suit. Now give me your hand, you wicked creature."

She did, and he held it so lightly she was sure he'd notice how it trembled.

He cleared his throat. "The last time I did this, I was

so distracted I'd no notion of what I'd said or promised. Distracted by you, of course, but that is beside the point."

He reached into his coat pocket for another ring, a new one, and as he slipped it onto her finger, she realized that his hands were shaking, too.

"With *this* ring, Serena Fairbourne," he said gruffly, "I thee wed. There now, it's done properly."

"Oh, Gerald," she whispered, staring down at the new gold band on her finger. "Whatever am I to say?"

She had never seen a ring like it. Not only did this one fit her without being wrapped with string, but the two tiny gold scallop shells that crowned the top proved how much he, too, remembered about the day they'd met.

"You might say you like the ring, Mrs. Crosbie," he said as he took back her hand and gently drew her face down to his. "That would be a fair beginning."

"It is perfection," she whispered with a little catch of joy in her voice, "as you know perfectly well. And so, Mr. Crosbie, are you."

She was near enough now that he felt the warmth of that little catch in her breath upon his cheek, promising an equally warm welcome between her lips. No wonder he'd lost interest in the ring. He had, in fact, for the moment lost every memory of it. His entire being was focused on her mouth so close to his, on how her hair had fallen into an enticing golden tousle around her shoulders, how one of those shoulders itself was bare where her shift had slipped to one side.

Her smile was charmingly lopsided with uncertainty. She shouldn't have doubts any longer about being his wife, but clearly she needed further reassurance. So, for that matter, did he. He threaded his fingers back through her hair, bringing her face closer to his, and kissed her.

He kissed her. That was the simple explanation for what he was doing, but it didn't begin to describe what that meant. Her lips parted immediately for him, her mouth warm and eager and infinitely soft and yielding, and she tasted of a thousand things, of salt-spray from the sea and laughter and wildflowers and spicy-sweet quiddany, which was to say she tasted of one thing alone, and that was herself. Knowing that she was his wife, his to enjoy and savor forever, was exciting in a way he'd never dreamed possible, and only made him want her more.

He slipped an arm around her waist, pulling her to her knees against him as he sank more deeply into the wonders of her kiss. Beneath the linen her body was soft and pliant, melding against his, and the musky sleeping-woman scent still clung to her skin. His hands slid lower, over the full curves of her hips and bottom, guiding her against the hard, ready proof of his interest.

"Wait," she said, her voice husky, pushing back away from him with her hands on his chest. "Gerald, please. This isn't fair."

"Don't tender philosophy to me now, Serena," he said as he ran his tongue lightly across the skin of her exposed shoulder. Its roundness had reminded him of a peach, soft and downy and glowing pink, and he was discovering to his pleasure how exceptionally apt an analogy this was. "Nothing could be more fair than being here with you."

"That's not what I meant," she said breathlessly as she ran her hands into his coat, shoving the heavy fabric from his shoulders, back over his arms, and down across his hands.

"No?" he asked as he impatiently shrugged his coat into a heap on the floor behind him.

"No," said Serena as she began to work her fingers down the long row of embroidered buttons that fastened the front of his waistcoat. "I am here in my shift alone, while you are shrouded in layers and layers of worsted and linen and probably some silk somewhere, too. *That* is not fair."

Nor was it fair that there were a great many buttons, tiny buttons, or that he was doing his concentrated best to distract her from her task. Not that he objected to being undressed by her—far from it—but as he slid the hem of her shift higher he could see, and touch, the long, clean line of her bare legs. He loved this first, private glimpse of her legs without stockings or garters, pale and sleek, and making his thoughts race ahead to consider what lay at the top of her thighs. Heaven, he decided, pure heaven; he could scarce wait. Lightly he ran his fingertips along the back of her knee as he kissed the hollow beneath her collar bone. She gasped, resting her forehead briefly against his chest, while her fingers still fumbled gamely to undo the last few buttons.

"You are very . . . very *bad,*" she breathed, nearly incoherent with distraction.

"I try," he said hoarsely and without much modesty, and let his hand creep higher beneath her shift.

She made a little strangled noise deep in her throat as he did, and simultaneously the last button on the waistcoat gave way. Impatiently she shoved it aside, then with both hands grabbed the opening of his shirt beneath and ripped it down the front into two neat halves.

"From the first day I saw you," she said with a guilty giggle as she ran her hands across his now-bare chest, "I have wished to do that."

"Rourke," he said, "would die."

She ran her palms over the broad muscles of his chest, flexing her fingers into the dark whorls of hair as she explored the tantalizing differences between her body and his own. Her hand followed the narrowing path of the hair, along his belly, and he sucked in his breath at her touch. The differences were becoming more apparent by the second.

"Hang Rourke," she said succinctly, looking up at him from beneath her lashes. "I'm your wife, Gerald, and I can always sew you a new shirt. A hundred, if needed."

He envisioned a future of her ripping the clothes from his body nightly. His body responded further, and with ever-growing interest.

"Enough, Serena," he said roughly, taking her wrists in his hands. "Unless you wish me to tumble you here on the floor."

She frowned, perplexed, and shook her hair back from her face. "The bed, then?"

"An agreeable suggestion." He began to rise, then stopped and swore as the pain flared fast in his knee. It wasn't nearly as bad as the last time—he'd put his weight on it wrong, that was all—but it was enough to make him stop.

"Oh, Gerald, how could I have forgotten?" said Serena softly, though her disappointment was clear as she took his arm. "Come, let me help you."

He climbed gingerly to his feet, leaning his arm across her shoulder. She fit against him well, well enough that he felt the pain already fading from his knee. She was, he decided, an excellent size for a woman, with exactly the right degree of softness in the right places, too, places he intended to consider much more closely.

"Perhaps while we are here in Boston we should take you to a surgeon," she suggested, unaware of the sensation that her hip was causing as it pressed into him. "I have an interest in seeing you healthy, you know."

"Damnation, Serena," he growled. "Do you really wish me to end this here?"

"There will be other times," she said with noble resignation as she helped him hobble across the room toward the bed. "If your knee grieves you so, then we— *Gerald!*"

With one arm around her waist he neatly tipped her onto her back on the coverlets, letting her sprawl tumbled across the bed.

"You have a great deal to learn about me, Mrs. Crosbie," he said as he pulled off the rest of his clothes, "if you believe that your pleasure—and mine, too, to be selfishly honest about it—depend upon my blasted knee. My *knee,* for God's sake."

She grinned, her arms outstretched and her hair fanned about her head on the coverlet.

"Then it must fall to you to educate me, *Mr.* Crosbie, if I am so woefully ignorant of such things." She rolled over onto her hands and knees and began crawling up the bed, her shift tangling about her thighs, a sight that made him nearly groan aloud. "Here, let me snuff the candle."

"No," he ordered hoarsely as he dropped his breeches to the floor. "Leave it. I want to be able to see you."

She turned, leaning back with her elbows on the bolster behind her, and her eyes widened perceptibly as she studied him. The way she did it wasn't bold—he'd never cared for boldness in a woman, anyway—but her interest was considerable, and he liked that very much indeed, especially for a new bride.

Jesus, he'd nearly forgotten. This was their wedding night, and here he was rampaging about before her with all the snorting subtlety of the village bull. He could almost hear Anabelle scolding him. Serena was a remarkably brave woman, but she wasn't one of his usual worldly partners. He didn't want to terrify her outright, and belatedly he reached for the edge of the sheet to cover himself as he climbed onto the bed.

But instead of thanking him, she scowled, a close second to her brother's black stare. "Now that is not fair, either, Gerald, not fair at all. You are a beautiful man, and I should like to see you every bit as much as you say you do me, yet there you are, scurrying to hide your light, as it were, under a bushel."

Before he could answer Serena wriggled upright, grabbed the hem of her shift with both hands, and pulled it over her head in one fluid movement. She shook her hair free and raised her chin, determined to meet his eye levelly. But as a grown woman she had never been this exceptionally unclothed before anyone else, not even Abel, and she could feel the warm flush of discomfiture beginning somewhere around her chin and spreading both upwards and down, clear to her forehead and over her breasts as well. Yet she didn't flinch, or cover herself. This was Gerald, her husband, her love, and she smiled, albeit crookedly, at the thought.

And oh, Lord, he *was* such a thoroughly beautiful man, with his long dark hair loose over his shoulders, such broad shoulders, too, and arms that would do her sailor brothers proud, and his lean, flat belly, and—and all the rest of him, too, those fascinating male parts that she didn't know the proper names for. But she'd no doubt she would learn, and soon. *He* would teach her, and she felt that flush spreading further, into her very blood, and hot enough to make her wriggle a bit more.

He wasn't jesting any longer. The strangled look on his face was new to her, and she wondered if he was feeling the same peculiar but pleasant warmth that she was.

"I should like it very much if you kissed me, Gerald," she said shyly. "That is, if you please."

"My God, Serena," he said hoarsely as he reached to take her in his arms. "You should never have to ask."

As easily as he'd tipped her onto the bed he now rolled her beneath him, pressing her deep into the feather-bed. She'd thought she'd known what kissing him was like, but nothing they'd shared before had prepared her for the overwhelmingly new sensations of feeling his skin and his hair and his weight against her, his strength and the male scent of him, even the taste of his kiss, richer somehow in ways she couldn't explain.

His caresses were bolder now, too, sweeping along the length of her body in a way that made that first warmth in her blood glow hotter still, and when his mouth, wet and teasing, found her breast, she arched beneath him, instinctively seeking what only he could give her. She hadn't realized she'd let her legs fall open until he touched her there, too, and she cried out with surprise and pleasure at the way her heartbeat had seemed to shift to this magic place she hadn't guessed existed.

"Please," she gasped raggedly, not knowing what she sought, what she craved, as she clung to him. "Oh, please, please, *please*, Gerald!"

"Another moment longer, Serena," he said, his breathing as harsh and unsteady as her own. "I want to be sure you're ready, that you're—"

"Please," she gasped again, almost a wail, twisting

beneath him, and against him, until suddenly he was inside of her, deep inside, and the teasing heat and the fire ended abruptly before a new, unwanted pain that was there with him as well. He was, as she'd so often noticed, a large man, large in every way. She shifted beneath him as best she could, trying to ease the sharp ache of being so *filled* like this.

"Don't," ordered Gerald with a groan, his eyes squeezed shut. "Don't move, I beg you."

She froze. "It's your knee, isn't it?" she asked anxiously, her own discomfort temporarily forgotten. "I've gone and hurt you more, haven't I?"

"For God's sake, Serena, it's not my blasted knee," he said, breathing as hard as if he'd run a race. "It's you. You're so perfect, and I—oh, hell, I've made you cry."

He rubbed his thumb tenderly over her cheek, wiping away a tear that Serena hadn't realized was there.

"It won't always be like this, you know," he said, with a certain kind-hearted desperation, as if he were trying to convince himself as much as her. "You'll see. I promise."

That desperate little promise of a hope from him made the tears rise up fresh in her eyes, and before they betrayed her again she buried her face against his shoulder and pulled him closer. He groaned again, and gently began to move within her, long, slow strokes that miraculously eased the soreness. Tentatively she began to move with him, and to her great surprise the warm sensation of coiling pleasure began to build again within her. He'd been right to promise after all. She curled her legs over his hips, taking more of him, and the pleasure grew, faster and hotter and in a race with her heartbeat, until it burst within her with a suddenness that made her cry out with joy and release, a cry that was echoed seconds later by Gerald as he spilled himself deep within her.

Afterward, long after the last candle had guttered out, they lay tangled together, not speaking, not needing to, as one by one he kissed away her tears of happiness.

"I love you, Serena," he whispered against her hair, so softly he scarce heard it himself.

But she did. "I know," she said drowsily. "I always have known, even before you did. Though I do believe I loved you first."

"You did?" he asked, genuinely surprised.

"Aye," she said, curling closer with an extravagant yawn. "From the day in the boat. I loved you then, and I love you now, and I expect I'll love you even more as the years go by."

"Matched only, of course, by me."

A banshee's moan suddenly rose from the darkness, cutting off as abruptly as it had begun.

Gerald started, rolling Serena to one side. "What the devil—"

"It's only Abel," said Serena, giggling as she pulled him back down beside her. "Doubtless he's dreaming of more bacon from you. That means he's contented."

"I suppose it's better that all three of us feel the same."

She laughed again, a soft vibration in the dark. "You should be thankful he didn't decide to join us on the bed. He does that, too, when it's cold."

"I shall have to persuade him otherwise. Abel is as good a dog as there is, but I have married *you,* and not him." He lifted her hand to his lips and kissed it lightly, next to the new ring that symbolized so much. "In the old days pilgrims put cockle shells like those upon their hats to let everyone know they were on a journey."

She let her head tip sideways onto his chest, her eyes heavy-lidded. "A journey, you say."

"I say it because it's true, noddy." He ran his fingers fondly through her hair, brushing it away from her still-damp face. "It seemed only right to put them on your ring to announce to the world my wandering is done. And yours, too, for that matter, my fair mistress mermaid. Appledore was deuced dull without you. No more dashing away, mind? You must promise me that."

"I'll promise you anything you wish, Mr. Crosbie," she said sleepily. "I love you, and you're my husband.

And because I am your wife, and your *bella cicerone,* and your muse, and your nymph, and your mermaid, and goodness knows whatever else, I'm afraid I can do . . . I can do . . . nothing . . . less."

What she'd done was to fall asleep, her body soft against him and her breath coming in peaceful little wheezes that he was too charitable, and too much in love, to call snoring. He settled his arms protectively around her and smiled in the dark.

Oh, aye, his wandering days were done. And he didn't regret it in the least.

Sixteen

A fine day, decided Gerald with satisfaction as he walked along Lynn Street, as fine a day as man or beast or even a woman could possibly wish for in this life. The sun hung high in a cloudless sky, warm enough to hint at summer, and warm enough, too, to make even the pewter-hearted citizens of Boston smile and laugh as they went about their business. Gerald was happy enough to smile in return, to touch his hat with gallantry to soapy-armed laundresses, or toss a wayward ball back to the boys who'd let it slip away, or join in the delighted applause for a sailor's pet monkey dancing on top of a barrel. How could he not? If the entire city wished to share his joy this morning, then he'd be a hopeless churl not to return their good humor. And on this morning he was certain he was the happiest man in Boston, perhaps in all the colonies.

The happiest, and surely the most fortunate, too, and he smiled again at the thought of his new wife. Once he thought he'd never speak such words, and now he never seemed to tire of them. My wife, Serena: it had a most charming sound to it, and though he knew he was as hopelessly, unashamedly in love as a man could be, his only regret was that he hadn't come to his senses and married her earlier.

He pictured how she'd looked when he'd left her just now, sleeping with her hand beside her cheek on the pillow, her lips parted and her hair tumbled over her bare shoulder, the sheet over half her hip revealing as much as it hid. She'd been so enchanting that he'd almost considered waking her to demonstrate yet again the depth of his ardor; the only way he'd been able to let her sleep was to leave the inn entirely. God knows she needed it—the sleep, that is, though the ardor was likely a close second. A *very* close second. Except for the brief, necessary excursions with Abel, for the last five days he and Serena had scarcely left their room, much to Mrs. Whatman's delight, and scarcely left the big curtained bed, either. He'd every intention of returning there soon, too, as soon as he'd found more flowers, no small challenge in Boston, to bring back to Serena.

His dear, darling wife, Serena.

"Fresh China oranges, oh!" cried the buxom young woman to Gerald's left. "Fresh China oranges, fresh, oh, fresh!"

Though she winked broadly at him, hoping to entice him as much that way as with the glowing fruit in the basket on her arm, it was the baby she'd tied in a checkered sling to her back that caught Gerald's eye. A jolly, fat-cheeked baby with huge eyes and glossy black ringlets, intent not only upon wedging his entire fist into his mouth, but also in covering the whole of his mother's back with the resultant infant slobber. In the past Gerald would have found the baby a rather revolting example of why he'd stayed a bachelor; now he caught himself waggling his fingers beside his ears and grinning like a madman at the little creature.

"Have you wee ones yourself, sir?" asked the mother, no fool as she turned her back to better display her child to Gerald. "You have a way with him, no mistake."

"Not yet, no," he said, sheepishly dropping his waggling fingers to his sides where they belonged. "I am but newly wed, less than a fortnight."

"Then may God's blessings smile upon you an' your wife, sir!" The woman nodded sagely. "'Tis early days now, but a fine gentleman like yourself's sure t' sire a dozen children in no time."

"Early days, yes," said Gerald uncomfortably, and cleared his throat. How the devil had he fallen into such a conversation with an orange-seller on the street?

Yet what the woman said only echoed what had already been on his mind. In one of Anabelle's more unwelcome confidences, she'd told him that her child had been conceived within the first week of her marriage, perhaps even (and at least she'd had the decency to blush) before it. He and Serena were of exactly the same breeding stock as Joshua and Anabelle; wasn't it possible that Serena, too, was already on her way toward motherhood? It was a possibility—more a probability, really—that he found both terrifying and exhilarating, and he began studying the baby with renewed, if wary, interest.

"An orange for your lady-wife, sir?" coaxed the woman with another sly wink. "Fresh China oranges, sir?"

Gerald laughed. "I doubt they're either from China or fresh."

"Fresh yesterday from th' sloop that brought them t' port!"

"Fresh enough for me, then." He dropped the coins into her waiting palm and chose the two largest oranges, slipping them neatly into his coat pockets. Oranges would be a rare treat for breakfast, and besides, he'd had little luck finding flowers. "And I'll give my 'lady-wife' your wishes, too, along with your—"

"My Lord Crosbie!"

Even before he turned Gerald knew who it was, for only one person in his life had been so misguided as to give him a title that wasn't his. But what in blazes was Mary Sears doing here in Boston?

"Oh, my lord!" Breathlessly she hurled herself against

him, forcing him to hold out his arms to keep her from dropping to the ground. He'd remembered her as frail, but now she looked wretchedly unhappy as well, her narrow shoulders drooping visibly beneath her kerchief. And she'd been crying; he'd spent enough time in women's company to recognize the reason for her red-rimmed eyes and their puffy lids. The reason, yes, but not the cause.

"Here, Mary, come sit and ease yourself," he said with concern, taking her by the arm to guide her to a bench outside a public house. How he wished that Serena was here with him; Serena would know exactly what to do. "Let me get you a cup of tea or a glass of cider."

"You'll do no such thing, sir!" ordered a stern woman's voice behind him. "Remove your hand from that young woman's arm instantly, sir, or I shall cry loud and long for assistance until you do!"

The stern voice belonged to an equally stern woman with a grim visage to match, dressed, or rather upholstered, completely in dun-colored wool with a plain linen cap that tied beneath her chin. She swept her gaze from Gerald's shoe buckles to the crown of his hat, and made no attempt to hide her distaste.

"I know your kind, sir," she declaimed, rolling the syllables as fulsomely as if she stood in a pulpit, and loudly enough, too, to begin drawing a crowd around them. "Gentlemen such as you are the lowest viper to feed upon young women such as this one!"

"Oh, no, Mrs. Smather," protested Mary anxiously. "Lord Crosbie is not like that, not at all!"

"Lord Crosbie, hah," said the woman scornfully. "He would have lorded you directly to a brothel, Mrs. Sears, and then how would your poor husband find you?"

"I would most definitely have done nothing of the sort," said Gerald indignantly. "This lady is a dear friend of my wife's, and thus mine as well. If she is in need of assistance, then—"

"How can I trust the word of a glittering devil with cut-steel buttons on his coat and lace at his cuff?"

demanded Mrs. Smather. "And how can you, Mrs. Sears, after your recent misfortunes?"

"Your wife?" repeated Mary in complete bewilderment. "Jupiter, did Serena really marry you?"

"Hah, do not believe him, Mrs. Sears," rumbled Mrs. Smather ominously. "Doubtless this Serena is but another poor creature he has deceived and cast away."

And with that, Gerald decided he had had enough. "She is my wife, ma'am," he said, drawing himself up with all the hauteur of generations of Crosbies, "and this lady is my particular friend, and now my responsibility as well. Mine alone, ma'am. If this displeases you, ma'am, pray do find yourself the nearest sheriff, or magistrate, or whatever other grandee pleases you. But Mrs. Sears comes with me, ma'am, and with me she shall stay."

Even though she'd already begun to deflate in the eyes of the gathering around them, Mrs. Smather managed to glare down at Mary. "Do you then, Mrs. Sears, wish to damn yourself and go off with this impudent rogue?"

Poor Mary nodded and handed the market basket she'd been carrying back to the other woman. "I do, ma'am," she said in a tiny voice as she shrank back behind Gerald. "Lord Crosbie is a true gentleman, and no rogue."

"Then go," the other woman proclaimed as she swept away, "and may God find mercy for your miserable soul!"

"She is the one with the miserable soul," muttered Gerald as he hurried Mary inside the public house and away from the curious. "I have never seen such an ill-tempered, meddling old bit—ah, old woman as that one."

Mary sank gratefully onto a wooden bench, and though the room was close and warm, she drew her shawl higher over her shoulders as if she'd felt a chill.

"Mrs. Smather's not so bad as all that, my lord. She is a Christian woman who does much good, truly, saving young women who might come to ill here in this wicked place, and giving them a haven." Her voice shrank beneath the weight of confession. "She saved me from Ezra."

Gerald sighed. Such meddlesome, good-doing folks were to be found in every city, striving to save others and ensure their own place in heaven in the process. For that matter, he'd the uncomfortable feeling he was turning into an over-helpful meddler himself.

He beckoned to the keep for a pot of tea for Mary and strong coffee for himself, certain that he'd need its Turkish fortitude before this morning was done. "Who is this Ezra, Mary? And why in blazes would you need saving from him, anyway? For that matter, why aren't you still safe in that snug little cottage of yours?"

"Because of Robert." Mary's narrow shoulders drooped even further beneath the neat folds of her kerchief. "Ezra—he is Robert's brother—told me that he'd heard from Robert, that he was alive and waiting for me in Boston. And oh, my lord, I cannot tell you how happy I was! So happy that I did went with Ezra that very day, without heed to my doubts."

Gerald frowned. "But surely your husband's brother would not wish you harm."

"He should not, nay." She looked down at her tea. "But Ezra is not a good man, my lord. He is not like my Robert. There, I've said the worst of him, and I vow it must fall bad on me, but 'tis naught but the truth."

"Sometimes," said Gerald gently, "the truth is like that."

"You are kind to say so, my lord," said Mary without lifting her eyes to meet his. "Most kind. But Ezra is harsh, and mean, and lazy, and he blames Robert's misfortunes for his own. It is not my Robert's fault that Ezra's found no berth on a decent ship—how could it be?—but he will say so to any who'll listen. He would blame Robert for a day's cold rain if he thought he'd see profit from it."

Gerald took a long swallow of his coffee. It did not take an oracle to tell the rest of Mary's story. "And once you'd reached Boston, there was no sign of Robert, and worse, it had somehow become your fault, hadn't it?"

"Ah, my lord, you are so clever!" she said unhappily, as a bright glow of shame stained her sharp little cheekbones. "Ezra said I'd been disloyal to Robert and to him by being friends with Serena. He hates Serena for that, my lord, nearly as much as he hates her just for being Captain Fairbourne's sister, and he said if I wished to make it up to him, I had to—he wanted me to—"

"So you ran away instead," said Gerald quickly, sparing her. He could imagine well enough what price Ezra had wanted her to pay, and it angered him to think any man, let alone her husband's brother, would dare treat such a helpless creature as Mary Sears in this despicable fashion.

Mary nodded miserably. "We had scarce left the packet boat, and I had not even the fare for my passage home, but I couldn't bear to be with Ezra, not after that. I should have been wiser, and known how Ezra is and stayed home, as you said. You would not understand it, my lord, but oh, I wanted so much to believe that Robert had come back for me that I would've done anything—anything!"

"Ah, but I do understand, Mary. I've Serena to thank for that," said Gerald gently, reaching out to pat her arm. This was hardly the way he would have chosen to end their blissful wedding trip, but it was unthinkable to abandon Mary Sears now. "We'll see that you come back to Appledore with us, and I'll deal with Ezra myself."

Mary dared to lift her gaze from her tea. "Have you truly married Serena, then?" she asked uncertainly. "Jupiter, I never would have dreamed it!"

"Neither would I," he agreed, "but I'm powerfully glad that I came to my senses in the end. Now come with me, and Serena can explain it all to you herself."

It was the most delicious way to pass a morning.

Serena smiled and stretched luxuriously, basking in the afterglow of such infinite pleasure. Gerald lay behind her, his arms around her waist as he held her as close as a husband could, their bodies still intimately twined.

"Sweet Serena," he growled as he pushed her hair away from her ear. "My own wicked, wanton lass."

She laughed softly and pressed back against him, the way she'd discovered he liked best, and was rewarded by a warm, wet kiss on her neck, below her ear, a most sensitive place she newly discovered on herself as well.

"Who has made me so wanton, love?" she murmured. "Ah, Gerald!"

She twisted about to face him, seeking the kiss that could bring her such endless delight. But his mouth had somehow grown a great quantity of fur in place of his lips and whiskers, nor was the fragrance of his breath particularly beguiling as his tongue licked wetly across her cheek.

"Abel!" With an indignant wail Serena woke and shoved the dog back from her face. "Bad dog! Very, very bad dog, to climb on the bed so!"

Dejectedly Abel clambered from the high bed to the floor, his head low with contrition as he gazed up at Serena.

She rubbed her cheek with the edge of the sheet and sighed. It had been such a pleasant dream, at least while it lasted. But she could hardly blame poor Abel; there'd been a time, and not so long ago, either, when a morning kiss on the cheek from him would have been the most appealing one she'd be likely to receive. She flopped over onto her stomach, reaching out over the edge of the bed to scratch Abel's head.

"I am sorry, Abel," she apologized. "You startled me, that is all. I suppose all you wished is to go outside, hmm? Outside?"

The dog thumped his tail in eager response.

"Very well," she said. "Let me collect myself, and we'll be gone."

She sat upright and yawned, stretching her arms behind her back. She was not particularly surprised to find herself alone; Gerald had fallen into the habit of rising before she did and going out walking, and, she suspected, to a barber, for she'd yet to see him shave himself, much to her private amusement. Because he'd taken his watch with him, she'd no notion of the exact time, but from the bright lines of sunlight edging the drawn curtains she guessed it must be late morning at the very least. Not that she'd been quite ready to rise. Another morsel of sleep seemed an enormously wise idea, and after she let Abel out she'd every intention of returning to bed. If she were truly fortunate, she'd be there still when Gerald returned.

With a yawn she rolled off the bed, and instead of reaching for her own clothing, she took what was nearest, Gerald's gold silk banyan. She wrapped it tightly around herself, relishing how his scent had permeated the rich fabric, surrounding her body the same way he did himself when they made love. It wasn't the most respectable attire for a lady, especially worn over nothing but her own skin, but at this time of the morning she doubted she'd meet any of the servants or other guests on the back stairs.

"Come along, Abel," she said as she unlatched the door. "Outside."

The dog bounded obediently ahead, having learned well these past days the way to the turning back stairs that led to the inn's stableyard. Serena followed, the sleeves of the banyan drooping over her hands as she clutched at the heavy silk to keep from tripping over it on the stairs.

"You're growing quite portly, Abel," she said as she unbarred the back door. "Too much bacon and not enough rabbit chasing. If we don't return to Cranberry Point soon, you'll grow so stout people will mistake you for a small black heifer. Now go, run about."

She watched the dog go bounding across the walled yard, pausing here and there to investigate some particularly interesting bit of straw or horse leavings on his way to his favorite spot, the stables themselves. As Serena had guessed, there was little activity in the yard at this time of day; guests had either left or were yet to arrive, and the inn's staff was all occupied with either preparing, serving, or eating the midday meal. The day was bright, and she stepped outside the door, turning her face up toward the sun like a flower to feel the warmth upon her cheeks.

It was time she and Gerald returned to Cranberry Point, too. As much as she'd enjoyed their days and nights together here, as long as she'd treasure the memory, she still longed to return home so they might begin their life together in earnest.

Or at least that was the life she prayed they'd share; she knew how little certainty there was to such prayers. She and Gerald had never discussed such things between them, and she'd been too much a coward to ask him where they'd finally live. He'd made no secret of how much he loved journeying and how he craved newness and novelty. He hadn't offered to change his ways, and she didn't expect it. Wives were the ones to change, not husbands.

But how would Gerald fit her into such adventures? At least she knew she wouldn't be left behind like Mary or any other sailor's dutiful wife. He'd made that much clear. But to be borne about like some rootless gypsy, with no home to tend and call her own seemed like no real life at all for a woman, and as for children—she wanted their children to grow surrounded by friends and family, in the kind of home she'd always wanted for herself.

She'd never doubted she and Gerald would have children, lots of children, especially not after this time in Boston. She closed her eyes, remembering her earlier dream, and the blissful reality that had preceded it, and smiled to herself. Perhaps she was carrying their first child already, and once they—

The cloth that suddenly covered her face was wet, soaked with some sort of sweet-smelling oil that made her head spin and her knees grow soft beneath her. Yet still she fought, struggling to call for Abel, her fingers clawing weakly against the cloth and the smothering scent and the man's arm locked around her waist, pulling her down, pulling her back, drawing her at last into the black emptiness of oblivion.

"Oh, Mr. Crosbie, how glad we are to see you!" cried Mrs. Whatman as she rushed to greet Gerald in the front hall of the inn. "Such a trial we are having, sir, such a trial, and only you can help us!"

Gerald sighed. With Mary Sears trembling wide-eyed at his side, he believed he'd already had his fill of dutiful salvation for one day.

"You have always impressed me as a most resourceful woman, Mrs. Whatman," he said heartily, hoping to escape the landlady through base flattery, the way he usually did. "I greatly doubt I can remedy any crisis that has defied your supreme gifts for resolution."

"Nay, Mr. Crosbie, you are wrong there!" she said, waving her hands in the direction of the back door to urge him along. "You must come—you must! 'Tis your wife's great black dog, sir, gone wild in the stableyard, he has!"

"Abel?" asked Gerald with disbelief. "Why, Abel is the most even-tempered dog I've ever known!"

"Not now he's not, begging pardon," declared Mrs. Whatman firmly. " 'Twas only from concern of your wife's feelings that I forbid Mr. Whatman from taking his musket and putting the creature down. Snarling and slavering like the devil's own hound, he is, and gone and bitten one of the grooms something fearful. You must come directly!"

But Gerald was already ahead of her, striding toward the open back door and the commotion outside. A small ring of men, some holding wooden pitchforks, stood warily before the brick wall near the stable door, and above their excited voices Gerald could just make out a low, frightened growl that must belong to Abel.

"Abel!" shouted Gerald as he broke into a run. Serena would be devastated if anyone harmed her dog. And so, for that matter, would he. "Abel! Abel, here!"

The growl rose up into a yip of recognition and like a black bolt Abel shot through the ring of men and raced across the yard toward Gerald.

"Take care, sir!" shrieked Mrs. Whatman as she scurried for safety. "Mad dog!"

But as Abel came skidding to a halt, his whole body trembling with relief, Gerald could see at once that there was nothing mad about him. But the small smears of blood glistening on his back fur showed where he'd been jabbed with the pitchforks, and Gerald looked angrily to the men who'd done it.

"Why was my wife's dog mistreated in this fashion?" he demanded of the stableman who'd come running after the dog. "You are the mad ones, not he. If you'd but gone to Mrs. Crosbie first—"

"We tried, sir," said Mrs. Whatman, daring to return now that Gerald had his fingers looped firmly through Abel's collar. "I knocked and knocked at your door, but Mrs. Crosbie never answered. I believed her with you, sir."

"That is ridiculous," he snapped. "My wife would never go out and leave her dog behind."

Yet even as Gerald spoke a chill dread began to creep around the edges of his heart. It was true that Serena would never willingly go anywhere without Abel by her side, and conversely Abel would never let her go without him. When Gerald had left Serena, she'd been soundly asleep, with Abel in much the same state on the floor beside the bed. So how could Abel have come to be alone in the stableyard?

And where, dear God, was Serena?

He ran up the stairs two at a time, throwing open the door to the chamber he'd shared with Serena. Everything was exactly as he'd left it: the curtains still drawn across the windows, the hastily shed clothes tossed across chairs and the floor, the sheets and pillows mussed and tumbled.

Except, of course, that there was not the slightest sign of Serena.

"There's none of us have seen her go, sir," said Mrs. Crosbie apologetically, wringing her hands in her apron as she hovered in the doorway. "She couldn't have gone out without us noting it, sir, not out the front."

Gerald didn't hear her, as instead he struggled to make sense of what had happened. No, what *was* happening: he wouldn't give up Serena without a fight. There'd been no theft: his trunk with the small strongbox with his coins tucked inside was still locked, untouched, and the only jewelry Serena owned was her wedding ring. For that matter, the windows were locked, too, proving that no one had forced their way into the room.

But if Serena had left on her own, what in blazes was she wearing? She had brought few clothes, and all of them remained in the room, even to her stays and shift and stockings and the shoes that Abel was even now snuffling forlornly. She couldn't be parading along the streets of Boston like Lady Godiva.

He swore, and whipped back the bed's coverlet in angry frustration, and then, suddenly, realized that the one thing that was missing was his banyan. He'd often worn it to let Abel run in the yard. Could Serena, then, have done the same? He imagined the gold silk wrapped close over her naked body, and the dread deepened its hold on his heart. He could dismiss the idea of her being stolen from their chamber, but out-of-doors, from the stableyard, with her clad only in his dressing gown was altogether different.

He'd spent his whole life wandering, unaware that he'd been searching for Serena, the one woman meant for him. His Serena, his wife, his one love.

And now, through his own carelessness, she was gone, and all the joy, all the happiness he'd found with her came crashing down around him.

He looked to Abel, who'd gone from Serena's belongings to pacing back and forth before the doorway, pausing to look back over his shoulder at Gerald and whimpering anxiously for him to follow.

"Do you think you can find her, Abel?" he asked, immediately seizing on the possibility. He didn't want to admit it was the only one he had. Not that it mattered: he'd tear this entire town apart clapboard by clapboard to find her, and oh, how he'd make the man pay who'd done this to her, and to him. "Can you take me to Serena?"

"But I ask you, sir, who would wish to hurt a young lady such as Mrs. Crosbie?" asked Mrs. Whatman plaintively. "Whoever could wish her harm?"

Almost without thinking Gerald looked to Mary Sears. The answer was clear enough to him, and from the way she pressed her hand to her breast he knew it was clear to her, too.

"Ezra," she whispered hoarsely as she sagged against the mantelpiece for support. "Dear God, it must be Ezra."

"When do you think she'll wake, Ezra?" asked Robert with concern. "She's been asleep for so long it makes me fearful."

"She'll wake soon enough," said Ezra as he cut another slice of the cheese they'd bought for their supper. "The apothecary said the oil ne'er took the same on every person. Some sleep longer, some not. Our little doxie there be one of the ones that sleeps longer."

"Hush now, don't speak so o' her," said Robert uneasily as he turned the neck of the rum bottle around and around in his palms. He didn't care what the apothecary had told Ezra. It wasn't natural for anyone to have slept throughout the day without moving so much as a finger, and it wasn't natural sleep, either; it was quiet as the grave. She had the look of the grave about her, too, lying there on the floor of their small, mean hired room, still wrapped in the grimy old sail that they'd bundled her in while they'd carried her through the streets. Robert worried that they'd unwittingly smothered her, but when he leaned over her he could see the tiniest flutter of a breath from her pale lips.

"Taking a peek for yourself, are you now, brother?" Ezra chuckled lewdly. "I'd be looking for more o' a poke than a peek, myself."

"I told you, Ezra, none o' that manner o' talk about her," said Robert sharply. "She's a lady."

Ezra shoved his chair back from the table and came to stand beside Robert. "Oh, aye, that be the very image o' a fine Christian lady," he jeered, and before Robert could stop him he'd flicked aside the sailcloth. "The kind o' lady I'd want being friends with *my* wife. What kind o' lady dresses in a smock like this one, with nary a stitch beneath? Don't leave much to fancy, does it?"

And Robert did look, though it shamed him deeply to do so. Serena had always been kind to him, had never laughed at his tongue-tied ways, and she did not deserve to be ogled now. Yet he couldn't stop himself, not with her hair so wantonly loose around her shoulders and the full, rounded curves of her breasts and hips and belly accentuated by the shining golden silk that barely covered them.

"Don't matter now whether she's a Fairbourne or not," said Ezra hungrily, his pale eyes turning wolfish as he reached for the edge of the gold silk. "A hussy like her's made to give a man pleasure. Wouldn't you like to fill your hands with that pair, eh, brother, then fill her sweet nest besides? When she woke, she'd ne'er recall a thing."

"You leave her be!" ordered Robert furiously as he struck his brother's arm away so hard that Ezra fell and skidded back across the floor. "That's wicked wrong, Ezra, and the devil take you if'n you don't know it!"

"Don't turn pious on me now, Robert," said Ezra, panting, as he scrambled to his knees. "Or maybe you fear you're not man enough to take your turn with the wench, that the rum's left you too mealy and weakish to please a woman proper?"

"What you're talking has nothing to do with pleasure, Ezra Sears," said Robert, stung by the mocking reference to the rum, "and I won't listen to another foul word of it. When Serena wakes, when it's dark, we'll take her to the island, like we planned, and wait for the captain to come to us with Mary, and with the pardon."

"And the gold, Robert," said Ezra, rubbing his arm. "Mind in the letter I sent to Fairbourne, I asked him for gold, too."

"And the gold." Robert sighed heavily. All he'd wanted was to be reunited with Mary, and instead he and Ezra seemed to be plummeting deeper and deeper into deceit, so far down that he doubted they'd ever be able to claw their way back out. He didn't like it, not at all, but it was too late now to change his mind.

And still Mary would be his reward. Everything he did now was for her sake alone. His one prayer was that it would be enough.

"I'll take you back to the inn now, Mary," said Gerald as he paused to let Abel rest. "It's getting late now, and you'll be safer with the Whatmans."

But to his surprise Mary shook her head. "I'm staying with you and Abel, my lord," she said stubbornly. "I told you that before, and I meant it. It's because of me that Ezra took Serena, and because of that I'll stay with you until you find her."

Gerald sighed uneasily. The sky was nearly dark, the first lights already lit behind windows for evening. The air had cooled when the sun had set, and a light mist hovered over the water, hiding all but the brightest stars overhead. Darkness, fog, and a paucity of lights and torches did not, in Gerald's opinion, make for a reassuring combination. Though Boston was too young a city to rival the centuries of evil and misdeeds that permeated the waterfront streets of London, it still could boast a good—or bad—supply of drunkards, thieves, and other miscreants, especially in the low rum shops and taverns that he intended to visit next.

The three of them—Mary, Abel, and himself—had spent the afternoon crisscrossing the wharfs and the bent and winding streets, searching faces and asking questions and, in Abel's case, sniffing for any trace of Serena. If Appledore were less than a day's voyage—at best—away, Gerald would have sent for Joshua, too, but he had refused the search party that Mrs. Whatman had offered to assemble, just as he'd refused to go to the constable. Too often such well-meant help ended in bungled tragedy, and besides, this was between him and Ezra Sears. When they finally met, he wanted no one else in the middle.

He had allowed Mary Sears to come with him this far because she could identify Ezra and he could not, and also, though he'd never admit it, because he hadn't the heart to leave her behind. Together they were the two people in the world who cared most for Serena, and somehow it seemed oddly right to have Mary with him, almost as if there were a little bit of Serena there, too.

"I cannot countenance the risk to you, Mary," he said gently. Beneath the long tails of his coat he carried two pistols tucked into his belt and a knife as well, and he'd no qualms about putting them to use if necessary. "At night every city is a different place."

"One more time along the water, my lord, one more, I beg you!" cried Mary, anxiously twisting her hands in the corners of her shawl. "I feel sure that this time will be the one, and—and Serena would wish me to be here with you, I know it!"

Gerald sighed again, shaking his head. The worst of it was knowing that Serena *would* want her here. "You're two of a kind, you know," he said gruffly, "both of you stubborn and willful and too damned brave to last a day in the world."

Mary smiled sadly. "That is what my Robert said, too, though I know there's not a whit of truth to it. Serena is

Serena, and I am only Mary. But you would have liked my Robert, my lord, liked him just fine."

It was the first time he'd ever heard her speak of her husband in the past tense, and he wondered if she even realized herself that she'd done it. He understood now how she must feel; without Serena, he felt as if a part of himself were missing, gone, leaving an ache that wouldn't fade. "Only a good man," he said softly, "would have wed you, Mary."

"Oh, aye, so I told him often enough." Swiftly she looked away to avoid his pity, out over the wharfs to the water. "One more time along the shore, my lord, there where all the boats are drawn up for the night."

"One more time, and that is all," he said. He believed that Ezra and Serena were still on land, somewhere in the town, mainly because he didn't want to believe they'd escaped by water and to the sea beyond, where his search could become endless. "But only if you vow to stop this lordly foolishness, and call me Gerald."

Her eyes widened. "Oh, but I can't! 'Tis not my place to be so familiar!"

"You can," he said firmly, "and you will. God knows Serena will want you to do so."

She nodded and took a deep breath. "Aye, then, my— my—*Gerald.*"

"Alas, Serena's already spoken for me," he said, his smile falling short of his eyes. "Now one last pass by the water, and pray our luck has turned."

Seventeen

"Enough o' your sleepyhead," said the man's voice roughly. "Time to rise, you lazy hussy."

Serena's eyes felt weighted shut with sand, and though she tried to tell the man so, her lips were too clumsy to form the words. Her whole body ached, her joints sore from lying on the hard floor with only a piece of rough, ill-smelling canvas for covering.

"Up, I say." He slapped his palms against her cheeks and she groaned in protest. She *was* trying her best to do as he asked, and at last she managed to drag her eyes open.

"There you go," he said, his face so close to hers that his smirk seemed to fill the room. "Easy as pie, once you put your mind to it."

"I know you," she whispered, her mouth so dry she could barely make herself heard as she struggled to find the name that went with the face looming over her. Her mind wouldn't work right, either; everything seemed thick and slow as molasses in winter. "Aye. From Mary."

"Ha, brother, what did I tell you?" crowed the man as

he rose away from her. "The first words she can say are of your wife! We'll have Mary back soon enough now, Robert, and you've only your brother to thank!"

But before she could sift through this for meaning another face had come to hover over her, one that made even less sense than the last.

"Robert," she breathed, confused and troubled. "Robert? Dear God, am I dead, too?"

"Nay, nay, mistress," he said swiftly, his words coming in a rush of rum that turned her stomach, "though you may well wish you were, and how sorry I am for it, too!"

"Robert." She said his name again, making it more solid in her muddled thoughts. He looked older than she remembered, his face thin and lined, his sandy hair fading to gray. "Robert Sears. Why are you not with Mary, Robert? Why are you here?"

The first man cackled. "Ah, you could ask the same of yourself, couldn't you now, *Miss* Fairbourne?"

"No." The thoughts were growing clearer now, tumbling back into place with images to match. She wasn't Miss Fairbourne any longer. She was married, she was Mrs. Crosbie, and she was, she realized, in a great deal of danger. "Where's Gerald? What have you done with my husband?"

"Your *husband?*" Robert turned angrily toward the other man. "Did you hear this, Ezra? She's wedded. Now we'll have her husband after us as well as the cap'n, and still not a whisper of my Mary! Oh, I'm thanking you fine now, Ezra, real fine!"

"Ezra," said Serena slowly. Mary didn't like Ezra, for all that he was Robert's kin; she'd called him mean and wicked, and already Serena could understand why. "You were supposed to be bringing Mary to Boston, here to Robert. Where is she now, Ezra?"

Robert glared at his brother. "Aye, where is she, Ezra? You said Mary was with the Fairbournes, yet here's Serena asking you instead!"

"As if a Fairbourne would tell the truth to any Sears!"

Ezra spat on the floor next to Serena. "Maybe it's this husband o' hers who's got Mary now. *I* surely don't have her, if that's what you're trying to say. Whose word would you trust anyways, Robert? Hers, or mine?"

Repulsed, Serena pushed herself upright, away from the blot of spittle. "But I've not seen Mary for weeks! How could I—"

"Enough of your lies." He seized her by the arm, dragging her, swaying, to her feet, and the sail she'd had as a coverlet dropped away. "If you're wakeful enough to yammer so, you're wakeful enough to come with us."

Serena caught at the slippery silk, trying to tug it into some semblance of decency. Her face grew hot with shame as she saw how Ezra was watching her, and, appalled, she wondered what else he might have seen or done while she'd been unconscious. She'd no notion of the time or day, or how long she'd been here, or why these two men believed that she had done something to Mary, something bad enough for them to make her their prisoner in return. But she did know she was in trouble, perilous, desperate trouble, and that, for now, was more than enough.

And dear God, what Gerald must have thought to find her gone. She knew he would have begun searching for her immediately, most likely with Abel to guide him, but how were they to find her in this tiny garret room? Abel had the best nose of any dog in Appledore, but since she'd been wrapped in the foul-smelling canvas and carried, she would have left no scent, no trail for him to follow.

"Where are we going?" she demanded weakly. Not far, she hoped; she still felt lightheaded, unsteady on her feet. "I cannot go anywhere dressed like this!"

Ezra laughed scornfully. "You've come this far, haven't you?"

But Robert draped a dirty, worn cloak over her hair and shoulders, covering her both for modesty's sake and to disguise her, too. He gazed down at her bare feet and shook his head. "I fear we've given no thought to shoes."

"She don't need 'em." From inside his coat Ezra drew a battered old pistol, slapping the barrel against Serena's arm as he shoved her toward the door. "Mind you do as we say. One wrong word to anyone else and I'll knock you senseless, see if I don't."

She didn't doubt that he would, and her fear rose as they cautiously made their way down the winding back stairs. Back stairs, Lord help her: she'd never go down another set of back stairs again in all her life. A blowsy woman and a half-drunk sailor were coming up the same stairs, and as they squeezed past, Serena considered turning to them for help.

"Mind that I'm close behind you," whispered Ezra, squeezing her arm tightly. "Nary a wrong word, hussy."

Serena bowed her head, hating herself for being such a coward almost as much as she despaired of her own helplessness. But she was one woman against two men and a gun, and doubtless a sailor's knife or two, and there was precious little she could do to save herself. If Robert had been alone, she might have been able to sway him, but not Ezra. At least they didn't seem to intend to kill her, at least not right now, though that was cold comfort indeed. All she could do now was to pray that, one more time, Gerald would save her.

It was night, with the moon hidden behind clouds or fog, and from the salty scent in the air Serena guessed they weren't far from the water. As Ezra led her out into the darkened street, the hem of the gold banyan caught on the hinge of the door, and with a resounding rip, the silk tore, leaving a thin strip dangling behind.

"Oh, no, wait, please wait!" she cried, trying to turn back. The banyan was Gerald's, his favorite, and now she'd gone and ruined it.

"Come along now," ordered Ezra sharply. "No crying over a bit o' rag."

Yet as Serena looked back over her shoulder, the torn strip of silk fluttering forlornly in the moonlight, she realized she'd just discovered the way to mark a trail for Gerald and for Abel, too. She waited until they were near rough-hewn fence, and then she stumbled, making sure to snag the soft fabric again.

"Clumsy chit," muttered Ezra as he jerked her back to her feet as the silk ripped again.

"I can't help it," said Serena meekly. "I've no shoes."

He swore and pushed her along, unable to see the small smile of triumph hidden by her hood. If it would bring her back to Gerald, she was willing to stumble all the way back to Appledore, but every twenty paces or so should be enough, and in the shadow of the hood her secret smile grew with determination.

"There's nothing," said Gerald, letting his gaze sweep one last time the empty length of the wharf. "I've kept my promise, Mary. Now you must keep yours and go back to the Whatmans."

Mary nodded unhappily, staring down the wharf one last time for herself. The harbor lights on the two ships tied near the end glowed ghostly, the tops of their masts disappearing into the shifting fog. Snatches of a jig, played on an ill-tuned fiddle, drifted toward them from the open door of a distant rum shop as they turned back toward shore. They walked in silence, both too tired and too discouraged to do otherwise.

When they reached the street, Gerald whistled for Abel. The dog had wandered off again, though by now his steps dragged and his head drooped so wearily that Gerald was almost resigned to having to carry poor Abel back to the inn in his arms. Now he frowned, wondering why the dog hadn't rejoined them. Abel wasn't the most obedient animal in the world, but he generally did come when called, and with concern Gerald whistled again, louder this time.

A scrabbling of paws, an excited panting, and suddenly Abel was racing around the corner toward them, his earlier exhaustion vanished. He bounded up to Gerald, nearly prancing with excitement, and neatly dropped a long, wet scrap of fabric over the toes of his shoes.

"Oh, Abel," scolded Mary gently. "Gerald doesn't want your rubbish on his feet."

"No, lass, I rather think Gerald does." Gerald held the ragged scrap up to study it, running his fingers over the grimy surface. The color was barely discernable now, a sad, sorry remnant of the beautiful brocaille, but still he'd recognize it anywhere. "Here, Abel, you good, wonderfully good dog!"

Abel ducked his head with pleasure, his tail whipping from side to side, and with an impatient little whine he darted three steps ahead, then ducked back, waiting for them to follow him.

"*Supremely* good Abel!" praised Gerald, drawing Mary along as he hurried after Abel. "Lord Dog of dogs!"

Mary rushed to keep up. "What is it, Gerald?"

"Our first real blessing, Mary, our first clue. This mouldering scrap is part of my banyan, which Serena was—*mirabile dictu,* he's gone and found another!"

This scrap was snagged in the edge of the hoop of a sprung barrel, as hard to miss as a little flag. "Serena's left them for us," he explained excitedly as he tugged the fabric free. "Clever lass, and a vastly clever dog to find them!"

He watched as Abel, with a happy yelp, caught the trail of Serena's scent near the barrel, rushing ahead with his nose lowered. The scent was fresh, and he guessed they'd passed through this street less than an hour, maybe only minutes, before them. He could sense Serena's presence almost as keenly as did Abel, and his heart pounded with anticipation.

The trail ended at a low, short wharf with a handful of small boats tied loosely to the bottom of the ladder. The boats and their oarsmen were for hire, to take passengers back and forth between the larger ships moored farther out in the harbor. At this hour only two men, still hopeful of a last fare, remained with their boat and smoked their pipes by the swinging light of the lantern overhead.

"Have you seen a man and a lady come this way?" called Gerald. "The lady tall and fair, with gold-colored hair?"

The boatmen looked up impassively, considering an endless moment before the older one answered. "Nay, sir, not a lady and a man, nay, not this night."

Gerald swore with frustration. To have come this far and then nothing . . .

"But a lady and two men, aye," continued the boatman, nodding. "Aye, that we've seen, and not three minutes past."

"Two men?" gasped Mary, clutching Gerald's arm. "Brothers?"

The boatman shrugged. "Could be brothers, mistress. Could be not, as well."

"Three minutes isn't much of a start," said Gerald. "A guinea apiece if you can catch them."

The man nodded again, and began untying the boat, prodding it free of the others.

Swiftly Gerald turned to Mary. "You wait here where you'll be safe, with Abel, and I'll be back as soon as I can."

"No!" she cried desperately. "I can't stay here, not wondering and worrying whether it's my Robert that's out there!"

Impatiently Gerald glanced out across the water, wishing he could see through the fog and the darkness. He didn't want the responsibility of Mary in the boat with him, yet he understood all too well why she wished to come. He shook his head, warring with himself.

"Please, Gerald," begged Mary. "I vow I'll never ask another favor of you."

They were wasting time standing here, time Serena didn't have. Gerald took a deep breath, then held out his hand to her. "Can you manage the ladder?"

She was down the rungs in an instant, and he was beginning after her as he whistled again for Abel to join them. But instead of the eagerness he'd expected, Abel was huddled on the far side of the narrow wharf, shivering with his tail pulled between his legs.

"Oh, hellfire," he muttered crossly. He'd forgotten the wretched dog hated ships and boats, but if he left Abel behind now, after he'd been so helpful, Serena would never forgive him. He climbed back up the ladder, slung the front end of the trembling dog over his shoulder, and backed down into the narrow boat.

"Two guineas apiece," he said as the men slipped the oars into the locks. "I want to overtake that boat before they reach land."

"Aye, aye, sir," said the older boatman, bending hard against the oar with his first pull. "Won't be no challenge, that. Them two be rowing themselves, and one's shaking so bad from drink he worse'n that dog. We'll take them easy, sir."

Gerald reached down to give the terrified dog a reassuring pat. One of the Sears brothers must be in a sorry state indeed if he rivaled poor Abel, huddled behind Gerald's legs, pressing himself as low into the bottom of the boat as he possibly could.

"With Ezra rowing, we'll catch them," said Mary with grim certainty as she drew her shawl over her head against the spray. "Especially if he's been drinking. Ezra can't abide rowing or small boats, anyways, on account of not swimming."

Gerald glanced at her incredulously. "He doesn't swim? For God's sake, he's a sailor, isn't he?"

"Ezra doesn't swim, and neither does my Robert. Most sailors don't." She was staring hard at the water before them, clearly willing the other boat to become visible. "It's not proper. If our Maker wished men to fly, then he would have given them wings like birds. If he wished them to swim, then we'd all have gills, wouldn't we?"

"Though feet and hands make passable fins, in a pinch." Gerald knew she'd no more interest in the theology of swimming than he did, not now. He pulled the two pistols from his belt and began to reload them, wanting to be sure that the powder was dry and fresh. His guns weren't as ornate as Oliver Parrish's Groshicks, but they were every bit as deadly, and Gerald was acutely aware of Mary's watching, and of the men at the oars trying hard not to.

"I'd no notion you had those with you," she said, her voice strained. "Will you—would you use them?"

Gerald sighed, knowing everything she wasn't asking. "If I must, yes. Just like the wings, men don't have guns unless they intend to make use of them."

Likely it would break her heart now if the second man in the boat didn't turn out to be her husband, but in a way Gerald almost hoped it wasn't. Even at close range, a figure in a bobbing boat in the fog at night would make a perilously uncertain target. He forced himself to concentrate on loading the pistols instead, making doubly sure of his powder so they wouldn't misfire. Rourke had always done this for him in the past; now he'd have to rely only on himself.

The fog was oddly disorienting, swallowing up all the landmarks from the shore. Sometimes the sound of a ship's bell or a raucous laugh would drift their way, but the fog stole away most everything else into an eerie quiet. The only sure sounds were those of the two boatmen: the heavy rhythm of their breathing, the squeak of the oarlocks, the *shush* of the water as the oars themselves sliced through the wavelets again and again.

Yet for Gerald the fog seemed a welcome omen, reminding him as it did of the day he'd met Serena. No, *met* was not perhaps the best word. His ship had nearly severed her little boat in two. Lord, how furious she'd been at him! He smiled fondly at the memory, remembering, too, how he'd contrived some silly poem to steal a kiss. That kiss had been the beginning, really, for once he'd kissed Serena he'd found it impossible to put her from his mind again.

Jesus, what he'd trade now just to know she was safe.

"They're just ahead o' us, sir," whispered the older boatman.

"Are you certain?" asked Gerald softly, every muscle in his body on edge.

"Oh, aye, sir," said the man, almost apologetically. "From being on the river an' the harbor so long, you get to hearing things most folks don't. But mind how your dog can hear them already, too."

Abel had crawled out from beneath the bench, and was staring intently across the water, his ears cocked to catch the sounds that Gerald still could not make out. Beside him sat Mary with her fingers pressed over her lips in silent prayer as she, too, strained to hear the boat ahead.

"Shall I call out a hail for you, sir," asked the boatman, "or shall you?"

Gerald's fingers tightened around the butt of a pistol, and he shook his head. He turned in the direction that the boatman pointed and cupped his left hand around his mouth.

"You, there!" he roared as loudly as he could. "Stop at once!"

Serena gasped, and started up from her seat. "Gerald!" she cried without thinking. "Gerald, over here!"

Ezra's arm lashed out to knock her backward. "Quiet, damn you! Quiet!"

Yet Serena scarcely felt the blow or heard his warning as she scrambled back onto her seat. Gerald was there, and he'd come for her. "But that's my husband!"

"Your husband?" asked Robert with dismay. He was breathing hard, the back of his coat soaked clear through with sweat. He let his oar go still, and the boat lurched to a clumsy, rocking halt. "Your husband's come clear after you to here?"

Another woman's cry echoed through the fog. "Robert?" she shouted, her voice shrill with excitement. "Dear God, Robert, is that you?"

"Mary!" Robert twisted about excitedly in the direction of her voice, his face glowing with joy and hope. "Did you hear that, Ezra? It's my Mary! I'm here, sweetheart, I'm here!"

Furiously Ezra swung at him. "What the hell do you think you're doing? Have you gone daft, too?"

But Robert ducked the blow, struggling with his oar to turn the boat about. "All I've ever wanted was Mary, Ezra, and she's there, waiting for me."

"You damned fool, have you forgotten our plan?" demanded Ezra. "The gold, you ass, the gold!"

But through a strange trick of the wind the fog suddenly tore apart in straggling wisps around them. Now Serena could see the other boat clearly, and its passengers as well, oddly frozen in place, as if in a painting rather than life. Two strong-backed boatmen sat at the oars, holding the boat as steady as they could. Abel—how had Gerald gotten Abel into a boat?—was poised high in the prow of the boat like some sort of figurehead. Mary was clutching the side of the boat, one hand pressed to her breast and her gaze desperate for her first glimpse of Robert, and Gerald—Gerald was sitting straight and tall behind her, his body twisted slightly to steady the long-barreled pistol in his hand, his face as coldly impassive as it had been the night he'd outshot Oliver Parrish. Only this time his target wouldn't be a scallop shell, nor would this target sit passively waiting its destruction.

And Serena's heart dropped from wildest joy to sickening dread.

Then Ezra's arm was around her neck, dragging her off the bench to hold her head back against his chest. She squirmed, struggling to break free, until she realized that the cold metal pressing against her temple was the barrel of Ezra's pistol. Instantly she went still, still enough to hear how Ezra's heart was pounding beneath her ear.

"Let Serena go, Ezra," ordered Robert hoarsely. "Let her go now."

Abruptly the gun disappeared from Serena's cheek, and when she opened her eyes she saw Ezra had pointed it at his brother's chest instead. "You're a sniveling coward, Robert, and you always have been," he snarled.

"But you can't quit this time. Damn you, you owe me this!"

Shreds of fog were drifting back between the two boats, thickening again, and Gerald's frustration grew. He didn't dare fire at Ezra, not with Serena there like a shield before him.

"If it's gold you want, Sears," he shouted, "then name your price. But you must let my wife go free so we can settle this between ourselves."

But before Ezra could answer Robert had thrown himself at his brother, knocking him back into the bow of the boat with Serena still clutched in his arm.

Then, with maddening timing, the fog once again drifted between the boats, blocking their view.

"Row closer!" Gerald ordered the boatmen. "Damnation, *now!*"

As they leaned into their oars, there was a splash, and too late Gerald realized that Abel had gone over the side.

"He'll kill my Robert," whispered Mary in agony. "Oh, dear God preserve him now!"

But all that Gerald could see over the sight of his gun when the fog broke apart again was how vulnerable Serena was, clinging to the sides of the rocking boat as the two brothers struggled for the gun, heedless of how close they were to capsizing the boat.

If he could only get one good shot, one clean shot, then he'd be able to end this madness now.

Then, to Gerald's horror, he saw Serena tugging at the oar, trying to use it as a long, unwieldy weapon to strike Ezra, the same way she'd made use of the butter crock and the chamberpot another lifetime ago. His brave, foolish Serena: for as she pulled it back to swing, Ezra broke free of Robert and stood and aimed the pistol squarely at her as the boat rocked wildly from side to side.

"That's the end to it, you damned Fairbourne slut," gasped Ezra, his eyes wild as he rose unsteadily to his feet in the rocking boat. Behind him Robert lay stunned, tumbled in a heap. "The end to it, and the end o' you."

Serena froze, unable to move. But where, really, would she go if she could? Ezra was only an arm's length away from her: he would not miss. But she did not want to die, not here, not like this, not with so much life left in her, life she'd meant to spend with Gerald. She closed her eyes, unable to look at the gun any longer, and tried to make her last thoughts of him, the man she'd loved so very much. She could hear the click of the flintlock as Ezra drew back the hammer.

Oh, Gerald, I love you . . .

Suddenly the boat lurched to one side, and Serena's eyes flew open at the sound of the snarling howl that accompanied it.

"Abel!" she shrieked, terrified that Ezra would shoot him next. "Abel, no!"

The boat pitched back as, with an enormous effort, Abel scrabbled his paws over the side.

"Shove off, you damned cur!" shouted Ezra, kicking at Abel's paws with his foot as he struggled to keep his balance in the swaying boat.

But as the boat rocked down in the water toward Abel, the dog pulled himself up and sunk his teeth deep into Ezra's leg. Ezra screamed with pain and fell back, jerking Abel with him as his pistol went off. Serena had never seen Abel like this, growling through the haze of the gunpowder smoke as he worried and shook Ezra's leg like a mutton bone while Ezra screamed in agony, desperately trying to shake or kick the dog from his leg. The boat rocked precariously beneath his shifting weight, and before Ezra could catch himself he and Abel pitched backward over the side, into the water.

"Abel!" cried Serena frantically as she leaned over the side. "Here, Abel, here!"

The water churned where the two had fallen, white foam on the black water. There was nothing Serena could do to help either of them as the boat drifted away on the current, nothing except watch in growing horror. How could she have guessed that Ezra couldn't swim? She'd never watched anyone die, not like this, so slowly.

Over and over and over again Ezra's pale, terrified face bobbed up to the water's surface, his mouth gurgling as he flailed helplessly to save himself, until finally he came up no more and the waters were still.

But where was Abel?

"Abel," she whispered, her eyes filling with tears. "Oh, my poor, brave pup!"

She was still leaning over the side when the other boat bumped against hers.

"Serena, love," said Gerald, lifting her into his arms to cradle her there. "Are you unharmed? Oh, love, when I heard the shot—"

"Abel's gone," she said, her voice breaking as she buried her face against his chest. "Oh, Gerald, he saved my life, and now he's gone!"

"Oh, sweet, I'm sorry," said Gerald as he gently raised her from his chest to see her face. "Poor Abel! He was the best—"

But from the far side of the boat came an impatient bark.

"Where have you been hiding, you wicked dog?" scolded Serena through her tears as she and Gerald helped haul a thoroughly exhausted Abel into the boat—though not too exhausted to shower them both with wet water and dog hair as he shook himself and wriggled with delight before he settled himself at her feet.

Yet still Serena wept, tears of joy and relief and love and fear, too, of what might have happened. The feel of the pistol's cold muzzle pressed against her skin, the helplessness that had overwhelmed her, the terror in Ezra's pale face as he'd sunk into the water for the last time—these were all things that would stay with her for a long, long time, and with a shuddering sigh she curled herself back into the sanctuary of Gerald's embrace. Over his shoulder she could see Mary with Robert, his arms so tightly around her he might never let go again.

And so, she knew, it would always be with her and Gerald.

"I love you, Gerald," she said with a little hiccup of

emotion. "Oh, I was so afraid I wouldn't be able to tell you that again, and when Ezra—when Ezra—"

"Hush now, Serena," said Gerald, kissing her forehead. "It's done. You're safe with me, and I've every intention of keeping you that way."

"Then take me home, love," she whispered as she burrowed closer to him. "Take me home to Appledore."

Eighteen

As soon as her brother's house was in sight, Serena knew that something was wrong.

The lower windows were thrown open as they always were on warm days, to catch the breeze from the water, and the tall grasses around the apple trees in the front yard had been newly clipped. The first of the trees was in blossom, too, white and palest pink flowers enveloping the branches like sweet-smelling clouds, with stray petals scattered across the stone walk like an offering to a bride. Taking the sun on the granite step lolled Tomkins, the kitchen cat, his tail curved in an elegant arc over the edge of the step. Even the weathervane on the roof pointed unwaveringly to the east for fair winds. Together it made for a charming picture of peace and prosperity, yet it seemed to Serena the house was too still, too quiet, almost as if holding its breath for its occupants. Something had happened while they were away to bring this awful solemnity, she knew it, and with her heart pounding she gathered her skirts and broke into a run up the crushed shell walk, Abel bounding ahead toward the cat.

"Why the hurry, love?" teased Gerald as he stretched his stride to keep pace with her. "Is my company so unwanted that you'd run to shed yourself of it?"

"No, no, no," she said breathlessly, her mind racing ahead to all the grimmest possibilities: an accident on the docks or on horseback, a drowning, Josua or Daniel or Samson swept away and lost forever at sea. "But something's amiss, Gerald, I can feel it. I cannot explain it any more than that, but I know. I *know*."

Serena didn't bother to knock, instead turning the heavy brass knob herself and throwing open the door. At once Joshua stepped from the parlor, staring at her blankly with hollow eyes, his shirt mussed and open at the throat, his jaw unshaven, and a tumbler of rum clutched tight in his hand.

"Oh, Josh," she said, resting her hand upon his arm. To find him here now, in such a state in the middle of the day, only increased her fears. "Whatever has happened?"

"Happened?" he growled. "I'll tell you what's happened. Anabelle's time has come, that's what's happened. What's happen*ing.*"

As he spoke one of the doors upstairs opened and shut, but not before letting out a string of infinitely creative oaths that sputtered into a wail of pain, loud enough to make Abel bolt back outside past the open door.

Joshua's face went pale beneath his stubbled beard. "All last night and this day it's been like that," he said with a groan. "My poor little Anabelle!"

"Mrs. Crosbie, ma'am," said the midwife's assistant, dropping a quick curtsey from the landing of the stairs. "We saw 'twas you from the window. Mrs. Fairbourne has asked if you'd join her, if you please."

"'If you please,' ha," murmured Gerald. "Knowing Nan, there was no 'please' about it. Best to go to her, Serena, before she screams next for your head on a silver charger."

He gave Serena a quick kiss on her cheek as she hurried away, up the stairs after the other woman. As a spinster she'd never been included in a birthing before, and she approached this one now with a mixture of curiosity and trepidation. Of course she'd heard whispered tales grim enough to make her hair stand straight from her head, but then if her guess was right—and granted, it was early days, very early days—she'd be in much the same position by Christmas, and it was better to be prepared.

Prepared, yes, though nothing ever seemed quite to prepare her enough for anything involving Anabelle. She was sitting on the edge of the birthing chair with the midwife and another woman on either side. The fine lawn of her shift was drenched with sweat and plastered to her oversized belly, her face flushed and her hair hanging in one wet, disheveled braid down her back. But what amazed Serena the most was that, for the first time in her memory, Anabelle was actually working.

"Oh, Serena, you're here at last!" she cried hoarsely. "Come, come, you must sit by me and hold my hand and—oh, dear God, not again so soon!"

The midwife leaned closer. "You must push harder, ma'am, push. You're almost done, and the babe wishes to be born."

"No more dearly than I wish it," said Anabelle through gritted teeth, her eyes focusing inward and her grasp so tight on Serena's fingers that she feared for her bones.

As the pain faded, Anabelle's grip loosened, her breath coming in short, exhausted pants. "Quick, quick, tell me," she gasped to Serena. "You are with Gerald?"

Serena nodded. "He came to me in Boston, and we—"

"No, no!" cried Anabelle impatiently. "I want to know if my ninny of a brother has finally made love to you!"

The midwife and her assistant both looked up with interest. Serena blushed, an acute shade of embarrassed scarlet.

"Yes," she said, clearly, for the sake of Gerald's pride. "Yes, he has, and it was—is—most fine."

"For *them,* of course, it always is," gasped Anabelle as she braced herself for the next surge of pain. "And blast, double-blast, their wicked, handsome souls for having all the pleasure and none of this suffering!"

"I have killed her," confessed Joshua mournfully as he stared into the empty hearth. "As surely as if I'd taken a blade to her throat, I have killed her."

"I'd not be so blessed confident," said Gerald, sprawled in an armchair with his legs stretched before him. As exciting as all this was, he was extremely sleepy, having spent the night with Serena exploring the possibilities of a swinging hammock in a private cabin on board the packet from Boston. "Nan is wonderfully strong for so small a personage."

"That's it, isn't it?" said Joshua with a great rattling sigh. "She's such a dear, tiny sweetmeat of a woman! If I were not such an outsized hulk, then she'd never have been burdened with so large a babe to be delivered of now. Oh, aye, 'tis all my fault."

"If you wish to believe it, you will, no matter what I tell you," said Gerald, "but I'm just as certain that Nan will survive this most heartily and be ripe for another as soon as you're able."

It wasn't that he was unsympathetic toward Anabelle's travail—even though she was as sturdy and strong as a moor pony, he still wished her a swift delivery, with all his heart—but the more pressing truth was that he missed Serena. Even for this short a time, with her only so far away as upstairs, he missed her. It must have been at least an hour since he'd been able to tell her how much he loved her, and that was an hour too long.

Joshua shook his head, unconvinced. He thrust his hand into his pocket, searching for the comfort of his pipe, and instead pulled out a crumpled sheet of paper.

"Look at this, Crosbie," he said as he handed the

paper to Gerald. "As if I hadn't enough to trouble me now, some damned fool tried to play a jest, sending me a letter like that! He has Serena, he says, and won't give her back until I give him a pile of gold and pardon that bastard Robert Sears, may he rot forever in whatever deserving hell he's been cast."

A quick chill spiraled down Gerald's spine as he scanned the crudely written note. He told himself it didn't matter—the man who'd written it was dead, while Mary and Robert were safely on their way to a new life together on Martinique—yet still the chill persisted, a reminder of how much he'd nearly lost.

"The work of some malcontent," he said softly, returning the letter to Joshua. "I'd pay it no heed."

Joshua snorted with disgust. "Oh, aye, as if I would. They've asked me to send along Sears's wife, too, as if poor little Mary would ever do anything I wished. Mind you, I've tried my best to help her, being a widow and all, but she would never—Serena!"

At once Gerald was on his feet. He'd never seen Serena like this, her whole face seeming to glow with happiness when her gaze met his.

"Upstairs, the both of you," she said. "There's someone you must meet."

"Anabelle?" croaked Joshua. "Is she—does she still live?"

Serena laughed. "She is perfectly fine, you great coward. I vow she could not be better!"

And as they followed her up the stairs to the bedchamber and crowded all at once through the door, they could see the proof for themselves: Anabelle, her hair once again neatly braided and crowned by a ruffled cap, propped up against the bolsters in the middle of the bed, looking exceptionally tired and exceptionally proud of the tiny, squawking, red-faced bundle in her arms.

"Faith, Joshua, you can come closer," she said. "He won't bite, you know. He hasn't any teeth."

"He is a *he?*" asked Joshua in wonder. "A son?"

"I should hope so." Her smile wobbled. "Now come kiss us both, love, before we perish of loneliness."

And as Joshua did, climbing onto the bed to join them, Gerald slipped his arms around Serena's waist and drew her close. "Dearest love," he said softly. "Does all this put you to mind of a family for us?"

She blushed, something he hoped she'd never stop doing, and he kissed her with all the tenderness he possessed.

"So shall Serena be next, Gerald?" teased Anabelle with a wicked grin that had nothing of the new mother about it. "Now that you've seen your way to behaving like a proper husband, shall my babe soon have a cousin to bully?"

"More likely the other way about." He smiled down at Serena, marveling again at how well they fit together. No, more than that: how much they *belonged* together, and his smile widened even further. "Once I discovered how much I loved her, the rest followed with exceptional ease."

"Hah," said Serena, thumping his chest with her fist. "Once *you* discovered what I had known from the beginning. Very slow you were about it, too."

"But quick about the things that matter." He took her fist and kissed the knuckles, then used her hand to draw her back into his embrace. "Such as rescuing feckless mermaids whenever they wander astray."

"Wandering?" She frowned up at him, trying to look fierce, but the fierceness couldn't last, not when he held her like this, and soon it melted into a lopsided grin full of purest love. "I thought we'd agreed there'd be no more wandering by either of us."

"No more, sweetheart," he said softly as he bent to kiss his mermaid's grin. "We're home."

Miranda Jarrett

The Captain's Bride

The Dazzling Fairbourne Family Saga Begins!

"Miranda Jarrett can always be counted on for
the very best in romantic adventure!"
—Kathe Robin, *Romantic Times*

Now available from Pocket Star Books

POCKET
STAR
BOOKS

1459

Judith O'Brien

Judith O'Brien's books are
"Magical! Harmonious! Dazzling!"

—Marla C. Ferrer, *Romantic Times*

Ashton's Bride   87149-8/$5.50
Rhapsody in Time   87148-X/$5.99
Once Upon a Rose   50225-5/$5.99
Maiden Voyage   50219-0/$5.99
To Marry a British Lord
00039-X/$5.99

POCKET BOOKS
PROUDLY PRESENTS

EVENTIDE

MIRANDA JARRETT

**Coming early 1999
from Pocket Books**

Turn the page for a preview of
Eventide. . . .

1721

The sky over the bay of Ste-Pierre was close to black, dark with night and the clouds that hid the stars and moon, and a near-match for the black mood that bedeviled Samson Fairbourne.

"So help me, Zach," he growled at the younger man beside him in the ship's longboat, "if you were not kin, I would hurl your sorry carcass over the side for how you've shamed me this night."

For once his cousin had sense enough not to answer, instead steadfastly staring over the shoulders of the men at the oars to avoid meeting Samson's eye. That was fine with Samson; if Zach had tried to argue with him now, when his temper was still roiling so furiously, he might very well have tossed his cousin into the waves, blood kin or not.

It was bad enough for the *Morning Star*'s bo'sun to have to drag befuddled seamen from the rumshops, but for the captain himself to needs go brawling in the street to rescue his own first mate—and over some silly strumpet, too—was beyond bearing. Samson grumbled another oath to himself, tugging his cloak over the sleeve of his best superfine coat. The *torn* sleeve, thanks to Zach, torn and dabbed with the same street filth that dabbed his back and breeches and likely even his hat as well.

"I never meant to shame you, Sam," ventured Zach with an unfortunately accurate prescience of his cousin's thoughts. "All I did was bring Ma'm'selle Lacroix a cup of punch and dance one dance with her when the fiddler began. One tiny dance, Sam, I swear that was all. How could I know her brother and his friends would take such offense?"

"Her brother, hah." Samson glared at his cousin. "More likely her pack of bully-boys. 'Tis the last time I take you ashore for supper, Zach. Next time we're in port you'll stay on board, and the time after that, too. You won't set one wretched foot on land for the next year if I've anything to say about it."

"Aye, aye, sir," agreed Zach forlornly, hanging his head so that his long, dark hair fell across the blossoming bruise on his forehead. After losing both his hat and the ribbon that had bound his queue in the scuffle, he looked to Samson more like some disreputable stable boy than a ship's officer, and exactly the kind of charming, worthless rogue that drew low women like flies to honey cake.

Samson sighed again. "It's for your own good, Zach. To keep the strumpets from getting their greedy little hands on you."

"But begging pardon, Sam, you're mistaken about Marie—I mean Ma'm'selle Lacroix. She was a lady through and through, and—"

"And from the veryest moment she clapped eyes upon you, she felt only the purest love for your own dear person," said Samson wearily. Not a single man in the tavern had missed the little French chit, trying to outdo every other woman in the room in the amount of lace, furbelows, and breasts prodigiously displayed, but only his young cousin had been foolish enough to fall under her spell. "How much did you tell her, Zach? Did you brag about our profits for this voyage, or how you were the first mate of the finest vessel in the harbor? Did you jingle the gold in your pocket loud enough for her to hear?"

"I did no such thing," said Zach with all the wounded dignity his nineteen years could muster. "I didn't have to. She liked me for what I was, Sam, and that's God's own truth."

Samson regarded his cousin with sorrow, his anger now tempered with despair. Jesus, had he himself ever been this pathetically innocent where women were concerned? He *was* fond of the boy. He truly was. But though he was only seven years older than Zach, there were times when he felt as if a whole lifetime of experience stretched between them instead.

"You listen to me, Zach, and you listen well," he said sternly. "I don't care if that lass tonight was the granddaughter of the king himself. It makes no difference, mind? None at all! She'd still be a female, rich or poor, lady or otherwise, and as entertaining as females can be, in their place, there are still no more taxing, troublesome creatures to a sailing man on this earth. The sooner you learn to keep clear of them, Zach—*all* of them—the happier your life will be."

Zach stared down into the bottom of the boat, his shoulders hunched with misery. "I don't believe it, Sam," he muttered, and pulled a small rum bottle from inside his coat for solace. "Not even from you."

"Give me that!" Samson snatched the bottle away and poured the contents into the water for emphasis.

"What the devil's gotten into you tonight, anyway? Whoring and fighting and drinking—"

"What about your sister?" demanded Zach. "She's a woman, isn't she? Are you saying that Serena's naught but trouble, too?"

"You leave off Serena, Zach," warned Samson. No man said ill of Serena in his hearing, not even Zach. "Besides, I don't mean sisters. Sisters are different."

"Well, then, how do you find the different ones if you keep clear of them all?"

"You don't," said Samson decisively. "You can't. You'd sooner find a drop of fresh water in an ocean of salt than one good woman in the great sea of doxies."

"But why can't I wish—"

"Wishing means nothing with women, Zach. Less than nothing, else I'd—I'd—" He broke off abruptly, aware of how close he'd come to telling more of himself than he'd ever wish Zach or the other four men at the oars to know. His fingers tightened around the empty bottle in his hand, and impulsively he reached into his coat for the pencil he always carried for calculations. The only paper he had with him was the innkeeper's reckoning from their supper, and he drew that from his coat now, too, smoothing the strip across his knee to hold it flat against the breeze.

"I'll show you how much wishes are worth," he said, determined to make his point with his head-strong cousin as he swiftly pressed the words into the paper. "I'll wish to Neptune himself for the perfect woman. Look, here, I'm putting it all proper in writing: 'I, Samson Fairbourne, with all the ocean as my witness, do wish for a young woman sweet in temper & without vanity, modest & truthful in words & manner, obedient & honorable, to take as my lawful wife.' Is that a grand enough wish for you, Zach?"

But as he waited for his cousin's reply, the young man's startled face was suddenly washed with light, and swiftly Samson turned to look for the source. The full moon had at last shown herself, the dark clouds tearing into little wisps across the brilliant silver circle that now seemed to fill the night sky. As if awed by the moon, the waves went instantly, strangely still, as even and smooth as a mirror to reflect the skies overhead.

Mere coincidence, Samson told himself fiercely, coincidence and no more. How could one foolish oath have power over the sea? Yet still he felt the uneasiness prickle beneath the collar of his shirt, an uneasiness that was perilously close to fear.

"A most grand wish, Zach," he said again, though even to his own ears the brash words now sounded hollow. "Grand enough to not have a prayer of a chance of coming true, eh?"

"Nay, Sam, stop," said Zach quickly, his eyes wide as he, too, stared up at the moon. Behind him one of the men at the oars raised one hand to cross himself. "Don't do this. 'Tis wrong to make such vows, even in jest, and you know it."

But Samson shook his head, determinedly turning his back on that glowing witch of a moon. Damnation, he was a rational Englishman, a Massachusetts-man, his own master, not some superstitious heathen who'd cower and quake before a pack of wayward clouds. With a great effort, he forced himself to laugh.

"You are right, cousin, right to stop me," he declared. "This perfect woman I wish for must be a rare beauty in the bargain. I'll mark that down here on my list, after 'honorable.'"

He twisted the paper into a tight little scroll and stuffed it down the neck of the empty rum bottle, wedging the cork in tight to seal it. As he did, the tall, dark shadow of the *Morning Star* loomed beside them, the boat bumping gently against the brig's side. Samson seized the guide-rope that hung from the rail, braced his feet, and clambered easily up the side to the deck. In three long strides he'd crossed to the bow, ignoring the startled looks of the handful of crewmen on watch.

"Here, Zach, here," he ordered, his voice booming effortlessly over the water as his cousin hurried to join him. He was master now, master of his ship and the lives of those who sailed with him, and the knowledge renewed his confidence. Moon, hah. This was the Caribbean, with weather as changeable as a whim. Besides, all he really wanted to do was set his cousin on a steadier course, with a dramatic gesture the boy wouldn't soon forget. Where was the sin in that?

He swept the bottle through the air, encompassing the harbor, the sleeping town, even that infernal moon. "There! Even with all this as my witness, you'll see how empty such wishes for women will be!"

Before Zach could protest again Samson hurled the bottle as far as he could, far out over the bowsprit and into the water. It bobbed there for a moment, the neck spinning gently in the moonlight, then vanished down below the glassy surface so abruptly that it almost seemed to have been pulled from beneath by an unseen hand.

Samson frowned. A corked and empty bottle should float, not sink.

"Oh, hell," he muttered, all too aware of how every other man on the deck was holding his breath in anticipation, or dread, or fear, or maybe all three. "'Tis not natural for a bottle to—"

But his words were torn away by a gust of wind so

strong and so sudden that he had to grab at the foremast to keep from being swept over the side. Even with all her sails still furled tight for port, the *Morning Star* heeled before the wind's force, her timbers groaning in protest as she tugged hard against her anchor.

He squinted back over the water, struggling vainly one last time to spot the bottle in the wind-whipped waves. Yet the churning waves were empty, the brilliant moon still there to taunt him for his rash words.

Damnation, he would *not* be cowed! He would claim this wind as his, and tame it for his own purposes. None had ever dared question his courage or his wisdom before this. He'd no intention of letting them start now. He'd give orders for the *Morning Star* to sail at once, and with such a wind to carry them, they'd be clear of Martinique by daybreak. He'd prove to his men once and for all that he wouldn't quiver before superstition and a wayward moon.

And that idle, fool's wish of his could just as soon go to the devil, where it belonged.

Patience and grace were most pleasing virtues in a woman, or so Polly Bray had heard the ministers preaching from the high pulpit in the Marblehead meeting house. But if what those wise men preached was true, then on this cold, gray morning Polly knew she must be the most soundly unvirtuous woman in all of New England.

She braced the heels of her sea-boots against the low side of the *Dove* and, with a deep breath, she pulled as hard as she could on the heavy nets. Despite the bright October sun, her fingers in their mittens were clumsy with the cold, and her back ached from the hours she'd already toiled, ached so much she longed for the freedom to weep from exhaustion and loneliness.

Not that she would. She hadn't cried since the fever had taken Father last spring, and she wasn't about to begin now, especially not over a net full of codfish. Wasn't this the reason she'd sailed this early, anyway? There'd be little use shedding tears over a bounty like this, or feeling sorry for herself because Enos and Abe, the *Dove's* usual two crewmen, had been still too befuddled with rum to sail with her this dawn. All the more profit that needn't be shared: that was what Father would have said, and laughed merrily as he'd figured how rich they'd be one day, rich enough for Polly to be a lady in a silk gown instead of cut-down homespun breeches and an old knitted cap.

But the tears threatened anyway, brought there by remembering poor Father and his endless dreams. Furiously she blinked them back, wiping her jacket's rough sleeve across her eyes for good measure. Pretty dreams and memories wouldn't pay the debts her father had left behind. Only hard work and luck could do that, and with fresh resolve she threw herself against the weight of the nets and pulled as hard as she could.

And this time the nets gave way, the lines rushing over the side of the boat and onto the deck with the wriggling, glistening mass of cod trapped within. With a gasp of surprise Polly tumbled backward, sprawling across the deck beside the fish. Breathing hard, she slowly rolled over onto her knees and surveyed her catch.

"I've won this time, you little noddies," she said to the fish with satisfaction. "You're mine now, and I—"

She stopped, and frowned. Tangled in the middle of

the squirming silvery fish and netting lay a long-necked rum bottle. Not only did she despise strong drink for what it did to men, but she also hated what the very bottles themselves could do to her nets. Holes and snags and knots aplenty, she muttered crossly to herself as she worked to free the empty bottle, and all because of some careless, wastrel drunkard of a *man*.

But the bottle wasn't empty, not entirely, though through the dark green glass she couldn't quite make out what lay curled inside. A paper of great importance to be so carefully rolled and sealed, thought Polly, her imagination bounding headlong as she remembered Father's whispered tales of pirates' maps and hidden treasures. Swiftly she sat back on her heels, easing the cork outward with her thumbs. If not a pirate's map, then perhaps the paper would be the lost deed to a great estate, or some nobleman's will, or—

Or a water-stained tavern-reckoning. Glumly Polly stared at the blurry words: a roasted chicken, three made dishes, a cheese, two pipkins of ale, and a bottle of Madeira. So much for dreams, indeed. Even the gulls that wheeled and danced in the sky overhead seemed determined to taunt her, their raucous cries sounding like mocking laughter to her ears.

"So much for a fool's dreams, Poll, my girl," she murmured as the paper fluttered between her fingertips. "Next you'll be fancifying you're the Queen of Sheba her own self, and off you'll ship for Bedlam."

The wind folded the paper backward, enough for her to see the smudged words on the other side. Carefully Polly turned the paper over, holding it up to the sunlight as she studied the scrawling penmanship. Because of always following the fish with Father, her schooling had been slight at best, and though she could sign her own name and read plain-writ upright letters, more elegant handwriting remained a challenge, and this had also been blotched here and there with seawater.

Her brows came together as she concentrated, sounding the words aloud as she made them out. "'I . . . I' something, or someone, 'with all' . . . oh, bother . . . 'a young woman sweet in temper . . . truthful in words and manner' . . . what nonsense *this* is! . . . 'obedient, honorable, beautiful'—oh, bah!"

She wrinkled her nose with disgust. Whatever man had written such clod-pate drivel had most likely first emptied the bottle of its rum. Her fancies after pirates' gold were nothing besides this moon-calf's longings for a lady too perfect to exist outside of his own muddled head.

"'To take as my wife'—his *wife!* As if any woman with half her wits about her would take *him,* the pompous, puffed-up scrod! 'To take as my—'"

The gust of wind caught her by surprise, catching and filling the *Dove*'s single half-furled sail so suddenly that for the second time that morning Polly tumbled backward, this time onto the pile of wriggling fish. Careless, she scolded herself as she scrambled back to her feet, careless, *careless* to be so taken with the foolish note that she hadn't seen the weather changing. The morning sun had vanished behind a bank of black clouds, the water ruffling uneasily into whitecaps before the rising wind.

Swiftly Polly stuffed the bottle and the note into her pocket and made her way aft across the slanting deck, toward the *Dove*'s tiller. All she had to do was turn the boat into the wind to steady her, a task she'd done a thousand times before.

But as she reached for the tiller, another rush of wind caught the *Dove* broadside, filling the sail so abruptly that the lashed stay on the boom snapped beneath the force. Freed of the stay, the heavy timber of the boom swept wildly across the deck. Instinctively Polly ducked, but not fast enough. The boom struck her shoulder, lifting her off her feet, off the deck, and then, to her infinite surprise, clear over the side. For one instant she felt as if she were flying with the same grace as the gulls, hanging in the air where she could see the *Dove* and the angry clouds and dark waves draped with froth as white and delicate as lace.

Then she hit the water, sinking fast, and there was nothing delicate, nothing lacy, about it. Her boots and clothes were dragging at her, dragging her deeper into the icy darkness, her limbs already numbing with the cold even as she struggled, and she could not breathe from the weight of the water, and from the shock of her fear and the certainty of her fate. There would be no one to help her, no one to miss her, no one to mourn her when she didn't return.

But God help her, why did she have to die like this?

"You found him, then," said Samson as the two crewmen lifted the lifeless body over the *Morning Star*'s side. "Poor bastard. Leastways we saved him from being gobbled by the fishes, eh?"

It was all Samson had hoped for when he'd ordered the boat lowered after the lookout had spotted the body in the ocean. No one survived long in the open sea, especially not after the night-long storm they'd suffered through since leaving Martinique, but this way they'd at least be able to give the poor fellow a decent, Christian burial. Though drowning was a common enough death among sailors, it still wasn't an easy way to go, and Samson watched with genuine sympathy as his men laid the body carefully onto the deck. A small fellow, scarcely more than a boy from the look of him. Samson himself had gone to sea when he was younger than this, and only God and good luck had kept him from a similar fate.

"Not long in the water," he said as he looked down at the forlorn, water-logged figure curled on its side, its face mercifully turned away from him and further masked behind a tangle of wet hair and a shapeless knitted cap. The clothes were worn and homespun, clearly cut down from those of a larger man, though the patches on the coat and breeches were neatly made. Somewhere, thought Samson sadly, there'd be a grieving mama for sure. "Any notion of his ship or port?"

"Nay, Cap'n." Plunkett, the man who'd led the rescue boat, uneasily shifted his shoulders and stared down at the deck. "No notion, sir."

Samson sighed. Sailors were often leery of their dead fellows, and he guessed Plunkett was no better than the others who were keeping an overly respectful distance. "Ah, well, perhaps there's something on his person to tell us."

He knelt beside the body himself, reaching for the first of the horn buttons that held the coat closed.

"Wait, Cap'n, wait!" said Plunkett quickly. "There's something—something—you should know about that one."

Samson paused, his hand stilled, and waited expectantly for Plunkett to continued. But the man decided to think better of his interruption, only shaking his head as again he stared shame-faced at the deck.

"Very well, Plunkett," said Samson curtly, and

began to unfasten the dead man's coat. "I expect I'll find out your mystery soon enough for myself."

He slid his hand inside the sodden woolen coat, searching for a clue to the young man's identity. A letter from home, perhaps, or a purse marked with his name.

But instead Samson jerked back his hand as if he'd been burned. What he'd just discovered might not have told him the dead sailor's name, but it certainly explained Plunkett's distress.

"Damnation, man," he demanded. "Why didn't you tell me outright he was a *woman?*"